Do Try to Speak as We Do

Marjorie Leet Ford

Thomas Dunne Books

St. Martin's Press New York

Do Try to Speak as We Do

The Diary of an American Au Pair

The author wishes to thank Arnold Chamove for permission to use the untitled poem on pages 121 and 122.

THOMAS DUNNE BOOKS.
An imprint of St. Martin's Press.

www.stmartins.com

Title page and part title image used courtesy of Photodisc, Inc.

Book design by Victoria Kuskowski

Library of Congress Cataloging-in-Publication Data

Ford, Marjorie Leet.
Do try to speak as we do : the diary of an American au pair / Marjorie Leet Ford.—1st ed.
p. cm.
ISBN 0-312-26866-1
1. Americans—England—Fiction. 2. Culture conflict—Fiction. 3. Young women —Fiction. 4. Au pairs—Fiction. 5. England—Fiction. I. Title.
PS3556.O7126 D6 2001
813'.6—dc21 00-045963

First Edition: March 2001

10 9 8 7 6 5 4 3 2 1

For Phillip Lonnie Ford

Troonfachan

1

THE SKY ALTERNATES FROM gray in the day to black at night. Since we're five miles from the nearest village, two miles from the nearest farmhouse, and starlight doesn't come through the clouds, when I switch off the lamp the darkness will be as thick as India ink. In the morning the sky will rheostat into gray again. The mist seeps into the closets (or cupboards, as they say here), so the socks and underwear are damp. Even the sheets have a touch of wet, like ice, when I get up the courage to inch between them. Mrs. Haig-Ereildoun has let me use the heating pad she bought to soothe Grampy's rheumatism, which acts up when he comes to stay. He's only come here once in his life. In summer. He didn't like it. She says the central heating Granny and Grampy have at home is the root of her father's health problems. My weakness, in her eyes, comes from having lived a soft life in America. "You do have thin blood!" she sympathized today, glaring at my left hand ditched in my coat pocket as I laid the table for lunch. A cloud of white breath puffed out of her mouth with each syllable. In this house, all words come out with frosty white puh-puh-puhs. We keep the butter, which comes in a pound cube, next to the teacups in the hutch, and a knife saws off slivers so brittle they shatter. A steaming cup of tea is cold by the second or third sip. And taking a bath is torture. The water heater is tiny, giving enough for three inches in the tub. To get the contraption going, you go down to the cellar and build a coal fire, go up to the kitchen and pull a lever, and wait half an hour. (Mrs. Haig-Ereildoun thinks it's too complicated for me, so I've only watched. Same with the washing machine; that has to be operated with a hand crank.) When the water's hot, first I bathe the three-year-old, Claire ("bahth" her, I'm supposed to say—"Do try to speak as we do," Mrs. Haig-Ereildoun has requested); the water is cool before I can force Claire in, kicking: She kicks for fun, she scratches for fun, and when she triumphs it gives her glee to see my face and hands striped and dotted with blood. By the time she's sudsed and rinsed, a quarter of the tub's water is on me and a quarter on the bathroom floor, sloshing like melted snow around my knees; nine-year-old Trevor bathes ("bahths") in the inch and a half that's left, then eleven-year-old Pru, then Mrs. Haig-Ereildoun, then me. You can imagine how beige the water is by the time I get into it, but you can't imagine how cold. By the time I'm through, the water heater has warmed up a fresh tank for Mr. Haig-Ereildoun.

It's funny about good and bad. I've always thought bad was more interesting, but maybe good is. This just hit me because although I can hardly wait to get into the details of Mrs. Haig-Ereildoun's personality, I think of Mr. Haig-Ereildoun and feel my heart billow up with eagerness to get onto that subject. I'm pretty sure he has no idea the rest of us share freezing bathwater, and I hope he doesn't find out. Since the water heater is what it is, and he's as sensitive to people's feelings as he is, it's lucky that when it comes to practicalities he has a certain obliviousness. Unfortunately he's not here much; he's a member of Parliament and spends all day out chumming with his Aberdeenshire constituents. When he is here, for an hour or two after breakfast, he's locked in his study, writing a novel. He's written two—on Scottish history—and he says perhaps the third one will be the charm.

The other person who seems to notice how I feel is Trevor. Luckily for me, he's here all day, my constant companion. It's odd to have your best friend be a nine-year-old. I'm going to hold back, though, and not jump ahead and tell you about any of the Haig-Ereildouns, or even me, until I get you settled in here, where I am right now, in bed.

My method of getting into bed is to slip the heating pad, turned to high, between the sheets near where my feet will be; when my teeth are brushed and my face washed, I move the heating pad up to where my knees will be; when my shoes are off and my second layer of socks on, I move it up another length; then, under the tent of my coat, which I never take off except for a bath, I hurry to switch from my jeans into my pajamas and push the pad up again. Before I put my arms back into my coat sleeves and fumble the buttons with my numb fingers, I slip the pad a step closer to the pillow; after I've tied my long plaid scarf over my head and ears and wrapped the rest of it around my throat, I do a little jig to kindle up warmth and then move the pad onto the pillow as I slide under the blankets, double pairs of socks first, rearranging the bulk of my coat, which weighs five pounds and looks like Russian army surplus. When the heating pad has warmed the pillow, I scramble it back under the coat and pajamas next to my skin, taking care not to let any air in as I finish the adjustments. Tilting the lampshade by my bed to angle the beam through the crevice between top and bottom sheets, I take the writing pad and my pen under the covers with me. I brought *War and Peace* here, thinking I'd have plenty of time, but it's turned out almost all of the twenty-four hours are spoken for by Mrs. Haig-Ereildoun. I work almost three times as many hours per day as we'd agreed by letter that I would work for my pitiful pocket money but she says there's nothing else I could do here anyway.

Well, it's occurred to me I could take a walk. I'd love an hour or two outside this house, away from this family. My lungs long for some free air. I can just imagine how big and lovely the breaths would be, just walking along, swinging my legs, not being polite. I mean, right this minute, under the covers, I'm not being polite. But any second, someone could knock on my door, and I'd have to spring to politeness.

After a week here, I asked, in as nonchalant a way as I could fabricate, when it might be convenient for me to take a day off. Her answer was quick, with a scowl: "Wherever would you go?"

I couldn't think of any particular place, right off the bat.

"No," she said, "for the present I think a day off would be rather a waste of time."

I hate disagreeing with people. So I swallowed. It took another week or so, inside the house, feeling more and more pinched, always under her glance, to mention once again my idea—modified this time to just a couple of hours.

"I was thinking," I said.

She was at the kitchen table, leafing through the village newspaper, and I was finishing the breakfast washing-up. "I thought—one of these days I might just stroll around a little, with my camera."

"Well!" she said. "That's a splendid idea. But do wait for a sunny day."

I felt the swoon of black a prisoner must feel when someone nails a board over the small window high in the cell wall, shutting out the last beam of daylight. "Do you think we'll ever have a sunny day?"

It was a sincere question, but she thought it was a terrific joke, and she's repeated it to several of her friends.

I MUST ADMIT, WHEN I've finished the washing-up after lunch and bedded Claire down in her sea of blankets and Tin-Tin books, Mrs. Haig-Ereildoun usually puts a generous look on her face and says, "If you like, you're free to go to your room now, to write letters for an hour." A couple of times I settled down on my bed and tried to concentrate on *War and Peace*, but what I always really want is to sit at the little desk and write letters. My one day in London I bought five pads of beautiful blue airmail paper, a heavenly blue with the texture of silk. I get my daily letter to Tedward done: "Dear Sweetheart," and a page of whatever I can think of that isn't complaining; then I start a letter to whoever else I feel like writing and tell the whole truth about what's going on. The hour is maddeningly short. I don't get another one until all the children have stopped fighting and laughing and playing tricks on me. It takes a long time, and every night it seems like it'll never happen, but every night they give in to drowsiness.

I click my door shut. Energized by their absence, I want to stay up all night. The second I let myself doze off, the morning gray is back, intruding. I have to rush to get dressed, then get the three-year-old, Claire, dressed and fiddle with her hearing aid until it stops screaming, and then coax Trevor. He's like me, always daydreaming, so it takes him half an hour to put on each sock. Pru, thank heavens, is completely self-sufficient, or we'd never get to breakfast.

NOW I HAVE TO describe my room. It's big. The walls are painted Wedgewood blue, and the carved moldings are painted cream. The twin bedsteads are rosewood or something else gorgeous, carved by hand way before I was born, maybe before my great-great-grandparents were born. The bedspreads are thick, white, tufted, with voluptuous layers of fringes. A lady's writing table gets daylight from the window. A dressing table seems to curtsy, in a taffeta skirt, with an old mirror on a swivel stand, a china pitcher and washing bowl, and a set of silver brushes, combs, and a hand mirror. To comb my hair and put on lipstick, I sit on a small round bench with a taffeta skirt that matches the dressing table's. There are slipper chairs at opposite walls, and beside the fireplace two small armchairs face each other, upholstered in a print that reminds me of old Blue Willow china, all faded. The fireplace—too small for logs, no doubt meant to burn coal—hasn't been lit since I've been here, but it gives the feeling of a fireplace. Between the facing armchairs is a low, oval table, also of rich-textured wood, carved and polished to reflect colors in an abstract way. On the little table is a fancy white china pot, planted with brilliant pink cyclamen, and a small Wedgwood ashtray. Forgetting I have on my thick serviceable coat and letting my imagination put on an evening gown, I strike a wooden match from my yellow Swan Vesta matchbox, compressing my lips into a rosebud and pulling in on my short fat Silk Cut cigarette. Pretending long nails instead of my bitten ones and extending the cigarette fingers of my left hand, I bring the flame close to my lips for a blow and give the smoking matchstick a regal drop into the Wedgwood ashtray. I take another puff, and I stride (on my imaginary high heels) to the dressing table and exhale at my reflection in the antique mirror. I sit down and join myself for a cigarette. In this light, my brown hair is rich and shiny, my cheeks have roses, and you can't see any pimples.

Mrs. Haig-Ereildoun has shown with her glare what she thinks of smoking, but I enjoy it. Her husband smokes. She's always buying him pound bags of lemon drops and Pascall crystal mints, hoping he'll like those better than his Rothmans.

IF I WERE WHAT Mrs. Haig-Ereildoun calls a "proper nanny," I wouldn't get such a pretty room. Proper nannies have to go to nanny school, and when they qualify, they get jobs with half-decent pay and sleep in cubicles. "I have uniforms in all sizes," Mrs. Haig-Ereildoun's letter told me. The letter arrived in San Francisco after the phone call. If she hadn't added, "or, you may wear your own clothes if you prefer," I wouldn't have come.

Up until not so long ago, Mrs. Haig-Ereildoun says, the nannies from the best nanny school wore brown pinafores over crisp blouses of brown and white striped cotton, with starched white collars and cuffs. In Kensington Gardens the prestige nannies must have been as easy to spot as Kellogg's cereal boxes in the grocery store.

The ex–prime minister and his family visited Scotland, and their nanny wore a tailored gray jumper that looked like a uniform. In the kitchen, on our way into the dining room with the tea things, the ex–prime minister's nanny was horrified when she saw me put my face close to Claire's and exaggerate my lips to whisper, asking if she needed to wee-wee. "We *don't* say 'wee-wee'!" the ex–prime minister's nanny huffed.

"What should I say, then?" I asked.

"We say 'tinkle'!"

I saw Mrs. Haig-Ereildoun's eyebrows react. She was the one who had told me to say "wee-wee." (I'd said "pee.")

IF ANY HOUSEGUESTS COME to stay at Troonfachan, I'll be moved upstairs, to what I imagine is a cell. I haven't seen the little rooms on the third floor, because the door to the service staircase is locked. What I imagine is so ugly that I'm not even curious. There aren't any real servants living here now, although there are uniforms—small to huge—hanging in my closet. Mrs. Campbell comes every day to vacuum: she wears a sweater and skirt, and Mrs. Haig-Ereildoun refers to her as "my daily." I wear jeans, and she refers to me as "my American girl." I wish I could show in writing how Mrs. Haig-Ereildoun trills the "r" of American, making it start out with a "d" and following through with a resounding "h." When no one's around, I practice: *"Amed-h-hican."* Trying to speak as they do is one thing I like about my job.

I hadn't realized I was coming to a country where I didn't understand the language. I mean English. Not Scottish. Scottish would be impossible. In one of her friendly moments, Mrs. Haig-Ereildoun chuckled that I might write a book on the differences between American and English. If I stay here long enough, with a good enough stock of these heavenly blue notepads, maybe I will end up with something as long as a book.

The worst example of the language difference happened the night we got to Troonfachan. (It's pronounced TROON-fah-kon, by the way.) It gets dark around four-thirty in the afternoon, so the sky had been black the last hours of our drive. Rain, no moonlight. We were all tired, hungry, and we had cartons of groceries, linens, toys, and books to put away before we could fix supper. When our headlights hit the big old farmhouse, rain whipped at it, and the wind was so strong it was hard to open the car doors. The key to the front door didn't fit. "Honestly, Angus!" She grabbed his keys and the door simply opened. The light switch didn't work. "You don't even know what a fuse box is, do you!" she hissed at her husband. "Melissa, fetch me the torch." Torch? "Oh blast! You just stand there and contemplate while I fetch the torch." Her head tucked down against the rain, she came back from the car with a flashlight. So they call that a torch.

When she'd filled the house with electricity and I'd put away the children's clothes and made the three beds, I tossed a sheet on my own bed and heard footsteps racing down the hall. She banged on the wall next to my door, which was open.

"Melissa!!" (You should hear how she hisses the s in my name.) "Me*lisss*-sssa! You *didn't* make up the cot!" Her face was red as the bullfighter's blanket.

Explosions of fear went off inside me. I heard my voice quiver as I whispered, with all honesty, "Yes I did. I made up the cot."

"You did *not!*"

"But—I did . . ."

"You did *not!*"

She marched me down the hall. There, in the children's room, were the three beds, all made up with sheets, blankets, and pillowcases. One was the small bed, the kind Claire sleeps in in London.

"You did *not* make up the cot!"

I hardly had any voice, but I pointed to the small bed and eked out the words, "Yes I did."

She pointed to the crib and said, "You did *not!*"

"Oh!" I said. "The crib?"

She glared at me.

"I'm sorry," I said. "We call that a crib. *This* is a cot." I pointed to the undersized bed.

AFTER MAKING UP THE crib, I walked down the hall to my room and shut the door. Closing the collar of my overcoat snug around my throat, I sat on the edge of the half-made bed and frowned.

There is a phone in the kitchen, I said to the room. There is a phone book. Somewhere in this county there are taxis. I have traveler's checks.

I knew the address was: c/o Haig-Ereildoun; Troonfachan, near Bridie; Aberdeenshire; Scotland. I assumed Troonfachan was a small town. But it's the name of the house. The village, Bridie, is five miles away. That might sound close, except if you have a heavy suitcase, five shopping bags bulging (I *wish* I'd spent the money on a second suitcase), a tennis racquet, and no car. I'm not allowed to drive their car. And it rains. Getting here, I had the feeling it rained all the time. Now I know it only rains most of the time. The nearest actual town is ten miles away, but it has no train station. The nearest city is fifteen miles, which would be quite a walk, in the rain, with my stuff.

I went to the shopping bags, suitcase, and handbag stacked in the corner and dug out a Silk Cut and my yellow box of matches. Striking one, I said to myself, I can get back to London. Lighting the cigarette,

I thought, If she speaks to me that way again, I will use the phone book, the phone, the taxi, the train, and my dollars. My breath, as I blew out that match, had a satisfying whistle.

I sat on the bed and smoked and didn't unpack my suitcase.

The oddest thing happened. The next morning, I didn't say a word about my resolve. But she seemed to know. All that day, she spoke to me as one human being speaks to another. I wonder if my posture told her. After supper, I unpacked my suitcase.

MY WINDOWS ARE TALL and wide. To shut out the cold, you can pull thick curtains, triple- or quadruple-lined. In the morning I'll open the curtains, and although the sky will be pewter, the grass will glow with greenness. The light doesn't seem to beam down from the sky but up from the ground, like green neon. Two or three fluffy white lambs will munch. An organization of Scotch pine trees will poke their stout bodies up around the borders of the grass. Unfurled to the horizon will be folds of patchwork farmland, checkerboard squares of color: ochre, shades of green, and here and there, mustard. Through the branches beyond, I'll see glints of bright yellow daffodils.

Forests carpeted with daffodils. Those are the words that sailed into my mind the second I decided to come here. I saw the woods Lady Chatterley romped through wearing nothing but chains of wildflowers. I saw luncheons served on the lawn, as in Henry James and Merchant Ivory: wicker furniture and linen tablecloths and silver cigarette boxes. The second I decided to come here was when I heard the pretty music of Mrs. Haig-Ereildoun's English on the phone, transatlantic. "Hang on!" she said. "Do you play tennis?" "Then be sure to bring your racket, as we have courts in Scotland."

The tennis courts are a crisscross of weeds between chunks of cement. The lawn is too soggy for luncheons. The music of Mrs.

Haig-Ereildoun's voice is usually like a soprano hitting the wrong note. But I was right about the daffodils. The forest floor—all its rooms and corridors and crannies—is dappled with more brilliance than streets paved with gold. But without a lover, or a reason to romp, the daffodils give me an odd kind of pain. It's not exciting pain, not the pain so acute you forget everything. It's a dull, polluted disappointment.

I keep thinking of a poem about sadness. "Ode on Melancholy." By John Keats. I wrote a paper on that poem once, and I got so close to it that I think of Keats as John. He says if you want to face true sadness, don't look at the sad things: "Glut thy sorrow on the morning rose . . . Or on the wealth of globèd peonies."

He thinks that what really wrenches the heart is beauty. "Beauty that must die." But my problem is worse. In these misty forests with yellow dapples, I sense that this beauty is here and will be here, and that I am here and will be here, and that I won't be able to enjoy it. I don't enjoy it.

2

"BLAST!" SHOUTED MRS. HAIG-EREILDOUN. She slammed the front door. "Why don't *I* ever get any post?" She thwacked letter after letter at my place on the breakfast table.

We get two deliveries a day here, tied with brown string. Once in a while there's a letter or two for Mr. Haig-Ereildoun, but almost everything is for me. Today there were two postmarked Portland—a note card from my grandmother and a fat manila envelope full of letters from my mom's first-grade class. I had an air letter from Tukuyu, Tanzania—my friend Trish teaching English there—and four letters from San Francisco: one from the president of the advertising agency that fired me; one from his thirteen-year-old daughter; one from his secretary; and a joint letter (mostly drawings) from two art directors. I also got a thin envelope from my brother in Spindale, North Carolina. I can't read all that mail at breakfast. I have to supervise Claire's wild eating and gag down my own breakfast. Eating my breakfast, a totally liquid, barely warmed egg, is the hardest job of the day. The albumen reminds me of mucus. The little spoons we use, and the pretty eggcups, are nice. But I think Mrs. Haig-Ereildoun does one-minute eggs. She's always in a hurry.

I open my letters at breakfast and skim them, and read them after lunch. Trish is planning to get married, in a church with a grass roof. Grandmother says, "My thoughts are with you so constantly that I even *dream* about you." Mom's first-graders take home my letters about Scotland for their families to read; for me they print in big wobbly letters their news about Portland: "We spent Sunday at aunt Electra's, which spoilt the day." My old boss, who's about Mrs. Haig-Ereildoun's age—forty-four-ish?—says, "It seems you've found yourself in a pickle, as they say where you are, working for a demented Scottish family. And a child who pretends to be deaf. I advise you to use my special Berlitz system, which I use while traveling in countries where people pretend not to speak English. Just lean in close and *shout!*" My brother, Sam, who pleased half of Portland by getting a scholarship to Princeton and then became bad gossip by flunking out in a flash—like one of those nightmares where you're going to the final exam but can't find the building because you've never been there—has found religion. Even long before Princeton, since he was nine and Dad died, Sam's been finding religions. The latest one, though, is the scariest. Christianity. Hard core. His whole church moved to a farm in North Carolina. No one owns their own clothes, they just pick something from a common closet and wear it for the day. They milk goats and work in a cannery because it's wrong to engage their minds in anything except worship. Everything fun is wrong, even laughing. Laughing used to be what Sam did best. Now he sends quotes from the Bible.

If my mother were here, she'd say I get so many letters because everyone feels sorry for me. I'm sure that's part of it. When you lose your job and your apartment and your wedding is canceled, people do feel sorry for you.

THE AFTERNOON POST BROUGHT only a package from Ted and a letter. The letter, if you could call it a letter, was from this Abraham Lincoln–looking guy I met on my one evening in London, before we came here. He writes on memo pads from his lab. No "Dear Melissa." No "Sincerely Simon." His first letter was one sentence. Today's was two. It's fun to get these tiny notes afloat in normal-sized envelopes.

Ted's even less of a writer, so he sends presents. I wish he could write, because I miss laughing. Ted can be really funny. They say humor is the flip side of pain. A good laugh is like a good cry. Tedward has a lot of pain and anxiety, as his presents show. This time it was a quart-sized bottle of vitamin C. My first week here he sent a hot-water bottle. Last week I got wool kneesocks and a box of healing tea with a name full of x's and z's. I can't pronounce it. And I won't drink it. I won't take the vitamin C either. I eat oranges. Just to prove myself right, I held up the label on the vitamin C and read through the list of chemicals. I agree with Mrs. Haig-Ereildoun about one thing: The other day she got out the butter and said, "I can't see why anyone would think margarine more healthful than butter. Butter is a natural product."

Ted is afraid I'll get sick and die. At home, he was afraid I'd be murdered.

Of course, he had reason for anxiety about death. The year before I met him, his whole family had been wiped out. One death after another. First his older brother dropped dead from a heart attack, at the age of forty. No warning. A few months later his mother died. She was old—older than my grandmother. Then his sister was killed in a car crash. His father had died years before, and so had his grandparents. He had no cousins or aunts and uncles he was close to. So all of a sudden Ted was alone. No family except a little niece and nephew who are, to him, a burden. "I don't have anything in common with kids."

It was all these deaths that brought us together. The guy he shares his studio with—a sculptor named Hans Lundt, from Holland—was worried about Ted. When Hans met me, he thought, *Perfect!* He set up a lunch with his girlfriend, Ted, and me. I didn't know anything about the deaths until later. If Tedward was depressed, he didn't show it. All I knew was that he was a hunk. Shy eyes and a sly sense of humor. At lunch, he asked for two glasses of chardonnay. "How did you know I like chardonnay?" I asked. "Oh. You want some too?—Make that three." Then the waiter couldn't answer any of our questions about the menu and finally admitted, "I'm new." With complete seriousness Ted widened his eyes with understanding. Seeming to notice something, he said, "Oh *yeah!*" and made the motion of plucking something from the waiter's sleeve. "Your tag's still on."

I'm always a second late getting his jokes. In fact, I now have to thunk myself on the forehead with my fist. Duh. I am so slow! It only just hit me that when he gets out the brown mailing paper to wrap those vitamin C pills and the healing tea and the hot-water bottle, he probably has that wicked twinkle in his eye.

IT WASN'T UNTIL OUR first real date—dinner at Fleur de Lys, the fanciest restaurant I've ever been to—that he told me about all the people in his family who'd just died. I couldn't imagine surviving so much shock. It felt very sobering to realize how much good I could do for him. It was also at Fleur de Lys that he told about why Hans had introduced us. I was flattered that Hans had felt so sure I was "perfect." Now I know what was perfect. It was my body. Meaning my hips. Or to be more complete, my t & a.

I admit, Tedward's extreme need of me is very appealing. And his adoration is wonderful, even if it does have to do with aspects of me that aren't my favorite.

The whole thing may not be a grand passion, but it's sweet. One thing I've noticed about myself, as I get older, is that I'm developing good sense. Tedward is right for me. He's the safest man I've ever met.

. . .

I WOULDN'T STAY OVER at his apartment on Nob Hill because of the claustrophobia. Both rooms were stacked with all the furniture of all the households of the people who've died. He couldn't stay over at my apartment on Russian Hill because he said my mattress gave him a backache. So he used to bring me home, and there was a ritual. First, he insisted that I stand out on Leavenworth Street in the cold as he used three keys to open the knob lock, the standard bolt, and the extra-strong bolt he'd installed in addition. This was the exterior door, leading through a corridor, past a storeroom to the apartment itself. He turned on the lights to check out the hall and behind the boxes in the storeroom. Using three more keys to unlock the apartment, he went out to the deck and peered around the plants; inside he kicked under the clothes hanging in the closet to be sure no one was hiding, and he felt through the overhead shelves. It was romantic. He was so protective.

Ever since the day I met him, the songs that really get me are the ones where the sweetheart has died. Car crash, murder, a rare disease—at home I find myself standing by the radio, drenched in tears. They don't seem to have such sad songs over here.

I did break off the engagement. I returned the wedding presents. But then, luckily for him, I changed my mind. I think it's good for him to miss me for a while, but late this summer he's coming over, and we'll get married. Maybe in Paris.

3

ANOTHER DAY, GLUTTING MY sorrow on daffodils. Another night, pitch black outside. Another Silk Cut cigarette, in this Wedgwood-blue bedroom.

If the Eskimos have hundreds of words for snow, the Scots should have as many for gray. Today we took our umbrellas and had a picnic on a lake. The clouds were multileveled, both high and low, churning the spectrum: some smoky, some gilded, some luminous dove-white, some dull like molten steel, all moving with streaks and huffs and froth. They didn't seem to mingle but to decoagulate. The small lake was still as metal, each stroke of the oar breaking silence as we rowed our wooden boat through a screen of mosquitoes. Mrs. Haig-Ereildoun reached into the picnic basket and pulled out a pack of Rothmans! She passed cigarettes around to all the children, including Claire, and lit them with wooden matches. My mouth gaped as the children held cigarettes between thumb and forefinger and sucked and puffed, along with their mother. "Scares off the mosquitoes," Trevor explained.

The sky didn't make good its threat until after we'd finished our Scotch eggs, cold chicken, and apples—but then it attacked with the fierceness of the Pict and Scot warriors Trevor and I have been reading about in his history book. Instead of rain it pelted hail. Mrs.

Haig-Ereildoun rowed with all her might as the sky hurled white rocks at us. Being under our umbrellas was like being inside a war drum, with another battle going on outside—hail battering the lake, making explosions of white water everywhere, hail knocking the boat and bouncing off to plunk in the water, the oars creaking and clinking in the oarlocks and bashing the lake.

All in the course of a picnic, I saw the water change from obsidian black to inky teal to animated polka dots to a glowing swan white. Between the sky and the water, we get a full vocabulary of gray emotions.

WE HAVE LOTS OF picnics under umbrellas. This house sits on a large, flat knoll, and the hill behind us has a trail to the tumbling river, called a "burn" in Scotland. This burn stuns me with its likeness to the Deschutes River, in Oregon, near our summer cabin. The water of our Scottish burn rushes and jumps over mossy rocks and slippery fallen trees, absolutely singing as it goes. Before I came here I did imagine forests carpeted with daffodils, though no mental picture could come close; but I never thought I'd find my own Deschutes River in Scotland. The only difference is that in the summer in Oregon, sun spatters gold on ripples; here the sparkle on the water is just a brighter shade of gray. And in Oregon we don't have picnics under umbrellas.

How I long to be home. Both homes. Oregon and San Francisco.

TEDWARD AND I MADE a pact, when I left, that I'd call him collect every Sunday evening, just as he'd be waking up at ten in San Francisco. In these phone calls I try to twist the conversation to where he'll have to mention a street name, like Columbus Avenue, or a restaurant, like Domino Alley, or a landmark like Coit Tower or Washington Square or even the North Beach library. Just the sound of these names makes me swoon.

When I was there, actually walking down Columbus Avenue past Washington Square and the North Beach library, seeing Coit Tower, standing in line at Domino Alley and watching the cook take his salt can by the handle and toss showers of white over black-striped hamburgers and making flames shoot out of the coals, I could hardly wait to be in Scotland. Now I wish I could be at Domino Alley.

IT HAPPENED BANG-BANG-BANG. TOO fast for thinking. When the wedding was a month off I gave notice on my apartment and someone snapped it up. Then I was fired. It wasn't because I was bad; the agency lost its big account and a third of the staff was fired. "Laid off" is the polite way of saying it. Why me? There were lots of people they could have gotten rid of. I was the most junior person—the copy trainee—but I'd won the most awards. The people I worked with had become my family: the funniest, most wonderful family. Then I got fired. I mean laid off.

Luckily, I was getting married. And luckily, Ted had a trust fund.

Then he made his confession. He finally told me that he would never, ever have kids. He hadn't said that before. He'd said we could have only one. (I wanted three.) Then he reneged on having even one. After my other losses, and after all the dreams I'd given up by choosing him (instead of the handsomest guy in the world, instead of the smartest or the richest), I was not going to give up what I wanted most in life, children.

The night he told me, I was still awake and crying at four in the morning. Suddenly I pulled my face off the pillow and looked out my window at a light still on, a few buildings away. That minute, my fury and fear evaporated as fast as my tears. It hit me that I had lost everything. All of a sudden I had nothing to lose.

That felt great.

THERE WERE ALL SORTS of things I'd always wanted to do, but felt I couldn't. Now I could. No matter how badly it's turning out, I still think of this as one of my good moments. At four that morning, I was already congratulating myself on my good character as I pulled my address book off the shelf and made my first transatlantic call. My oldest friend, Mots, had dropped out freshman year to marry a lawyer in London (barrister) and had always wanted me to come spend a year in England. Her father-in-law, chairman of a huge U.K. corporation, had come over last year on a business trip and had told me he could get me a job anytime, with his company. He'd made me yearn for the adventure, but at that point I'd been hired for this great job in San Francisco. I'd rented my first apartment, I'd met Tedward, and, as they say here, I was booked.

Now, though, having failed at everything, I was free. When Mots answered the phone I said, "I'm coming over! Tell Mr. Hedrick to get me that job."

"Sorry," Mots said. "I'm afraid Mr. Hedrick can't help you now. He retired last month. You'll never be able to get a work permit. The only thing for you is a nanny job."

I told Mots I didn't want a nanny job.

She explained how strict the laws are, keeping people like me from taking work from citizens. "Au pairs can work here legally," she said.

Really. Even though I'd lost my job in San Francisco, I had accomplished something in my year and a half there. The youngest and least likely to succeed, I'd won five awards. One statewide. I could turn on A.M. America any A.M. and see a commercial written by me. I was a little above being a nursemaid.

I went back to packing up wedding presents and taking them to the post office, along with notes that made me sound less pathetic than I felt. Luckily, since the wedding dress had fit perfectly right off the rack, Saks took it back. Secretly, I didn't mind about the dress. Ever since my father died, my mother has been pinching her pennies, and the limit of what she was willing to spend wouldn't buy quite the gown I'd always imagined. It was Saks, but Saks's cheapest. And I think it made me look fat. Naturally, I didn't say anything. I had a few dollars saved up and could have contributed toward buying a better dress, but Mom would have felt moralistic about the waste of money. ("You only wear it once.") Her feelings would have been hurt. I didn't feel I had a choice. I admit, I wasn't crazy about the idea of walking down the aisle in that dress.

After Mots's bad news about jobs, I went back to setting up appointments at the various advertising agencies in town. I think I probably limped in for all my interviews, which may have had a bad effect. I did a little better with TV stations and newspapers, because they were exotic to me. I had a great interview with the *Chronicle* food editor. Harvey, his name was. But like everybody else, he didn't have any jobs.

I called an employment company that specialized in clerical temp work in London. Even though it was temp, for visiting Americans there was a set salary. When I heard how much, I couldn't continue the conversation. What kind of neighborhood would I have to live in with that kind of pay?

Just three days after I'd talked to Mots, though, she called with news. She'd found me two jobs. The best, she said, was right across the street from her, a banker's family. I reminded her I didn't want to be a nanny. "The other," she said, without pausing, "has disadvantages. You'd have to spend half the time in Scotland. The husband is an MP."

When I found out an MP was not a military policeman, I told

Mots to tell them "yes" even before she told me that the main thing they needed was somebody to teach their deaf three-year-old how to speak.

How interesting! How would I do it? I was trying to figure that out at the same time as I was trying to figure out how I'd get both winter and summer clothes into my suitcase, so I may have missed some of what Mots had to say at the end of the conversation. As for the clothes, I got a genius idea. Shopping bags. Much cheaper than a second suitcase.

Two days later I picked up the phone and met Mrs. Haig-Ereildoun, with her chirrupy English voice.

One more transatlantic call to Mots: "Is there an English Miss Manners?"

I could hear the smile in her voice. "Sorry. The English don't have things like that. I'm afraid they reckon either you were born with it or you weren't."

Mots always uses words like "reckon." To me that's a cowboy word, but when Mots moved to England and brought a few people back home for visits, I found out "reckon" was also an English word. She's picked up no English accent at all, but she uses all the words, like "petrol" and "fortnight" and "reckon." Also, she's picked up all the inflections, like not putting a question mark at the end of her questions.

AS FOR MY MANNERS, I finally found an American book of etiquette in my grandmother's bookshelf, copyrighted before my mom was born. Emily Post. She had lots of rules for teas and balls—and a chapter called "The Butler in the Dining Room." She gave the hierarchy for seating at White House or United Nations dinner parties. Just in case, I memorized the correct modes of address for dukes, duchesses, marquesses, marchionesses, and of course Your Royal Highness.

The rules are strict. Emily says if I'm introduced to royalty, I must wait for the royal person to speak first, and let the royal person choose the topic of conversation. I could really see myself slipping up on that one. But over all, I thought I'd do okay. I'd been to debutante parties and knew which fork to use. And if they had a few different forks in England, I'd follow Emily's when-in-doubt advice and use the same fork my hostess was using.

One thing Emily finds appalling is what she calls "zigzag eating," where you cut a piece of meat, set down the knife, and switch your fork to the right hand ("prongs up") to get your food to your mouth. "Though not seen at the tables of fashionable people," she says, "zigzag eating is a custom seen often enough in this country to be known to Europeans as 'the American way of eating.' "

Obviously Emily hadn't been to Portland. Or San Francisco. On the West Coast even fashionable people eat that way. But then neither, probably, had my future host and hostess been to the West Coast. I immediately began to practice non-zigzag eating, training my ditzy left hand to find my mouth instead of my nose.

4

LETTERING LANE WAS AN L-shaped street off the Queen's Way, with what seemed by lamplight to be a single building, bent to line both legs of the L. A series of gates in a long, L-shaped fence of wrought iron opened onto short brick paths through gardens of gravel to stone porches with trash cans by the door. Mots's headlights spotted a red door, a blue one, a black, an ochre, and a purple door before pointing to the yellow blooms of the street's only foliage, a scrubby forsythia by the dark green door marked, in brass numbers, "11." Mots got my suitcase out of the trunk as I bent over the front seat to gather my tennis racquet and assortment of shopping bags from the back. It took a while to line up the handles. Mots was the one with the free finger to ring the doorbell.

The woman who answered didn't look anything like the woman I'd talked to on the phone. By then we'd had two conversations. The second had just been about how to get to Lettering Lane from Mots's: landmarks like a road that "squiggles," a stoplight that "winks," and an old vine that "scribbles" on a wall. I love people who use lively verbs. The woman at the door didn't seem about to use a lively verb or noun or adjective. She didn't smile, she just assessed me. What I think happened is, her whole self stopped chirruping the moment she set eyes on me. She saw me and I saw her and I'm sure my expression, like hers, registered innate, involuntary dislike.

Her gray wool sweater hung from shoulders that pointed like a coathanger. There seemed to be no hips or thighs at all inside her straight tweed skirt. How I envied that. My hips have always been my problem.

"You must be Melissa," she said, setting her mouth in politeness and extending her hand. I had to put down all the shopping bags to give her my right hand and introduce Mots. "Won't you come in," she said. It took some time to refind the many handles. Mots hoisted the suitcase over the threshhold and we stepped in.

The front hall was done in linoleum, yellowing white and black squares. The walls were bare but for a row of nails, for coats. Paint had blistered off the walls, and a couple of rungs had been knocked off the banister. Up the middle of the stairs, the stained carpet was worn almost to see-through. The temperature must have been just a degree or two above freezing.

"May I take your coats," she asked.

Mots took hers off and handed it over, but I said, "Oh no, thank you, I'll keep mine on."

The displeasure on Mrs. Haig-Ereildoun's face showed I'd made a mistake.

I should describe her face. Long and pale. Tissue-paper skin, just about to crinkle, but not quite crinkled. Her forehead showed a history of eyebrows raised a lot. Past smiles and frowns were also recorded—but faintly. Perfect cheekbones. Perfectly straight little nose. Long chin. Water-blue eyes. Hair lank and pale, like spun glass, hanging to her jawline.

"The children are sleeping," she said, "but Mr. Haig-Ereildoun is in the drawing room. Do leave your things for him to carry, and come up." I remember following her up the stairs that night, trying to find an indication of a butt inside her skirt. (My hips really are a problem.) She led us into a room the size of a deteriorated ballroom, painted the gray of a drydock submarine. On entering, the vastness of the room, nearly empty, amplified the click of our steps. It was like being inside a bell. A small Persian rug floated like a raft on a sea of marred hardwood. A velvet sofa had dark spots where heads had rested. Two tattered armchairs sat within shouting distance of each other, one with its tall back to the doorway, the other facing us, spewing stuffing from its shoulder. In front of the fireplace stood an electric heater, obviously not turned on. The isolated pieces of furniture in such a big space gave the effect of a warehouse that had been emptied of everything but the stuff not worth taking. There were no throw cushions, no magazines or coffee-table books, no family photos. The only decorations were a tiny brass coachman's clock, ticking loud from its place on the mantel; and a dark painting the size of a paperback hanging crooked above the sofa: a nighttime landscape of black hills, storm clouds swallowing a blueish moon, and in the foreground a small, bruise-colored dog with its ears pressed back, seeming to howl.

"DARLING," MRS. HAIG-EREILDOUN SAID. Like a jack-in-the-box, from the tall armchair with its back to us, sprang a tall, lanky gentleman in baggy tweeds, letting a book drop from his lap.

"Well well well!" he said, pushing back the salty red hair that fell over his forehead. He dipped to pick up the book, then straightened to shove his hair back. He loped over with his long arm out. "Which one of you is Melissa?" I gave him my hand. "How do you do," he said, with a firm grip. "May I take your coat?" Unlike his wife, or Mots, he did put a question mark at the end of a question. It made me feel at home. About the coat, though, I looked over at Mrs. Haig-Ereildoun with a silent apology and said to him, no thank you, I am fine. My answer made his eyes smile. "A bit warmer in California, I venture." He shook Mots's hand with vigor and asked if he could tempt us with a whiskey. Mots said no thank you so I did too, although I wouldn't have minded a glass of whiskey. "And you, darling?" he asked his wife, who pursed her lips and said her no thank you without a word, or a glance in his direction. Her eyes were fixed on me. They hadn't left me since we'd entered the room. Mr. Haig-Ereildoun put the book back down on his chair and walked to a cabinet in the corner. Without measuring or anything, he poured from a bottle into a glass. He dribbled in some water from a little pitcher and swirled his glass for a taste. "In America you take ice, don't you?" he said. "We don't need that here!" He had a nice laugh. Rich voice. Very English and aristocratic.

As the rest of us chose places and seated ourselves primly on the edges of our cushions, he strode back to his armchair and, pitching the book to the other chair, tossed himself into the seat and threw his head back to rest it. His long legs, in loose tweed pants, sprawled far apart. He took another sip and balanced his drink on the chair arm, letting his own arms fall loose, his fingers barely touching the glass.

I heard Mrs. Haig-Ereildoun say to Mots, "And so, Mrs. Hedrick . . ."

Relieved to have her talking to Mots instead of me, I said to him, "I thought you were Scottish."

"That I am," he said. "Scottish I am indeed."

I'd assumed so. His wife's letter had said they lived half in London half in Scotland because he was a member of Parliament with "a Scottish seat."

"But you don't sound Scottish," I said. He sounded Shakespearean.

A chuckle rumbled up. "I suppose I *don't* sound Scottish!" He swirled the drink in his glass. "That would be because I was educated in England. Everyone in my family has been educated in England, for at least the last hundred and fifty years. Before that, they probably did sound Scottish." The look on his face, as he watched the liquid circle the sides of his glass, showed it amused him to imagine relatives of his sounding Scottish.

I could see Mrs. Haig-Ereildoun watching me as she asked "Mrs. Hedrick" if they'd thought, yet, about what schools they would consider for their baby. I leaned forward and accepted a Rothman from the bent pack Mr. Haig-Ereildoun held out to me. I thanked him for lighting it—feeling the disapproval on her face without looking over to see it. He asked me about my flight. Hearing, with one ear, Mots's reply about the schools, I gave him at least a fast sketch of how bumpy my flight had been, and he said, "I had rather a nasty flight myself last week, coming back from Cairo." He rearranged himself, tossing a leg over an arm of his chair. "I had a good meeting with the president, though, and got some good footage of him. One night we'll have to show you the video." To free both hands to illustrate his description of the president's personality, he set his drink back down on the arm of his chair.

"Angus!" his wife said, flashing her eyes at the drink. "Do be careful."

Even as she finished that sentence, her eyes traveled from the tip of my toe to the top of my head, taking in once again the bitten nails, the flaming pimple on my chin, my missing coat button, and the smoke coming off the cigarette.

She had a basket beside her, full of children's socks and nametags. She barely glanced at her work of sewing on nametags, barely glanced at Mots as the two of them talked: She moved her needle absently and pierced me, with her half frown and her water-blue eyes. As Mr. Haig-Erieldoun mused that Oregon must be similar to Scotland and that San Francisco must be "the most geographically blessed city on earth," I remembered being twelve and reading some book about a governess, and how her prospective employer asked her to take off her gloves in order to have her fingernails examined.

Before the little brass clock had done many ticks, Mots, who has never been able to tolerate small talk, stood up and said that she had to get back to her baby and her husband. With my eyes I pleaded with her to stay a little longer. But even while I was silently begging, I remembered how, after she'd lived in London for just a year, she'd come home for a visit, full of observations on how much better England was than America, including the complaint, "Americans take so long to say goodbye."

"WELL, MELISSA," MRS. HAIG-EREILDOUN said, clicking the front door shut, "Mr. Haig-Ereildoun will take up your case, and I'll give you a peek at the children and go over tomorrow's schedule [shedjool] with you. It will be quite a busy day. Your first task this evening will be to lay the table for breakfast. Then I'll show you how to work the electric kettle, the washing-up machine and the cooker, how to set out Claire and Trevor's clothes—the elemental procedures of every day."

The children were nestled all snug in their beds: Christmas-card children with long, lush lashes and cheeks like roses, the girls with gold ringlets, the boy red-headed. I learned where their clothes were kept—three-year-old Claire's in the nursery on the ground floor, although she slept on the third floor; nine-year-old Trevor's upstairs in eleven-year-old Pru's room, although he slept on the second floor; and Pru's in her father's wardrobe on the fourth floor, one story up from her own room. It struck me as illogical. I'd be spending a lot of time running up and down stairs. I learned how to check the battery on Claire's hearing aid, and that I must set it at "naught" when I took it off to put her to bed. They're not sure she's totally deaf, or if the hearing aid helps or confuses. They hope it helps. She can't tell them.

. . .

HALF THE KITCHEN WAS papered with a print of Delft blue and white, and then right in the middle of one wall the paper changed to buff and brown tones. Seeing me notice, Mrs. Haig-Ereildoun said, with pepper in her voice, "I started repapering a few years ago, but I ran out. Originally, the print that's now brown was the same blue as the new paper." A large sheet of painted pegboard was nailed above the stove, pots and pans and spatulas hanging, along with spats of grease and cobwebs and a few dead bugs, plus a live one, struggling. The wooden table was square. "This is the cutlery we use for breakfast," Mrs. Haig-Ereildoun said to me, pulling six sterling knives, forks, and miniature teaspoons from the drawer. She walked with me, looking over my shoulder as I set them out. When I was through, she repeated my path around the table, switching the knife to go outside the spoon at each place setting. "This is how it is done," she said kindly.

"Really?" I said, interested in this little difference. "In America we put the knife inside the spoon."

She gave me a look. Examining.

"We put the knife inside," I said. "Next to the plate."

For an instant she looked surprised, then apparently realized that I was wrong, and that there was no need to embarrass me. "How interesting," she said.

You might think only butlers would be insulted. But table-setting is something I know. About England I know not, but I am right about table-setting in America. I felt a heat build up under my skin.

"And the napkins?" I asked.

"Oh, we don't use them."

MY ROOM WAS THE only nice one in the house. It was tiny, painted peachy pink, with a single bed, a peach-pink bedspread, a one-row bookshelf stocked with paperbacks, a framed botanical drawing of a rose, and a vase of camellias on the bedside table. I checked out the paperbacks. A book about gardening, the short stories of Turgenev, some travel books by someone called Baedeker, a book of Tennyson's poems, and a Penguin pocket book of *War and Peace* exactly like the one I'd brought for myself, except this one was fat with having been read.

My first mistake in English was the last thing I asked Mrs. Haig-Ereildoun that night: Where's the bathroom? She showed me the door, right across from my room. She said she was going up to bed then and would switch off the hall and stair lights when she got upstairs. "Please don't switch them on again tonight, as it will wake the entire household. Sleep well. I'll need you to be at your best tomorrow."

A moment of panic struck when I entered the bathroom. Tub, sink, cupboard, chest of drawers. Period. In the dark, I felt my way along the walls, down the staircase, around the ground floor, back up another flight and a half, until I came to the room I should have asked for.

When I got in bed, a rumble built up and the vase rattled, then steadied itself without spilling. I've lived in California for a year, which is long enough to get used to earthquakes. But I hadn't expected one in England. In the morning I woke up to another shake.

"Oh, that's just the *underground*!" Pru squealed, at breakfast. "The Circle Line makes a path *directly* under our *house*!" Pru is at that thrillable age. Her school uniform, gray wool over a white blouse, could have been a prison matron's. Instead of detracting from her prettiness, such a stern uniform set off her radiance. Pru has the plump rosy face of a cherub about to blossom into Botticelli's Venus. Taking up her little spoon (these English teaspoons are so cute), she leaned toward me with sparkling eyes. "I absolutely can't *wait* for you to tell me every single *thing* about America!"

Her mother said that might take a few hours, and we had very little time to get through breakfast. She said we'd have quite a few hours in Scotland. I didn't realize at the time what an understatement that was.

MY FIRST DAY IN London was to be our last full day in the city for a month. "When you've cleared the breakfast things and done the washing up, made up the children's beds (I'm afraid that means a change of sheets today), and have scrubbed the nursery floor, you'll set the table for lunch, pack the children's cases, take Claire for a walk in the park, come back to prepare lunch, and give Claire her rest as you finish the washing-up and clean out the fridge. Trevor has a half day, as it's last day of term, so when you've done the washing up he will show you the way to the library to stock up on books for Scotland. Pru has her own, but I've prepared a list of the books Claire and Trevor should get, as well as any additional ones that catch their eye. Trevor is particularly keen on the American Indian. I assume you're an authority, and you'll be a great help at selecting the most exciting books, for a boy his age. As we'll be gone for five weeks, you'll need to fill out a permission form to extend both the number of withdrawals allowed and the due date. I've written a note, but just in case, you should bring your passport for identification. After the library, you must exercise Claire again, as being deaf gives her far too much energy. It has something to do with the effect on the mind when one hasn't the use of words. Trevor will be a help with the exercise, today, in the park. You mustn't let him push Claire too long in the swings, though, because it does something to her eustacian tubes, and the same is true for the merry-go-round thingy that the children push themselves. Keep in mind that you must be home in time for tea, at half past four. Normally tea will be your responsibility, but I'll prepare something simple this afternoon, as you have your work cut out. As for the children's supper, they'll have boiled eggs. You can boil eggs, can't you? Normally, you'll have eggs with the children, but for your first supper here I've bought a cutlet for you. And yes, I've talked it over with Mr. Haig-Ereildoun, and it will be all right for your to accept your invitation to attend the symphony with your friends tonight, as it will be your last evening in London. That means, though, that you'll have to be extremely well organized with the supper and the washing up, and the bathing of the children. The performance is at eight, and you won't be able to leave until Claire is in her bed and you've had your cutlet. Trevor can watch his program for the half hour, Pru will have her reading, and I can put the two older children to bed. I will require, though, that you come home immediately after the performance and be in bed with your light off by half-ten. Tomorrow will be even more demanding than today."

My mind is still on that cutlet. It was the smallest lamb chop I've ever seen, a scrap of bone with so little meat I couldn't believe anyone would bother to cook it. Most people would throw it away.

IN TEACHING CLAIRE TO speak, I started with a blank book. She knew only three words: "Hhhoo," for Pru (with a prolonged, grunted "h," almost like the beginning of a retch, starting back where her tongue was attached); "*Hhheh*-hhhuh" for Trevor; and "No!" She was very proud of "no." Her pronunciation was perfect. As I dressed her for breakfast that first day, she marched around the bathroom shouting "No! No! No!"—looking at me to see if she'd achieved the desired effect. It put her off that she hadn't. I wasn't impressed one way or the other, but she recovered and marched around the bathroom anyway, continuing the chant. I know what that's like, since I'm usually the only one who gets my own jokes.

She's had three and a half years to learn to speak. I'm not sure how long I'll be here, but it occurred to me the first morning that if

I wanted to double Claire's vocabulary, I'd only have to teach her three words. I started. In the bathroom, after tying her shoes, I pointed to myself and said, "Melissa."

She looked at me and yelled, "No!" She ran about, laughing. "No! No! No!"

Still crouched at shoe-tying level, with my face at the same height as hers, I pointed to my nose and said, "nose."

Aha. This was a good one. "No! No! No!" she shouted.

"Pretty *good!*" I said. *"Nose!"* I pointed to her nose.

"No no no no no no no!"

"Pretty *good,*" I said.

I knew something had happened when she got to the breakfast table and pointed to Trevor's nose, shouting, "No! No! No!" She then touched her own nose and shouted the same thing.

"What *have* you done to her," Mrs. Haig-Ereildoun snapped.

After doing the breakfast washing-up and changing all the sheets but my own, I helped Claire into her cute little red coat and tried "nose" again. I got the same response from her ("no!"), and she got the same response from me: "pretty *good!*" I thought of trying "mouth" next, but that would be too hard, so I held her head in my hands and said, "head!" She said, "No! No! No!" When I didn't say "pretty good," she gave me an annoyed look, like a reprimanding professor over the rim of his eyeglasses. Taking her head in my hands again, I said, "Head." Then I held my own head and said, "Head." One more time I took hers and said, "Head."

"Hhheh!" she said.

I picked her up in my arms and swung her, laughing. We were both exhilarated. "Yes, yes, yes! Head!" She grabbed my head and said, "Hhheh!"

Boy, were we doing good. On the way to Kensington Gardens I kept stopping her stroller (or "pushchair," as they call it) to move around to where I could put my face up to hers, so she could see my lips as I pointed at things. Exaggerating my pronunciation, I said, "Bus!" "Man!" "Truck!" "Taxi!" She seemed to enjoy this, although she didn't answer back with word sounds, just with laughing. When I got to "nose," though, she went into her no-no-no's and clapped her hands. We tried "head" again. At first she didn't remember, but it came back to her, and she got a great laugh. *Hhheh!*

Getting closer to the park the skyline became a charcoal sketch of bare trees, and the words became "Dog!" "Squirrel!" "Statue!" Inside the big gate, I unstrapped her seatbelt and let her run wild, chasing squirrels in her chubby red coat, her strap-buckled shoes flying every which way over the lawn, as we passed a dignified man with a pheasant feather in his hat putting his Irish setter through an elaborate drill. Off the leash, the dog adjusted his step to keep his nose in line with his master's left knee. Told to sit, the dog's haunches sank to touch the lawn and his front legs stayed stiff, his muzzle high, facing forward. At the word "stay," the alertness in the dog's face intensified almost to a shiver, and a slight tail vibration hit my heart: I'd never seen such an anxiety to please. The man threw a weighted thing, and as it soared, even the muscles in the Irish setter's tail stilled. The object landed and the dog remained frozen until the man murmured, "Fetch"—a quiet word as powerful as a starting gun. I watched the russet body and tail fly over the green grass with grace like something in *Swan Lake*—a dip to pick up the object, a wide, free turn, and the flight back to the master, to hand over the prize. Another throw, the dog quivering in erect obedience, an imitation of patience as he waited for the word "fetch" to free him again.

A straight-backed nanny pushed a pram. A boy with nose rings and a black velvet cloak floated by, trailing a guitar behind him. A couple kissed. The couple kissing (and kissing) made me think of Tedward for the first time since breakfast. Claire running far ahead,

I slowed my steps to watch the kissing as long as possible, savoring both the envy that swashed through my body and the swoon. No wonder there are peeping toms.

Claire sped on, her feet at home with the path, and soon we were at the shore of a huge, round pond. "Duck!" I shouted. I took her shoulders, put my face up to hers, and said, more quietly, "Duck." Families of ducks huddled together in the icy slush around the shore. Claire ran to the pond, clapping her hands, sending a small flock into the air. What power she had. She ran around the pond from cluster to cluster, disrupting the peace. I sat on an ice-cold bench and lit a cigarette, thinking of the kissing couple, and Tedward. It hadn't been that many hours since I'd been kissing him like that. I'd almost missed my plane.

When it came time to buckle Claire back in her pushchair, I took her head in my hands. "Hhheh!" she shouted, "Hhheh! Hhheh! Hhheh!" She grabbed my head and said, "Hhheh."

I PUSHED HER AROUND the bend of Lettering Lane just in time to see a black station wagon pull up in front of the forsythia tree to drop Trevor off, after his half day. There's something irresistible about a nine-year-old in short pants, knee socks, blazer, necktie, and little round spectacles, carrying a briefcase. Latching the gate behind him, he walked the eight or nine steps to the forest-green door, put his hand on the knob, and turned back. At the gate, instead of opening it, he touched it and slowly pivoted, returning to the brass knob in the center of the door. He seemed to be in a daze. He touched the knob and turned again to the gate, touching his fingers to the latch but not opening it. He looked at the ground and didn't see us as he went through his paces, gate to door, door to gate; and he didn't seem to hear Claire shouting, "*Hhheh*-hhuh! *Hhheh*-huh!" (that means "Trevor") as I said, "Trevor?"

"Mmmm," he said, ducking his head, and slipping the briefcase handle over one wrist, he pushed both hands into his pockets.

"Something wrong?"

"Mmm."

"What?"

He didn't raise his head. He mumbled something like, "My report."

"Report?"

"Mmm. We got our reports. I don't want to show Mummy." He swung up his briefcase, heavy with books, and pulled out five crumpled booklets, like the blue books we used for exams at the University of Oregon. Each blue cover had four blanks. The first blank on all five was filled in, "Trevor Haig-Ereildoun." Next, the name of the subject, then the name of a teacher, and finally the letter "F."

I stifled a gasp.

"There are five marks you can get," he told me. " 'O' for outstanding, 'E' for excellent, 'G' for good, 'F' for fair, and 'P' for poor."

The inside pages of each book were filled with handwriting that I didn't have time to start, because at that moment the front door opened. Mr. Haig-Ereildoun stepped out.

"Hello," he said. "We seem to have a conflagration. What's this?"

Trevor took the books from me and handed them to his father. Pressing his chin against the knot of his tie, Trevor mumbled, "My reports."

Mr. Haig-Ereildoun browsed each cover with eyebrows slowly rising. "Hmm," he said. He said "Hmmmm" again, making it longer. "All fairs." He scratched a place between his eyebrows. He looked at the top of Trevor's head. "I, I-I-I say. All fairs?"

The pain in Trevor's eyes, as he met his father's.

The father screwed his eyes to see his son clearly, the boy with shame written all over his body.

"All fairs," the father said. "I say. I say. I say, that's . . . That's *fair*-ly good!"

Trevor stared at Mr. Haig-Ereildoun with a stunned look, and then he laughed. We all broke out laughing, especially Claire.

Shuffling through all the pages, Mr. Haig-Ereildoun said, "This should make quite stimulating reading. Meanwhile, I'm quite late getting to the House of Commons. Cheerio." He wheeled his bicycle through the gate, clicked it shut, and mounted the bike. As he rode off, we watched the front of his tweed jacket flap backward.

I LOVED THE KENSINGTON Library, a real ye olde library. And this time, at the park, Claire got part of "duck." In fact, she got a hint of the final consonant, if not the first. It must have been that the way I exaggerated my lips on the "k" sound made an impression, because she said, "Hhhuggh," making that beginning of a retch sound at both ends of the word. She ran to Trevor, who had his hands in the pockets of his short gray pants, watching an old woman throw bread to the ducks. Claire pointed to the ducks and shouted, "Hhhuggh! Hhhuggh!" He looked at her, confused. She socked his knee and pointed again to the ducks. "Hhhuggh!" His eyes, behind the glasses, had that fuzzy look—until he saw the ducks and snapped into focus. "Oh," he said. He patted her on the head and said, "Duck. Well done." He might have patted my head, too.

Nose, head, and duck? I'd doubled her vocabulary the first day.

IN THE NURSERY, WITH Trevor sitting on the floor next to the ironing board, his illustrated *Life of the Iroquois* spread open, I pressed hard on the iron. Spending three days in my suitcase had left the white linen collar of my navy blue dress so wrinkled I needed all my weight to force the linen smooth. I was afraid the new pleats in the skirt would be permanent. The eggs were getting hard-boiled in the kitchen, but Mots's father-in-law, Mr. Hedrick, had given us his box-seat tickets at Festival Hall, and I couldn't sit in Mr. Hedrick's box looking like a bag lady. However, after Mrs. Haig-Ereildoun stepped in and instructed me about the sequence of people to use the same bathwater (first Claire, then Pru, then Trevor, then her, and me number five), I decided I could get by without a bath. I hadn't realized England was such a poor country.

Mots says it isn't. Not anymore. "Some people just don't take to change."

"TREVOR," SAID PRU, BRUSHING past the ironing board with an imperiousness she must have been trying on, like clothes from her mother's closet, "Trevor. Have you decided what you want done with your remains."

"Remains?" Trevor, his pink knees poking left and right, looked up from the book. His red-tipped eyelashes brushed the perfectly round little lenses of his spectacles.

"Your body. After you're dead. What do you want done with your remains. Do you want to be buried or cremated."

"Neither," he said, going back to the Iroquois.

"Buried or cremated," Pru repeated. "You'll have to be one or the other."

"No. I want to be et."

"What!" Pru gasped. "Et! How hideous!"

"Not really," Trevor said. "I've thought about it. I don't want my body going to waste. I want to be properly cooked, with wine. I want someone to enjoy me."

"Oh, *ghastly!*" Pru gave him one last despising look, raised her chin, and floated out of the drawing room.

She poked her head through the doorway once more to add, "Absolutely un-English."

He looked up at me from his book. He let a little smile grow.

. . .

IN MY DRESS AND my nice flats, I put my coat back on for warmth and pretested the water for Claire. One memory I won't forget from being a child is the terror of getting into the bathtub. It could feel like being boiled alive. In some biology class I learned that what makes a tiny person so sensitive to temperature has something to do with the ratio of total volume to total surface area. The smaller you are, the more of you is total surface area: exposed nerve endings. I wanted to let Claire test the water with her foot so I could adjust it before she had to get in deep. Claire, though, is not a normal child. Take her anywhere near a bathtub and she wants to use her powers to get all the water out of it. Getting naked and wet is the starting gun for a wild time. It was lucky the house was so cold I'd had to keep my coat on, because water dribbles off the wool the way it dribbles off the ducks in the pond. However, the blood that dribbled from my chin as she dug her nails in so happily—just missing the red-hot pimple—dried into small scabs, and I was going to have to sit in Mr. Hedrick's box looking like a battered woman.

Mr. Haig-Ereildoun passed by the open bathroom door on his way up the stairs and raised his voice to call out, over Claire's screams of delight, "I hear you're going to the symphony. LPO or LSO?"

Holding Claire's hands still but being careful not to let her drown, I had to think this out. It was the London Symphony. I said . . . "LSO!" The LPO must have been the London Philharmonic. I felt like Claire, learning "Hhheh!"

"Bravo," said Mr. Haig-Ereildoun, continuing his loose-tweeded lankiness up two steps at a time.

RUPERT HAD MADE IT a foursome by inviting a friend. Simon. A tall, bony guy with incredibly blue eyes. Simon's suit seemed to be from the Salvation Army. He obviously hadn't tried to iron it. Who was it that described Dylan Thomas as looking like an unmade bed? Extra-long, in Simon's case. He's doing a PhD at London University, in psychology. He has lived in America, though. He got his master's in Michigan. Working with monkeys. In London, for his doctorate, he's reduced to rats. He told me about an American at his lab who'd made an interesting mistake in English, regarding bathrooms. At the registrar's office, he asked the receptionist, "Do you have a rest room?" The receptionist went blank. She left, to consult with a few people. The American stood on one foot, then the other. At last the receptionist got back, triumphant. "Yes! We have a rest room. This way." She led him down a long corridor and opened a door, ushering him in and closing the door. It was a darkened room, with several beds.

This was my last night of being my own person—of being with people I knew, who knew me, who treated me like myself.

5

TROONFACHAN WAS SIX HUNDRED miles away, and we were splitting the journey, spending the weekend at Mrs. Haig-Ereildoun's parents' house in the north of England. All I knew about her mother and father was that they lived in a place called Phillingsford, that they had a "brilliant" television, with a "vast" screen. I pictured a little town in the north of England, sort of like a small town in the north tip of Oregon—Scapoose or Clatskanie or Svensen—and a little square house with a triangle roof and a big antenna.

Pru sat in the front seat. Her long curls are so fine and blond they glisten even without sun on them. Trevor, Claire, and I spread out in the back of the station wagon with our books. I pointed to pictures and exaggerated my lips to tell Claire the words. She studied first the picture, then my face, with intense interest, although she didn't try to copy. We turned the page to an apple-cheeked, helmeted man with a blue uniform and a badge. "Bobby!" I said. Mrs. Haig-Ereildoun stopped her conversation with Pru and turned her head to the back. "I don't think you should teach her the word 'bobby.' "

"Really?"

"No. That's something like the American word 'cop.' We say, 'policeman.' "

"Policeman!" I said to Claire. "Policeman!" I repeated, with enthusiasm. She gave me a blank look, and we turned the page. "Truck!" I said.

Mrs. Haig-Ereildoun turned back: "We say, 'lorry.' "

The scenery on the A–whatever was disappointing when we drove out of London. Housing developments. Neat, compact houses of yellow brick. Identical, boring little rectangles one after another. The streets were geometrically laid out, with no swerves of imagination. No greenery. But as we got farther from London, the road got thinner and the green got thicker. It got gorgeous. "Cow!" I said to Claire. "House!" "Lamb!"

"These hills are called wolds," Mrs. Haig-Ereildoun called back from the front seat. "Wolds are hills that are barely hills, just lovely big lumps." The lumps were lovely. Her voice had cheered into the one she'd had on the phone to San Francisco.

We stopped and spread the rug under a clump of bare elms. (A rug is a blanket.) The hamper was full of pleasures, like crispy brown ovals that glistened gold—edible, organic, Faberge eggs. Beneath a shell of toasty breadcrumbs were concentric surprises: a ring of crunchy sausage, and deeper inside, another ring of hard-boiled egg white, then the round powdery yolk. These little treasures were called Scotch eggs. There was cold chicken, like no chicken I'd ever tasted the juice of. "So tasty!" I said. "Our English chickens are far better than yours," Mrs. Haig-Ereildoun agreed. She told me she had lived in New York City for a year, after finishing her degree at Oxford. She'd worked as a fact-checker for *Life* magazine. "The American chickens!" She smiled to show she was teasing and said, "I realize that you Americans are compulsively clean and sterile, but it amazes me that you take it so far as to pull all the flavor out of your hens." For dessert we had shortbread cookies and apples, also more delicious than ours. "Cox orange pippins!" Pru identified with patriotic pride. They weren't half as pretty as shiny red delicious, but they had a bouquet. The tart-sweetness was nectar.

Back behind the steering wheel after lunch, Mrs. Haig-Ereildoun returned to her tense self. She got tenser and tenser. Claire, on my lap, churned in her sleep. Trevor, on my other side, had closed his Iroquois book and sat stiff. The front seat conversation had stopped, and the only sound was the occasional inhale from Mrs. Haig-Ereildoun, extra loud, and then a blow from her lips. I tilted my angle so I could see her face in the rearview mirror. Her expression was, as Mr. Haig-Ereildoun would say, very very unhappy indeed. She blew up from her lower lip, as if trying to blow wisps of hair off her forehead, but there were no wisps of hair on her forehead. By a grove of leafless hardwoods, she swerved the car to a stop. "I'm sorry!" she exploded, turning to the backseat. "I've endured it thus far, you being an American. But I can't take it any more."

My heart stopped. What had I, or my country, done?

"We *must* go to the loo!" she said. "I'm *sorry*. But that is a fact. We *must* urinate."

I had felt under pressure to urinate myself. What did this have to do with America? I'd been wondering when we'd ever get to a gas station. Having started to learn the language, I said, "When will we get to the next petrol station?"

"Petrol station!" She shot the words. "I'm talking about the need to urinate!"

I closed in my shoulders, all compressed and petrified.

"You Americans are such prudes, you can't *go* by the side of the road. What on earth *do* you *do*?"

I was thinking, we go to a gas station, but apparently these petrol stations didn't have toilets, so I told her what we'd do instead: "We go in the woods."

She heaved a great sigh and restarted the station wagon to steer it into a thicker clump of hardwoods. "You're lucky this isn't France," she snapped. "You might *die* of shame! They just *wee*-wee right on the edge of the road."

Why did she think that would kill me?

I said nothing and found a private thicket for me and Claire and used a leaf to dry myself. Of course, I had to unpin Claire's diaper, because her lack of speech makes potty training impossible, even though she's three. Her nappie was wet, so I'd brought a dry one from the car. She did have enough urine left in her, though, to copy my squat and pee in the bushes. I handed her a leaf.

"Well done!" I said, as I fastened the fresh nappie. To show her affection, she dug her nails into my chin, again just missing the pimple.

WE WERE PICKING UP Mr. Haig-Ereildoun at the train station in Stanford. He'd given a speech there the night before. The most interesting thing about Stanford was the women's loo at the train station. Someone had written a story across all the walls, floor to ceiling and all around the interior. The writing was supposedly by a secretary whose boss closed the office at half past four every Friday, making everyone leave except himself and her, the secretary. Her handwriting, drifting across the walls from stall to stall, told of how her employer then commanded her to come stand by his massive boss's chair. "Like a throne," it was. He pulled her closer and pulled up her dress and pulled down her tights and panties. He made her turn so that he could examine her bare bottom. He then asked her to bend over, onto his lap. At that point he began to spank. She described the sound ("thwank") and the feel ("hot and stinging") of his large, meaty hand on her bare skin.

As I held Claire's hand and followed the handwriting around the walls, the pulse in my throat throbbed, and the pulse in a place deeper than my own bottom. I tended to Claire and used the loo myself and rushed out dragging Claire.

Typewriter in one hand, Mr. Haig-Ereildoun leapt off the train and landed on two feet. He would use a typewriter. "I find the touch of a computer very unsatisfying indeed," he says. Such a traditionalist. But not prim. You should ride in a car with him. With him at the wheel, the road winding through the wolds became the Grand Prix. "Angus!" commanded his wife, as we whistled within an inch of an oncoming Rover. He laughed and took the next turn on two wheels. "Daddy!" Pru scolded, at the same time as Trevor shouted, "Well done!" and Claire clapped her hands. I sat erect, barely touching the seat, brittle enough to break as we overtook every car that poked along at forty-five miles an hour. We skidded to avoid a cow. I gave silent thanks to God every time we didn't crash. I could imagine Tedward being there, with Mr. Haig-Ereildoun putting my life in danger. Tedward would clock him.

We whizzed by a road sign that said Phillingsford twenty miles, then Phillingsford fifteen miles—ten, five, three. Now and then after the twenty-mile sign, Pru or Trevor would point and say, "Cossle!" I picked out faraway towers and turrets poking up through a fuzz of wiry branches, across miles of plush green pillowy wolds.

Phillingsford one mile. Then quick as a wink a small wooden sign indicated a narrow side road leading to Phillingsford. In the rearview mirror I could see Mr. Haig-Ereildoun's face savor the squeak of the wheels as he spun the corner into a forest. The road from there was straight, crowded by thickets of twisty bare branches reaching for the sky. Mr. Haig-Ereildoun managed to make our Volvo roar like a jet, then screech to a slowdown. A clearing. The station wagon went almost silent to make part of a *ronde-de-jambe* onto a yellow gravel drive circling a vast lawn with a mirror globe centerpiece, on a pedestal, reflecting a shimmering blend of greens and silvers and all the colors in this peaceful atmosphere. Beyond the reflective centerpiece stood a grand red brick manor house with tall windows and a grand set of doors opening, an old couple stepping out—tiny people, compared to the doors. The four doors of the station wagon flew open, and Pru and Trevor shot out, running. Grampy, tall and spindly as one of those cartoons from the old *Vanity Fair,* lifted his stick to wave as he opened his other long, long arm to Pru. Granny, plump and rosy in a cloud-pink sweater, reached out to let Trevor skid to a stop and pump an exaggerated handshake. She lifted pudgy, stumbling Claire to her bosom. I took in the chuckling and cooing, and the inscription way up above the door-case of the house: 1585.

When Trevor shuffled back to me, hands in the pockets of his short pants, I asked, "Where is the town?"

"What town?"

"Phillingsford," I said.

Trevor looked puzzled. He shrugged and pointed to the house. "This is Phillingsford."

"Mother," said Mrs. Haig-Ereildoun, "I'd like you to meet my American girl, Melissa. Melissa, this is my mother, Lady Chipchase, and my father, Sir Chester."

Well. This was more like it. This was the kind of lawn Henry James might have chosen for his lunches.

WALKING INTO PHILLINGSFORD. MONUMENTAL hall. A lake of polished wood at our feet, reflecting our silhouettes. Grand portals opening onto the west, east, and south wings. Tremendous staircase, gorgeously carved.

Trevor and Claire were running past us up the stairs, clattering floorboards. The slower strikes of Sir Chester's two feet and cane thudded up after them, so that the boards responded to him not with clatters but with groans.

"I trust you've hidden the remaining swan away, Mother," Mrs. Haig-Ereildoun said, nervously watching Claire disappear up the stairs. "I'll never forgive myself for Claire's breaking the neck of the dear old husband."

"But nonsense, Philippa. Claire is far more dear than a marble swan. This time, Mr. West has removed everything breakable."

"Where is *Mrs.* West?" Mrs. Haig-Ereildoun asked, sounding startled at not seeing her.

"Pru," Mr. Haig-Ereildoun said. "Why don't you come with me to the kitchen to hunt up Mrs. West?" I noticed adoration in Pru's posture as she looked up at him and fell in step, like a puppy proud to heel. When I was eleven (and other ages) I felt that way about my father—that specialness at being singled out even for a walk into the kitchen.

Lady Chipchase turned to me with a rueful smile. "I won't tell you the value Christie's assigned to the pair of swans. Poor Claire didn't mean to kill the husband. She banged into him quite innocently. Afterwards we wondered how he could have survived even a couple of centuries on those spindly legs." Lady Chipchase had a gentleness. I tried to put my finger on the difference between the softened way she pronounced her vowels and the brisker way Mr. and Mrs. Haig-Ereildoun whisked them out. In the few words he'd said, I'd noticed the same languishing quality in Sir Chester's speech as in Lady Chipchase's. "Lyanguishying." Or "thyank you." The grandparents preceded each vowel with a hint on a "y." Well, not all vowels. Like "Phyillingsford." The "phill" had a "y" ("phyill") but the "ings" didn't, and the vowel in "ford" wasn't pronounced at all: "fd." This was the way Sir Kenneth Clarke spoke, in those PBS tapes on art history. Very cultivated. ("Cultivyated.") It seemed that Granny and Grampy and Sir Kenneth Clarke had more leisure to spend on a syllable than the Haig-Ereildouns had. In just one generation, things had sped up enough to change the language.

"Melissa!" gasped Mrs. Haig-Ereildoun, suddenly aware of me, standing there. "*Whatever* are you doing."

Heart hiccuping, I jolted to attention.

"Melissa, hello?" Mrs. Haig-Ereildoun said.

Could she see the terror in my eyes?

"Melissa, you're *wanted upstairs!*"

On my way up I heard Mrs. Haig-Ereildoun sigh, "That girl!"

"But Philippa dear," Lady Chipchase calmed. "We were talking with her. And your father is upstairs with the children."

"Nonsense, Mother. Why do you think I have an American girl."

I was trying to keep my feet from creaking the old boards, as if silence would make me invisible to the four eyes following me. Being so quiet, on my long, winding way, I heard other shy footsteps tiptoe across the entry hall.

"Mrs. West!" Mrs. Haig-Ereildoun sang, all chirrupy again. I looked down to see the top of a gray head: a woman wearing a sweater, a tweed skirt, and a flowered apron.

"Ah, Philippa, it's a joy to see you. I've prepared you a lovely tea."

I stopped at the top of the stairs to hear Mrs. Haig-Ereildoun say, "And where is old Nanny?" and to hear Mrs. West answer that she'd spotted her from the kitchen window, making her way to the door. "Nanny walks very slow now," Mrs. West said.

Lady Chipchase told her daughter, "I'm frightfully keen to show you the rooms we converted for Nanny, over the stables. The renovation has been quite a project, and we're all of us a bit thrilled with the outcome. She's lived in her new flat quite independently for nearly a month now, and she's close enough for Mr. West to keep her fire going and for Mrs. West to slip over with her supper."

"Melissa!" Mrs. Haig-Ereildoun whipped her head up to see me sprint from my place at the landing. "That girl!" I heard her say, again.

"I suppose I see what you mean," I could imagine Lady Chipchase saying, but I didn't hear it, because by then I was in the room with Trevor, Claire, and Sir Chester.

. . .

IT WAS A BIG room, at the top of the stairs, with carved paneling and a covey of easy chairs and sofas huddled at one end—warm Persian rugs, some lamps, and the big television. Claire sat on her grandfather's bony knee, next to the cane resting against the cushion, reaching with both hands to feel his bald head and his sandpaper cheeks. Trevor stood facing Sir Chester, his long-socked feet planted far apart, his eyes wide behind his spectacles: "And then, Grampy, the Iroquois poured pitch all over Gabriel L'Allemant. And they forced Jean de Breboeuf to watch them light Gabriel L'Allemant on fire."

"Ah. Burnt him alive, did they," Grampy asked, acknowledging my entrance with his eyes.

"Yes, but Grampy, I think it was far worse, even at that moment, for Jean de Breboeuf than for Gabriel L'Allemant, who was covered in flame like—like a human candlewick. Because I think by the time they lit Gabriel L'Allemant on fire he must have wanted to die, and death is always worse for the people who are still alive than it is for the dead person. I mean, if you're already dead, why would you care? And if you've been set afire, you want to die, I'm sure, but it was quite terrible for his friend, Jean de Breboeuf, to see Gabriel being burnt. And Jean de Breboeuf *said* the Iroquois were wicked, he *shouted* it out. He screamed at them how evil they were, so they sliced off Jean de Breboeuf's *lips!*"

"Good heavens."

"Yes. Really. And then they forced a red-hot iron down his throat."

"Oh, good heavens."

"And that wasn't enough for them. While Jean de Breboeuf was still alive, still struggling to tell them how wrong they were, even though by then he didn't have any lips, so he must not have spoken very clearly, they cut into Jean de Breboeuf's heart and drank his blood."

"How did it taste?"

Trevor stopped, startled. "The book didn't say. But I imagine they enjoyed it."

Sir Chester smiled. Claire went into convulsions of giggling.

"What I wonder is, Grampy, what do you think about dying? Is it worse for the dead person, or for the people who miss the dead person?"

"I can't say, Trevor, as I haven't been dead yet."

"Yes," Trevor said, thinking hard. "That's the problem. Because once you're dead, you can't describe it for the rest of us, can you?"

6

"NORMALLY YOU WILL SLEEP in the nursery." With a brisk step, Mrs. Haig-Ereildoun led the way through the dining room, passing a table as long as the one in the Mad Hatter's tea party, surrounded by portraits bigger than people; through a tiled kitchen with shelves so high I couldn't imagine what ladder could reach them; to a skinny back staircase and up to a linoleumed room the size of our high school gym, with a kitchen at one end and a dormitory of cramped little bedrooms at the other. In a cubicle with no windows she pointed to the lower bunk. "This will be your bed. Claire will sleep above." She opened a door to show the closet. "There's plenty of room in the cupboard for your things and hers." One by one she opened the drawers of the chest. "Two drawers will be Claire's, two will be yours. You will unpack her case first, then Trevor's and Pru's." Leading me into a second tight room, then a third, each with two sets of bunk beds and two chests of drawers, she said, "As it's only us this weekend, Trevor will have a room of his own, and Pru will be over here." Pru's was the only room with a window. "Often we have a much larger menagerie of children here, and my nieces and nephews have their own nannies, so who knows where everyone will sleep when we're all here together. This weekend, I'm afraid, you'll have your first experience of being displaced."

Displaced to where?

"Old Nanny wants to stay in the nursery this weekend. I'm afraid you'll have to give up your bed—the one below Claire's. That's been Nanny's bed, after all, for most of her life."

I imagined spending my life in that compartment.

"She *does* miss the children," Mrs Haig-Ereildoun continued her apology, "and after all, this is her domain. So for this weekend my mother has found a place for you in the wing where the rest of us sleep. Before you unpack the children's cases, I'll show you to where you'll be."

"Who is old Nanny?" I asked, as we clattered back down the stairs meant for servants and children.

"Who is old Nanny! Oh! She's been my family's nanny for forty-four years. When we were small, she took care of my brothers and me, and then as we married and had our own children, she took turns with each of us as we needed her." As we made the trek through the kitchen, hard heels resounding on the tiles, she said, "Nanny took care of Pru and Trevor, and later my eldest brother's first two, and then my next brother's first son." Whizzing through the dining room, portraits of the ancestors blurring by as I tried to keep up with Mrs. Haig-Ereildoun, she continued: "We do seem to have spaced our children rather handily for Nanny. Now she has trouble with her legs, and Claire would be too much for her." We paused in the entry hall, with the various portals leading to parts unknown. "I'm afraid my brother Humbert, who is the baby of the family, will miss out altogether, as he's not yet married." Like small chipmunks skittering up a big tree, we climbed the staircase. "It's his room you'll be sleeping in." She led me down a corridor. "Don't worry," she said with a smile. "Humbert won't be here. He lives in London. He has rather an important job, in the city."

. . .

IN THIS HOUSE, I could take off my coat. Each person got fresh, hot bathwater. In fact, I got my own bathroom (not just my own loo, but my own room for a bath). Humbert's bedroom was still furnished with plaid chairs and plaid blankets and hundreds of books, from Ben Jonson to Sir Walter Scott to James Herriot. I looked for Hemingway, Faulkner, Hawthorne, any American, but found none. I looked for a woman writer: Jane Austen? Emily Bronte? George Eliot? Barbara Pym? Nope. The bed was a funny, bloomphy pudge, so I bopped on. Yikes. It was like falling from skis and sinking in powder. Feather mattress. It hadn't occurred to me that anyone in real life ever slept in a featherbed. My fireplace had a blackened brass plate on the hearth: 1698. This seemed wrong to me, since the house was built in 1585. But at tea I asked, and it turns out that all the fireplaces at Phillingsford have blackened brass plates inscribed with the dates they were installed. "Fireplaces were quite the luxury, back in the sixteenth and seventeenth centuries," Sir Chester said. "Even in the large houses, like this one, a family could only afford to add perhaps one each generation."

It was at tea that I first met Nanny. Our London tea had been milk, tea, and biscuits at the kitchen table. (Not cookies. Trevor and Pru think the American word "cookie" is one of the funniest sounds they've ever heard.) Tea at Phillingsford was high tea. Chafing dishes of scrambled eggs, sausages, poached eggs, and ham were brought to the center of the table by Mrs. West, in her sweater, tweed skirt, and apron. Silver toast racks sat at each end of the table, cooling thin slices of toast with their crusts removed. Beautiful china and cutlery.

Nanny, with downy white hair and candy-apple cheeks, even a crab-apple pink chin set atop a pillowy white pile of under-chins, sat between Claire's antique high chair and Pru. I sat between Pru and Trevor. Nanny wore a snowy cardigan clean as a baby's blanket, over a cotton dress whose print reminded me of a summer sky with powder-puff clouds. She kept her conversation scant and low volume, aimed only at the children, unless asked a question by another adult. Her accent was Cockney, like an old Eliza Doolittle. She served Claire's, Pru's, and Trevor's plates, and then her own dab of scrambled egg, a lone yellow polka dot on a large china plate. When Sir Chester protested, "Come now, Nanny, you must have more than that!" she answered, "I eat like a bird, I do. Always 'ave. Like a lih-hl bird."

The other adults would get a good supper, so we had only tea and cake. "You Americans don't normally go in for sweets in the afternoon, do you, Melissa," Lady Chipchase asked. Sir Chester answered for me: "They make up the calories they miss at tea by having a few martinis before supper." Everyone laughed, and Lady Chipchase looked at me closely. Of course Mrs. Haig-Ereildoun was watching me too, but I'd started to get used to that.

Nanny had cut up Claire's sausages for her, and she shot me a silent criticism as she leaned her heavy bodice past Pru's plate to Trevor's. She was struggling to attack his sausage with her knife. Her pointed look at me implied that I needn't be so lazy: He sat next to me, and couldn't I see that she had her hands full with Claire?

Trevor was nine. He had his own knife.

Mrs. West's poppyseed cake was scrumptious—and plenty—but when urged I also accepted one of Mrs. West's lovely lemon bars. I should be cutting down on these things, but I told myself I was easing Lady Chipchase's worry about saving up for martinis.

When the children had satisfied their appetites, Trevor said, "Granny, may we please get down?" Funny. Children do put question marks at the ends of their questions.

"First say grace," Sir Chester reminded.

It was a quick grace, led by Trevor: "Thank you, God, for this food." And they were off. Nanny dabbed her mouth with her napkin and Mr. Haig-Ereildoun helped her out of her chair so that she could hobble outside for the play on the lawn. Every few steps, as we walked out together, she dug both canes into the ground and rested, saying, "Aow, milegs!"

At the evening meal, no children, no Nanny. Just the Haig-Ereildouns, Sir Chester, Lady Chipchase, and me in my dress again. Mrs. West served "the joint": a lovely leg of lamb. It was not cooked to sawdust, the way you always hear English meat is served, but pink and juicy. In fact, the whole meal was pretty gourmet. Lady Chipchase proudly admitted that she had made the mint jelly herself, and there were compliments. ("Oh, but I say, you know how I like mint.") It wasn't sweet, like the kind we get in jars. The mashed potatoes had a bitter little bite to them, really wonderful, and I was told that I must be tasting the celeriac. (Celeriac?) The carrots had been browned with the lamb, with a caramelized crunch on top, not boiled to mush the way I'd been told to watch out for in England. The vichyssoise we had for a "starter" was even better than the one I'd made for Tedward, using my mom's most complicated cookbook, *Mastering the Art of French Cooking, Volume 1*, by Julia Child. As I remember, just reading the recipe for that took about half an hour. This Mrs. West was amazing.

The conversation at dinner was even more amazing. Almost from soup to dessert, it was a debate between Sir Chester and Mr. Haig-Ereildoun about what Queen Elizabeth the First's naval policy should have been: where she succeeded with the Spanish Armada, where she blew it. At Trevor's age I'd been as swept away by Queen Bess and her red-headed tempers as Trevor now is with the Iroquois, and I'd got almost drunk reading about Henry the Eighth's beheadings; but I hadn't paid any attention to the naval strategies. I had a hard time following Mr. Haig-Ereildoun's and Sir Chester's this-ship and that-ship (they knew all the names), this-sea and that-sea (they knew all the winds), but I hoped to understand, to learn something. Every time I glanced over at Lady Chipchase, her eyes were following my head, as it moved like a spectator at a slow-motion tennis match from the old man to the younger man, and back and forth. Her head didn't turn, it stayed fixed on me. She seemed displeased. Her daughter's vigilance, assessing me, was intense as ever. I felt a little sorrow at Lady Chipchase's rudeness to me, because from the first second I'd seen her I'd known she and I were of a kind, somehow. Like Trevor and me. Also, I was puzzled. I had always thought the English had the best manners of anyone on earth, and I would have thought that the particular English around this table would be the best-mannered in the kingdom. So why wasn't she embarrassed to stare, with the expression of a judge on her face?

Her approval of me didn't grow when Sir Chester told a story that must have been for my benefit, since the others had heard it. One year he realized that, with his and Lady Chipchase's rheumatism getting worse, not to mention old Nanny's, it was finally necessary to get central heating at Phillingsford. He couldn't imagine how he'd raise the funds. "Then one day, I was looking through one of the antiques magazines that I read, and I happened to glance at the adverts at the back. A black-and-white photograph of a ceramic artichoke struck me as familiar. I knew I'd seen it somewhere. It was so ugly one wouldn't forget it. A collector was searching the mate to this miserable object. I decided to have a look about, which involved several days and the use of a ladder. But at last, at the far back of the highest shelf in the nursery, lo and behold. I rang the number in the magazine, packed that dreadful artichoke in yards of gauze, string, brown paper, more string—repulsive as it was, I was not about to break it. Carrying it in both hands, I took it on the train to London, keeping it on my lap throughout the journey. And, to make a long story short, Staffordshire. 1667. That's how I paid for the central heating."

My interest in the story displeased Lady Chipchase.

At dessert it got worse. (They call it pudding. Or, as Mr. Haig-Ereildoun calls it, "pud." ("What's for pud?") At pud, I made my *pièce de résistance* of a faux pas. Mr. Haig-Ereildoun led me into it with the best intent, and I could see him smart, along with me, at the result.

Lady Chipchase blushed a little when she announced that she had made the pudding. It was a mint mousse. Heaven. All this whipped something, or whipped nothing, like a cloud. Flavored with mint, which evaporates when it hits your tongue. It was ethereal.

"I don't like it, Mother, I'm afraid," said Mrs. Haig-Ereildoun. "It tastes like toothpaste."

Everyone laughed.

"What about you, Melissa?" Mr. Haig-Ereildoun asked. He wanted to make me feel included. "Do you think it tastes like toothpaste?"

He hadn't meant to stick me in the middle of a fight. But since Mrs. Haig-Ereildoun had mentioned it, and I didn't want to disagree with her, I could see how the mousse tasted a little like Colgate.

Not quite knowing how I'd end my reply, but sure I'd think of something, I started out, "Well, I guess it does, a little . . ."

Lady Chipchase's eyes really shot me then.

"The most heavenly, ethereal toothpaste I've ever tasted," I concluded.

That wasn't quite enough.

She scowled into her plate.

7

AS PART MEMBER OF the family and part servant, half of me has risen to a much higher class. This is the class I feel naturally cut out for. The other half of me has sunk. The people I've met have not seen me as a little bit of each class; each has put me in one slot or the other. It's the males who seem to see me as I see myself—as one of their own. The females almost uniformly see me as their inferior. I'm not sure about Pru or Mrs. West, but even Nanny looks down on me.

KNOCK KNOCK. THE DOOR cracked open. "Good morning, I hope you slept well?" (Mrs. West.) "Good. Lovely. I'm to tell you that Mrs. Haig-Ereildoun is having a lie-in this morning. Breakfast will be served in the dining room in thirty minutes. Nanny is seeing to the children. And since this is a special day, she'll be breakfasting with the family."

Lie-in. What a nice word. A relief, too, because I'd worried I wouldn't be able to find the nursery again.

A few more minutes. Nothing like a featherbed, for a lie-in.

. . .

LADY CHIPCHASE AND SIR Chester sat at opposite ends of the Mad Hatter's table, with places set between for Nanny, the children, and me, and lots of spaces between the places. We served ourselves from the sideboard—again chafing dishes with eggs, poached or scrambled. Bacon, ham, and sausages. The toast racks. The cold toast.

"Americans always ask why we like our toast cold," Sir Chester told me, "so I'll spare you the trouble. If the toast is warm, the butter melts. It's as simple as that." He bit into his slice, chewed with relish, and swallowed. "We like the taste of cold butter."

"Did you get some of Nanny's Seville marmalade?" Lady Chipchase asked. "I think it's the best marmalade in England."

"My speciality," Nanny admitted, leaning across Pru's place to spread some on Trevor's toast. "No other oranges will do for good marmalade. Only Seville." They pronounce it with the accent on the first syllable. *Seh*-vil.

All three children wore fisherman's knit sweaters. "Nanny made them for us," said Trevor. He beamed at her.

"For Christmas!" Pru chirped. Pru is the absolute opposite of blasé.

"Oh, I'm 'andy with the needles I am. And these are my loves." She put a big, spotted hand over Claire's little fat one. "Made a pullover just like these for Mr. 'yge-Er'ldoun too, I did, a couple o' Christmases back."

I NOTICED LADY CHIPCHASE'S frown of concentration on my knife and fork as I ate my egg and sausage. I prayed for my left hand to make it to my mouth, instead of to my chin or my nose. I wanted her to be relieved of worry that I'd set an example of the American way of eating.

I did find, later, that my speech bothered her. That was after tea, after I'd given the children to Nanny for their supper of boiled eggs. As I was dressing for the grown-ups' supper (same dress), Mrs. Haig-Ereildoun knocked on my door. "May I come in?" She sniffed the air and wrinkled her nose until her eyes found the Silk Cut butt in the ashtray on the desk. She frowned. "May I sit down?" She sat in one of the plaid armchairs and bade me to sit in the other. "Mother and I were passing on the landing this afternoon, as you sat by the fire, reading to Claire. We stopped and listened, and we couldn't help but notice that as you broke off to stir a log, you said to Claire, 'fy-er.' We say, 'fah-ah.'

"Mother pointed out that, as learning to speak will be particularly difficult for Claire under any circumstances, it would be a pity to have her learn your pronunciations, instead of our own. And so, I was wondering. Could you be an angel, and do try to speak as we do?"

"FOUR HUNDRED ACRES," SIR Chester said. All of them green. Gentle green, rolling green, glowing green, under the silvery sky. We were walking to the aviary, Pru and Trevor running ahead with egg baskets, Claire stumbling along beside Sir Chester and me with a huge bag of stale bread, tearing off bits to throw on the ground and giggling as birds swooped and flew off with their cargo. "This is the church, and the graveyard." The church was a box, rectangular as a kitchen matchbox turned on end, made of square stones, with a squat square steeple. From the ground at the back of it, gravestones poked up like row upon row of gaped teeth. The simple slabs were packed in, too many to count. "I'm afraid that after four centuries it's so full that when it comes to our turn we'll have to move out a few bodies," Sir Chester said. We passed a croquet court and went under an arched bower covered with vines. Sir Chester moved at a clip, using his cane to propel his stork legs. Instead of guiding me along the path leading to the grass tennis courts he led me up to a wider path lined with cages, like a zoo. The cages held big exotic birds, all brilliant, like Joseph's coat of many colors.

"Our eldest son Harry manages the farm. He and his family live at the far corner. Four kids!" Sir Chester seemed to relish this American slang, as he pointed across the rolling green wolds in the direction of Harry's house, beyond our line of vision. "As the eldest son, Harry will, of course, own Phillingsford one day."

Primogeniture! I remembered that, from History 1A. But to hear of this law in reality, in this century, struck me. How could they give all this to one child, leaving the other three without? Sir Chester seemed to read my thoughts. "In America you don't have this custom, do you. Nor do they on the Continent. It's turned out to be quite a healthy tradition, part of what makies England great. No worthless young brothers lolling about the estate. The young ones are forced to go out and fend for themselves. From the time of Elizabeth, the young ones have become lawyers and shipmasters and clever doers who have often outdone their landed elder brothers." Sir Chester rested on his cane and absorbed himself in watching Pru and Trevor move through the chicken coops, plucking eggs from nests.

"Trevor," Pru quizzed. "Do you remember the names of each of the Banty hens?"

"Of course. Here's Gertrude, here's May, and Agatha—"

"Oh, Trevor." Pru was disgusted. "You have it all wrong. Agatha is dead. Don't you remember? We et her. This one's Mrs. Bobblington."

"Dreadful mistake, naming farm animals," Sir Chester said to me. "Because when it comes time to eat them, one loses one's appetite. My son Harry's little girl once named a calf Babyface, and when it came time to eat him the children bawled so, they had to leave the table without a bite of dinner. 'No, no! Not Babyface!' they sniffled and wailed. I don't know how this business got started."

Sir Chester saw the gardener, Mr. West, at the far side of the aviary and excused himself to scuttle up there—something about mending a fence. He used his stick like a third leg. As he got small and distant, I watched the chickens scramble for the hunks of bread Claire tossed them. She couldn't have heard their cackling, but she carried on conversations of noise with them, her own not completely human. She joined them in their snack, tearing off a bit of bread for the chickens and a bit for herself, a bit for them, a bit for herself.

"What in 'eaven's nyme are you doing!" Old Nanny threw her voice ahead of her as she struggled to move her unsteady legs up to the aviary. Panting, she stood with her hands on her canes and glared at me.

Me?

Nanny threw her canes down and grabbed Claire in her arms and hugged her, smoothing her hair with her spotted hands. "Poor lih-hl thing. There there." To me, " 'Aow could you leh 'er eat that bread! I saw 'er! Eating that style bread! I reckon you don't care if she's ill for a week. I s'pose you don't care if the pooh thing eats poison!" She let Claire go. I picked her canes off the ground so she could struggle after Claire, back to the house that someone built in 1586.

AT LUNCH MRS. HAIG-EREILDOUN emerged from her lie-in, looking all cheerfulness and wearing a different gray sweater. The one she had been wearing since the evening I'd met her—first with a skirt, then with jeans—was storm gray, a rough wool; but this was more like pussy willow, with a radiance like the sky at Phillingsford. She'd also changed into a skirt with a less old-maidish cut. Her silver-blond hair was clean and fluffed, shiny as cellophane. On the way in to the dining room she whispered that while I wouldn't be called on to make beds or help with the washing-up at her parents' house, it would be kind of me to help old Nanny with the children. "Normally, I'll try to give you an hour after dinner to write letters, but while we're here . . . Old Nanny wants so to be with them, but her legs make it difficult. Would you be an angel, and be Nanny's legs for the rest of the day?"

"I'LL 'AVE YOU GAOW to Mr. West str'ight off and ask 'im to bring up a load of wood." I wish I could write the way Nanny sounds, but it's impossible. She told me that even though we have central heating now, it doesn't seem right not to have a fire in the nursery on a cloudy day; that when I got back I could straighten the cupboards and drawers; that Trevor'd already made a mess of his. "Then iron fresh frocks for the girls, to be ready for tomorrow. We won't be having high tea today, just a cozy tea in the nursery, but there's church tomorrow. And Sunday dinner has always been a grand occasion in this house, and milady likes to see her granddaughters wearing their pretty frocks. Oh, look at this! Claire, you naughty hooligan, look at this hem! You'll have to mend it, Melissa. I'll show you to the threads—Trevor! You've had quite enough reading about the American redskins for one day. Run out and play before the rain comes."

It was odd to see the adoration in Trevor's eyes as he protested. "There's no one to play with, Nanny."

"Nonsense! Melissa will play with you. She's very good at soccer, aren't you dear. Melissa, after you—*and Trevor!*—have gone and picked up the wood from Mr. West, you can change out of your dress and entertain the young master and mistress here, out on the lawn. Take Claire with you. After the games, you'll have plenty of time for your sewing and ironing and general housekeeping." Nanny really took to having a servant.

. . . .

OUR COZY TEA WAS at a child-sized table in the nursery. Pru and I sat with our knees almost as high as our shoulders. Saying, "Aow, milegs," Nanny couldn't lower herself into one of those little chairs, so she presided from an adult's chair at the end of the table. Mrs. West had brought up a full buffet of chafing dishes. After serving each child, Nanny put about five SpaghettiOs in the center of her large, shiny plate, and talked about her bird-sized appetite. She ate only two SpaghettiOs. When I carried the serving dishes, still half full, to the nursery kitchen and brought Mrs. West's plate of biscuits to pass, Nanny said, "Aow, not for me! Puddings and biscuits go straight to my waistline."

After tea I washed the glasses and plates, but Nanny told me to leave the serving dishes and leftovers be—Mrs. West would take care of them. She ordered us out to play again. Trevor had picked up his book, and with that same loving shine in his eyes, he whined, "But Nanny, it's raining!"

"A little rain never hurt a healthy young man like you. Put on your Wellingtons and skidaddle!"

Trevor tried to sulk, using his long, red-tipped lashes to hide the merriness in his eyes. He wanted Nanny to win.

This time Trevor, Pru, and I played badminton, me against them, in our boots and anoraks with the hoods up. The three of us big kids were just hitting our stride when Claire started shouting and running toward the house. I dropped my racket to skip off and escort her inside. She tugged at me to be picked up. Getting what she wanted, she cuddled in, sucking her thumb. In case Nanny was having a nap, I tiptoed. From the doorway I saw her wide backside bending over the little table to pluck the last three lemon bars off the plate. Before I could turn away, she'd eaten those (inhaled them through her mouth) and had scooped all the remaining ginger biscuits into one hand, straightening to shove them in. So fast they disappeared, down the gullet! Only the macaroons were left on the plate. I hadn't liked those either.

Being a cookie thief myself, I knew the worst thing I could do would be to catch her in the act, so I turned on my toes and carried Claire back down the steps to visit Mrs. West in the kitchen. After a conversation of coos, she excused herself to go up to the nursery with a big empty tray, to carry down the remains of the tea. I felt embarrassed, not offering to help her, but I knew it was best to keep myself absent from the nursery for a few more minutes.

"Rain!" I said to Claire, pointing out the window.

"Hhghay!" she shouted, pointing.

"Very good!" I took her out to the kitchen porch so she could feel it. I got down on her level and held her shoulders, to help her focus on my lips: "Rrrrrain." She concentrated. "Rrrrrrrain," I repeated.

"Hway," she said.

I clapped and clapped. Almost a consonant. Other than the "n" of no, or nose, and the "ggggh" at the end of duck, this was a first. I shook her hand. Grabbed her shoulders again and compelled her to watch my lips: "Rrrrrain."

She said, "Hway!"

We were out on the porch clapping and shaking hands when Mrs. West returned. "I'm quite flattered," she said, looking down at her tray of empty plates. "I thought I'd supplied enough for two teas, but the children scraped all the serving dishes clean. All but a few macaroons. The country air does something for their appetites."

The rest of the afternoon was spent mending hems, ironing dresses, straightening drawers, and bathing children. "What!" Nanny huffed in horror as I started to put on Claire's sock. "Let me see that foot." She made a face at me as nasty as a bullfrog. "What's the matter with you! You didn't dry between her toes!" She picked Claire up and hugged her tight. "Fetch me that towel from the bathroom."

Lovingly, Nanny bent to dry the spaces between the toes, looking up every now and then to shoot me scorn.

MY SURPRISE CAME AFTER supper that night, when I met a completely different Nanny. Mrs. and Mrs. Haig-Ereildoun had gone with Lady Chipchase to a neighbor's party, and the two older children sat in their pajamas with Sir Chester and me to watch a BBC drama about Oliver Cromwell. When Trevor and Pru began tossing in their chairs and rubbing their eyes with their fists, I took them off to the nursery and Nanny. After the long journey back to the television room, I found Sir Chester's mouth hanging open, his eyelids fluttering. Hearing my steps, he jolted to attention and shook his skinny jowls awake. He nodded toward the screen. "A bit stuffy, this. Would you mind if we change it to two." His posture picked up when I switched the channel to *Ironsides.* That was my dad's favorite show. We watched the reruns when I was Trevor's age. It's about a detective in a wheelchair.

"I daresay this is your city, isn't it," he said. It was San Francisco. I strained to see if I could identify any of the scenery. "Jolly good program," he said, leaning forward to concentrate. It was funny to see how little the buildings were then, compared to now. I was hoping they'd have my street, or at least my neighborhood, with all the views of water and bridges and Coit Tower and St. Peter and Paul's, so I could show Sir Chester. All I recognized was the street in front of the unemployment office, where Tedward had taken me when I lost my job. (I only got one check, I must point out. I was only unemployed for two weeks before I came here.) Tedward had had to escort me when I signed up, of course, because he was afraid I'd be held up at gunpoint.

"Can't understand a word they say," Sir Chester growled. "Damned American accents."

"Ah!" he smiled, when Mrs. West suddenly stepped in, carrying a tray. She brought a dish for me and a dish for him. "I say. *Goose-brihs!*" He accepted his dish. "Could I trouble you, Mrs. West, for some cream to go with them?"

Reddening, and apologizing, she reminded him of what Lady Chipchase had said, having to do with cholesterol.

"Nonsense!" Sir Chester rumbled. "I'm slim as a schoolboy and my heart's as strong as a racehorse. I want cream." He scowled, thinking about it. "Double-cream!" To me he said, "You must taste these gooseberries with our English double cream. I don't think any other country produces a cream that compares with it."

I went downstairs with Mrs. West to bring back some cream. Leaving the kitchen with a pretty balik creamer in my hand, I spotted a transparent canister of lemon bars on the counter of the pantry. Mrs. West had her back turned, hanging up her apron, so I swerved a couple of steps from the logical path to dip into the pantry and pick up a lemon bar. In the front hall I bit in. Licking some buttery crumbs off my top lip, I looked up to the top of the staircase and who did I see looking down but old Nanny.

On my way up the stairs my pulse raced. Should I offer the uneaten half of the lemon bar to her? Should I pretend I was bringing it to Sir Chester? (What would Miss Manners say about giving titled personages half-eaten cookies?) Should I pop it in my mouth? Why not. I chewed casually.

"I see you like a nice biscuit," Nanny whispered, when I got to the top, holding only the batik creamer. "I was just headed down to the kitchen myself, for an apple. I like an apple at bedtime." I agreed that an apple was good at bedtime.

Then she surprised me: "When you're through with him, why not pay me a visit in the nursery? I'll get you some lemon bars. And do you like those nice ginger biscuits?"

. . .

WHEN SIR CHESTER HAD excused himself to go to bed, I passed through the endless dining room on my way to the nursery. The lights were off and the floorboards groaned. I felt my way to the kitchen and groped the walls to find the pantry. Shutting the door, I found the light switch. Just curious. The canister wasn't on the shelf anymore. When I found the door to the back stairway, I found a light on behind it.

"I should have left all the lights on for you," Nanny said, sitting by the electric heater in her fuzzy blue bathrobe, "but you might not've known where the switches are, to make it dark again when milady gets home.

"Naow," she said, passing me the biscuit plate. "Let's have a talk. How do you like working for Mrs. Haig-Ereildoun?"

My bones froze. "Oh," I said, "it's very interesting."

"Ye-es?"

"It's a very nice family."

"But Mrs. Haig-Ereildoun?"

"It's an adventure for me, getting to know this family."

"Is it pleasant, working for her?"

No! I wanted to say.

That was what she wanted me to say.

I couldn't. "Oh, I'm learning so much!" It hurt to keep my feelings inside. It was an actual, acute pain. I could only calm myself by eating a biscuit whole.

"Mr. Haig-Ereildoun, now, he's a bit of a hunk, wouldn't you say?"

Now she was looking for a scandal! I laughed. "Hunk" is not a word I would have chosen for this stork-legged Englishman in baggy tweed. I don't think of hunks as starting their sentences with "I say," or "I-I-I daresay," or the cultivated stutter Mr. Haig-Ereildoun uses when he's about to be emphatic ("W-w-w-well!") or the prolonged throat-clearing: "Ah-uh-uh yes. P-p-precisely." It would be almost impossible for an upper-crust Englishman to be a hunk. But I didn't want to hurt Nanny's patriotic feelings, so I said what I did find attractive about him: "He's incredibly smart . . ."

"Oh yes. Had a first at Oxford, he did. Read history. Quite a brain he is."

"And he's funny and charming—but the main thing I like about him is, I think he's very kind, from deep down. He cares about people's feelings."

"Ah, that's a good thing." She leaned forward, pushing the plate of biscuits toward me again. "And Mrs. Haig-Ereildoun? Do you find her kind? Does she care about people's feelings?"

Oh, God. I had another biscuit.

"Kind and gentle?" The shine in Nanny's eyes was almost lascivious.

Aching to burst out, I looked away. "So you've worked for the Chipchases a long time?"

She frowned, her eyes focused on the door to the children's rooms. "Oh, yes, a long time." She was disappointed in me. "Since Philippa was just a wee little tyke. In fact, since before Philippa was a twinkle in the eye.

"Aow, it's nothing like it used to be." She was perking up. "England has changed. Changed for the worst."

"What was it like before?"

"Aow. Lovely. It was lovely! We had a woodsman, a gamesman, a whole staff of gardeners—we had upstairs maids and downstairs maids, and a couple of sculleries, besides the cook and head housekeeper. We had a chauffeur, four footmen, and a butler. We had a stableman and groomsmen. I was the nanny, and I had two undernannies. Now you see what's happened." She hung her head and rolled her chin on the pillows of flesh underneath.

She pushed the plate of biscuits toward me. "In America you have black people working in your homes, haven't you."

I blinked. "Some people do."

"We English haven't come to that." She paused, then said, "I've been to America, you know."

"You have?"

"Aow, yes. One of my boys married there. Harry. His wife's from New York. Long Island. Beautiful, green country there, in June. A bit like England. But they had a black cook. I lost my appetite. Tremendous big wedding it was. High society. But I never did like the American accent. 'Arsh. Very 'arsh."

Suddenly I remembered something. "I didn't used to like English accents."

She opened her mouth, her eyes twinkling with greed for more.

"I thought they were funny. One day my father picked me up at school and told me he'd just heard Queen Elizabeth on the news. He imitated a high, ladylike voice: 'Eh-oh, it's *love*-lih to be he-ah.' I said, 'Oh, Daddy, stop! Queen Elizabeth doesn't have an English accent!' "

Nanny laughed until tears came. "Come, come!"

"I looked up to her, so I assumed she'd speak normally."

After our laughter subsided, and we'd sat quietly for a bit, Nanny said, "My boys and my girl made a pool and bought me a pass to go all over America on the Greyhound bus. Excellent boys I've reared. Harry, Jeremy, and Humbert."

" 'Umbert." I smiled.

"Naow, *'Umbert!*"

"I mean Humbert," I apologized, actually very embarrassed. I hadn't meant to mock her. But the name seems funny.

"An excellent Chipchase name," said Nanny. She was looking at the biscuit plate. I'd had half a dozen, not counting the one I'd swiped when Mrs. West's back was turned. But Nanny hadn't had one. Her hand went out slowly, then jerked itself back to clasp the other hand, in her lap.

"I found Americans to be very nice people after all," she said. "I didn't think I'd like them. I met some during the war. Soldiers." She began to chuckle. "Oh, they were funny. Bumptious! Americans are all so bumptious! Better than Pakistanis though. I'll take an American any day, over a Pakistani."

I HAVE TO DESCRIBE those lemon bars. Shortbread crust, all buttery. It's a mystery how the crumbs can be so crisp and so soft-satin-rich at the same time, and so breakable that some lingers on the hand you're using, some on your lips, to lick off. On top of the crust, this thick puddingish goo of bright yellow—another mystery, how the sourness of the lemon and the bitterness of the rind, plus a hint of sweetness, can all be together in one creamy taste. The dusting of powdered sugar on top also comes off on your hand and your lips, giving you more to lick. "Won't you have one?" I asked.

"Aow, well."

I tried not to notice her fingers flutter with tension as she touched down on the yellow square and brought it to her lips. While eating, she wouldn't look me in the eye.

"Well dear," she said, "it's soon morning, isn't it. And we'll have our hands full tomorrow."

I stood up and reached for the plate to carry down.

"Never mind those, Mrs. West will tend to them in the morning. We've had a lovely chat now, haven't we."

I gave her hand a touch. She pulled it away, but she said, "And just remember, don't let Philippa hurt your feelings. Just remember

I told you, she always was a hard girl. Ever since she was a little tyke." She frowned down. "A hard, hard girl."

SUNDAY MORNING NANNY AND I dressed the children for church. After breakfast we all went into the morning room to wait. The children, in their good clothes, were like the room itself: orderly and sparkling and comfortable at the same time. "Such a pretty name for a room," I said to Lady Chipchase, looking around at the graceful shapes of the chairs and sofas, the pastel silks upholstering them, the polished woods, the soft colors in the rug patterns, the light-filled oil paintings of people and countryside. "Why do you call it the morning room?"

She thought. "It's because this is the room best situated to catch the morning sun. When there is sun. At other times, well—simply that lovely gentle light of the morning."

Just then we heard the vicar rattling up in his old French deux chevaux. Trevor, Pru, and Claire ran to the window, and Lady Chipchase took the hat she had been holding in her lap—a pink felt hat, with a floppy silk rose cocked off to one side—to the mirror framed with gold leaf. As she adjusted her hat, I buttoned on Claire's chubby red coat, restringing the wire of the hearing aid in her dress pocket, and straightened Trevor's tie. Since there might be no heat in the stone church, I fetched my overcoat from the armoire in the foyer. Nanny waited for Lady Chipchase to get her hat straight before she went to the mirror herself and adjusted the brim of her navy blue hat to flatter her face. Sir Chester, leaning on his cane at the doorway, stood ready to offer his arm to Lady Chipchase. He looked at me and said, "I give my *left* arm to my lady, to keep my sword arm ready to protect her." With his right hand he chopped his cane through the air like a sword. Mrs. Haig-Ereildoun wore no hat, and she didn't take her husband's arm.

The family filed out the front door and walked the stepping stones round the side of the house to the stone church. The pink-cheeked vicar, somewhere between my age and the Haig-Ereildouns', grinned at Sir Chester and Lady Chipchase and the rest of us filing in. Turning back to me, Lady Chipchase said, "Do you see these chairs? They were the chairs our party used at the coronation. Queen Elizabeth the Second, in 1953. Afterwards, we were given the opportunity to buy them. Perfect for the church, don't you think?" I love the friendly way she often puts question marks at the end of her questions. The chairs were plain wood, with rectangle backs and the ER-II emblem carved into the wooden band at the tops—about thirty of them. This little stone box of a church had no pews, and these chairs did the job. Lady Chipchase and Sir Chester preceded the rest of the family, plus Nanny, the Wests, and me. We filled the first two rows of chairs.

The service lasted only fifteen or twenty minutes, without the usual Episcopalian choral reading of I-believe-that-this-and-that (all things I don't believe). The vicar gave a lesson from the Scriptures, we had a couple of responsive readings, we heard the world's shortest sermon, recited the Lord's Prayer, and sang no hymns. Maybe because of the Chipchases' age, the service was arranged to have no kneeling and getting up and kneeling and getting up. And of course there was no collection plate.

Before even Claire could get restless, the vicar left the pulpit and moved to open the door. First Lady Chipchase and Sir Chester left their chairs, then the rest of us. The vicar shook all our hands. Lady Chipchase's cheeks blushed rosy as she thanked him for coming. He seemed truly pleased to have been there. Then he was gone.

"He comes here?" I whispered to Trevor. "Just for us?"

"Mmm," he said. Thinking. "But you see how quickly he drives off. Now he has to give mass in the village."

The sun didn't shine on Sunday, but the rain stopped. Mr. West carried chairs to the lawn for the adults to sit in, and the children played kick-the-can with Mr. Haig-Ereildoun. He wore a fisherman's knit sweater like the children's—the one Nanny had knit him. Sir Chester stayed inside, and I sat on the lawn chairs with Lady Chipchase and Mrs. Haig-Ereildoun—all of us in coats.

"What's Nanny's name?" I asked.

They froze. Lady Chipchase's eyes blazed at me. Neither she nor Mrs. Haig-Ereildoun said a word.

"She's called Nanny," Lady Chipchase said at last.

"But before she was Nanny, she must have had another name."

"Just Nanny."

I realized I was on thin ice, but it seemed important to get an answer. "I just wonder what *I* should call her."

Lady Chipchase's and Mrs. Haig-Ereildoun's eyes riveted to the game of kick-the-can. They'd heard my question and hadn't liked it.

I had to explain: "It seems wrong for me to call her Nanny, because she's not *my* nanny." At that moment I wasn't looking at Mrs. Haig-Ereildoun, only at Lady Chipchase. She was the one I trusted. Her face was clearly disturbed, but I repeated my question. "Does Nanny have a name?"

"Call her Nanny," said the firm voice of Mrs. Haig-Ereildoun.

8

AT TROONFACHAN EVERY SUNDAY is alike. The first thing is always Mrs. Haig-Ereildoun's suggestion that I go to church with her husband, and the second thing is always my saying no thank you. She knows my calendar isn't full. She must think I'm an avid atheist. I wonder if it's crossed her mind that showing up on her husband's arm might make me uneasy, even though everyone knows I'm just the American au pair.

It *isn't* an awkward situation. He's so smooth he'd make it comfortable, introducing me to all the villagers. I'd love to see the inside of the church. I wonder if the ceremony is totally different from what I'm used to.

I'd probably be able to hold up a short conversation alone with him. If I couldn't he could carry it. But church is the kind of situation where I'm a little frightened of feeling more than I want to feel. I mostly don't like organized religion; but sometimes, in churches of all kinds, and for some reason especially in synagogues, a feeling of mysterious awe washes through me. The music has something to do with it, but I can hear that same music on the radio and not feel anything. I think being packed in a room with people whose hearts are seeking the same thing touches off that oceanic feeling Freud and Jung used to argue about. Freud thought it was nonsense. Jung thought it was real and universal. Maybe I think like Freud and feel like Jung. I can choke up in churches. I can feel like crying without any reason. My mother is the same way. I don't like to sit next to her in church.

I wouldn't want to sit next to him in church. The problem is, I do kind of adore him.

Mrs. Haig-Ereildoun doesn't go to church. But whether it's raining or just misting, she spends Sunday morning out in the garden, lovingly planting or tending flowers around the borders of the lawn. The lambs don't seem to notice she's there. She doesn't work in the garden any other time of the week. I watch her through the window and feel a kind of happiness.

I don't do anything special, in a private spiritual way, on Sundays. But three things are different. First, there's no mail. Since I usually answer letters the minute I read them (because I can't wait), Sundays are a day off from letter writing. Second, on Sunday afternoon we always have a joint at Granny Aitchee's—Mr. Haig-Ereildoun's mother: Aitchee is the children's way of saying H-E. Third, at six P.M. I make my weekly call to Tedward. Collect.

Our rule is, there's no time limit on these phone calls. It would be hard to relax, if you kept thinking about how you were spending a pound a minute. If I were paying, I'd run through a week's salary pretty fast. But I'm not paying. You have to decide that keeping up the relationship is important, so don't think about what it costs. It may be easy for me to say. But he has a trust fund (a *small* trust fund, he keeps reminding me). And yet it's hard to relax anyway. We talk about how much we miss each other, and I always feel uneasy because I'm not sure it's him I miss. I miss everything about home. Tonight I manipulated the conversation around to where he gave me a view of Grace Cathedral, and that beautiful park across the street on Nob Hill.

Mostly, in our conversations, he tells me about the conflicts he has. Right now it's his landlady, in this apartment I twisted his arm into renting, since we were getting married. He never wanted to live there. He doesn't care enough about an apartment to spend fifty dollars a month extra for a beautiful one. (Of course, with his furniture, even the most beautiful apartment could not be beautiful.) He says the landlady is crazy. I can imagine what she says about him. What a shock it must have been to rent out a lovely apartment and see it stacked with junk furniture all the way up to the ornate Italian chandelier. She says all his stuff is a fire hazard, and he's almost sure she sneaks in when he's out. He says yesterday he definitely left the red socks on top, and when he opened the drawer in the evening the red socks were under a pair of brown socks. I can feel he is blaming me, that it's my fault his landlady sneaks into his apartment.

I told him about Granny Aitchee's garden, the lunch she fixed. The lunch got his attention. "How's your weight problem?" he asked with a lascivious voice.

He loves to think of me getting fatter and fatter. He adores every dimple of flesh. At home he was always taking me out for French dinners and begging me to eat, eat. "Round and voluptuous" is how he likes a woman. I read a book by one of Picasso's ex-mistresses, and Picasso was the same way.

I'm the kind who's round and voluptuous at a hundred and eighteen pounds. And it's almost impossible to stay only that round and voluptuous. I usually weigh about a hundred and twenty-three. When we first got to know each other, Tedward told me I'd be perfect if I'd gain fifteen pounds. He had a very appealing twinkle in his eye. To me it was something that made me laugh almost as much as Claire laughs when she says the naughty words she's just learned, "Shut up." One of Tedward's goals for me has been to get me up to a hundred and thirty-three.

Of course I resisted. Quelle nightmare.

A nightmare on the one hand, but on the other, those French

restaurants. If you're going to get fat, might as well get fat on foie gras.

I've been on a diet, breaking it and getting back on it, breaking it and getting back on it, all of my life. At first, it was a thrill to be given permission—or not just permission, but encouragement—to defy all the rules my diet-conscious mother had taught me, and the rules I'd learned myself, reading book after book on nutrition and calories, making charts of my daily vitamins and proteins and minerals. I was always learning something, like how amazingly good for you an orange turns out to be. Vitamin C is just the beginning. And yet. There was sumptuous abandon in throwing all that anxiety out the window. So, with Tedward's influence fighting my willpower, it was back and forth, five pounds this way and five pounds that, over and over and over. I'd hit one-twenty-seven again by the time I left home. But the stewardess on the plane asked me if I was Miss February (she actually thought I was the one in the *Playboy* centerfold!), so I couldn't have been as fat as I thought.

Here, the scale measures in stones. One stone is fourteen pounds. So you need to use arithmetic to figure out how much you weigh, and luckily, my arithmetic's awful. But one thing is easy. Ten stone is a hundred and forty pounds. When we got to Troonfachan, the needle edged just past nine. Two weeks later it was almost halfway to ten. Today it was three quarters of the way—*before* Granny Aitchee's shortbread.

Even though I don't like to talk about it, I admitted this to Tedward on the phone. His voice almost dripped with what he calls "horniness." I hate that word. And I hate his proprietary concern with my body. Every stone of me crawls. One thing I don't miss is sex.

"Love you," I said.

"Love you," he said.

. . .

GRANNY AITCHEE IS THE exception to the rule that all the women in Britain look down on me. In the literal sense, she has to look way up to me. She comes to my chin. She's very slim, but not wiry. She seems all litheness and softness, flexible as a long blade of grass. Her white hair shines—tidy but with some tousle and sway. When she comes for a day at Troonfachan, she follows me around the kitchen as I do my work. "Is it true that in America even ordinary people have washing-up machines?" She's amazed when I say yes. "And that they have washing-up machines that can clean saucepans?"

"Granny!" Mrs. Haig-Ereildoun inserts. "In England even ordinary people have dishwashers too, in this day and age."

I feel like swooping down, my large presence, and hugging Granny Aitchee's tiny presence, clothed in plaid.

Every day she wears her family's tartan, the MacLaren plaid. It's tan and a pastel aqua green. Sometimes she wears it in a mid-calf kilt, sometimes in a dress. She seems to have just these two outfits. (One of Simon's short notes to me said, "Quite naff, these tartans.") Granny Aitchee sounds English, but so does everyone in the Haig-Ereildoun circle, including the three-year-olds. She is, though, completely Scottish. In her dining room she arranges flowers reciting Robert Burns: "My love is like a red red rose." Her favorite book is *Ivanhoe*. She makes delicious scones, and shortbread that tastes ninety percent butter.

Her two dogs are Scottish deerhounds. I can't imagine less practical dogs for Granny Aitchee. She's tiny and they're tall—on stiltlike, weak-looking legs. They're scruffy-furred, gray, and they run like gazelles, never coming when you call them. But they're Scottish. The old female is named Mary (as in Queen of Scots); the young one is Bruce, as in Robert the. Both dogs dwarf Granny Aitchee and almost dwarf her house.

It's tidy and white, with windows of a hundred tiny panes held together by thin strips of lead. The strips, shaped in diamonds, are greenish with age, setting off the brilliance of the thick old glass, which is wavy and full of rainbows.

Outside her grounds, it's fields of grass and daffodils and sheep. Hedges of yew and rosebushes are the fences that enclose her abode. Inside the borders, her garden is her private paradise. She's shown me every flower and every flower-to-be. ("Spring is coming," she says every day.) The entry to her garden has a story. There's a very old iron gate, prettily scrolled. It's framed by two rowan trees, trained to twine together. She says it's an old Scottish belief that when two rowan trees are so intertwined, no witch or fairy can come through the arch.

She has a book of tartans, and she shows me which plaid is the tartan of which friend I've met. Even Mrs. Campbell, our daily, has a family tartan, although she doesn't wear it. I love to think of these plaids, like family flags.

For Sunday lunch, Granny Aitchee serves a joint. And beautiful gravy. Even her roasted potatoes seem to have a special taste. But her pride and joy is consommé. Why, I'm not sure. She strains it several times through many layers of cheesecloth and then further cleans out the sediment with egg whites. After all this work, it ends up tasting uneventful. It's pure, though, and clear. She must like that.

She isn't Catholic, but she knows some of the catechism. She told Trevor and me her favorite part. There's a question: "What is man's chief end?" The answer is, "To love God and enjoy Him."

IF I HAVE A religion, I learned it from my grandfather. Grandpa Pomeroy used to carry around dozens of poems in his head—maybe hundreds. At breakfast he might burst into "Evangeline," reciting stanza after stanza until Grandmother said, "All right, Bill, that's enough." If he could memorize so many poems, at least I could memorize one. There was one called "Abou Ben Adhem."

Abou Ben Adhem, may his tribe increase!
Awoke one night from a deep dream of peace,
And saw, within the moonlight in his room,
Making it rich, and like a lily in bloom,
An angel writing in a book of gold:—

Exceeding peace had made Ben Adhem bold,
And to the presence in the room he said,
"What writest thou?"—The vision raised its head,
And with a look made of all sweet accord,
Answered, "The names of those who love the Lord."
"And is mine one?" said Abou. "Nay, not so,"
Replied the angel. Abou spoke more low,
But cheerily still, and said, "I pray thee then,
Write me as one that loves his fellow men."

The angel wrote, and vanished. The next night
It came again with a great wakening light,
And showed the names whom love of God had blessed.
And lo! Ben Adhem's name led all the rest.

When I got to college I found out this was by an 1800s poet named Leigh Hunt, and that my English Romantic Lit professor thought it was a simpy poem. Everyone thought it was sappy, wimpy, and goody-two-shoes. That hurt my feelings. I still like Abou. But he's at the root of one of my main problems. If it's my religion, so to speak, to love my fellow man, I'm a failure. I don't love every single one.

Granny Aitchee's Scottish catechism lets me off the hook a little. To love God and enjoy Him includes the shortbread and the daffodils. Maybe even glutting my sorrow on the morning rose has to do with enjoying Him. And seeking out songs that will make me cry. If part of loving God includes the sadness beauty can stir up, maybe loving God also includes even such an imperfection as not being able to love Mrs. Haig-Ereildoun. Maybe it even includes continuing to try to love her, and failing.

9

THIS MORNING I'D SWEPT the floor, as usual, and put the broom away, as usual. Mrs. Haig-Ereildoun opened the broom closet, grabbed the broom, slammed the door, and came charging at me, waving the broom, brush-side up. "What is *this!*"

It's one of those big pusher brooms, like the kind janitors use. Her face was flushed and furious, as her thin arms swished the big thing through the air.

"Is *this* how you put it away?" She slapped the brush part. Little pieces of dust flew off. "Like *this!* Is *this* how you do it in America?"

She told me I'm supposed to comb the broom, with my fingers, before I put it away. I never knew this.

Later, I was pressing the iron to one of Claire's socks (it's so damp here the clothes never get dry, so I have to iron not just shirts and trousers but the terry cloth towels and even Mrs. Haig-Ereildoun's bras) when she picked up her car keys and gave me my instructions for lunch. I was to slice the leftover mutton and set the platter in the oven at Mark Two (the ovens are different here—you don't set them by degrees but at various marks, ranging from one to five); shell the peas; and prepare the new potatoes. I did this, and everything was ready, the table laid, when she got back. She saw what I'd done and blasted into rage. "You *don't peel* new potatoes!"

Her face was hot and her voice shook. When she gets this way, my voice comes out in creaks. "What do you do with new potatoes?"

"What *is* the *matter* with you!" She frowned into my face, her mouth turned down at the corners. Pulling herself together, she blew up from her lower lip. She does that to calm herself. "You don't *peel* new potatoes, you *scrape* them."

I DON'T KNOW MUCH about potatoes. My mother always thought they were high in calories ("starch"), and we didn't have them that often. When we did, she fixed them.

I thought you peeled potatoes.

I don't like this.

I started thinking about taxis.

I MANAGED TO HIDE my feelings through the meal and by the end to take part in conversation. Trevor said, as usual, "May I get down?" and his mother, as usual, said, "First you must say grace." As usual, he said the quick "Thank you God for this food" and ran outside. This was Claire's signal to climb into her mother's lap and snuggle in, as she does every day, after lunch. I love to see the look on Mrs. Haig-Ereildoun's face as she smoothes Claire's hair, soft as baby bird's fur.

"Isn't that funny," I said, clearing plates. "In America, people get *up* from the table. Here they get down."

Mrs. Haig-Ereildoun said hmmm, kissing the top of Claire's head.

"And in America," I said, gathering up silverware, "we say grace *before* the meal."

At this she froze. "Well," she said hastily. "I must explain." She raised her head from Claire's and blew up from her lower lip to whish those imaginary hairs from her brow. "I must explain." Then she rubbed her whole face. She's always rubbing her face.

She shifted Claire's position in her lap, to keep up the cuddle but give full attention to me.

Wondering what in the world she had to explain, I dropped my handfuls of silverware in the sink and returned to my chair, facing her.

"I must explain," she said. "Oh, dear. I lost my Dutch girl this way. She was from Holland, she was before you, and she left after only ten days. I always thought it was a tremendous mistake that she left, because I think that if she could have worked it out, she'd have grown very much as a person, from the experience, but she insisted, she had to go home. She was from a very religious family, and . . ."

"Oh," I said, "I didn't mean *that!* I just meant that, *you* say grace at the *end* of a meal. If *we* say grace at all, we say it *before* the meal. In my family, we only say it at Thanksgiving and other special occasions, except if my brother Sam is there, because, since all of a sudden he's become involved with a very weird religion, kind of ultra-Christian, and he's become super self-righteous and sanctimonious, my mother tries to please him and show that she's a Christian too. But we never said it at all till he got so critical. All I was saying was that when people at home do say grace, we usually say it before the meal, instead of after. Just like we get 'up' from a meal instead of 'down.' "

"Oh," she breathed out, with immense relief. "Well, this Dutch girl . . ."

She resumed stroking Claire's hair as I rinsed dishes. She told me how foolish she thought this Dutch girl had been, to leave so soon, without really giving it a chance, how her religious convictions had been offended, how she'd let a small matter . . . And it was the same with the girl before her, from France, and the one before that, from Switzerland. In the case of the French and the Swiss girl, it hadn't been religion, it had just been intense homesickness, but still, they would have been far better off . . . Before that, it had actually been an English girl who'd left before giving it a month. So many of these girls, nowadays, had no spines, no interest in staying with a thing. In the last six months, four in a row had left without giving it a chance. She'd had to go weeks at a time with no au pair or nanny at all, and then she had all the breaking in to do all over again, and again.

So I wasn't the only one. I didn't say, but I thought: You don't have to worry about me. I promised I'd stay here at least six months, and—I keep my promises.

Just like my promise to Tedward. Right now, I don't feel anxious to spend the rest of my life with his furniture, but he's counting on me, so I will. I keep my promises.

OH. ONE MORE INTERESTING thing about today. My letter from Simon. Seven provoking words: "Why not ask for a hard-boiled egg?"

10

"DEATH ISN'T SAD FOR the one who dies," Trevor says. "It's only sad for the ones who don't die." We sit in the drawing room of this drafty old farmhouse, sheets of rain making what seems like a second pane of moving glass behind the windows. "If Mum died, or Granny or Grampy or Granny Aitchee or Nanny, I wouldn't be sad for them. I'd be sad for myself." He makes his declarations with the confidence his father must exude in the House of Commons, then checks with me, to see if he's correct.

"If I died," he says into my eyes, with a statement that's a question, "I wouldn't be sad, but they would be."

He's not naive enough to think I know how death feels. He just likes to check his thoughts. There's always a chance someone else knows something he doesn't. I'm afraid I don't.

It doesn't seem odd to me that death is on Trevor's mind. I must have been around nine when I zeroed in on it. I used to lie in my bed, not sleeping, trying to imagine. The thought of me dying was the most untouchable concept I'd ever tried to grasp. It still is, but I don't try anymore.

I'm not sure how I found out about death in the first place. It must have been very early. The wicked stepmother had a poison apple that would kill Snow White. The three blind mice ran away from the carving knife. My bedtime prayer ended, "And if I die before I wake I pray the Lord my soul to take." I do remember thinking what a horrible thought to put in a child's prayer. It didn't scare me, because I couldn't imagine it, but I thought it would scare most children.

Maybe the reason death isn't on my mind much now is that I tried to imagine it and I couldn't.

Also, I don't believe in death, the way other people do. I don't know if I ever did. Probably Trevor doesn't, and that's why he wants to think about it.

ONE DAY WHEN I was a couple of years older than Pru, my father and I took a walk before breakfast. It was the fourth of April, and people's gardens were coming out. Dew made the lawns extra green. Morning walks were something Dad and I did sometimes, when we woke up earlier than the others. Side by side, swinging our legs, we took in beauty and air, and felt pleasure we would have felt alone—magnified a thousand times by having each other to feel it with. If we talked while we walked, I don't remember a word. On his way to work this one day, April fourth, he gave me a ride down the hill to school. That afternoon he was dead.

It took a long time for me to feel whole-hearted again. But my spirit must be strong. Mom's is too. I don't know about Sam. I hope. I hope it's just taking a little longer for his spirit to show its strength. But I don't worry about Dad. It's preposterous to think that, because of some physical thing like a car shattering the body, the soul of a person stops. The great miracle isn't those miles of blood vessels that carry chemicals around, and nerve endings that react and brain cells that work like machine parts. The real miracle's the spirit, and no study of the physical universe can explain it. It doesn't seem logical or probable that something as mindless as a car, or a bullet or a cancer, could put an end to the miracle.

Obviously the life's transformed, or transported—carrying on in a realm we don't know anything about yet. What I feel is too strong to be called a "belief."

I don't talk about this to people.

Sometimes, on these long dark days, I help Trevor with his history lessons. If he gets a head start on next term, he may get better than an F. Since I know hardly anything about British history, he reads ahead and tells me the stories. He's surprised how exciting it is. For instance, the first people on these islands were "swarthy and squat." They wandered over from Egypt. Then about three thousand years ago some tribes trekked over across the Alps, with herds and children and wagons. These turn out to be a little like the American Indians Trevor likes, except they were tall and fair, with light blue eyes. They painted their bodies blue! So they were called the Brythons, which meant "painted people." The Brythons were living here with the squat swarthies, and the Celts, and the Gaels, when the Romans sailed over and conquered and named the whole place after the Brythons: Britannia. This was in A.D. 78, about forty years after Jesus was executed. The Romans stayed in power on these little islands for four hundred years, and I think they left their secret here forevermore. Their secret (this is my guess) was that they were nice. They built beautiful villas, gardens, and baths. So the natives built villas and gardens and baths. And fresco paintings and even underground heating. The Romans brought with them a system of justice that helped everyone get along. They founded schools, so the people could use their heads. Other rulers had done the opposite: tried to keep the people down by giving their brains as little as possible to work with. The deprived, ignorant people were very fierce and effective at overthrowing the ones who tried to keep them down. But the Romans treated the people of Britannia like friends. Pretty soon, the British people were wearing togas and speaking Latin.

According to Trevor's history book, the current British people are pretty much a mix of races, invaded by each other and influenced by each other. But, says the book, "If you should see a tall Scot with red hair, chances are he's a true Celt." "That's Daddy!" It's nice to see that with all this mingling, a few pure characteristics hold forth. The Haig-Ereildouns just went to a party where the men wore kilts, and you should have seen his knees. Blue, with freckles. A true Celt.

The Romans remind me of Mrs. Haig-Ereildoun. When she isn't on the war path, she can be nice. If I say I have a headache, she heaves a sigh of self-pity, but she insists that I spend the morning in bed. Every Sunday she asks if I'd like to go to church with Mr. Haig-Ereildoun. A couple of times she's invited me to sit with her at the kitchen table and have a cup of tea. One day our conversation went to when she was a debutante, and wore a white gown and took her father's arm to be presented at court. Her knees cracked so loudly they echoed through the hall. "We have pictures of Mother," she said, "at her debut. This was in the thirties, right before the war. A slinky vamp, she was." It wasn't hard to imagine the plump-cheeked Lady Chipchase a vamp. She must be more beautiful now though, filled out and aged. Another day Mrs. H-E told me about her shock on arriving in New York, seeing how savage people were in fighting off others for a place on the bus. "It took only a few days, though," she told me with a sly smile, "for me to knock old ladies aside as easily as everybody else did." On our way up from London she took side trips partly so that I could see certain museums and castles and famous houses. We toured one that belonged to a friend. ("A lot of our friends," Mr. Haig-Ereildoun had told me, "have found that the only way they can keep up their houses is to donate them to the National Trust. That way they can keep living there, but they must allow groups to come through.") From the north of England into Scotland Mrs. Haig-Ereildoun was almost thrilled to drive me, the newcomer, on the Roman roads—roads so straight they seemed to have been drawn by a ruler, going up hills and down them without a swerve, like a roller coaster uncurled. Pru said, "Quite rigid, these Romans must have been. Quite lacking in imagination." "Not at all, I'm afraid, darling," answered Mrs. Haig-Ereildoun. "It was technological. Their wagons had fixed axles." When she's nice, Mrs. H-E takes pleasure in her generosity. I feel I must be good to her in return. I'm almost sure that the people who now rule these islands keep their power by following in the Romans' footsteps: They're nice part of the time. Trouble is, though, I do think they have fixed axles.

ON THESE RAINY DAYS, we have lots of time. This family doesn't play dominoes or Clue, but there's a game I played first with the children, then with all of them. I call this game "You're Out Walking." It's a bunch of questions, and answers you interpret. Everyone's answers were interesting, but Mrs. H-E's the most.

Q's:

1. You're out walking. You come upon a house. Describe the house.
2. Inside, there's a table. There are three objects on the table. What are the objects?
3. Outside, you see a bear. What do you do with the bear?
4. You find a cup. Describe the cup.
5. What do you do with the cup?

And now, to interpret.

A's:

1. The house is yourself.
2. The three objects on the table are the things you do best.
3. The bear is a problem, and what you do with the bear is what you do with a problem.

4. The cup is your love.
5. What you do with the cup is what you do with your love.

It's amazing, the answers people give. One boy I went out with at U of O described the house he saw as "a three-two." I asked what's a three-two? He said, "Oh, a three-bedroom, two bath." "Any trees?" He shook his head. "A garden?" He didn't see one. I couldn't draw out of him one feature that interested either him or me, although the clicker to open the garage perked him up some. His cup was one of those mugs from the gas station, with the Union 76 logo. And what did he do with it? He filled it with hot water from the tap and mixed in a spoonful of instant Maxwell House. It was flattering not to hear from him again.

The house I saw was a storybook house: an English cottage, centuries old, with a thatched roof and wild roses—all kinds of flowers. The three objects I saw were three vases of flowers. The vases were different and the types of flowers different: one formal and crystal with orchids and lilies and exotic things you pay a lot for; one a crude pottery cup full of wildflowers; one in-between-sized and full of garden roses and forget-me-nots and other flowers that had just been picked. The trouble with my three objects was that they all added up to the same thing: beauty. And it doesn't go with me. I'm not a beauty.

Trevor saw a sixteenth-century abbey. A monastery. That seemed just right to him. "A place to think, to understand life."

Trevor's cup was "Nanny's! It's the great china coffee bowl with the bluebird and the thistle painted on it." He filled Nanny's china cup with milk and drank until he had to lick the last drops from around the rim. "It means that your love will be prickly and sweet, like Nanny," Pru interpreted. "And that you can't get enough of it."

Pru's house was an ancient French chateau, from the time of Louis the Thirteenth. "My favorite king!" Pru was delighted that her self was full of history and aristocracy.

"Just like you, Lady Pru," Trevor grinned.

Her three objects were a fancy dancing shoe "from the period"; a garland of flowers ("fresh! with silk ribbons hanging down"); and "a great tome, leatherbound with gold lettering and gilt-edged pages—it's an illuminated manuscript!"

How apt, for Pru the social butterfly, to see dancing shoes. Especially dancing shoes with history. And the garland. She's such an old-fashioned, fresh-faced beauty. Garlands are associated with honor, too, and she wins every prize at school. Her mother has told me about how Pru's brilliance has actually posed a problem: she finished all the requirements a year before she was old enough to enter the next school. They'd had to search quite a while to find a school in London that would allow her to attend this year, a year of killing time.

As for me, I keep dreading the day when Pru finds out that I, twice her age, don't know half as much as she does.

About the bear, Pru did what I did. Well, almost. I went out to make friends with the bear. Pru went out and danced with it.

Her cup was the silver chalice from the church at Phillingsford. What she did with the chalice was go off to seek as many people as she could, to drink from it.

One thing Trevor's and Pru's answers made me think of was how often the cups people see are related to home and family. My cup was a tin dipper that had hung on a nail in a tree by the creek behind our cabin at Moose Lake since Grandpa Pomeroy had first hung it there, when my father and aunts were young. What I did with the dipper was hide it, in a memorized place, so I could easily find it when the time was right. I had no idea when the time would be right—but somehow it rang a bell, when I first played this game, that it wasn't the right time yet.

The really interesting thing was when we played the game with Mr. and Mrs. Haig Ereildoun. His answers fit him wonderfully. His house wasn't a house, exactly, but an ancient inn, with a tavern like the kind Falstaff must have drunk in: "Very merry indeed!" His cup was a loving cup to share all 'round. When it came to the bear outside he said, "Of *course* there's a bear outside. Why do you think I came *inside*?"

"Typical, darling," Mrs. Haig-Ereildoun said when the meanings were revealed. "You always hide from problems."

Her answers, though, were what made me think of fixed axles. The house she saw was tall, narrow, elegant, "A Queen Anne, I think." But it was being "mod'nized." "They're tearing out fine, old, leaded glass windows and installing sheets of plate glass. Picture win dows, one calls them." She almost shuddered. "They're installing built-in cupboards, totally out of character with the original architecture, and a wing of concrete and glass—American. I want to tear the hammers right out of the builders' hands!"

As for her cup, it was filled with plaster dust from the remodeling. What she did with her cup was take it to the sink and begin scrubbing "with all my vigor."

Pru, having played the game before, asked with an anxiousness in her voice, "Does it ever get clean enough for drinking, Mummy?"

"I think it will, darling. That's why I'm working on it as I am."

11

CLAIRE IS LEARNING NEW words even faster than I'm putting on big hunks of stones. I can't count how many words she knows. It might be a hundred. "Hhhuh hupp!" she chants, marching in a circle. She *hup*-two-threes up to Trevor, puffs out her chest, shouts, "Hhhhuh hupp!" and runs away squealing with joy. "Shut up" is a forbidden phrase, considered very rude. Trevor must have taught it to her, but I must admit I taught her to say the final "p." Those consonants are hard, but she was motivated. I thought it would help her learn "push," "pull," and "please."

This is the first time she's ever had someone spend hours and hours a day teaching her. Her eyes get bright as a baby animal's when I put my face near her and mouth the words so she can lip-read. It's actually easy, in this place where there's nothing else to do, and teaching her is the challenging part of my job. Most of the time I spend with her I spend talking, repeating, listening, and cheering.

"Puh" turns out to be the easiest consonant sound. I'd have thought "sss" would be, but that relies on hearing. (I remember learning "s" in first grade: The first day, the teacher made an "s" that looked like a snake and said, "Sss!" Such a thrill it was to learn that, right off the bat, a major step on the way to reading.) But your lips don't do anything special when you say "sss," and your breath doesn't come out in a dramatic way. I haven't figured out how to get

Claire interested in "sss." To say "puh," though, you have to close your lips before you start, and use a burst of air to pop them open. Pop! If you put your hand near your mouth, you can feel the air come out in a blast. I put Claire's hand by my mouth, so she could feel the "puh," then got her to try the same thing against her hand. Puh. Shut up-puh!

It pops. "Pop" is really an onomatopoetic word, with two blasts in a row.

Now Claire can say "pea" (please), "pea-huh" (peanut), "pooh-puh" (purple), and "pikk" (pig). Claire can say "pop." The whole word—the consonants on both ends of it: *pop*-puh.

The hard part of "pop" was showing her what it meant. I clapped—pop! But she didn't hear the clap. I pantomimed socking Trevor on the chin, and he pantomimed falling over. Pop! She liked that one, but she thought "pop" meant sock. I got some popcorn in Bridie and popped it on the stove. As kernels popped, I said, "Pop! Pop! Pop!" and she could say it back, with enthusiasm. She might have thought "pop" meant getting puffed up. We have a cap gun. "Pop!" But she can't hear it. When she shoots it herself, though, she can feel the trigger. Pop. We have a jack-in-the-box. "Pop!" She seems to realize that "pop" is something sudden. "Pop" is my masterpiece.

She likes it, but it's not nearly as good as "shut up."

It must be a wonderful mystery, when everyone is trying to get you to speak and you master a word that gets you a scolding.

"No!" was the first one that delighted her. "Shut up" is better because it's more complex. About the scolding. Her mother and Mr. Haig-Ereildoun only pretend to scold her; same with Trevor and Pru: Claire can tell they're secretly very happy for her when she says shut up. The responses she gets from no and shut up must be the most complicated communications Claire has ever been able to stir up, verbally.

She knows many kinds of words now. We can open a book to a random picture, and she knows the word, even if she can't say it the way we would: "*Hhh*igh-huh." (Tiger.) "Hhhaa." (Cat.) "*Eh*-eh-fuh!" (Elephant.)

"Fuh" is the other easy consonant. So she can now say "fah," which is pretty close to how they really do say fire.

"Fuh" is so easy (and "ggkkk" is so easy) that I hate to think what her next masterpiece might be.

I don't know who will teach her that one, though. That's one word that doesn't seem to be in the language here. I mean, I know it's used. I've seen English movies like *Laundromat* and read modern English plays, and that word's even in the old book *Lady Chatterly's Lover*. But in this family, and this family's circle, I've never heard one expletive of this sort. For me, after my year and a half in the advertising agency, the absence of that word here, plus the one that starts with "shhh," is culture shock.

TREVOR AND I WERE petting Granny Aitchee's huge old Scottish deerhound, Mary, and she was talking to us. Hrrroo!

"She thinks she can talk," Trevor said. "You notice how she listens. How many words she understands." Mary knows "out," "walk," "sit," "stay," "come," "thirsty," "water," "hungry," "food," "cat," "ball," and lots more, especially "Mary." "Why can't dogs talk?" asked Trevor.

"I think it has to do with their tongues," I said. "That's supposed to be one of the things that set human beings ahead, in evolution. Humans' tongues, that can do so many movements, make more complicated sounds, end up in a complicated language, to say more complicated things."

"Oh," Trevor said, interested but easy, like his father. "Yes. The things dogs say are all things where you don't have to move your tongue at all. Like 'Rrrr.' And 'How-oo.' You see? 'Ruff-ruff!' You don't have to move your tongue."

I tried it. It's true. But I'm not sure, then, why vowels are easier for Claire than consonants. Her difference from Trevor and me is not like a dog's difference. Dogs can hear, and imitate to a degree. My great uncle, Uncle Lou, had a dog who could say, "Hello Lou!" just the way Claire would say it: "Eh-Oh, Oooh!" Claire has a human tongue, but can't hear, to imitate. What she can do is see. She sees how we hold our mouths when we say hello Lou. She can't see our tongues, when we make a sound more complicated than eh-oh, Oooh.

Maybe I should try showing my tongue. That's hard, because my tongue's behind my teeth.

L. "L" is a consonant that shows your tongue. My old boss, the one who fired me, used to love the first words of *Lolita.* Nabokov. "Lo-lee-ta: the tip of the tongue taking a trip of three steps . . . to tap . . . on the teeth." I'm not sure about the third step, the "tuh," but "lo-lee" should be easy for Claire. She won't be able to feel it, with breath, but she might be able to see it. My tongue flicking the backs of my top front teeth. The problem will be to find the L word that's interesting to her. Little. Unfortunately, she already knows "ih-uh" now. To get her to think "llllih-uh" is an improvement may be hard. (Heavens! I hope it won't be hard to get her to improve on all the words she's proud of so far. Like *Hhhheh*-huh for Trevor and *Hhigh*-huh for tiger. I assume this is a beginning and there will be more progress.)

"Love" is another L word she might find interesting. But I've noticed that love, like the expletives people here don't say, is a word that hasn't been used in this house. I don't mean to say they don't feel it. They just don't say it. And to tell the truth, I'm not sure it makes a difference, whether you put that one into words or not. You feel what you feel. You sense what you sense. You probably communicate what you feel. Words or no.

. . .

LOVE AND TREVOR. I would never end a conversation with him by saying, "Love you." Why wouldn't I? I do love him.

Maybe this is a big subject.

I've never seen Mrs. Haig-Ereildoun hug or kiss her husband, let alone Trevor or Pru. Mr. Haig-Ereildoun never hugs or kisses them either. Between those four, the only touching I've seen is a touch on the shoulder. The exception to the family's no-hugging-no-kissing rule is Claire. I'm not sure if it's because she's still so little or because she's deaf and touch is the best way to communicate with her, but her mother holds her on her lap every day after lunch for about half an hour, hugging and kissing, mumbling little things and both of them laughing. This is Mrs. Haig-Ereildoun transformed. I can feel something like lively love from her as she verbally jousts with her other two children, but when she cuddles Claire, Mrs. Haig-Ereildoun seems soft. Peaceful. She also seems a little poignant. Claire becomes sweet then, too.

I admire Claire, because in spite of her deafness, and her lack of words to express her thoughts—or even to formulate thoughts—I suspect she's got the family brains. For some reason, she reminds me of Sir Chester! She's also got the family guts. Spunk. But "sweet" is not a word I'd use for her, except in that half hour after lunch, when she's cuddling with her mother.

I don't know what Pru does for cuddles, but I know what Trevor does. Every night, at bedtime, he starts picking a fight with me: a play fight. A light of excitement ignites his eyes, and I can see the wrestling match coming. We begin by boxing. He punches, I counter. His giggle gets more delight-filled as his punches get rougher. When I finally have to grab his wrists, his tussles get intense. Finally I have to wrap his little body in my arms and hug it tight. This makes him unspeakably happy. And I love hugging him as much as he loves being hugged. It's a ritual that goes on night after night. We both know what to expect, but every time it feels like a surprise. He shakes with laughing when I encircle his small shape in my larger shape, and he twines his arms around me and presses his soft cheek to mine. We rub cheeks and make sounds like little squeals and titters, mock-struggling until we fall on the floor or onto his bed, where we lie and rock, clasped, breathing hard and laughing.

It would never occur to me to say "I love you." And why not is what I wonder. It might seem improper, in this situation, me the outside person in this family. But I don't think that's it. I don't think, either, that my reason is that all the millions of times I've mouthed those words to Tedward has worn them out. I think it's that Trevor and I don't need those words.

My mother says, "I feel you say love with actions, not words."

When I analyze how she says I love you, I have revelations. Even buying me the wedding dress I didn't like, for marrying someone she didn't like, was an action that said love. She didn't do this with any you-should-be-grateful undercurrent. She did it because she cared about my happiness. The unspoken "I love you" I remember with the most emotion would be hard to make someone understand, but I'll try. When I was in kindergarten. I had a winter cold most of the year and never had enough Kleenex. So in the school yard, I used to blow my nose on the lining of my coat sleeve. When my mother found the evidence, dried mucus in the silky lining, she told me how important it was to take the time to run inside and get more Kleenex. She explained, with feeling, "People will make fun of you." I looked into her eyes as she said that, and I saw how much it meant to her to keep me from unhappiness.

Me.

The word "love" didn't come into my head, but the appreciation I felt was grave.

I suddenly remember another exchange with my mother, about

that same time, having to do with the winter cold. I coughed and coughed. I hated coughing. One thing I loved was singing. When my mother tried to sing, along with the rest of us when Dad played the piano, her notes were so far from the right notes that we had to laugh. So when we gathered around the piano, my mother stayed silent. One day, when I was coughing, my mother said, "But you can sing! When I was little," she said quietly, "I would even have had a cough like yours, if I could have sung." I looked at her. I couldn't imagine such a thing. "You would even have had a cough like mine?" "Yes," she said. "If I could have sung." Then I could imagine how much she must have wanted to sing. And she couldn't. That was absolutely true. She couldn't. My heart almost broke for her.

At that moment, she didn't say I love you. I didn't say I love you.

12

TODAY, AS SHE SET stacks of post on the breakfast table, Mrs. H-E said, "Mr. Haig-Ereildoun is going to the coast this morning—a charming little town called Kinturriff. Perhaps you'd like to tag along!"

Even as she started the question, my lips prepared the words, "No thank you." I wished she'd stop asking me, because it embarrasses me to say no all the time with obviously no excuse.

"It's one of my favorite settings," she said, putting the dreaded egg at my place. "He goes there quite frequently, to chum with the fishermen and bring home some fish. I can't believe it hasn't occurred to me until now to suggest that he take you with him. You must see Kinturriff."

"Oh, Kinturriff!" Pru swooned, cracking her own egg without the fear I feel when I embark on one.

Instead of saying no thank you to my hostess, I said, "What's it like?" Instantly I chastised myself for letting those words out. It was like someone inviting me over for dinner and me replying, "What are you having"—and *then* saying no thank you.

"It's heaven!" swooned Pru.

"Quite good," said Trevor.

"It's just quite an ancient harbor," Mrs. Haig-Ereildoun said. "A place hardly any outsiders visit, for some reason. I think you'll find it quite special."

At that point Mr. Haig-Ereildoun entered, and she said, "Angus. Melissa was thinking of accompanying you to Kinturriff."

"Splendid!" he said, sitting down to his coffee.

AFTER HIS BACON AND eggs and newspaper, he had to put in his hour at the typewriter. I ironed while the Beatles on the Golden Oldies let loose: "I Wanna Hold Your Hand."

I tried to plan what we'd talk about in the car. I haven't read either of his novels. I gather very few people have. Since other people don't want to read them, I'm afraid that after a couple of pages I'd see why. And I couldn't just sneak a copy and skim it on the sly. He doesn't keep either of his books at Troonfachan—or at Lettering Lane. He says. "To quote your John Cheever, 'We don't like unfinished things lying about the house.' " If I asked for a copy, chances are good that I'd have to say, "I *started* your book . . ." Risky. I can't even get through the first chapter of *War and Peace*.

I haven't been interested enough in John Knox or Robert the Bruce to learn anything about them in all the years I've lived so far. It could be hard to hold up my end of a conversation. But—I could ask him! He already knows I'm completely ignorant of Scottish history. I have been reading *Mary, Queen of Scots*. Not exactly reading it, but reading at it. I like her because she, too, was a prisoner in Scotland. She didn't like it either. When she was here, the island was nearly bald. Rocks, mostly. Some ugly scrub brush. She ordered pine trees.

Well, we talked about her, in the car. He and Mrs. Haig-Ereildoun know the author, Lady Antonia Frasier. "A bit heavy going, that book," he said, zipping the station wagon around a curve of road, now crowded in by pine trees that look as if they've always been here.

As for his new book, he said he didn't like to discuss what he was working on until it was finished, but that he would say it was a new look at King Macbeth. (I could see Mrs. Haig-Ereildoun as his wife.)

Mostly, he was pleased I was about to see Kinturriff. "I say, it will be novel indeed, to hear you converse with the fishermen. They speak quite a different language."

"It is English, though?"

"Technically," he said. "But I'll wager you won't be able to understand a word."

I said I'd just let him talk. I'd stay back with my camera.

YOU WOULDN'T BELIEVE THE pictures. In the first place, the streets are cobblestoned and the edges go right up to the water, where they become a tall, stone wall against the sea. Bright-colored fishing boats bob at anchor, way down there in the harbor. Since everything else is gray or black (the sky, the water, the cars, the people's clothes), the reds and yellows of the boats are as surprising as sunshine would be. The streets are skinny and there are hardly any cars, but the ones you see are antiques. The men are antiques. They're tough as New York dock workers, with unsmiling faces and stubble on their cheeks. They sit outside in rows, on benches, wearing those herringbone walking caps with short bills. They snug their hats tight over their ears and sit for hours in the cold, smoking pipes and talking. I tried to stay back in the distance, with my camera, but Mr. Haig-Ereildoun wouldn't let me. Somehow, without touching a hand to my shoulder or elbow, he managed to pull me in close, to talk with them.

He was right about the language being like nothing I'd ever heard. Mrs. Campbell, our daily, speaks English with a Scottish accent. These guys speak Scottish. It's so different from English it could be Martian. They sound a little like Claire: lots of "hhhekkh"s.

They got a good laugh at the way I sounded. Mr. Haig-Ereildoun had to translate. It's amazing they understand him.

I think the thing I'll remember longest about my day in Kinturriff was seeing how the fishermen lit up when they saw Mr. Haig-Ereildoun coming toward them. They seem to feel about him the way I do, only less shy. The pleasure between Mr. H-E and those men was raucous.

We brought home bundles of fish, wrapped in the *Kinturriff Observer*.

13

EVEN MR. HAIG-EREILDOUN, WHO can sit right at the same breakfast table and still be in another country and another era, notices how Claire's progressing. Today she banged her spoon on her egg and shouted, "Hhhekkkh!" His eyebrows went up. "Why, very good. Egg! Very good indeed."

I don't worry that it takes a specialist to understand what she's saying and that I'm the specialist. Trevor, Pru, and Mr. and Mrs. Haig-Ereildoun pick up bits of Claire's language, and I understand her almost perfectly. She's only three. Pretty soon the words will get more developed. She's mastered the consonants "puh" and "fuh." She's working on "tuh." But the main thing is the meanings, and her awareness of meanings grows faster and faster.

This week she has a new favorite word. Or sentence or phrase. It's her three-syllable masterpiece. She got it from a wonderful story. Trevor and Pru have a book they've wanted me to read since we got here, and we finished it last night, each of us taking turns reading aloud. Even though Claire couldn't hear, she went from lap to lap and "listened," laughing when we laughed. "Nanny is quite fond of this book, isn't she, Mum," Trevor smiled, quite fondly. "So am I," said his mother. It's a children's book by a French philosopher named André Maurois: *Fattypuffs and Thinifers.*

There are two brothers in the Double family: Terry Double is skinny and tense; Edmund Double is chubby and relaxed. The two brothers go down the escalator into the Underground (subway), and the escalator splits off in two directions, taking these boys into two different worlds under the earth. The fat boy finds himself in the world of the Thinifers: very stern, energetic, fussy people. The thin boy finds himself in the world of the Fattypuffs: happy-go-lucky people who don't have much ambition but living, loving, eating, and drinking. The Fattypuffs and Thinifers have a war, and of course the Thinifers, so much more efficient, strong, and spartan, win. But that's not the end. Once the Thinifers have conquered the Fattypuffs, the two types occupy the same land together. The Fattypuffs, being dominated, are forced to take on some of the ways of the Thinifers and in spite of themselves become more disciplined. The Thinifers can't help but be beguiled by the Fattypuffs' joie de vivre, so the Thinifers learn to ease up, to relax and celebrate life.

All through the book, the rallying cry of the Double family is "Hoi! hoi! HOI!" Since we started reading it, "hoi-hoi-hoi" has become the rallying cry of the Haig-Ereildoun family. "Hoi! hoi! HOI!" Trevor says to Pru at the breakfast table. "Hoi! hoi! HOI!" she says back. The wonderful thing is, "hoi-hoi-hoi" is easy for Claire: her three-syllable masterpiece.

I'M TURNING INTO A Fattypuff. Maybe not so mellow, but definitely chubbed. A Fattypuff in a family of Thinifers.

I haven't stepped on the scale this week, because I'm afraid.

It has occurred to me: The scale here may be wrong.

However, it's hard to sit down in my jeans. And the top two buttons won't fit in their buttonholes. It's not because my waist's so much bigger, but all the flesh from below is squeezed up to make a bulge. Although my metabolism may be adapting to the climate, or my fat may be insulating me so that I don't have to wear my coat inside, I do have to wear a few big old sweaters—which is lucky, or everyone would see that the seams of the denim are very stressed and that I've popped the two buttons. One more and we'll have to go all the way to town, wherever that is, to buy me a new pair of jeans.

I might like going to the town, but maybe not. You'd think I'd like the village, the stone streets winding like ribbons, walled by crusty old buildings with gold lettering on the doors, lettering done by some actual person who probably died a hundred years ago—but I don't. I see this charm and wish it was a picture in a magazine instead of my real life. Everything pretty intensifies my awareness of how alone I am. I am grateful for the shop in the village, where I load up on these heavenly blue notepads and buy my Silk Cut cigarettes. They sell them mostly in cute little packets of ten, but they have giant-sized packs of twenty, too. We go once a week, so I get two packets of twenty, and the chemist gives me a disapproving look. I've thought of buying four packets of ten, but extra packaging seems a waste of cardboard. The bakery is the other thing I love in the village, the place where I stand longing. But Mrs. Haig-Ereildoun never goes in there, never even slows down her steps as she passes. She just gets presliced bread from the other tiny food store in Bridie. She's a natural-born Thinifer, and the trays of plump jelly doughnuts glistening in the window don't even catch her eye.

EATING IS ONE OF the true satisfactions I get here, each day. I'd meant to write down a few recipes, because we eat Scottish things that are delicious.

Kedgeree is the best. We make it with the delicious smoked herring Mr. Haig-Ereildoun brings home from Kinturriff. We flake the fish into a pot of rice, melt in a hunk of Aberdeenshire butter, and jumble in some hard-boiled eggs cut into quarters. If we have a lemon, we squeeze it over the dish. Kedgeree tastes like Scotland.

Mrs. Haig-Ereildoun loves what they call smokies, a special kind of smoked haddock that Mr. H-E gets from the fishermen. She uses it to make "smokie mousse." That's only for parties, like the time Granny and Mr. H-E's brother and sister-in-law came for supper, and we had smokie mousse for our starter. I'm sure both the Kedgeree and the smokie mousse taste better because we know how bright the fishing boats look in the gray harbor, and what tough old characters catch the fish.

The other thing we have a few times a week is cottage pie. It's not really a pie—or if it is a pie, the top and bottom crusts are mashed potatoes. First, the bottom layer of mashed potatoes. Second, the mince: Mince is what they call hamburger. You cook the hamburger with some onions, fine-chopped carrots, and sometimes a little diced celery. You drain the fat and spread the mince over the mashed potatoes. You smooth on the top "crust" of mashed potatoes, making some peaks and valleys that will get varying degrees of brown when you bake the dish in a Mark Four oven. It's not so special, I suppose, but here where it's cold, it hits the spot.

Menu Number Three: Chicken. You can't do that in America. You don't have the chickens.

You should taste these chickens. We always bake a few at a time and have chicken around to slice and warm, or to slice and not warm. It's so cold in the pantry we don't have to keep the chicken in the refrigerator, and when everyone's asleep I go downstairs and pull off strings—or hunks—to eat in the dark. I don't think I'll be caught, because I can find my way without turning on any lights at all, and Mr. and Mrs. Haig-Ereildoun sleep far away from the kitchen.

Also, there are potatoes in many forms. Mashed potatoes. Baked potatoes. Scalloped potatoes. And you know about new potatoes. And . . . chips. Chips are something I wouldn't have dreamed of eating before I met Tedward. Then, with Tedward, I had them at Domino Alley: french fries. But these Haig-Ereildoun chips are miles above french fries. We have them almost every day. Even with cottage pie or kedgeree. You fill a pot halfway up the sides with vegetable oil and heat it on the cooker. You take a bunch of peeled baking potatoes and cut them into thin strips. Like fingers. You have a metal basket, with a handle, that fits into the pot. You fill the basket with potato fingers, lower the basket into the hot oil, listen to the sizzling for a few minutes, then lift the basket out and shake off the loose drops of oil. This is pretty much what they do at Domino Alley, so I wonder why the french fries at Domino Alley taste limp and stale, compared to our chips. The thing must be the immediacy—that you eat them the minute they're cooked. It's easy to explain why the texture is different. But I can't understand why the flavor, when we do it here, is so much more potatoey. Potatoes here have a great taste. You can taste it in crisps, which is their name for potato chips. These crisps are not only crispier, they're more distinctly a form of potato, with the flavor of earth.

The most boring thing we have is called "Apple." It's boring because we have it for dessert almost every day. First, you peel a million apples. Slice them. Cook them a little in a pan with some water. Then you grind the slices through this thing called a moulie, a colander with a handle and moving parts, and you lay the mush in a souffle dish. Sprinkle sugar and cinnamon, dab on some dots of butter. Beat some egg whites stiff, add some sugar, beat still stiffer. Spread onto apple. Bake at Mark Five for half an hour or so. Meringue. It's okay the first few times.

Another thing we have every day, with tea, is biscuits. Store-bought biscuits. We usually have a selection from many packages, most of them really average, like Mother's cookies. But they're better than nothing. The kind I do like are called digestive biscuits. They're not too sweet, and I don't know what kind of flour they're made of, but it has a texture. You can't get enough.

Since I spend a lot of my time in the kitchen, I dip into the tin now and then. Yesterday afternoon, after tea, Mrs. Haig-Ereildoun lifted the tin and gave it a frown, then a shake. She seemed to find it light. She pried off the top, looked inside, and found the level shallow. She lifted each remaining biscuit out one by one and made a low pile on the counter. "One. Two . . ." up to "Thirteen. Fourteen. Fifteen." She pierced me with her eyes and put all the biscuits back into the tin.

This afternoon before tea, she opened the tin and counted out the biscuits again: "Seven, eight, *nine*." Her look sprayed me with words she didn't have to speak.

ABOUT THIS EATING. I figured out something strange. It seems to be the only way I can assert myself. I try to get permission to take a walk, and when it's denied me, I suffer inside but don't put up a fight. I act like I agree with her, that I should only go off and explore the countryside when it's sunny. Which it never is. And we both know that. I let her man all the controls and actually work to let her believe that she's right. To save her feelings I act as if I'm perfectly happy abiding by her decisions on my behalf.

Now, by counting the biscuits, she has confronted me in another area, a private area. I assume she's more concerned with her grocery budget than with my weight, but she has almost put into words that she does not want me eating so much.

I don't want me eating so much, either. By the time we get back to London, I'll be f-a-t.

Mots will be horrified. Simon won't recognize me.

Still, just because Mrs. Haig-Ereildoun is onto me, I may not stop eating biscuits on the sly. This may be where I draw the line.

14

MY HERO HAS FALLEN. Mr. Haig-Ereildoun got drunk tonight. I could say tipsy, but he was almost toppling. That isn't why Granny Aitchee was mad though. She and Mrs. Haig-Ereildoun were both furious, because Mr. Haig-Ereildoun made a fool of himself over the sheriff's daughter.

The sheriff, Adam Foxwell, is probably the family's closest friend. Mr. H-E says the sheriff here is something like the county judge at home. Mr. Foxwell's wife died last year, and the Haig-Ereildouns try to see a lot of him. His daughter, Lucinda, is about my age but hasn't finished school yet. She had two years at Brighton, in England, and wasn't happy there, so she took a year in America at Radcliffe and another in Paris at the Sorbonne. When her mother died, she came home to stay with her father, but she'll probably go back to Brighton next year. Mrs. Haig-Ereildoun has often told me what a dear sweet girl Lucinda is and how much she and I have in common, since she spent a year in America, and how Lucinda wants to meet me. Mrs. H-E has tried before to get us together, but Lucinda spends a lot of time down in Edinburgh, with friends at the university there. Tonight, just before we'll be leaving for a short vacation on an island in the Hebrides, Lucinda and I had a chance to meet.

It was a gin-and-tonic party. The whole du Dordoigne family, Mr. Haig-Ereildoun's brother and sister-in-law, and all sorts of people were coming. Granny Aitchee, Mrs. Haig-Ereildoun, and I worked most of the afternoon arranging flowers and getting the smokie mousse and cold pheasant ready to go on the crackers. Granny Aitchee wore a special medallion with her MacLaren plaid dress. At the last minute Mrs. Haig-Ereildoun changed from her jeans into the tweed skirt she was wearing the night I met her. It's a very dowdy skirt and makes her look like the kind of librarian who's always saying "Sssh." I wore my navy blue dress with the white collar and the short pleated skirt.

Lucinda arrived all in black. Black turtleneck, tight black leather pants. A gold necklace, matching her long golden hair. I'm sure she thinks of it as golden.

I think she looks like a witch. Her hair is bleached and full of split ends. It doesn't seem like a living part of her body. Like a lot of the Scottish young people I've met, she looks unhealthy. You should see the children at the public baths, how whiter-than-white their skin. Like blemished dough. People cough as regularly as they breathe. "I've never seen so many ill-looking people," Mrs. Haig-Ereildoun said one day as we walked down the cobblestones in the village. I had the feeling she noticed only because I, such a robust American, was there. But they do look ill. And Lucinda fits right in.

Lucinda and I had a conversation. About potato chips. She said, "My most vivid memory of America is that the crisps are always stale."

She is so thin. Maybe she weighs seventy pounds. I pick a number, any number, because when you get down as low as what her weight must be, the numbers don't mean anything. All I can say is, she makes Mrs. Haig-Ereildoun look almost fat. You can imagine how she makes me look.

. . .

"I THINK IT'S MENTAL," Granny Aitchee said in the kitchen.

"It usually is," Mrs. Haig-Ereildoun agreed, very controlled, "when someone cannot eat." She was methodically lining a tray with crackers, around a tureen of smokie mousse. She stopped and ate a cracker. "No one has explained to me exactly the *type* of trouble she's had at these various colleges."

"I feel sorry for her!" said Granny Aitchee. "She looks positively grotesque." Granny Aitchee hacked like a killer at the pheasant carcass. She slammed down the knife and stomped across the kitchen to get a sharpener out of a drawer.

TEDWARD TELLS ME I'M cute when I'm mad. He doesn't take it seriously. So I'm terribly sorry to say this, but Granny Aitchee is adorable when she is angry. She's so small, and so passionate.

"Hello, Mother," Mr. Haig-Ereildoun beamed, sweeping into the kitchen on rubber legs, lurching downward to give her a kiss.

"Angus, get away from me!"

His face was red, and his grin got even sillier. "Now, Mother . . ." he moved in on her again.

"Angus! Off!" She ducked and began slapping slices of pheasant onto a platter, her eyes concentrating on the meat, her mouth in a purse.

Laughing, he landed a smack on her cheek.

MRS. HAIG-EREILDOUN WAS SO mad she didn't say or shriek a word.

Back in the drawing room, he had been almost drooling over Lucinda. At one point in the evening he'd backed her into a corner and, one hand on the wall to balance himself, the other hand holding his drink, he'd leaned so close to her face that I didn't know whether he was going to kiss her or lick her.

She seemed to enjoy it.

My own reaction surprised me. I was mad too. Drunkenness didn't become him. But that wasn't really why I was mad. I was mad because it was Lucinda he lost his dignity over. Do I have to look like a skinny witch with hair like white string to be adored by him?

15

UP UNTIL TODAY, MY most provoking letter from Simon had been the one that said why not ask for a hardboiled egg. It took me five pages to answer that eight-syllable question. I fill mailboxes around the world with descriptions of Mrs. H-E having a cow. But today, I got from Simon a two-sentence whammer.

It made me wonder if Mots and Rupert had told him I was engaged. We didn't talk about it that might in London—in all the newness of being in a different country, the subject of Tedward didn't come up. And I don't wear my ring. From Troonfachan I write only about the here and now.

In London Simon didn't treat me like a date, taking my elbow or anything—except at street corners, where everyone had to grab me, because I never remembered to look for cars driving down the wrong side of the road.

Today's note, though, on a very fancy little notepad he'd got at a hotel in Marakesh, made me worry. He said, "Maybe what's bothering her is the MP. Maybe she senses that the MP wants the soft breast of Melissa."

Hah. What the MP wants is the washboard breast of Lucinda. My worry is, what is it that Simon wants? My next letter to him had better be about Tedward.

. . .

LONG INTERRUPTION HERE. I wrote so many letters I used up my last notepad days before our weekly trip into the village. You'd think I'd therefore have made great headway on *War and Peace,* but no.

I did send Simon my letter about Tedward, explaining the depth of my commitment, etc. In the p.s. I told him my theory about the safety of the situation with Mr. H-E. The p.s. turned out much longer than the letter. I told Simon about what Margaret Meade says about incest. She says that in all tribes, incest is taboo. And in all tribes, incest is defined not by blood relationships at all—but by living in the same house. Except for the husband and wife, people under the same roof cannot have sex together. I think in some families I know, even the husband and wife are awkward about it. At least, once my cousin Pete's wife, Sally, told me she would love to sleep with her brother. "But that's incest!" I said. She said, "If you think that's incest, what do you think it's like having sex with Pete?" Be that as it may, there is such a strong sense of no-no-no between the au pair and the husband that I bet people don't act on their attractions very often. I bet the exceptions to this rule are as rare as what is legally defined as incest. I know some people don't think that kind of incest is rare either, but I think what those people mean is, it happens. Sometimes. I'm not saying hidden things don't happen. I just think certain bans are pretty effective, most of the time, and most people don't violate them. I've heard incest referred to as "crossing the line." There is a line. It applies to everyone living under the roof.

Although this p.s. about Mr. H-E and Margaret Meade and me took more pages than the main part of my letter, the point of writing at all was to let him know how I felt about Ted. I wanted to make it clear (without saying it) that there couldn't be any romance between us. Just in case he was thinking such a thought.

Simon didn't answer that letter.

But almost immediately, a big envelope came from him—the English version of a manila envelope, made of lighter, crinklier paper with a little cocoa in its color. Inside were three pages, all of them whole and unfolded. On top, there was a cover torn from *Nature* magazine: a picture of a fossilized frog. Prehistoric. Some archaeologists have just dug it up, after it lay in mud for millions of years. Paper-clipped to that there was a letter, and then a poem.

First, I have to describe the gorgeousness of the paper. Instead of using memo pads, he wrote on onionskin, very sheer, from the Hotel Shah Abbas, Isfahan, Iran. The first page, with his note, had the hotel's name in English, although the lettering style (in gold so heavy you can feel it with your finger) was very Arabian looking. There was a crest, like a coat of arms, in a very ornate obelisk, surrounded by a grand block of royal blue that had an intricate design of shapes embossed in gold. Weighty gold. Rich, rich, rich. Simon's letter, on this full piece of paper, was almost as short as his usual notes on memo pads. He said when he saw this frog on the cover of *Nature,* it reminded him of me.

The paper with the poem, though, was more mysterious. It had the same exotic design, in gold on royal blue; but the letters were, I assume, Arabic. If it weren't for the first page, identical except for its lettering in English, I might have thought the second page of letterhead had no words, only a fabulous decoration.

The poem was in Simon's mysterious fountain-pen handwriting, and consulting with Trevor, Pru, and everyone, we finally decided the first word is "light." He didn't give the poem a title, so it looks like the title is the decoration at the top of the page—those magnificent gold swoops and swigs and dots in gold against the royal blue.

Light of the Jurassic—
who awaited your touch
who sang for release
who gave life for your love in the dried grasses?

Memory etched in granite—
when cold nights and colder days
when blood flows slow
when eyes look elsewhere in their sightlessness
and clocks cease to draw together

The truth preserved but—
how much distorted
how much retained
how much reflected   like the outline of the ring of a bell

Were you the world for one . . . or two—
sunken in soft
sunken in heavy
sunken in crisp and open to the skies?

You might have, must have been more—
essence hidden in brief encounter
What delight in macromolecule
How much completeness you had to give
when needy searched for rounded flesh

Who has you now
pads sunken with delight
And where is truth
after countless years of sediment?

Kirriebairne

16

NOW I AM LIVING in a place far more to my liking than the freezing farmhouse. Now I am living in a castle.

Here, we dress for dinner. Tuxes and long dresses. We spend the days in jeans at the beach, and every day Mr. Haig-Ereildoun wears the same wool shirt of faded Stuart plaid. He's rangy enough to seem almost gangly, but with shoulders. All his clothes fall loose on his body. In his baggy London tweeds he looks like a rumpled aristocrat, and in the faded plaid he looks even more rumpled, and more aristocratic. But at dinner, in black tie, I say.

Damn my navy blue dress with the short skirt and the white linen collar.

"ISN'T IT AMAZING HOW different these buildings look with sun on their faces?" Mrs. Haig-Ereildoun said, as we drove through Bridie on our way here. I never thought I'd see the sun on Scotland, but it happened the morning we left Troonfachan. First we drove through farmland, getting *inside* the patchwork I see from my window. Later thickets of heather and broom banked the road—the ochres, rusts, and mauves of the nubs in Scottish tweeds. In fact, we crossed over the Tweed. And various riverlike bodies of water they call firths. Firths are much wider than burns, really big estuaries, where the seawater seems to come inland like finger lakes. Some have graceful modern bridges like the Golden Gate, and others have bridges made of stone, enormous ancient arches with flat tops, straight roadways for horsedrawn wagons. Imagine what the builders of these old bridges would think if they could see our Volvo fly, Mr. Haig-Ereildoun's foot flooring the gas.

We're spending a week with some friends named von Teplitz, on the Isle of Islay. Pronounced EYE-lah. In the Hebrides. It took us less than half a day to get from one side of this country to the other, and we didn't even cut straight across but made a long diagonal from northeast to southwest. The sun made sparklets on the lochs and the lazy flat waterways that meander into and out of the lochs, all blue that day—and it had been so long since I'd seen blue sky, the countryside seemed like a new planet. We passed abandoned crofts—stone cabins with square holes, glassless windows, cut into foot-thick walls. I just wrote Tedward that we may want to move here and live in a croft.

At a seaside town called Port Tarburt (I took lots of pictures), we drove onto a ferry. It was a stout ferry with a cheerful paint job. Below deck was like an underground parking lot, and up on deck the children and I moved from inside seats to outside benches, to experience the view from every vantage as we cut across the Sound of Jura. When we got close to the Isle of Jura we moved to the railings for a closer look. Jura was just a yellowish, flat-topped rock with nothing on it, sitting out in the water like the back of the Loch Ness monster. Maybe that's what all of Scotland looked like when Mary Queen of Scots got here. The bigger island in the distance was our island: Islay. Our Islay was very green with lots of zigs and zags on its coastline. Trevor and Pru had been to Islay before, and as the ferry's engine purred along the outline of the shore, past deep coves and inlets, Trevor pointed out the sights: "Cossle!" Then another one: "Cossle!"

Much more cool, with the breeze breathing through her hair, Pru tapped both of us on the shoulder and pointed across the mirror we were cutting through. "This is ours." She was pointing at a castle.

Really? A castle?

"Forty-one rooms," Trevor said. "Brilliant for hide-and-seek."

"We're staying in a castle?"

"Yes!"

"Yes!"

"It's not a real castle," their mother said, smiling down. "It's a Victorian."

It didn't look like what I think of as Victorian, but I suppose she meant it was built during the Industrial Revolution, by some self-made millionaire who wished he were a duke.

"Neo-Gothic, I daresay," daresaid Mr. Haig-Ereildoun.

WE GLISSED PAST OUR second-rate castle, past a village cozied into the seawall, past another castle. (Real?) The engine was chugging now, chopping rather than gliding past this last castle, from a more respectable era, and by the time we turned into the harbor at Port Askaig the engine had putt-putt-putted off for a silent landing. The seven von Teplitzes met us at the harbor and cheered as Mr. Haig-Ereildoun drove the station wagon down a long platform and off the boat.

When we circled the drive at Kirriebairne, the housekeeper opened the door to wave, and even through the window of the station wagon I could feel a sense of efficiency and energy coming from her. (Hoi hoi hoi, a Thinifer.) She wore a short-sleeved black uniform and the whitest, crispest apron I've ever seen—ironed eyelet ruffles at the borders. When we did step across the threshold, after the band of clattering kids, she ushered us in with a strange blend of cordiality and standoffishness.

In the background, two old women in uniforms knelt at places on the staircase, one near the top, one at the foot. They held cloths, and apparently they were polishing the banisters in slow motion. So far these old women have been here each day, slowly, slowly doing housework; but from a distance they don't seem to be moving. They don't talk to any of us, and none of us talks to them. I've never seen them talk to each other. They remind me of those statues of little black manservants some people have on their lawns in the South: They're a symbol of something.

WITH THE SUN OUT, it doesn't seem like Scotland. Certainly not like my imaginings of the Hebrides. I think of *To the Lighthouse,* with fog so thick the beacon can barely slice through. There are lighthouses here, on cliffs at the edges of the island; but no fog. I could swear I'm in Pebble Beach. The feeling is the same, with woods behind the house and water in the front. The Islay birds tweet through the quiet like Pebble Beach birds. The grass sloping all about the castle could be a golf course. The only big differences are, they don't have lambs on the lawns in Pebble Beach, or the Isle of Jura sitting across the sound like a big gold molar on a mirror.

I spend a lot of time gazing out at that big bare rock across the water. My bedroom window looks out on it, but usually I'm gazing from the big yellow bathroom. With eight children to bathe, I spend a lot of time in that bathroom. The von Teplitzes have five children, and they've left their nanny and their two au pairs at their house in London—"ill." All three of them.

Before we set out, Mrs. Haig-Ereildoun assured Mrs. von Teplitz that it would be no trouble at all for me to take care of the von Teplitz five, as well as the Haig-Ereildoun three. And of course, it's fine. The more the merrier. I have nothing else to do.

Fabulous, this house is, like color page after color page in a magazine: walnut paneling, or teak or something, that is perfection; no old paint anywhere; no faded furniture or frayed spots on the Persian rugs. But the most stupendous thing is the shower, set in that vast and beautiful bathroom.

Ever since we got here yesterday and I saw this bathroom, in the back of my mind and sometimes in the front of my mind I've been trying to figure out how to describe the color. One of my favorite books is by a Scot named James Barrie: *Sentimental Tommy.* (James Barrie also wrote *Peter Pan.*) Tommy always failed in English composition, because halfway through the second paragraph he would stop. His teachers saw him chew his pencil and frown out the window, and they thought there was something wrong with him. They didn't understand. He was trying to find exactly the right word. They didn't realize that this was the sign of a writer. I liked that book because I was a little like Tommy.

The color of this bathroom is driving me crazy. It's definitely something edible. It's not like lemon custard: On the one hand it's not so creamy and on the other not so sharp. I could say it's like butter and be done with it, but it's brighter than butter, and the texture is different. (Of course, think how many textures butter has, depending on how cold it is, or if it's melted.) This yellow is brighter than butter but nowhere nearly as bright as an egg yolk. The only comparison that satisfies me is something only cooks would understand. In my mom's favorite cookbook, *Mastering the Art of French Cooking,* Julia Child teaches you how to make crème anglaise: You beat egg yolks with sugar and then cook them over a double boiler, cooking and whipping until the mixture "forms the ribbon." That means you get the sauce base to a consistency that, when you pick up a spoonful and dribble some back into the pan, it doesn't land in droplets anymore but winds steadily from the spoon in a thin stream, like a ribbon. And instead of disappearing instantly back into the rest of the sauce, the ribbon lingers on top a second or two before the outline fades. At the ribbon stage, there's so much air whipped into the egg yolks, along with white sugar, that the thickness is satiny, and the color is exactly the shade of this bathroom.

The window is enormous: not little leaded panes but a great sweep of glass so clean you only know it's there because it steams up when you run a bath. You look straight out on the mirror of the sound, and the Isle of Jura. If you stand close enough to look straight down on the lawn, you see white lambs, fluffy as clouds. The bathroom is as big as the living room in a normal San Francisco apartment—but no furniture, just air and light. I haven't counted the towel racks, but there are rows of them, all highly polished brass—and they're heated! The hot water runs through the towel racks and warms up the towels. In America this would have impressed me, but imagine the difference between wrapping up in a heated towel here and shivering after a murky ice bath at Troonfachan. The warm towels at Kirriebairne are white as a cloud in a storybook sky—double-thick and double-size.

The shower itself is big enough to bathe all eight children at once, although the way we've done it so far is the von Teplitz and Haig-Ereildoun girls first, then the Haig-Ereildoun and von Teplitz boys—except the oldest von Teplitz, Matthew, who is thirteen and wants privacy. Thank heavens. Something about him bothers me.

It's a treat for Claire to stand in the shower with the big girls. They're very sweet to her. The Haig-Ereildoun children love being the guests in this huge shower almost as much as the von Teplitz children love being the hosts. It's like a porcelain room, more spacious than the entire bathroom at Troonfachan. And water can come out from every direction. The overhead nozzle is shined up like a huge brass serving plate, with such a vast spread of holes you stand in a gentle downfall of delicious, warm rain. For the sides of your body, there are holes up and down the porcelain walls that shoot warm water at you horizontally. It works especially well for a group of naked children.

The base of the shower is a tub, so you can just loll in there as if it were a hot swimming pool. There's a brass nozzle, on a brass hose, and you can hold the nozzle in your hand and move it around to rinse your hair. You can slide a brass magazine rack (with built-in soap baskets on the sides) to the most comfortable reading position and engross yourself in *War and Peace*. Or, if you're not into *War and Peace,* you can pick from a stack of magazines the von Teplitzes have here on a corner stand. One thing that strikes me is that American magazines like *Time* and even *Cosmopolitan* are tossed on tables all about this castle: They're a status symbol. Built into the bathtub reading rack there's a basket of sponges, brushes, and loofahs and a place to rest your glass. As the bathwater cools to tepid, you can replenish with fresh hot. There's no shortage of teakettle-hot water at Kirriebairne.

There's a hair dryer for every guest.

DRINKS ARE SERVED IN the drawing room at half past eight, to the minute. (Mr. von Teplitz is German and the housekeeper is Scottish.) To me this exactitude is amazing. My grandmother is so much against lateness that she sets her watch ahead half an hour, so if you're not half an hour early, you're late; but her kind of punctuality is not the same thing as being on time.

This schedule gives me precisely what I need to get the older children in their pajamas or nightdresses and their dressing gowns, the smaller ones tucked into bed with their books. I'm so glad the English don't have that stupid, stifling American idea I was brought up with, about total sensory deprivation at bedtime, whether you're sleepy or not. Books in bed are the best idea, for avoiding those long boring fights: Especially with *eight children*. They read until they want to sleep, and then they're asleep.

Supper is served at nine. Each evening I check my watch. So far, the announcement from the housekeeper comes when my second hand gets to the top. This says something for my ten-dollar watch.

Mr. von Teplitz seems like he was born in a black tie. And in fact, on the beach in his plaid shirts, he looks uncomfortable, as if he's put on somebody else's clothes. He's what you would call handsome and suave: tallish, pale skin, dark hair, a well-cut moustache, alert little black eyes with lashes like tiny hard bristles. Miss Manners would look up to his manners. But even when he's sitting back in a chair and swirling his cocktail, you can tell his buttocks are clenched. Although he's from Germany, and talks about Germany, he has not a trace of an accent. His wife is English, and Kirriebairne belonged to her father, Mr. Skychurch. The old man bought it in World War Two and moved his family up here, to keep them safe from the bombing. She and her sister inherited the house, but her sister never comes here. Mr. von Teplitz does seem to think of it as his house. Not her house or their house. And every single adult here, including me the newcomer, knows it's not.

I'm more aware of this than I normally would be because one day when Mrs. Haig-Ereildoun and I were alone in the laundry room, she lowered her voice and told me about an incident at Kirriebairne, a few years ago, when the old man, Mr. Skychurch, was alive. The old man liked to take his supper separately—boiled eggs in the kitchen with the housekeeper—before the others had their five-course meal in the dining room. One night the four of them (von Teplitzes and Haig-Ereildouns) were enjoying a most splendid claret with their supper when the old man strode in, standing tall. "Where did you get that wine?" Mr. von Teplitz had got it from the cellar. "That is my wine! I did not grant you permission to rob my cellar!" Mrs. Haig-Ereildoun said the old man was so angry he shook. Her fear was that he would strike his son-in-law. Mrs. v.T. later confided to Mrs. H-E that her fear was that he'd have a stroke. "It was quite unpleasant," Mrs. Haig-Ereildoun said.

. . .

MRS. VON TEPLITZ I like. She has big teeth, like Princess Anne or Eleanor Roosevelt, and a thoroughbred's bone structure. She's almost as tall as Mr. Haig-Ereildoun, and all her angles jut out like the studs of an unfinished building: Her clothes drape in points over shoulders, hips, elbows, and knees. Tonight she wore a long skirt, hand knit from nubbly wheat-colored wool yarns and gold twine, with a matching knit camisole and long matching cardigan. Even I could tell she didn't get this at Peter Jones, the department store where Mots and Mrs. Haig-Ereildoun shop. This was one of a kind. She wore no bra, and the weave was so loose that I worried Mrs. von Teplitz's nipples, as well as her hipbones, would wear holes into the fabric. Even though she dresses like an actress, her personality is never on stage, except for the awkward moment when she enters the room, dressed up: She seems almost painfully conscious of her clothes. Once she's been seen and complimented she forgets about how she's striking everyone and becomes completely straightforward again: raw, solid. Her voice is almost as deep as a man's, with a roughness that makes a counterpoint to her queen's English accent. At least *she* likes my navy blue dress. "Supah!" she said, the first time she saw it. And she loves to laugh. With those big teeth.

She's not very old. She mentioned that she was only twenty when Matthew was born, which would make her thirty-three. Mrs. Haig-Ereildoun seems much older. At least forty-three.

Mr. and Mrs. von Teplitz seem to like talking about America, both looking down on it. (But then they do have all these American magazines). The first night Mr. v.T. told me, at gin and tonic time, that before they were married, just after her debut, Mrs. von Teplitz lived in New York for a year, and that to get a green card she'd had to sign a paper saying, among other things, that she'd never practiced prostitution and didn't plan to begin doing so. He snickered. What a country. At dinner he told me that when he's not using Kirriebairne for their family week in spring or his all-male hunting week in fall, he occasionally lets the house out to groups of Europeans. "Europeans!" he emphasized. "I would never let it to an American." I really didn't care, but I could tell he was eager for me to ask. "Because you have no culture!" Actually, I'm not sure Miss Manners would give him straight A's.

Last night Mrs. von Teplitz wore slinky silk jersey, black, like a floor-length T-shirt, with a rope of pearls. She certainly has sharp nipples. "In America you're always changing your names," she said, "aren't you."

Changing our names? Thoughts zipped through my brain, wondering what she was talking about. Our family hasn't changed ours. Except! My Norwegian great-grandfather (Mom's grandfather) did change his at Ellis Island, from Stokkeland (too hard to spell—in fact I'm not exactly sure how it was spelled—Stockeland?—Stokkelund?) to Nelson (easy to spell). And all the people from very very foreign countries—like my friend whose Russian Jewish grandfather had, as a thirteen-year-old immigrant, dropped the unpronounceable bag of syllables he'd come with and chosen Gold, for the hope it symbolized. And Grandpa Pomeroy's friend Mr. Todd changed his name to Tod, "because if one 'd' is good enough for God it's good enough for Tod."

As I mused out these things they all laughed. Superior. "And you actually give your babies Christian names that are like our titles for nobility, don't you," Mrs. von Teplitz said. "Like Earle."

I realized this was true. I didn't tell them my grandmother's maid's name: Queenie.

AS FOR THE KIRRIEBAIRNE suppers themselves. This is nothing like what they tell you about English or Scottish food. This is like Paris probably would be if you didn't mind paying as much for your dinner as you paid for your plane ticket. First, soup. Morag's cream of mushroom is nothing like Campbell's. For one thing, real cream, whipped a little. There was something like sherry or port or Madeira. And the mushrooms. "Supah!" said, Mrs. von Teplitz, tasting. Mr. von Teplitz thought my naivete amusing when I sighed. He seemed especially superior when he explained what was different about these mushrooms. They grow wild on the island. The feeling I got from him was that they have little elves (or maybe those same old ladies in the uniforms) crawling on their knees in the woods, with magnifying glasses, searching out these scrumptious little umbrellas. For the main course we have fabulous, buttery carrot purees, and celeriac julienned in mustard sauce, and green beans with so much inborn sugar (and added butter) they could be candies. And those extra-earthy-tasting potatoes, from mashed (with port-flavored gravy) to glistening oval-shaped jewels. The first night the meat was pheasant, shot here on the grounds; the next night we had Scottish salmon (wow), and tonight we had a kind of wood hen found only in the Hebrides, also shot by Mr. von Teplitz. "Supah!" Mrs. von Teplitz says, pretty often.

I must say I do contribute something to these dinner parties, because Mr. von Teplitz gets great pleasure in displaying how much better they eat at Kirriebairne than we do in the United States. I don't mind. I love the food. And there must be some price for coming from the richest country in the world.

The game part of the menus, though, the part he's most proud of, is not foreign to me. My father was a hunter. Kirriebairne pheasant tastes like Dad's pheasant (which may be why I love it), and the special woodcock that lives only in the Hebrides tastes almost exactly like the wood hens we used to help Dad pluck in our garage in Oregon. The first time I had wood hen was when I was little, and the family had a goose at Christmas, but Dad saw to it that there was a special tiny wood hen just for me. Now a lot of my friends at home think hunting is barbaric, but I can't agree—partly for logical reasons, and partly because I can't condemn my gentle father. These tastes, of pheasant and woodcock, make me ache, missing Dad.

On to the next course. Salad. Once watercress, once endive (pronounced onnh-*deeve*), and tonight these many-ruffled leaves.

And then the fruit and cheese. All kinds of squat little wheels, with powdery crusts casing lusty creams—French names like Pont L'Evêque—plus the tall wedges of bright ochre and ivory pale Islay cheddars. The oldest von Teplitz girl, Josephine, told me her father had cut out an article from an American magazine saying that Islay cheddars were the best in the world. She had stars in her eyes as she told me this, and I bet when she grows up she'll get stars in her eyes tasting Islay cheddar just the way I do tasting wood hen.

After Morag clears the cheese plates, she brings on the fruit basket: a glut of glistening gorgeousness, always served with a little pair of sterling silver scissors for the grapes. Mrs. von Teplitz presides over the scissors, handing each person a clump of fat juicy marbles to put on his plate. ("Philippa?—Melissa?—Angus?—Darling?")

As if that weren't enough, coffee is served by Mrs. von Teplitz, from a silver tray brought in by Morag. The pot is sterling, the cups demitasse, of that china so thin you want to bite into it. Every cup is a different design, each so delicate, and the coffee itself is a special filter. Mrs. von Teplitz passes a bowl of huge brown sugar cubes, all flaky, with their corners bumped off. No one has milk or cream with this coffee.

The coffee is apparently a rest, before the final course. It may be a dessert ("pud"), or a savory (savoury, it's spelled here). These savories are the most exciting thing. I've never had mushrooms for dessert, until last night, when Morag served thin white toasts without crusts, with those wonderful Hebrides mushrooms spooned onto them. Period. No herbs, no sherry or port, just mushrooms sautéed in butter.

"And to think," Mrs. von Teplitz said. "She's never been off the island."

THE MOST SIGNIFICANT THING I've learned at these dinners is that English men (or maybe European too—Mr. von Teplitz is German) seem to have a different attitude toward women than American men do. They don't seem so drawn to youth. Here I am, Miss February, but the woman Mr. von Teplitz can't get enough of is Mrs. Haig-Ereildoun. I admit, in my bathing suit at the beach, he ogles me till not only my face is red but probably the skin all over my body. It might not be so embarrassing if I hadn't just put on these piles of extra bosom and bottom, but under any circumstances I think I'd be mad if someone invaded me the way Mr. von Teplitz does with his eyes. My body is none of his business.

Only at the beach does this happen. At cocktails, he pays attention to me and to the general crowd. Same with the soup course. By the middle of the main course, his head is leaning over toward Mrs. Haig-Ereildoun's plate, and their conversation is private, hushed. As the courses continue his interest intensifies. By coffee, you'd think Mrs. Haig-Ereildoun was Michelle Pfeiffer.

Her eyelids are usually lowered as she listens to him. When she raises her eyes to answer him, there's usually some amusement in her face. She's like a girl, having a safe flirt. It's obvious she's in control.

Mr. Haig-Ereildoun gets a bang out of Mrs. von Teplitz. They seem to have a lot to laugh about. But he doesn't *need* her (and she doesn't need him) the way Mr. von Teplitz needs Mrs. Haig-Ereildoun. He's such an all-powerful type, a master from the master race. And yet he almost grovels to keep Mrs. Haig-Ereildoun entertained. She seems to enjoy it. She likes being in control.

. . .

DIFFERENT AS WE ARE, I suspect Mrs. Haig-Ereildoun and I are attracted to the same men. I don't think she's attracted to Mr. von Teplitz.

I'm trying to figure out why he tries so hard. It isn't youth and beauty. I wonder if there's some relationship between what makes him so urgent to please her and what makes me so afraid to displease her. And I wonder why Mr. Haig-Ereildoun is neither afraid to displease her nor urgent to please her. Maybe that nonchalance is the secret of his success.

17

LAST NIGHT MRS. VON Teplitz did something that made my heart stop half a second. Mr. Haig-Ereildoun froze.

Morag brought on the tureen of soup. Mrs. von Teplitz ladeled some into the first soup plate and handed it across the table to Mrs. Haig-Ereildoun. Then, looking me straight in the eyes, she filled the second soup plate and handed it to Mr. Haig-Ereildoun.

Not everyone may know this—but whether most people know it or not, or care or not, Mrs. von Teplitz knows, and she cares: You're supposed to serve the women first. Serving Mrs. Haig-Ereildoun very first is according to the etiquette: Mrs. H-E is the female guest of honor. But to skip the other lady present (me) and serve a man next is a statement.

She was stating: As we all know, you do not belong at this table, on a par with us. She had a defiance in her face, and she didn't unlock her eyes from mine as she handed the soup plate to Mr. Haig-Ereildoun.

When he saw the soup coming toward him, his eyes blinked in embarrassment. His face muscles tightened, a trace of hurt mingled with shock. The shock disappeared fast (faster than the ribbon on the crème anglaise), but a hint of a frown lingered and confronted Mrs. von Teplitz as he handed me his soup, making a contradiction to the statement she had made.

"Melissa," he said, his eyes on Mrs. von Teplitz.

18

TONIGHT I'M GETTING AN early start on my blue notepad, because of a so-called headache. Skipped dinner. Hard day at the beach.

I had a bowl of soup in the kitchen with Morag. The funny thing is, she knew about what had happened on the beach. No one had told her, but she knew. Up until today, I hadn't thought of this place as dangerous, but it is.

WHEN I TOLD MRS. H-E I had a headache, I could see she was thrilled. I wonder what would have happened if I'd just said, "I'd rather have a bowl of soup in the kitchen with Morag tonight." Would that have offended anyone? Probably what would have happened is that Mrs. Haig-Ereildoun would have explained to Mrs. von Teplitz that I had a headache, and Mrs. von Teplitz would have been pleased.

Morag. I told you about that thing she has, a balance between cordiality and standoffishness. It's such a precarious balance I thought it would be hard to pull off. After getting to know her a little, tonight, I think the hard part for her is the cordiality.

To give you an idea of Morag, I should describe not just the three-star dinners but all the meals. Breakfast, of course, is breakfast. Silver chafing dishes on the side table, the usual serve-yourself—but there's everything to choose from: all kinds of fresh fruits and juices, pastries and toasts, poached eggs and omelettes and all the breakfast meats, along with hot cereals and cornflakes and a choice of granolas. Yogurt. Cheeses. Lunch is on the beach, in wicker baskets: the Scotch eggs, the pork pie, the sandwiches, the crisps—all assembled by Morag. She serves high tea for the children, egg dishes and hot breads and pasta dishes and fabulous puds (apple pies, long wedges of buttery shortbread, meringue cups filled with berries). Tonight she explained—or complained—that each bottle of milk and every apple and salmon and roast of beef has to be ordered far enough in advance to be brought over on the ferry, which only crosses the sound on Mondays and Wednesdays. If she runs short of an ingredient, there's no remedy for her mistake. Counting the hot meals for herself and the two old housemaids, it turns out Morag has to serve sixteen people three times a day. That's forty-eight meals every day, three hundred thirty-six meals a week. If I were more in the mood for arithmetic, I'd count how many courses.

It's quantity. But the stunning part is the quality. If she's never been off the island, how did she learn to cook like this?

"I've learned a lot from booooks," she told me. I won't keep up trying to pronounce her words in spelling, though. All her pronunciations are Scottish. Hebridean! It's lucky she's so interesting.

"I've worked for Mr. Skychurch—Mrs. von Teplitz's father—since I was a girl (and she was a girl too), and he noticed me looking through his library. He wanted to know what books I was interested in, and I told him the few. He got them out and made a stack and said, 'Read them, and tell me what you think.' On hearing my reactions to the first books, he told me others he thought I might like. I read those, and I had things to say to him about them. He told me, 'I hope one day you'll read every book in this library.' *That* was ambitious for him to imagine! He'd moved back to England by then, except for holidays, but after his wife died, he moved up from London and lived here full time, in the gloom—it's sunny now, but you can't imagine how gloomy it is most weeks of the year—and each day I cooked his supper and after he'd eaten, he invited me to sit across from him at his desk in the library, and we discussed a particular book. Sometimes it would be a book I'd read, and sometimes it would be a book he'd cared about—and that I therefore vowed to read. By the time he died, I still hadn't read all the books, but now I have, and I've gone back, rereading. It's a fine library, he has here."

I knew, because I'd been in it. Pru and Josephine had pulled me in. The room filled me with awe, too: It was rich and warm, with a beautiful desk and leather chairs and four long walls of books, floor to ceiling—a tall ladder of polished wood to get you to the higher shelves.

"Most of the cookbooks that taught me were books he ordered up from London. In this way, he gave me my career."

Morag told me her family thought she was crazy, living alone in the castle, all winter long. They all live on the island, but "in reasonable houses. Cozy." She told me I couldn't imagine how loud the wind, how fierce the rain. How rare in a year a day of sunshine. "You can't imagine how cold it gets." I remembered taking a bath at Troonfachan and thought I could imagine. "The mist is so thick, most days of the year, that you cannot see the sound. You cannot see the lawn nor the lambs. Even in a cozy house, it's eerie on Islay. Here, with forty-one rooms and each of them banging and creaking and whistling, it's hard not to believe you're in the company of ghosts. And I don't mean well-meaning, friendly ghosts. My family may be right when they say I'm crazy. If I wasn't before, I must be now."

Ah. I imagined curling up in a blanket on that leather sofa in the library, with the wind yowling and the ghosts prowling and a fire going, a book in my hand.

"They say I'm crazy, but the von Teplitz family's only here two weeks out of the year. That's the part I don't like. The rest of the time, I like it. And so, for the most part, my sister and brother, my mother and aunts and uncles and cousins, they leave me be."

"How has it been for you here?" she asked, suddenly serious. Her face looked concerned, almost grilling me. "With the children."

"Oh fine," I said.

"No trouble?" She was grilling me.

"No . . ."

"What about Matthew. Any trouble?"

Matthew is the thirteen-year-old. He looks like a younger, fattish version of his father. His little black eyes are stuck in his face like raisins in dough. When he gets excited, they glitter and twitch like flies trapped in dough. Today I decided he's like Piggy in *Lord of the Flies*.

Yesterday he raised his double chin and told Trevor and me about Christmas at the von Teplitzes' in London: "First," he said, in his peculiar, shrill voice, "we have a tree on Christmas Eve, with the nanny and the au pairs and all of the servants. Every one of them gets a gift. Then on Christmas morning we have our family celebration." His sense of superiority almost changed the direction of the blood in my veins. Putrid conceit. I wanted to pinch my nose.

Then today he really did it. After the picnic the eight children and I tromped up and over a cliff to another beach, far from the adults, and found the ruins of an old castle, with jagged stone walls no taller than me, all soft with green moss. Rocks from this castle were tossed all around the beach, but for some reason the remains of what must have been a turret was left standing tall (and eerie) above the rubble. Stubs of the ground-floor walls still stood sturdily, so we could map out the rooms, now fantasies in the sand. We decided to play house, each child claiming a room as his house. Pru and Josephine von Teplitz were protective of Claire, seeing that she got the nicest room, the one with half a window frame left, moss padding its stones. "Hoi! hoi! HOI!" Trevor shouted across to me from his "house." All the children enjoyed knocking on imaginary doors to pay visits, serving tea in imaginary cups—except Matthew, who'd apparently had a better game in mind ever since we'd gone out of sight of the adults.

I felt uneasy as I saw him whispering in his sister's ear, his black eyes darting, flying with excitement that struck me as not healthy. Josephine shook her head no, and more buzz-buzz went from his mouth to her ear. His fat little body twitched with excitement. He hustled over to his two younger sisters and got them squealing; he ran to Trevor, getting a skeptical frown to begin with, then, with some whispers from Josephine, raised eyebrows and a grin. I didn't know what was being said, but I knew I didn't like it. Still, there was nothing concrete to confront. From room to room in the moss-covered castle there was a stirring. I felt my authority threatened, and it seemed like time to get out of there. "Back to the family!" I yelled, beckoning them all to follow me.

They followed me—but running, fast as bats. "Get her!" Matthew yelled, his voice climbing beyond the usual shrill into a vibrato. I ran with all my might, a sheer wall of sand in front of me. It took more breath than I could get to pull my weight up the side of the cliff. I couldn't move my feet fast enough. Each gulp of air had to go so deep it seemed to rip tissue. "The knees! The knees!" Matthew yelled, from way behind the others. I heard feet thumping close. Up, up I struggled, in a panic like drowning. "Collapse her! The kneeeees!" Even on my stomach, body on body pouncing onto my back and legs, I couldn't gasp air fast enough. "Well done!" Matthew clapped as I flipped onto my back, freeing my arms for a moment's struggle until the army of five pinned them to the sand. "Well done, chaps, well done!" From under the gang of strong young bodies I picked up my head to look back at him, halfway up the cliff, bouncing from his heels to his tiptoes, heels to tiptoes, screaming. "Get her jumper. Good, good!" He started his feet up again, moving toward us. "Pull harder, you fools. Harder!" Matthew's two oldest sisters had the bottom of my sweater and Pru and Trevor had each grabbed a cuff. "Off with it! Off with it!" Matthew cried, almost writhing in glee down there, the way I was writhing in sand and trying to kick them off me. Matthew trudged close enough for me to see the sweat beads on his face. Behind him the little von Teplitz boy and Claire—Claire's little body, in her sundress—frolicking up. Claire was as ignited as the rest.

"Off with it!" shouted Matthew, standing high above me in the sand, high above his troops. "Off with the jumper!" Against their tugging I clenched my chin to my collarbone, so determined to keep my dignity that they'd have had to pull off my head to pull off my sweater. They had it bunched up around my neck and shoulders, and Matthew shrieked, "Forget the pullover. You have her! Can't you see she's exposed. Get the shirt!" As I flung my arms at Pru and Josephine, the eight-year-old ripped the buttons to tear my shirt open. "Stop it!" I hissed. "Stop!"

Matthew was the image of power, standing so tall in the sand with the sun behind his head. His fat-breasted chest pulled his green T-shirt taut. He jiggled with excitement.

"Stop!" I shouted, very loud, as one sister tore at my bra.

My panic worked like a sprinkling of gunpowder on their flame. All of the children flickered up and blazed, joining efforts to rip off my bra.

"Trevor." With my eyes I reached for his eyes and spoke in as normal a voice as I could. "Trevor, you will not do this. Trevor, you must not join in this."

Trevor wasn't Trevor. His eyes glistened. He loved this.

I took an enormous breath, stopped struggling, and pronounced,

"Trevor, wake up. Wake up. This is me. Melissa." I put every ray of human energy I had into my eyes, working to magnetize his. "Trevor?"

I'm not sure if it was my imposed calm or my intensity that made these agile children fumble, but in getting my sense of humor back, they remind me of that Monty Python sketch of the upper class twit, trying to get the bra off the dummy. They didn't have a clue about sliding the bra up to expose a nipple (that's what I would have done)—they just went on grappling in a way too frantic to have an effect.

Trevor did meet my eyes. He was taking deep breaths through the nostrils into the chest.

"Trevor, this is me and you cannot let me be hurt. You cannot let me be shamed. That would hurt me. We are friends. I could not let you be hurt. By anyone. You cannot let me be hurt. By anyone."

The glee in his eyes was changing to fear.

"Especially by you. Trevor. Get your mother. Now."

For a moment the children were paying more attention to Trevor than to me. His feet were like tree roots, in the sand. Behind the perfectly round lenses of his glasses, I could see his eyes struggle to refocus, like a drunk blinking.

"Trevor, please hurry."

Eyes narrowed for an instant, he pivoted and shot toward the picnic site, his rubber soles kicking right and left behind him as he climbed the sand.

"Trevor you fool!" screamed Matthew. "You cretin!" By now the children had let go of me to watch Trevor. Matthew was sputtering. "You *pansy*. Trevor."

Without refastening the buttons that remained, I tugged down my sweater and stood up. I had only a flicker of eye contact with Matthew—and I'm sure my eyes flashed as much hatred as his—before he turned to the others and ordered, "Get him!"

They ran, but Trevor had a big lead. "*Get* that faggot and pull down his pants!" Up they ran. Claire, the little von Teplitz boy, and I struggled after, sand in our shoes. Matthew was back there somewhere.

At the crest of the cliff, I looked down at the beach: water with whitecaps, creamy sand, a cluster of bright-colored blankets. The adults were four stationary specks, with one speck moving toward them: Trevor.

Down the sandy wall would have been a delicious flight, and it was hard to hold down my wings in order to stay behind with Claire and little von Teplitz. Matthew waddled down ahead of us, the fat on his back bouncing under his T-shirt, which fit him like green paint. Mr. Haig-Ereildoun sat in the sand, reading his book; Mr. von Teplitz was sleeping with his face on the rug; Mrs. Haig-Ereildoun and Mrs. von Teplitz made a long, hyphenated diagonal on another plaid rug, facing each other with heads propped on their wrists; and Trevor was almost up to them.

"Trevor!" yelled Pru, and he spun back to face her.

"Hello, you!" called Mrs. von Teplitz, rolling from her stomach onto her back and lifting her head off the sand. "Had an adventure?"

Still running with the pack, Pru cupped her hands to her lips and shouted, "We found a brilliant castle."

"All covered with moss," Josephine amplified.

"Supah!" said Mrs. von Teplitz, rolling back onto her stomach.

"SO," MORAG SAID, SETTLING her teacup into the saucer and leaning her face in closer to mine. "No trouble with the children?"

I was frowning into myself. "No," I said.

"None?"

"Well."

If I told her, she might tell Mrs. von Teplitz. It wouldn't speak well of my ability to handle the children.

"Nothing too bad," I said.

"I thought so." Her scowl was furious. Her eyes glistened almost like Matthew's fly eyes. "It was Matthew that started it, wasn't it."

I didn't answer.

Her eyes left mine and she frowned at some spot behind me. "They do it to everyone."

How alone I've been, on these islands. Things like the new potatoes—the broom, the cot—hit me like nerve gas. Even old Nanny barking at me about letting Claire eat stale bread and not drying between her toes, Mrs. von Teplitz and the soup plate—Lady Chipchase's piercing stare—maybe these things shouldn't hurt as much as they do, but they do. And there's no one to talk to. Well, these blue notepads. But they don't answer back. All my comforting is silent. Mr. Haig-Ereildoun and Granny Aitchee, and Trevor—they do seem to feel for me, but I could never have an out-in-the-air conversation with any of them about these hurts. Nanny helped, by at least trying to get me to talk, but I couldn't talk about Mrs. H-E to her. I couldn't talk to Morag about what the children did to me, or almost did to me, on the beach, either. But at least she exposed the truth for me, so that I didn't have to say it to have someone know and comfort.

Such a rush of relief I felt, after my talk with Morag. Such a feeling of freedom. So it's odd how it's left me not satisfied, but wanting more. More understanding.

19

MRS. HAIG-EREILDOUN'S CLOTHES AREN'T at all up to Mrs. von Teplitz's. Mrs. v.T. has a new outfit every night, but Mrs. H-E has brought, apparently, only two dresses—although it's possible she's kept one in reserve. But I doubt it. Fashion is not her thing. All I can hope is that she likes her two dresses. They're both flowery cotton prints, with skirts to her shoes, high necks and lace collars, lace at the wrists. One has a navy blue background with pink flowers, the other apple green with pink flowers. They're the opposite of her personality. Maybe that's why she likes them. If she does.

When she walks into the drawing room at gin-and-tonic time she reminds me of the part in *A Christmas Carol* where Dickens describes the many many ribbons Bob Cratchitt's wife and daughters wear on their cheap party dresses. It is in keeping with Mrs. Haig-Ereildoun's personality not to fit in with this century. But sociologically these dresses seem wrong. She has class.

And she's not silly. Her dresses are almost even too silly for Pru. They accent how uncomfortable she seems to feel about being herself. Mrs. Haig-Ereildoun's true personality is, I think, absolutely ribbon-free. But maybe she wishes she were the flibbety-jibbet type. I feel exasperated sympathy.

Yesterday, while I was getting the girls dressed up for tea, Pru and Josephine von Teplitz were talking. Josephine proudly told of her father's degree from a German university, and the girls giggled at the funny pronunciation of its name. "Mummy didn't go to university," Josephine said. "For years, she didn't even have to go to school at all. They lived up here, and she and my aunts had a governess to teach them all their French and maths and history."

"Oh, God, what bliss!" Pru sighed, and the two girls clasped their hands and looked to the heavens. (Honestly, they do that. Did I ever do that?) They sigh and make sounds like tortured cats, then giggle.

"Mummy and Daddy both went to Oxford," said Pru. "They both read history. Daddy had a first. Not Mummy, though." Pru seemed proud of her Mummy's—uh—scholarly restraint.

I suspect young Philippa had to work pretty hard to avoid getting a first.

THAT TIME IN THE drawing room at Troonfachan, when the children were drawing or reading and spellbound and uncharacteristically quiet, and I went up to my room and brought down *War and Peace*, Mrs. Haig-Ereildoun saw the cover and sighed. "It's the best book I've read. I think it may be the greatest novel ever written."

I didn't want to hurt her feelings and tell her the critics say *Anna Karenina* is better. I don't have an opinion. I haven't read that either. The day of this conversation, I'd probably read the first chapter of *War and Peace* ten times without taking in a word. I don't know what keeps me from concentrating, but I still haven't made any progress.

"I'm not sure I've read one book since I had the children," she told me that day. "I *can't* read any more." Then she gave me a searching look: "Can you?"

There I was with *War and Peace* on my lap, about to open it to Chapter One again. Still, I look down on myself for not being able to read now. I wasn't going to admit it. I went only so far as to admit reading *was* hard, for some reason, all of a sudden. I opened the book to about page eight hundred and pretended to read.

Another time, eating breakfast at Troonfachan, I asked her if she'd ever had a job since she was married. (I knew about the magazine job in New York, before they were married.) She said, "Well, once. For about seven months." She gazed into the distance as if recognizing a blissful memory. "One of Mr. Haig-Ereildoun's friends, Russell Churchill, hired me to do some research for a book he was doing . . ."

"She was happy then!" Mr. Haig-Ereildoun said softly. He got a similar look of pleasure on his face. "Weren't you, darling."

She smiled into his eyes and said, simply, "Yes."

THIS MORNING, IN THE hallway outside all the bedrooms, she stopped me. "Are you enjoying it here? Are you happy you've come?"

"Yes!"

"I must say," she said, "I find it a bit tense at Kirriebairne. I think Mr. von Teplitz holds quite a high standard. I fear that if Claire or one of the other children should make a sound at tea, he might be dreadfully put out."

"He is a little scary," I said.

She laughed. Relieved.

20

THE OLDEST VON TEPLITZ girl, Josephine, is exactly Pru's age, and she's just as enthusiastic about Every Single Solitary Little Thing in Life! Both of them are blond and rosy-cheeked. The two giggle and shriek and whisper secrets. They call each other "Thingy." It took them only about fifteen minutes of being together before they were calling me Thingy too. I like it.

"Thingy? What's your favorite course in school?" Pru asks Josephine.

"Hmm." Josephine thinks. "I'm not sure I like any of them."

"Mine is history. What was yours, Thingy?"

"Not history," I answer. "I think English. Everything having to do with stories and writing. I really liked philosophy, too, though. And anthropology."

"Mine is history," Pru states again, indisputably. "I inherited it. My grandfather's favorite subject was history. Have you talked with Grampy about history?" Her eyes sparkle with family love and self-love.

I nod, remembering the long debate about the Spanish Armada. The information about fireplaces in the sixteenth century. The discussion of primogeniture.

"And then history was my mother's favorite course too!" she exclaims. "*And* my father's."

I remember how I hated arithmetic, but my parents told me I'd love algebra and geometry. "It's fun!" they both said. And believe it or not, it was fun. I shocked myself by being a whiz. I think it was partly because of their enthusiasm, and their taking the fear out of it for me.

Pru, with the family she has, is almost disgustingly lucky.

WE'RE ALL IN THE nursery, which is like an upstairs drawing room for children. No ugly furniture here. No linoleum. The girls and I are sitting on a Persian rug, so not-antique it's still fluffy, and I'm just licking the stamps for my letter to Tedward.

Leaning in close to me, Pru takes the most intimate, excited tone: "What's your favorite part of French history?"

French history? My pulse stops. I can't remember a thing about French history.

"Oh, come on Thingy. Tell me your favorite king."

"King?" Not a name comes to me. The conversation can't go on.

"Go on. Pick one, pick one!"

"Uhh, the Sun King!"

"Oh, yes! He's my second favorite! I just *love* the French Revolution, don't you?"

"Who's your *very* favorite French king," Josephine asks Pru.

"Louis the Thirteenth, of course. The idiot child. I just love to think of an idiot child being king of one of the greatest empires in European history. Isn't it fun!"

"Oh look what she's written!" squeaks Josephine, grabbing my envelope. "Ted Doyle, 1278 Lombard Street, San Francisco, CA 94109 U.S.A.!"

Pru grabs the envelope from Josephine. "Oh *mon dieu*, oh *mon dieu!*" she sighs, pressing the envelope to her breast. "CA 94109!" She rubs it up and down the washboard, her rib cage.

"Oh, *mon dieu!*" Josephine plucks the envelope from Pru and copies. "Have you ever seen anything so romantic!"

"CA 94109!"

"May we mail it? Oh please, please!"

So in a wake of white eyelet ruffles, they're off to the post office, half a mile down the road, promising to be back in time for tea. ("We promise!" "We prrr-romise!")

THAT WAS A CLOSE one. I'll have to get Morag to find me a book on French history in Mr. Skychurch's library. But when can I read? To save time, maybe Morag can give me a quick brush-up course.

Meanwhile, I'm pretty pleased that my envelope will be postmarked Port Askaig. That *is* romantic. I told Tedward about my idea to have our honeymoon on Islay, instead of in France. There's a bright-painted inn, with beautiful grounds and white lambs, right on the harbor in Port Askaig. Morag says the sun we're getting this week is a rarity. But can you imagine how romantic it must be when the mist is so thick the lighthouse beacon can't slice through it? The inn has lots of chimneys, so I'm sure the rooms have fireplaces.

21

I'VE ALWAYS THOUGHT THAT if I had so much money I didn't need a job, that if I never had to worry about being fired, that if I had so much money I could pay other people to do all my boring chores, I'd be happy. That's why coming here has been disillusioning. Mrs. von Teplitz has these things, but she isn't happy.

These two women, Mrs. v.T. and Mrs. H-E, are more uptight than the account executives in the advertising agency. They worry-worry-worry over every detail of the day. After breakfast I happened to walk past a room off the kitchen where Mrs. von Teplitz crouched with a fraction of her bottom touching the edge of a straight wooden chair. Her back was rigid as a yardstick. Morag perched tense on the edge of another chair, facing her. Both held pencils and pads. Mrs. von Teplitz's usual rasp had turned to a creak, like a flabby old violin string. "Four dozen eggs? You're quite certain that will do for the rest of the week?" She started scribbling on her pad, I assume adding up people and multiplying days. "All right. If you've taken into account the baking. Have you?" Morag looked her in the eyes and gave her chin a jerk: yes. "And what about the ducks. Will they be defrosted in time." The mood was more fraught than it is in the conference room at the agency the night before the presentation.

At our picnics, Mrs. von Teplitz and Mrs. Haig-Ereildoun sit with eyes darting child to child. If a breeze blows the corner of a picnic blanket, gasps go up and hands pounce. Sand might get on a Scotch egg. Mrs. von Teplitz sits taut, watching, as Mr. Haig-Ereildoun runs for the soccer ball and falls into the sand, children running to him, hooting, trying to bury his plaid shirt in more sand. "Be careful!" Mrs. von Teplitz shouts, with what sounds like terror. Careful of what?

A child might start to answer a question before swallowing the last of his bite. Or take a drink of lemonade before the last trace of a bite has gone down the throat. (Never, says my grandmother's *Book of Etiquette,* under any circumstances, take a sip of any liquid if the least bit of food remains in your mouth. It says the purpose of manners is to protect people from anything "ugly.") No wonder they don't need books of etiquette here to advise them. (As Mots says, "I reckon the English just think either you have it or you don't.") Mrs. von Teplitz and Mrs. Haig-Ereildoun have the rules programmed into their DNA, and they take every measure to ensure these same manners are part of their children's makeup. Futures are at stake.

We take a cooler to the beach, and Mr. von Teplitz hands Mr. Haig-Ereildoun a beer. The men pass the beer opener between them and draw in the foam spouting from the mouths of the bottles. Ahh. "Be careful!" says Mrs. von Teplitz. Maybe she thinks they'll get some bubbles on the blanket. We, the women, aren't offered beers. A beer sounds like a good idea to me, on the beach in the sun, with Scotch eggs. We, the women, get a choice of mineral waters.

And with someone to look after the children, someone to do the cooking and the dishes, someone to clean the house and get the groceries, someone to iron, and all these lovely hours of leisure on the beach, what do these women talk about? Housework. Mrs. von Teplitz sits erect on the sand and calculates how many loads of wash will have to be done when we get back from the beach. She frets over whether the boat will arrive safely with all the right ingredients for the rest of the week's menus. She knows to the halfpenny what she's paid for every bag of chips, and she can't get over "the horror of it."

Mr. von Teplitz radiates tension. You should see him at tea. He's like the chief of police. All of us, except Mr. Haig-Ereildoun, sit rigid, eyes going from Claire to Matthew. The children, so dressed up, eat in silence. Even Claire. The only relief is when Mr. Haig-Ereildoun says something. "This morning's *Times* came in this afternoon. Did you see? We seem to be doing rathah well. The temperature in the Hebrides yesterday was warmer than in the Adriatic." Even he is reduced to talking about the weather. Maybe it's more fun than talking about the price of potato chips.

AFTER THE DAY THE horde of children threatened to strip me, I'm not about to take them out of sight of the other adults again. The beach today was not a cliff-boxed cove but a very long and expansive strip, like Waikiki Beach without people. The water was the turquoise I imagine the Caribbean to be. There were plenty of shells to pick up and compare. If Matthew was bored, I didn't mind. It was warm enough to wear bathing suits again (at least the children and I wore bathing suits); and we let the waves swish our ankles and knees and found a conch to listen to and arranged our handfuls of shells into something like a color wheel; and, above all, the nine of us didn't go where no one could see us. I actually took a dare and went in for a swim. That was five seconds of sharp pain. No one could breathe in cold like that. Talk about sting. It did earn me cheers, though.

The beach was very long, so we went quite a distance, for our shell-seeking and my swim (so-called). On our venture back from this adventure, the parents becoming less like just shapes and more like human forms, I took a step and felt myself sinking. "Quicksand!" The children ran up close to me, and I was thrilled as the sand level rose from my feet to my ankles and I felt myself not just sinking but being sucked down! The power pulling me was strong, but slow, so I knew I could get away if I had to. When my knees were buried, and the lower inches of my thighs, the sucking force stopped. Completely. The children screamed with joy as part after part of me disappeared, but alas, I didn't quite vanish. I felt solid ground.

Until today, my knowledge of quicksand was from comic books, where the sand sucked you down until your head was lost and pretty soon you were in China. Trevor stepped closer, and I held out my hands to him. He began sinking. Holding my two hands, he touched solid ground just as the sand surpassed the cuffs of his bathing trunks. One after one, each child came in close and joined us, and each was pulled down, giggling. The only one who stood to the side was Matthew, with his arms crossed. "That is very very dangerous indeed!" He ran off to his father, shouting, "Quicksand."

I wasn't worried. I held Claire's hand as she stepped closer and got pulled down. "Quicksand!" I said, my mouth close enough for her eyes to read as she felt the suction. "Quicksand." Sinking, she spoke: "Hhhhighh! Hhhaa!" Pretty good. I wondered if the suck of it was something she'd remember until the next time she heard the word. Probably, or at least I hoped, the next time she heard it, she'd have mastered more of the consonant sounds, and she'd put the sounds together with this memory of feeling. The pull stopped just as the sand buried her belly button, but while it lasted, it was an amazing feeling.

"Quicksand?" His voice a roar, Mr. von Teplitz rushed toward us, fast as he could make his feet go in the sand. "Quicksand! What in God's name are you doing!" He was almost spitting his fury. "You have taken my children into quicksand?" His fists were clenched. "*Get* my children out of that quicksand!"

"Come on in," I invited.

"Out!" he commanded, yanking his little son by the arm. "I don't know who you are or where you came from or what you think you're doing with my children. In quicksand!" His eyebrows would have crisscrossed, if they could have, and his nostrils got so big I could see the hairs inside. His nose made noises.

The quicksand seems to occur in pools. Like whirlpools. The rest of us used our leg muscles to climb out of this quicksand tub and followed Mr. von Teplitz back, but in zigs and curls, because we were trying to find more quicksand.

For some reason, he doesn't scare me. He doesn't even scare me the way he scares Mrs. Haig-Ereildoun—although she scares the life out of me.

The von Teplitzes' Land Rover has doors that slide open with a rumble that ends in a thwack. As soon as we arrive back at Kirriebairne, all four doors slide r-r-r-rumble-thwack. Part of the packed-in swarm shoots out; the rest tumble out. At the thwack, Mrs. von Teplitz and Mrs. Haig-Ereildoun's faces tighten, their minds on laundry. Upstairs, on getting first the girls then the boys into the big yellow bathroom, I have to gather up all the sandy clothes and have Trevor run them immediately downstairs to the laundry room, where the two women divide up loads.

I finish bathing and dressing the children, and when Pru and Josephine are dry and in their dresses, I put them to work with a book for the little ones, so I can go down to the laundry to help out. There's a dryer, but these people don't believe in it: There are clothespins.

"What are you doing?" Mrs. von Teplitz asks me, at the clothesline, wrinkling her nose and smiling.

"I don't know. Isn't this right?"

"Haven't you ever hung clothes on a clothesline?"

"No."

"What do you do in America?"

"Well, when I was growing up we had a dryer. Now I live in San

Francisco, in an apartment with no washing machine. So I take things to the laundry and they do them. I mean, wash, dry, fold."

Mrs. von Teplitz and Mrs. Haig-Ereildoun exchange looks.

"It'd take my whole Saturday afternoon to sit in the laundromat."

Their eyes connect again. No wonder she's hopeless, their eyes say to each other.

But I do know how to iron. Here I get extra practice, with these eight children, and all of them having to be presentation perfect at tea. This afternoon Mrs. Haig-Ereildoun asked me to be an angel and do some of her things too, as well as a shirt for Mr. Haig-Ereildoun.

It was brand new, never worn. (Mrs. Haig-Ereildoun said he didn't like the feel of new cotton—it had to be washed first to disguise the newness.) It was black with tiny white dots and no collar—pretty hip, for him. "Supah!" Mrs. von Teplitz said when she saw this shirt going into the washing machine.

Supah is not Mr. Haig-Ereildoun's style. His two tweed suits, he told me, were made for him fifteen years ago, when he came down from Oxford. I thought, "So cool." He probably hadn't had many new shirts since then, either—and probably never one that was in style. He's one of those people who could never go out of style because he's never been in style. I wonder if he bought that shirt, or if she bought it for him. Because that shirt is in style. Or maybe somebody else gave it to him. Because in style is not her style either.

Today the iron here decided to go nuts. You set it on cotton and it heats up to something that might melt metal. It's okay on the first few things, but after it gets going, the heat escalates. I'd saved Mr. Haig-Ereildoun's new shirt for last, and the crisis came up.

Mrs. von Teplitz walked in just as a thread of smoke sailed up from under the iron. "What's this?" she said, waving the air. The strip that would attach the collar of Mr. Haig-Ereildoun's new shirt, if it had had a collar, had puffed and browned like the crust of a pie.

I looked at this shirt. It would never be worn. I looked at the black bottom of the iron. I looked at Mrs. von Teplitz.

"How much does a man's shirt cost?" I asked her.

She looked concerned. The figure she quoted was twice my salary.

"I suppose I'll have to pay," I said.

I always try to seem as if things don't really bother me.

She didn't try to seem as if this didn't bother her. She shook her face, mouth closed tight over all those teeth. She looked down, then at me. "I suppose you'll have to," she said, and bowed her head and walked quickly out of the room.

Honestly, I think she did feel sympathetic.

Upon hearing her opinion, though, I felt resolved: I wouldn't pay. It would be unfair.

I took the shirt to Mrs. Haig-Ereildoun. She looked distressed but didn't say anything. I told her about the iron being set at cotton. It burned.

"It's not your fault," she said.

"I'm sorry," I said, meaning it.

"It's a shame," she said, meaning it.

22

"YOU SOUND WEIRD," TEDWARD told me on the phone tonight.

"Weird?"

His chuckle is raspy and adorable. "Eh-oh, eh-own-lih a bit pe-kew-liah," he said. "Pah-haps you're plahnning to run fo' queen?"

I work so hard not to pick up this accent. One thing that makes it hard is the "do try to speak as we do" rule, when I'm talking to Claire. I say a sentence to her in Oxford English and then immediately switch to American to say a sentence to Mrs. Haig-Ereildoun. Sometimes I don't make the switch fast enough. Another thing that makes it hard is that I like the way they speak. In fact, I just love it.

Still, I really don't want to go home sounding pretentiously English. I work to keep my American pronunciations. "To-may-to!" Mr. von Teplitz mocked today. Young fly-eyed Matthew laughed so hard his mother said, "Be careful."

IT WAS FUN MAKING my call tonight, because it gave Mr. von Teplitz a start. When we reported for our cocktails at half past eight, I was two and a half hours late for the call but calm enough to sit through a few sips before stepping to the phone. Mr. von Teplitz has taken to educating me on the superiority of liquors made in Great

Britain. He takes a brass key from his pocket and opens the leaded glass door of the bar to ponder gleaming bottles with labels of all colors. The first time he did this he chose something called Irish Mist. It tasted just like its name. He enjoyed my reaction; so now, each evening, he pours from a different bottle. He's most proud of Islay's famous single malts. Tonight it was Caol Ila. The other Islay Scotches I've had are called Lagvulin and Bunnahavhain. He measures an ounce and pours, lining the bottom of the glass with a skin of amber. Then he adds a few drops of water, thinning the color. He hands me the glass. It gives him pleasure.

Tonight I enjoyed my sips of Caol Ila even more because I knew I'd soon be asking to use the phone. When I did, the von Teplitz mouths opened involuntarily. If she thinks the price of potato chips is a horror . . . Mrs. von Teplitz stood up to lead me into the library, and as we left the room I heard him grumble, "Where's she calling? I hope not California." When I called back that I *was* calling California, I enjoyed his scowl. I hope nobody explained that I call collect.

IN MR. SKYCHURCH'S LIBRARY, my eyes went from the shiny black telephone on the desk to the Persian rug to the row upon row of books bound in leather or cloth: so much civilization put in such careful order. I heard the rings that must have been sounding in Tedward's apartment, with ratty chairs stacked on beat-up tables, and the past month's dirty socks and *Chronicle*s and empty Chinese food cartons strewn over and under it all.

This time Tedward didn't crab about his crazy landlady or how much he hates the apartment I forced him to rent. I could actually see him, his funny smile, his teddy-bear body in his cozy brown sweater. We had some good chuckles, and it reminded me of everything I've always liked about him. Maybe it's a good idea to call late like this, and give him a chance to wake up. Maybe a *short* conversation isn't a bad idea either.

As soon as we'd said, "Love you," "Love you," Tedward was six thousand miles away again.

23

I HAVE SEEN THE Haig-Ereildouns' bedroom. She asked me to be an angel and run in and pick up a cardigan she'd left on the back of a chair. I took a quick look around the pretty room, with lacy inner curtains veiling the Alice-blue sound, and noticed the paperback open on their bedside table. The cover showed a strong man's hand with hair on it clasping one globe of a smooth, beautiful female bottom. The title, in cheap chromey emboss, said, "Lady Priscilla Asks for a Spanking."

I wonder what Old Nanny has seen, in her forty-four years at Phillingsford.

Or Morag, at Kirriebairne.

"MRS. VON TEPLITZ FEELS sorry for Mrs. Haig-Ereildoun," Morag said, handing me an ashtray and sitting down across the table with a silver-polishing cloth.

"Why?"

"Because they don't have any money."

An anger ripped through me. How dare Mrs. von Teplitz feel sorry for Mrs. Haig-Ereildoun. Her pity made me realize how much Mrs. Haig-Ereildoun did have that Mrs. von Teplitz didn't.

"They won't even have the money to send Trevor to a public school," Morag said, working on the handle of a pretty little creamer.

Huff, I thought. Bother.

Proper boarding school. Mots's letters to me in San Francisco were full of this subject. Even though their baby hasn't hit one year yet, she and Rupert are into fights about how much of their lifetime income has to be devoted to this baby's schooling. Mots can't buy a new skirt this year, next year, maybe ever. According to Rupert, every spare penny and then some will go to schools. According to Mots, this is too much. Of course, Rupert knows the country. "Here," Mots says, "money doesn't get you prestige. Where you went to school is what defines you." Mots says, begrudgingly, "In England, education is everything."

From studying history with Trevor, I know that Oxford was here while Chaucer was writing. He wrote about French and Saxon words being mixed into "the English tongue that all understanden." That was the dawn of the language, and Oxford was there even for that. Eton got going while the black plague was on. The males in the Chipchase family have gone to Eton and Oxford for so many generations that some of them might have graduated in the first class of each. The men in Granny Aitchee's clan go back only a century and a half at those two institutions. Still. Even here, a century is something.

Mrs. Haig-Ereildoun must feel threatened, to have her son be the first in almost a thousand-year line to be squeezed out of his class. It may explain a few things about her.

But I don't think she has to worry. Maybe Lady Chipchase can sell that swan, or Sir Chester can find another artichoke. If not, though, I will not be so condescending as to feel sorry for Mrs. Haig-Ereildoun. As for Trevor, never.

. . .

I WISH WE DIDN'T have to pack today and drive onto the ferry tomorrow, because Mrs. Haig-Ereildoun isn't quite Mrs. Haig-Ereildoun here. Part of it is probably that she's on her best manners, and that extends even to me. Another part is, here she doesn't have to supervise the kedgeree or cottage pie every day. Maybe she gets bored having Apple for dessert, too. And even if she'd never admit it, there is something about hot bathwater, heated towels, and even central heating. Not to mention sun.

24

"MELISSA, IT'S FOR YOU." My first and only telephone call in this country. Simon. He had to do some detective work to find out the number at Troonfachan. Even Mots didn't know it. But she knew someone who knew someone.

So my first day off back in London is booked. It's funny to think how one day off a week sounded like not enough. Now it seems spectacular. Every Thursday I'll have one. I think Thursday was Mary Poppins's day off, too. Simon's going to give me a guided tour of his town.

Of course I dread what Mots will think when she sees the new me, rolling my big round hips behind me, leading with my ballooned-up bust. She was born thin and *still* she diets. She doesn't go in for lectures, but I know she'll give me a look.

AS A SURPRISE, AS soon as we got back from Kirriebairne, Mrs. Haig-Ereildoun gave me a surprise: four days off, and a ride to Edinburgh. Lucinda was driving up. In Edinburgh I was so happy I didn't write one word. And in Edinburgh it hit me that I actually like this family. I got presents for everyone and bought wrapping paper, ribbon, and Scotch tape (Cello tape, or celly, in Scottish); I sat on the bed in the closet-sized room in my bed-and-breakfast and wrapped my presents, including some placemats I'd found, with color photographs of Holyrood Palace and all the sights. Mrs. Haig-Ereildoun always uses placemats with hunting scenes, so I thought she'd like a change. They're all so proud of Scotland, I thought she'd like to serve meals on mats that showed the most historical sites.

You should have seen her face, unwrapping her package. She looked from one bright photograph to another: the changing of the guard, the Edinburgh Castle lit up with torches at night, the flowery park on Princes Street—there were six. She didn't smile. She looked very concerned. "You mustn't do this," she said. "You mustn't spend your money on gifts for us. Please."

I could see she felt bad that I'd spent more than a week's pay on the various presents—but she didn't understand, I'd brought some money from home. I thought she'd love them. And she'd have them long after I'd left. She didn't have to feel sorry about the money! But I also got the feeling she wasn't pleased with the placemats. I will say she hasn't used them, and she didn't pack them for London.

THIS AFTERNOON SHE ASKED me to take a minute away from the children and join her for a cup of tea, alone at the kitchen table. "Melissa," she said, "I must explain something to you. When I wrote you in America what your salary would be, I meant while we were in Scotland. As we're going back to London now, I'll be forced to cut your salary by five pounds a week."

I put my teacup to my lips and tried not to show how surprised I was. It wasn't the money. The mystery was, how could such a trifle make such a difference to her?

"You see, I knew that in Scotland, you'd have to be on duty full time, whereas in London you'll have some time off. And in Scotland I have Mrs. Campbell, at a very good price, but in London I'll have to hire a daily, which means I won't be able to afford to pay you the full amount you've been receiving in Scotland. The only thing I could suggest is that if you'd be willing to pitch in with the housework . . ."

The salary's so pathetic anyway that to me, five pounds up or down is like the difference between a dollar ninety-seven and a dollar ninety-nine. Or, zero vs. zero. What seemed important was that I was a guest in the household, and—"Oh, I don't mind housework," I lied. "I do it for myself at home . . ."

It seemed only polite.

She gave me a big smile. "Wonderful!"

Lettering Lane

25

LONDON. BLOSSOMS EVERYWHERE. COLUMNS of flowering fruit trees line the sidewalks like oversized sticks of cotton candy. I wheel Claire under and through clouds of puffy pink ruffles. The buildings so old and solid, the blossoms so new and airy.

The days are long. At eight P.M., the sky's still blue. When I put Claire and her books to bed, and slip down the stairs and click the door shut and skip down Lettering Lane, the floating clouds are just getting rosy. They have such shapely clouds here. As I move down the Queen's Way toward Mots's, the powder blue deepens by shades into purple, and the clouds go ruby coral.

I feel so light it's hard to believe I am almost up to ten stones now. As my feet fly, I don't feel like a great gallumphing girl in a Russian Army surplus coat, I feel like I have no body, just eyes and thirst to drink in the blush of the blossoms, the greens of the squares, the dandy tulips standing just inside the wrought iron fences. I love the way they've arranged this town—neat emerald squares with locked gates—set like jewel cases amidst the stern architecture.

We've been back three days now, and every afternoon I've pushed Claire's wheels down to Mots's house to play with the baby; and after I've tucked Claire in at night I've gone back to Mots's. My extra stone didn't seem to bother her; she just laughed. Mots, Rupert, and I laugh so much I get a side ache. I must have stored up a lot of laughing, in jail.

I've figured out what I'm going to do with my days off. I'm going to cooking school. The London Cordon d'Or. Mots took the whole year's basic professional course, eight A.M. to five P.M. five days a week. She wore a chef's uniform. I'm going to take the dilettante's version, where regular people can sit in on Wednesday afternoon classes. No uniform. So, after this Thursday, which Simon has already arranged to take off from the lab, my day off won't be the traditional one for people like me and Mary Poppins. Mrs. Haig-Ereildoun doesn't mind.

There's only one bad thing about being back in London. Every morning you'll find me with bucket and mop and a frown on my face. I don't mind being the nanny, but it turns out I don't like being the maid. Instead of working five hours a day for my pocket money, I'm on duty eleven hours a day. It would be twelve, except Mrs. Haig-Ereildoun still gives me an hour after lunch to go to my room and write letters.

26

YOU WON'T BELIEVE WHERE Simon took me today. A dungeon full of snakes. We went to the reptile cave at the zoo. That's Simon's favorite place in London. We went for the feeding. That's Simon's favorite time there. The snakes eat live rats and mice. Whole. In a gulp. You watch the mouse struggle, then disappear and turn into a bulge moving down the body, still kicking on the way down. You see the outline. You hear the screams only until the mouse is in the body. The bulge is slowly pulled by some force of nature, like quicksand, from the snake's throat region down toward what must be its belly. Maybe the whole length of the snake is its belly. I didn't ask. It takes the snake's body about a week to digest the rodent. The whole thing was such a shock that I didn't ask or notice if the snake breaks the rodent's neck right away so that it's dead by the time it's being digested. It does go down fitfully.

The reptile cave was dark and wet. You got the feeling of water collecting on the top of the cavern and the worry that drips of slime would get on you. The only light came from the cages. They're not really cages, just cavelets with windows. Every time I looked up at Simon, he was watching me instead of the snakes. Simon already knows every detail about snakes. He's like Trevor with the Iroquois.

Then we went from the pits to the heights: this amazing aviary designed by Lord Snowden, like a conservatory, open air in parts, where you actually climb a high footbridge, like an overpass, to be up there with the birds. They're daintily caged in, or you are, so they don't fly onto you. Simon knows almost as much about birds as he knows about reptiles.

We strolled and strolled, past Monkey Island (Simon knows quite a bit about monkeys), and into Regent's Park. It's huge and grand and green—Londoners really care about their parks. Simon told me about how the park had originally been hunting grounds for King Henry the Eighth and his friends. As a man pushed a snack cart down the path, Simon didn't seem to see it or hear its cheerful bells. "Can't you hear those little beagles baying and barking and chasing the deer around in circles, the tips of their tails fluttering like small white flags amidst the shrubbery, and the ladies and gentlemen riding easily along on their horses, bows and arrows in their hands? And Lady Jane Grey begging off, staying inside and reading Plato?"

I didn't know Lady Jane Grey read Plato. My head was beginning to feel too full of facts, and my stomach very empty of food. We'd walked a lot, and since it was my day off, I'd been free to skip the dreaded breakfast.

Trouble was, I had no say in when Simon and I would eat or what or where. I'd spent all my pounds, and I'd planned to take a traveler's check into the Bureau de Change near the tube station. Simon didn't want to take the time, said he had plenty of cash for both of us. But not having any money, I couldn't ask for any lunch.

I do love it, though, when the man pays for everything. There was something almost sexy about being helplessly in his hands, as he measured out pence for the tube and reached in front of me to put coins in the slot, and took my ticket from my hand and kept both till we emerged at Regent's Park Station, where he shepherded me through the stile again. Simon was disappointed to find that I've already mastered the money thing, but the money's the same in Scotland. It's lucky Simon's going to be a professor, because he loves to inform.

We get along, because I like being informed.

But I was more interested in food. Simon is keen on eating, but not on a daily basis. He knows about the cuisines of places like Rhodesia and Malaysia, he likes eating things like snakes and beetles. But like a reptile, he goes great periods without food. He doesn't believe in wasting money, and to him it's a waste to eat if it isn't an adventure—a bizarre and enlightening cultural experience. He wouldn't think of chowing down a sandwich or a candy bar. I can't tell you how many of those carts we passed, in the park, selling Cracker Jack–like things and ice cream. Well, no ice cream for Simon. No lunch! Instead, we sat under a tree and talked. Lucky he wanted to sit down, because by then I was faint.

IT TURNS OUT SIMON can listen, too. He probed about my past, my present, my future. I told him more about Tedward, about my old job, my mom, my dad, the University of Oregon, and Mrs. Haig-Ereildoun.

He'd heard about her plenty already, but when he met her today I got the feeling he dismissed my complaints as exaggerations. Funny how only seeing is believing. And when he met her, for a moment this morning, I could tell she seemed as darling to him as she did on the phone with me, before I came to live in her house. Her charming self is incredibly charming. And of Simon, I got the feeling she approved. She had *perked* up talking to Mr. von Teplitz at Kirriebairne, but she *lit* up talking to Simon. She knew that his father was the ambassador to Gambia. She and Mr. Haig-Ereildoun had once gone to Gambia and met several of the top people in their government. It turned out Simon knew all of them, at least slightly, so they had characters to talk about. With her, Simon took on extra magnetism.

So tall he is. And that nose, and all those bones, his body almost lost in his clothes. Rumpled. In one of our silent moments, under the tree in Regents Park, my hand was on my knee and he picked up my wrist and measured my palm against his. How large his hand was, compared to mine. His fingers are very long. Slender but big-knuckled. My fingertips barely made it to where his palm ended. It gave me a swoon. I pulled my hand away, because it felt too much like flirting.

I'VE BEEN WANTING TO go to the changing of the guard, or to the queen's gallery in Buckingham Palace, or to the Tower of London or Picadilly Circus. Simon doesn't go to those places. After Regent's Park we got back on the tube and went out to Kew Gardens. It turns out Simon knows a lot about plants, too. He knows the Latin names. Of course, it's cactus he's most attracted to. I like lilacs. Fluff. And what other people call a teddy bear cactus Simon calls an *Opuntia bigelovii*.

"HUNGRY?" HE ASKED, AT last, after the gatekeeper had come with his keys and shooed us out, closing Kew.

"Are *you* hungry?" I asked.

"I was asking you."

It's true, I'm always so polite. Always trying not to seem like I don't have any needs of my own. And still, I didn't want to say I was famished. Especially since I had no money. "I am a little hungry," I admitted.

"All right. I know a Pakistani place. Very cheap."

That was a relief. Until I saw the place. After another hour on the tube, and a lesson on how to follow the red, yellow, and green lines on the Underground map, we walked about fifteen blocks through a slum (they call them council houses) to a door with some Pakistani words on it. Inside, more dirt and grease and dangling insects than I've ever seen outside Mrs. Haig-Ereildoun's kitchen. Suddenly I wasn't so hungry after all. You order dish by dish, about three things making up a meal. I ordered one thing, the cheapest. Because I knew I wouldn't eat it. I took enough bites to be polite. Since his eyes never left me, I'm sure my lack of appetite, after saying I was hungry, registered.

After a movie, at an art cinema (another tube ride from the restaurant), we walked home. It was a long way, but this theater was actually in some far corner of the borough of Kensington-Chelsea, so it wasn't like a hike across the whole city of London. After so much walking, and then so much sitting in the boring movie (old, French, long, by Claude Renoir, supposedly funny), I was tired of walking.

THE LIGHT WAS STILL on in the drawing room. We went up, and Mrs. Haig-Ereildoun was sitting there by herself, in one of those greasy velvet chairs, reading a book! I've never seen her read a book. It was a hardback, one of Mr. Haig-Ereildoun's. She was dressed very fetchingly, in a navy blue suit with a pleated skirt that came to slightly above her knees. I'd never seen her legs before. They're beautiful. Sort of kick-up-your-heels legs. Very graceful ankles. She was wearing high heels! Well, not high, but medium—much more flattering than any shoes I've seen her wear before. When she stood up, offering to take Simon's coat (she knows better than to ask for mine), she looked absolutely girlish. She'd done something different with her hair, too. It had that super-shine, and she'd pulled the top part back in a grosgrain ribbon. I commented on her suit, how pretty she looked.

"Oh, I had a meeting today at Pru's school," she said. "Rather out of date, this suit, I'm afraid."

"Why?"

"Oh, you know, the skirt's too short. Last year's at least, or the year before."

So she finally got a chance to say what she's been thinking about my clothes.

The main thing, though. I don't question that she dressed up for the school meeting. But that had to have been over by four or five in the afternoon. I knew beyond doubt that she'd stayed dressed up to look pretty for Simon. Pretty she looked, and pretty she acted. She had that kind of wise-woman glow.

I felt like a plain Jane beside her. A fat Pat. A Carol the barrel. Marge the barge. And speaking of names. When the three of us went to the front door, and Simon said, "Good night, Mrs. Haig-Ereildoun," she said, "Oh, please. Call me Philippa." That woman just totally forgot herself.

27

I JUST FOUND OUT Mr. Haig-Ereildoun's salary. Usually I don't read the *Times,* I just put it in the dustbin after Mrs. Haig-Ereildoun has left to drive Claire to nursery school. She manages to scour every page of the paper while sorting the post, preparing two breakfasts (a fairly elaborate one for Mr. Haig-Ereildoun), and shooing Trevor and Pru out the door to their carpools. But this morning a headline grabbed me, and instead of having the washing-up done by the time Mr. H-E shuffled down the stairs in his comfortable old shoes, today I was standing by the sink reading. Luckily he doesn't read the *Times.* I don't want him to know I know. Members of Parliament make less than I did as the lowest paid person at the ad agency.

They must have outside incomes. Mr. Haig-Ereildoun has his novels. But I worry. He told me his first novel, on John Knox, sold several hundred copies. He couldn't understand why his publisher wasn't more pleased. The second, on Robert the Bruce, sold a few hundred more. "Getting up near a thousand! Quite impressive, I daresay, to think of nearly a thousand blokes spending their hard-earned quid to read of someone who hasn't been in the news for two hundred years." His publisher said the sales didn't cover the cost of the ink. His new manuscript, completed at Troonfachan, came back yesterday.

Taking his bacon and eggs from the warming oven and filling his coffee bowl with the cafe au lait his wife leaves over simmering water for him, he spread out his own newspaper, far more crowded with type than the *Times*, and cut off a bite of bacon. I tended to the kitchen cleanup, hoping to get upstairs fast, to tuck the pajamas under the pillows, make the beds, sweep, vacuum, and dust. It takes all morning, and I have to have dinner ready by the time Mrs. H-E and the children get home at noon. It bothers me that Pru, who is eleven, can't make her own bed. I even asked Mrs. Haig-Ereildoun why not. She got a dreamy look and said, "Well, I suppose I don't want her to. *I* never had to . . ."

Looking up from his peach newspaper he said to me, or to the *Financial Times*, "He says it needs pacing! I thought I'd paced it rather cleverly."

"A review? I thought it hadn't been published yet."

"No," he said to the *Financial Times*. "My editor." He reminded me of Trevor, avoiding eye contact when he showed his reports.

To look at Mr. Haig-Ereildoun any other time, or to listen to him, you wouldn't get an inkling that he has a tremor of anxiety in his whole system. "Rather a dire situation this time, I daresay. I can't afford another dud." He poked his knife into both egg yolks, flooding the plate with yellow. I concentrated on balancing the tiny eggcups in the upper tray of the washing-up machine. "He's tolerated two failures in the marketplace. I'm afraid this is my last chance."

Mr. Haig-Ereildoun may be like me. Full of charm, winning everyone's affection, but somehow not quite doing the job. I can *say* that the advertising agency chose me to fire because I was the youngest and the one who had the most to learn—who needed the most teaching. But I know it was more basic than that. I did win awards. But I lost hours, days, weeks, trying to make jewels out of the twenty-five-cents-off coupon ads. Everyone loved me, but in a practical world I wasn't what they needed. It's hard, actually scary, being the kind of people Mr. Haig-Ereildoun and I are.

Walking around the table to hang a saucepan on the pegboard, I got a glance at his jaw, chewing. He faced the *Financial Times*, but his eyes weren't reading. Ache and anxiety overwhelmed my body like nausea. A possibility I'd never thought of hit me like lightning: He could lose Mrs. Haig-Ereildoun.

Still chewing, he pulled a Rothman from his pocket. Lit it. Placed it in the saucer under his coffee bowl. I watched him cut a square of yellow and white, move fork to mouth, set down the cutlery and reach for the cigarette with his knife hand. Before completing each swallow, he pulled smoke into his lungs. Before exhaling the smoke, he put another bite in his mouth.

SHE'S BACK TO HER old self. "Melisssssa!" she called out yesterday, in that tone she gets. "Melissa come here at once." I found her in a remote corner of the drawing room, rubbing a finger on a windowsill. Eyeing the dust on that finger with revulsion, she hissed, "It's a pity you don't qualify for the National Health, as it's quite apparent that you need glasses."

She brought me a basket of old blouses to darn. Darn? She handed me a darning egg, needles, and a box of threads. I'd never heard of darning a blouse. She showed me the underarms, where the fabric had gone thin. "How do you do it?" I asked. Once my grandmother had shown me how to darn socks, and I vaguely remembered, but I never knew you could darn delicate cotton. Mrs. Haig-Ereildoun went red. "I suppose in America you just *throw* things *away*?" When I answered the truth, she whipped around and marched out of the room. I tried to do it right. I spent an hour in the afternoon, hours in the evening, but I made a mess of the darning. She didn't comment. Maybe that's how it always looks.

When she scolds me, I bow my head. They say, "she bowed her

head in shame." I bow my head because I don't want her to see the fear in my eyes.

Luckily I have Mots. She tells me she wouldn't have known how to scrape new potatoes before living here awhile, and she doesn't comb her broom after using it, and she certainly wouldn't know how to darn a blouse. As to the way Mrs. Haig-Ereildoun treats me, Mots thinks she's "probably mental."

"Philippa has always been a 'ard, 'ard girl." Nanny told me that time. So maybe she was born this way. I do think, though, that she's disappointed with her lot in life.

When we stopped at Phillingsford, on our way home from Scotland, Lady Chipchase kept staring at her daughter in the intense way she had stared at me, at first. Staring at me her expression was probing, evaluating, gathering facts. When she steadily watches Philippa, her eyes have that same hunger to know, but mixed in with her puzzling there's pity. Worry. A sorrowful anxiety. When Lady Chipchase was her daughter's age, she had woodsmen and gamesmen, grooms and a butler and footmen. She had upstairs maids and a kitchen staff and undernannies for her nanny. Philippa can't afford even one proper servant. She has to maintain two households at once, on his pittance. A deaf child puts another kind of pressure on the family. And I—used to a one-room apartment with almost no chairs, just huge floor cushions I made from burlap coffee bags—find this house appalling. Think of what Lady Chipchase must think.

Mrs. Haig-Ereildoun, I imagine, is not just disappointed with her lot in life. I think she is furious. When she nags at him, it's worse than when she nags at me. Her voice is more sour. Her anger flares up at even more irrelevant things, such as a dangerously long ash at the tip of his cigarette.

I wonder if some straw could break the camel's back. One last shred of suffering added to her long-suffering list, and crrr*rash*! Or

I wonder how she'd react if some unmarried Mr. von Teplitz type came along and offered to take her away from all this.

HE SAT AT THE breakfast table not reading the *Financial Times,* not aware of my presence. Silently rubbing a saucepan dry, I watched his eyes, not reading. The fork in his left hand put a chunk of bacon in his mouth and he chewed, chewed long past when that piece of bacon must have been pulverized. Seeing that the cigarette in the saucer had gone out, he struck another wooden match and scowled at the black smoke as he relit the butt. That's what his life would be like if she left.

IN LONDON, THE TENSE moments between them are few. That's because they don't seem to have many moments together. He doesn't get up until after she and all the children have left the house. He takes his breakfast from the warming oven, eats alone, and goes into his "office"—really the dining room. He shuts the door, and still he fills the house with the thundering of his typewriter. About noon he opens the door, his pent-up cigarette smoke escaping into the hallway as he clicks the front door shut and pedals off on his bicycle to the House of Commons. A few minutes later Mrs. Haig-Ereildoun returns with Claire, the older two are dropped off by their carpools, we eat the hot dinner I've fixed, and the children's carpools return to take them back to school. He has lunch at the House of Commons. According to Mr. von Teplitz, the meals there are splendid, with good wines. When he's not in a session, Mr. Haig-Ereildoun reads in the library, which Mr. von Teplitz says is quite a comfortable room, with a fireplace and leather chairs and waiters passing through, offering glasses of whiskey off silver trays. Voting is at ten, so Mr. Haig-Ereildoun has supper at Whitehall. Why come home in between? By the time he arrives, his wife and children are sound asleep. On Thursdays he doesn't come home at all. He takes a valise and his typewriter and gets on a sleeper to Scotland. He keeps a car at the train station and spends the weekend at Granny Aitchee's. Monday mornings he rolls in just after Mrs. Haig-Ereildoun and the children have left the house.

She's been spending her afternoons painting. She started prepping the front door on Friday, the morning after Simon was here, and she worked away all weekend. When Mr. Haig-Ereildoun got here on Monday morning, he was astonished to walk through a yellow door as bright as the sun. She wasn't here to see his pleasure. I was. "I say, what's this?" His voice boomed through the house. "Mrs. Haig-Ereildoun did this? Wuh-wuh-wuh-well done! I'd say while I was having tea with Granny Aitchee, she raised the quality of the neighborhood and gave us the smartest house on the lane!" But by the time they next saw each other, awake, he'd probably gotten used to it.

28

"MELISSA . . . ?" FOR ONCE SHE made my name sound pretty. "Melissa, would you care to join me in the garden for a cup of tea?"

It's a sad garden. I've always thought of it as a light well. It's about two square meters of brick, caged in by four walls. There's a rhododendron bush that doesn't bloom. Even the weeds don't do well. We sat in two tipsy chairs of old plastic and balanced our cups and saucers on our knees. Pru, Trevor, and Claire had already had their tea and were inside, watching the only television program they're allowed to watch in the daytime. Mrs. Haig-Ereildoun had primer paint on her shirt (one of those that I'd darned so badly) and on her tattered plaid shorts. After her success on the front door, she didn't waste a day to get going on a truly huge project. I do think the celery color she's picked out will be an improvement in the drawing room.

Almost joyous to be off the ladder, she settled eagerly into her chair, handed me my tea, and amazed me by jumping right into girl talk. "Tell me about your young man."

"Which one?" I nearly said. I caught myself in time and said, "Ted?"

"Yes," she said. "I'm sorry I haven't asked you before. It seems all I know about him is that he has a great concern for your health.

But I don't know who his parents are, what he read at university, what he does for a living. Do you have a photograph?"

I don't have a picture, but I loved conjuring one up in my head. I could see the twinkle in his eyes, the tangled eyelashes, the adorably unkempt eyebrows. The great strong cut of his jaw. "He's built like a teddy bear," I said.

"So you like his body?"

I just smiled. If there's one thing I do like, it's his body. For cuddling. If you could have that without sex, it'd be perfect.

She smiled in a shy way, her bitten-lip smile. "I think Mr. Haig-Ereildoun has quite a nice body." I love the way she pronounces body. It's somewhere between body and buddy. And he does have a nice body. It's funny how she seems to be in love with him whenever he's not around—and angry with him when they're together. The only time I've seen her take out a cookbook was last Wednesday, when she spent most of the day making three little *gallettes au Camembert,* one serving of *poussin chaud-froid,* one *tomate farcie,* and one *baba au rhum classique*: "a picnic for Mr. Haig-Ereildoun's train journey tomorrow."

Maybe it's smart of him to stay away.

Reaching over to pluck a brown leaf from the rhododendron bush, she said, "Simon has an entirely different sort of body."

Actually, it worries me how much I like Simon's body. All that length and all those bones. His bones stir up quite an interest in me; but I don't think they would if they weren't attached to Simon's head. I definitely didn't want to get into that, so I told her more about Ted.

It seemed to worry her that he was an artist. It's lucky I didn't expound and tell her he specializes in nudes. And it would have sounded defensive to mention the trust fund. I feel almost sure it's not just the thought of poverty that makes her think art is irresponsible.

"What does your mother feel about him?"

Oh, heavens. Mom doesn't like him at all, but she wants me to marry him. That was the hard thing to explain, because it seems to reflect some sort of idiocy on Mom's part. So I got into this twisty explanation of what could possibly be wrong with my mother. "I think she wants me to marry him because she believes in marriage. She's upset by this no-commitment thing. She's very strong willed, and she thinks she can force me into acting the way she wants me to act. Even though I'm an adult now. She's absolutely determined that I get a marriage license, even if she has to resign herself to a son-in-law she's uncomfortable with."

"Why is she uncomfortable with him?"

"Because he's uncomfortable with her." Those were the words that popped out of my mouth, and they were the truth. He feels, somehow, guilty in her presence. He doesn't say that. He says he feels bored. She talks about things that don't interest him. But the emotion that actually drives them apart, I think, is guilt. Blame and guilt. But in this case, I think guilt precedes blame. She senses his guilt and blames him. And it's hard to put my finger on why he feels guilt.

Well, alone with my notepaper, I might as well be brave. He feels guilt because he does not honestly want to marry me.

When I told my mother the marriage was off, she said, "Is it because you're always losing your keys?" She lives in constant anxiety that she's failed as a parent, that everything that goes wrong in my life is because I've turned out badly. It makes me afraid I've flopped as a person. But I haven't, completely. Tedward doesn't want to be married because, he says, he's never met a person with a happy marriage. It has nothing to do with me. In fact, the sad thing is, he doesn't even know me to like or dislike. He doesn't understand the thoughts I have. His vocabulary isn't up to it. I don't mean that his vocabulary of words is like Claire's. I just mean he probably wouldn't be able to understand a conversation between Trevor and me.

You might wonder why *I* want to marry *him*. And the answer to that is easy. I'd never have to worry about him leaving me. He absolutely needs me. Marriage is the price he has to pay. It won't kill him.

"Let's have a second cup of tea," Mrs. Haig-Ereildoun said.

Painting the drawing room must be good for her—even if it's just that painting is such hard work you'll do anything to postpone getting back to it. I really liked her in this mood.

"Do you have special schools for deaf children in England?" I asked. I've been wondering why Claire goes to a normal nursery school with normal children.

Mrs. Haig-Ereildoun frowned, seeming to concentrate on the taste of the tea she was sipping. At last she swallowed and spoke. "The family of every deaf child in the Commonwealth comes to London, for the free, specialized schooling. The rooms are a hodgepodge of Nairobe and Pakistani dialects, everything but English." Her face had the look of a person who has decided to take a risk and wants confirmation that she's made the best choice. "English is what Claire needs, and I'm afraid she won't find much of it there." It seemed to me she was right.

About sign language. "Nobody understands it except the deaf." This is another area where she and I agree, although at home it's become a fad to learn it. Really, though, not many people do. Not enough to make a difference. It does seem better to equip Claire to be a part of the world at large, the world that includes us, than to confine her to the small group that communicates with hand signs. For Mrs. Haig-Ereildoun to take this stand is a statement of hope.

Claire was born with a sturdy ego (it seems to be in the genes); but her self-image grows each time she says something like her version of "Marmite, please?" and all hands reach across the breakfast table for the jar. And Trevor and Pru are so pleased. They treat her like their puppy.

"Do you have any idea why Claire is deaf?" I asked.

She widened her eyes, almost rolling them, and blew that imaginary wisp of hair off her forehead. Before she spoke, she used a hand to wipe off that imaginary wisp. "When I was three months pregnant I had rubella." A tension had come into her throat, and her voice got so quiet I had to lean forward. "If I'd had it earlier in the pregnancy it would have been a certainty that the child would be handicapped, and I'd definitely have had an abortion. But at three months, the doctors said there was a fair chance the fetus would not be affected. I elected to take the risk." She looked into her teacup and said, "Now I wish I'd had the abortion."

I'M STILL STUNNED. WITH her, in the garden, I tried with all my might not to betray my shock. I was very careful not to say anything that would sound like, "Look on the bright side." I know how my cheerful love of Claire upsets Mrs. H-E. She thinks I'm a Pollyanna and that I have no idea how much she suffers.

But she loves Claire too. Claire makes her laugh. Claire is cute! She is one of the prettiest, cutest little girls I've ever seen. It's true that in a way, the hearing aid makes her less picture perfect. But in a way it makes her cuter. Like Trevor's glasses make him cuter. She's so cute everyone in the world wants to grab her and squeeze her.

Also, Claire is happy. I think her hearing handicap is outweighed by her natural inclination to be happy. In her inclination to be happy, she's way above the norm. She joins in with people even though she doesn't understand them. She struts her stuff. She shouts, "Shut up!" or "Hoi-hoi-HOI!" She has a fabulous spirit.

The only thing I can think is that Mrs. Haig-Ereildoun thinks life is not worth living unless you're a winner. The university has to be Oxford or Cambridge. The degree has to be a first, if you're a man, and if you're a woman it can't be a first.

At least Claire probably won't have to worry about disappointing her mother by getting a first at Oxford.

I always see the bright side.

"I wanted to ask you," Mrs. Haig-Ereildoun said, still quiet, but with the croak in her voice replaced by that musical English she gets. "Would you like to come to a party? Mr. Haig-Ereildoun and I are going to give quite a grand supper party, and we need an extra woman. Would you?"

I was flattered to death already, but she went on: "It should be quite a smart guest list. The Tory whip will be coming, and a Cambridge don, and some UN delegates. The du Dordoignes will be here—and a first cousin of the queen."

My heavens! Like, a prince or a duke or a duchess or something?

When I'd accepted, she said, "Excellent. Also, I was wondering. Although Wednesday will now be technically your day off, I hope you'll be home by half-six tomorrow, to babysit. Mr. Haig-Ereildoun and I are invited to quite a special party at the Italian consulate."

Mots was having a dinner party. I'd already accepted.

"Well!" Mrs. H-G's tea-in-the-garden mood erupted into anger. "If only you'd *told* me, a week ago, that this was happening, you could have given Mrs. Hedrick plenty of notice, so that she could could have rescheduled her party for almost any other evening. I could have arranged to let you off, for a special occasion. Then you could have gone to your party."

"But it was already my day off," a normal person would have said. I said, "I'll call Mots and tell her I can't come. She won't mind."

Mrs. Haig-Ereildoun went into a frowning state. I realized she was imagining a terrific guest list and lots of courses. "You *should* have consulted with me first!" When I told her the party probably was just a little salad and pâté in the garden—Mots, Rupert, Simon, and me—Mrs. Haig-Ereildoun gave a great sigh of relief and smiled. "Well then. It's all right."

. . .

MOTS IS MAD. IT'S not about her dinner party. It's about my wimpiness.

It's hard to be guest and servant in one. But also, I have a thing about work. At the advertising agency, when I found out the cute receptionist was getting paid more than me, I mentioned it to my boss. "Ah," he said. "It's the end of the line for her, isn't it?" She also set quite an example of a person who wouldn't go far, absolutely refusing to stay one minute past five. I was the opposite. If you refuse to go the extra mile, you're at the end of the line.

"So you're ambitious to climb the nanny ladder?" Mots says.

It must be a habit, this need to do a job well and completely, no matter what the job. Mots doesn't seem to understand. Missing the point completely, she gets on the subject of how it's *illegal* for an employer to deny an au pair a full day off. In fact, she says, most things about the condition of my employment are illegal. I'm supposed to be on duty for five hours a day, and instead I'm on duty eleven hours a day. Didn't the government handbook say "a maximun of thirty hours per week"? And do I not work between sixty and seventy hours per week? For virtually nothing? I point out that I can't do the job well and completely in less than sixty or seventy hours a week. Mots pays no attention to that, just says I should write a letter to the *Times*, addressing the problem of abusing au pairs. She says it's rampant. It should be exposed. And this is an *M.P.*! I should write an article. She knows they'd publish it.

An exposé on Mr. Haig-Ereildoun is the last thing I'm about to do.

"From now on, when you tell me anything this woman has done to you, I'm not going to listen. I've told you you should stand up to her. And I honestly believe you can't. So in that case, you should quit. You know what she's like. If she hurts you it's your fault."

"But what about Claire!" I said. "And Trevor."

"Oh, bah!" Mots said. "Those children are her responsibility, not yours."

"Also," I told Mots, "I promised I would stay through the summer."

"And she promised you five hours a day, one *full* day off a week, and five pounds a week more than she's actually paying you. She never said she'd reduce your salary if you didn't also take on the job of the daily. You should be getting an extra thirty or forty pounds a week for that. More! Nobody has a daily who actually comes daily."

I couldn't deny what Mots was saying. But I had promised.

And another thing. I saw in *Time Out* that there's a class on Picasso, Saturday mornings at the Tate. "You should go!" Mrs. H-E said. She's actually going to take the children for six Saturday mornings in a row.

About Mots's dinner, I really was conflicted. I had promised Mots I'd be there. But this was work. Also, I felt for Mrs. Haig-Ereildoun. It was quite important for Mr. Haig-Ereildoun and her to go to this party at the Italian consulate. Instead of the usual black tie, this was white tie.

She doesn't know any other babysitters.

And besides, she can't afford one.

And she was so nice to me, in the sad, cramped little garden.

29

SORRY I CAN'T WRITE about yesterday's great adventure at the Cordon d'Or, but I already did. I had to *tell* someone. So I wrote a long letter. I put the Eaton's blue airmail pages into an Eaton's blue airmail envelope and dropped it in the pillar box. Now I wish I hadn't. At least I wish I'd xeroxed it. When I reread it in the morning, before sticking it in the envelope, I loved the way the words had come out. I laughed when I was writing it, and I laughed when I read it. The way Granny Aitchee loves her own cooking, I confess that sometimes I love my own writing.

The person I just had to "talk" to last night was Harvey Frankelman. I've only met him once, on my spluttering swan song of job interviews before I landed here. But Harvey liked me. Respected me. For some reason. And he *loves* food. The best things in his food section are the ones that tell you more about the cook than the cooking. I thought he'd like to know what the world-famous Arabella Tuckett is really like: the way she hovers over her assistant, hissing complaints at almost every slice and chop; the way she looks down her nose (literally!) when she talks about modern ideas of cutting out fats—although she herself must not eat, because she's skinny as a rail; the Cordon d'Or's golden rule that all vegetables must be boiled a long time before you even start the recipe, so that the flavor of the actual vegetables won't overwhelm the taste of the sauce. Though the only restaurants I've been to in London are the cheap ones, everyone says this is the new food capital of the world. I probably could have found a more au courant cooking school, but I wanted the *classique*.

I wonder if Nanny would like to have an afternoon at the Cordon d'Or. She's coming for a visit. She certainly wouldn't be up to taking the tube at night, so she won't be able to see any plays. (I've been going to plays. I love London for the plays.) Nanny won't want to go shopping, and I think her legs would get tired in museums. The Cordon d'Or might be the treat Nanny and I could take in together. The Cordon d'Or is theater.

30

YOU SHOULD SEE THE way she captivates. Every time he comes over (twice now) she shows her legs. First the short skirt with kicky pleats just meant to call attention, then the black linen shorts.

Simon was taking me to a sitar concert. I mean, escorting me. I'd made sure to have plenty of pounds, because I wanted to pay my own way this time. For myself, I'd never pay to hear a sitar concert. My brother, before he was a Christian, used to be a Hindu. I liked the Indian religion better, but the music at the holy roller church is a big improvement on those sitars.

Mrs. Haig-Ereildoun's now priming their bedroom. She's been painting in shorts, but just before Simon was due, she took a bath. A fresh tub for herself. Of course I bathed after her, in her painty water. She dressed in fresh, sort of resortlike shorts with no paint on them. It hasn't seemed to me warm enough for shorts anyway, but it had *really* cooled off by seven, when Simon arrived. Even for a person with her metabolism. There was no reason for shorts except to show off. She wore sandals, and she'd painted her toenails. She never gets any sun, so her legs are like alabaster with the faintest rose tint. Not one flutter of cellulite. And for some reason she doesn't get goose bumps. When he got here (*she* answered the front door), she asked him where the concert was. Since it was in Kensington Church Street, she said, "Perfect. You'll walk. It won't take a quarter of an hour. So Melissa, the water heater must have warmed plenty of fresh water by now. If you'll be an angel and bathe Claire, I'll serve Simon a gin and tonic in the drawing room. No need to worry about Pru and Trevor. I'll see to their baths." She offers a favor after she's made a command. Or sometimes it's the favor first, then the command. Always the two go together.

With her instruction, she pointed out to Simon my role: the servant girl. She pointed out her role as the lady. Which would you have a natural inclination to respect more? To find more scintillating?

From the hall, holding Claire by the hand, in her nightdress and woolly blue dressing gown, I saw through the doorway that Mrs. H-E's head and Simon's almost touched as both sat on the sofa, leaning over a book on the coffee table. There was never a book on that table before. Maybe she put it there to distract from the shabbiness of the furniture, in this room freshly painted celery green, the crown moldings now glossy white. They were speaking in low tones, turning the pages of the picture book, and as Claire and I stood at the threshold, a great laugh went up from the two of them. He said something to her I couldn't understand, and another tinkling laugh went through her. She answered something I also couldn't understand. Claire broke loose from my hand and toddled over saying, "Muh! Muh!" A word I'd taught her. Mrs. Haig-Ereildoun swooped Claire into her lap to cuddle and over her soft little ringlets said something else incomprehensible to Simon. He smiled and held up the book cover to me: a picture of the Acropolis with the title in Greek letters.

Oh. I'd never heard that language spoken. They went on talking to each other in Greek a few sentences more, this time not laughing, before acknowledging me again.

At the door he said, "Good night, Philippa." At least I restrained myself from saying, "Good night, Mrs. Haig-Ereildoun."

. . .

THE SITAR CONCERT WAS as droning as I knew it would be. Actually, I didn't listen. My head just buzzed with anger. Not anger with him. Anger with her. But it turned into anger toward him. What about that poem you wrote me when I was in Scotland? I thought it was a witty, original way of comparing this male-female thing between us to time immemorial. Did you in fact mean to compare my looks to a fossil frog's?

After the concert we went to the wine bar next door, in Kensington Church Street. He had a mineral water (probably because it was the cheapest thing), and I had a glass of wine. Since I knew he'd be careful about splitting the tab according to items drunk instead of fifty-fifty, I didn't feel guilty. I had a second glass of wine and smoked. He didn't have a second mineral water and he lectured me about smoking. He knows all kinds of facts about disease.

"How do you feel about rats?" I asked, getting the subject back to him.

He cocked his head and squinted.

"I mean, how do you feel about them? You work with them all day. Do you think of them as your coworkers?"

He picked up his empty glass and seemed to examine it for drops. "Do you think of Claire as your coworker?"

Well, suddenly I was telling him about how Claire *is* my coworker. We have a project that we both participate in. Every accomplishment is a triumph we share. That must be why I like her so much. I think she likes me too, but she likes everyone.

Simon wanted to hear every detail of how I work with Claire. As I explained the methods that seem to work and the ones that don't—which intuitions succeed and which fail—his expression was like a person *eating* my thoughts. He's interested partly because he's a psychologist working with "cognition," but also, he has a human streak. We sat in the wine bar until it closed, and he surprised me by paying the whole tab. He gave me absolutely no choice. For some reason I liked that. And it turns out that he does, in a way, develop an emotional relationship with his rats. He has a favorite, whose name is Ratty.

Saturday morning I woke up feeling furious with Mrs. Haig-Ereildoun for trying to charm Simon away from me. I almost let my irritation spill over to Claire as I dressed her. I had to get to my Picasso class at the Tate, and the damn battery in her hearing aid was dead. I caught myself—well, to tell the truth, I caught the hurt, confused look on her face, and I collected myself.

At breakfast Mrs. Haig-Ereildoun surprised me by being sweet. (Why am I always surprised? I sound like Simple Simon was a pie man.)

"Remember, Melissa, that recipe you showed me from your cookery school? The stuffed lamb? How would you like it if I purchased the ingredients while you're at your art history class? You might enjoy having a practice session tomorrow, and we could have it for dinner. And what was that starter you told me about? The crab and orange salad? Perhaps if you'll fetch that recipe, I'll get the makings for that one too. And what was the pudding?"

Oh, I've been dying to cook these things. Even if it amazes me that they use canned vegetables at the Cordon d'Or, the taste was absolutely wonderful—but each person only got dabs.

"Perhaps you might invite Simon, for your Sunday supper."

NOW HE'LL SEE ME as the cook, as well as the nursery maid.

But if this turns out, and I think it will, there's nothing wrong with being seen as a Cordon d'Or chef.

Of course there's no way to reach him, unless he goes into his office on Saturday. He doesn't have a phone in his rooms. But I called the lab and there was someone there who said he'd be in, that he's always there, Saturdays and Sundays as well. I left a message for him to call the house. At one, when I got back from the Tate, Mrs. Haig-Ereildoun had cottage pie ready. And Apple, for pud. She told me, "Simon's a go, for Sunday dinner."

THE TATE WAS GREAT. There's a whole basementful of classrooms. You thread down the shabby, subterranean hallways, such a contrast to the grand rooms upstairs, into a scuffed-up schoolroom with student desks and a blackboard and screen and projector. It was all older people, with clipboards. The teacher was a Cambridge professor, full of wit. I love London.

MRS. HAIG-EREILDOUN WAS STILL in her nice mood Sunday morning, except for one moment, which really wasn't that bad. She stood by the cooker, handing me ingredients, interested in what I was doing. It was just when I asked for a cup of white wine that she blew up. "I'll *not* waste good wine on your recipe!" That's another difference between England and California. Wine is a rarity here. Moving to the refrigerator she said, "You'll use cider." Scowling, she opened a bottle, measured a cup, shoved the cork back in, and virtually hurled the bottle back into the fridge, clanking milk bottles and slamming the door to clatter more jars.

I learned something from this, though. A recipe can be as good if you substitute ingredients. The cider might have gone even better with the corn stuffing than wine. Anyway, I think my *Epaule d'Agneau* tasted better than Arabella Tuckett's.

The meal—so many steps! Arabella Tuckett has a sous chef. I finished cooking an hour later than I'd planned, so Simon and Mrs. H-E had two gin and tonics in the drawing room. We'd had to clear Mr. Haig-Ereildoun's typewriter and stuff from the table to make a dining room. Other than my little bedroom, his office is the nicest room in the house, with that blossomless rhododendron pushing its leaves up against the many-paned window. Mrs. Haig-Ereildoun wore those black linen shorts and the sandals, and a pretty top, but at least when I was around, she didn't flirt. They did burst into Greek for a minute, and she did fly up from the table to find a book about Greece he simply had to read; but mostly we all just enjoyed the children. Claire is learning food words (lamb is "baah! baaah!" tomatoes are "taaah-toe"), and she entertained us with her famous "shut up." Pru started a conversation about how Henry the Eighth used no cutlery and neither did Louis XIV and Trevor enjoyed talking to Simon about death. Simon agreed it might be nice to eat Trevor when he dies. But he thought he might taste better cooked in cider, instead of wine.

SIMON THANKED ME FOR the culinary experience, thanked Philippa for lending him the book, and left at about half-five. I made my collect call to Tedward, telling him about the Cordon d'Or lunch I cooked. I told him "Simon, a friend of ours," had been here. Tedward went immediately on guard. Wanted to know everything about this Simon. Age, height, weight. Ted doesn't like anyone I've met over here, even Mr. Haig-Ereildoun. Especially Mr. Haig-Ereildoun. And now he doesn't like Simon. Of course he's jealous, but I also think he believes that if they have English accents, they're phony.

31

THE NEWS IS, I have news. I stopped by Mots's tonight after cooking class and found out Mrs. Haig-Ereildoun had called her in the afternoon, saying a man in uniform had knocked the knocker and presented a letter packet for me marked urgent. Should she open it? And read it to Mots? Mots said no, she didn't think that would be necessary. Mrs. Haig-Ereildoun said it might be important, she thought she should read it. "Such a busybody," said Mots. "I'm afraid I quite shamed her. But imagine. Opening your courier letter."

Mots, in her way, can out-snob Mrs. Haig-Ereildoun.

I actually wished Mrs. H-E had opened my letter and read it to Mots. Now it would shame Mots if I called from her house and had Mrs. Haig-Ereildoun read it to me. So I had to fly home, without my evening with Rupert and Mots, to read my urgent letter.

Mrs. Haig-Ereildoun stood over me as I opened it. Wonderful bright-colored things these are, these Fed-Ex overnight letter packets. Shiny cardboard sheathing a single sheet of paper. Nobody's ever sent me one of these. But we don't have faxes and e-mail at this house.

It was Harvey Frankelman, Food Editor at the *Chronicle*. He was in a hurry. He wants me to—I'll quote: "Great letter. Mind if I print it? Send more. One per week if you can. Just write letters to me. Keep gossipy. Include recipes. 700–800 words. Your first check is in the mail."

So now I'm a foreign correspondent. Reporting on the Cordon d'Or for the San Francisco *Chronicle*.

Mrs. Haig-Ereildoun was unimpressed. You should have seen her forced smile. Patronizing. I even saw a hint of a shrug.

I wish I could ring Simon, but he doesn't have a phone.

Today we learned to do a pie crust Arabella Tuckett's way. She uses a steel bowl, set in a huge dishpan full of crushed ice. Cuts in the butter with two special knifelike instruments, making smaller and smaller pebbles. Works fast. Much strain. Tension. Arabella's face very hot. Heated reprimands to poor assistant. Must write Harvey.

NOW IT TURNS OUT Mrs. Haig-Ereildoun is planning a trip to Greece with her husband. The most interesting thing about that is that she left her passport out today, by the phone, and I looked inside. She's thirty-eight years old.

I'd have guessed older. Much. It's all those hissy fits that age her.

Simon is twenty-eight.

She's found a package tour to Crete, for three weeks. Showed me the pictures. Little stone bungalows by the sea. Each more than a thousand years old. She asked my permission! She had to make her reservations today. They'll leave in three weeks.

Mots was horrified. "Leaving you alone with the children? Boy, does she know a good thing! She knows she'll never have another opportunity like this one. An au pair who speaks English? And who's willing to work a twenty-four-hour day? She's going to milk every last ounce out of you."

Such a funny reaction. I saw it as a window of bliss. No Mrs. Haig-Ereildoun for three weeks.

. . .

THE ONLY THING I haven't figured out yet is who will take care of the children when I'm at the Cordon d'Or. Since I have a job writing up these classes, I can't cut. Pru can go to Camilla's house every Wednesday afternoon, that's no problem. Or to Pamela's or Sarah's or Cristina's. She goes to a different friend's house every day anyway. But Trevor and Claire have no friends. It's funny how I hadn't zeroed in on that until this question of what to do with them came up. But really, every afternoon, Trevor, in the short trousers and pullover of his school uniform—everything but the tie and blazer—kicks a soccer ball from one end of Lettering Lane to the other. He kicks and chases, kicks and chases. All by himself. After tea he watches the special educational show his mother allows, sometimes with Claire or Pru, sometimes by himself. Then he goes to his room with his books or his toy soldiers.

It's easy to see why Claire has no friends. But I don't know why Trevor doesn't have any. I must say, his mother doesn't push it.

Mrs. Haig-Ereildoun pooh-poohs my foreign correspondent job so much, if so subtly, that I haven't figured out how to approach her on this. I don't want a full-blown pooh-pooh. I don't think I'll bring up the problem until I've come up with the solution. It will come to me.

It crossed my mind that Nanny could stay on, or come back, to take care of my problem. She arrives on the train in a few days. But if she stayed here when the H-Es went to Greece, she'd be more trouble to take care of than all three children. And I'd be her servant.

Mrs. H-E says the place they're going to be, on Crete, has no telephone, so I won't be able to reach them. But if any problems come up, I can call Granny and Grampy at Phillingsford. If there's a problem, I wonder what Granny and Grampy could do? From their four-hundred-acre island in Yorkshire. But I can't imagine any problems coming up.

. . .

TODAY WHEN I WHEELED Claire through the gate, after the park, Mrs. von Teplitz was ringing the front doorbell. Mrs. von Teplitz. The solution? She has a little boy Claire's age. Trevor and Justin von Teplitz go to the same school. Trevor could go home with him, Claire and I could take a taxi from her school to the von Teplitzes' house, and I could continue on to my school. After, we could all come back on the tube. The von Teplitzes' nanny (and their au pairs) could take care of two more children. After all, I took care of the von Teplitzes' five, as well as my own three, for seven days at Kirriebairne.

I like Mrs. von Teplitz, even though she was rude to me that one time. I think Mr. Haig-Ereildoun shamed her that evening, and she felt the shame. I think she'd like to make up for it. And there was one other thing that endeared her to me. One time, a few days after the soup plate, the children were asking me about my job back home, and I said it was writing adverts, and I saw her raise her eyebrows, signaling to Philippa, "Uh-oh. You'd better be careful." Mrs. H-E didn't get it at first, so Mrs. v.T. leaned in closer and whispered, ominously, "A writer, Philippa." To me that showed respect.

"PHILIPPA, DARLING," SHE SAID when the door opened, the two of them kissing on both cheeks.

I don't think Londoners very often make surprise visits. Mrs. Haig-Ereildoun looked stunned. She was, again, painting. This big party of theirs is coming up, before they go to Greece. Now she's tackled the front hall. There was a ladder up, and drop cloths. She had paint all over her skin, a paint-spattered kerchief covering her hair. She whipped off the kerchief, and the two of them looked at each other and laughed.

"I say," said Mrs. von Teplitz. "The color is supah!"

For the front hall, Mrs. Haig-Ereildoun has settled on a dramatic claret. It'll shrink the size of the space, but it's so huge anyway. The rich dark color will look pretty homey, I think, and accent the glossy white she's going to paint the banisters. I don't know what she'll do about the broken rungs, or the torn stair rug or the cracked linoleum. She has taken the coat nails out of the walls.

"I've just dropped two chairs at the repairer," Mrs. von Teplitz said, "just round the corner in the Queen's Bench. Rather exhorbitant, the prices." She looked at me and said, "Pretty soon we'll all just start doing what you do in America. Throw things away!"

She and Mrs. Haig-Ereildoun had a giggle. I would have joined in except it's actually not part of my experience. I don't own anything yet. Well, those floor cushions I made out of old burlap coffee sacks. I wonder if Tedward has thrown those away. If so, it'd be the only thing he's ever thrown away.

I hope he hasn't thrown them away.

"We're going to Greece!" Mrs. Haig-Ereildoun said.

I felt my opening coming.

When Mrs. von Teplitz asked Philippa what she was planning to do with the children, and Mrs. H-E told about me, I said, "There's only one problem."

I hadn't expected to stop the whole gleeful conversation.

I told Mrs. von Teplitz about my cookery writing. "Supah!" she said to both of us, as if Mrs. H-E would share her enthusiasm. Then to me she said, "I suppose you can't take the children to the Cordon d'Or."

I shook my head. I hope not too pitifully.

"Well send them to us!"

Mrs. Haig-Ereildoun protested and protested, but Mrs. von Teplitz insisted and insisted. So Wednesdays are settled.

. . .

MY FIRST LETTER TO Harvey was easy. Just a letter to Harvey. My second letter was easy too. I knew what he wanted. One of those lively, honest, firsthand things. The hard part was counting the words: 361, 362 . . . I spent more time counting the words than I spent on the writing. First I came up with 903 words, so I had to cut. In the rereading I found redundancies or stupidities that I had to rephrase. In the end I had so many carets and arrows and additional sentences in all the margins that I had to recopy the whole thing. So in the morning, I asked Mr. Haig-Ereildoun if next time he'd let me use his ancient typewriter on Thursday afternoon—during my usual letter-writing hour.

He was amazed to hear of my assignment.

I thought she would have told him. But then, they never see each other.

He says I can use his typewriter any afternoon. "Or any morning," he added. "For that matter."

I'd been wanting to ask him how his rewrite was going but didn't have to ask. I haven't heard a sound from his office since the day his manuscript came back.

I thanked him and left the room. From the kitchen I heard, "Melissa?" He stood in the door to his office. "Melissa, well done."

Depression washed me. It seems so wrong of me, to succeed when he is failing.

32

"THE FRENCH ARE DIFFERENT from us, aren't they. The Frenchmen can have all the affairs they like. But not the French women, can they. It's not like that here, is it."

I'd been wondering.

"Here neither one is supposed to, but both do." Nanny's eyes laughed. "Don't they."

Do they?

Nanny lived in Paris with baby Pru and the Haig-Ereildouns, the year Mr. H-E had a job with a French publisher. Mrs. Haig-Ereildoun says Nanny hated every minute of it, but now she remembers it as the time of her life. In honor of Nanny's nostalgia, and maybe her own, Mrs. Haig-Ereildoun took us to Harrod's on our way home from collecting Nanny at Paddington and got half a wheel of Brie. "In Paris we ate Brie every day, didn't we, Nanny." Nanny had made friends with a widow named Madame Olivier, and the two of them walked together, pushing Pru's pram, and sat on the park benches in the Louvre garden and talked all afternoon. Possibly about romance. Love and sex are what Nanny likes to talk about, as I iron and she knits. If she's had any firsthand experience, she hasn't told me about it, but hearsay is worth repeating.

. . .

NANNY ISN'T THE ONLY one who likes to talk about sex. Simon has started talking about it, too. I don't like it.

I don't know why I don't like it.

Freshman year in college, when half of us were still virgins, we all loved talking about "going all the way." (Nanny was rapt when I told her about this. She lost count of her knits and purls so many times she finally set her needles and yarn on the table and did nothing but listen.) One girl, Sheila, had done it, and she loved to tell all. Our favorite thing, on a Sunday afternoon, was to gather in someone's room and plumb Sheila's wisdom. Everyone who'd done it said it was impossible to describe, but Sheila tried to. She always had new information for us. Like how, if you don't want to go all the way, be careful of the skin on your bottom. "Don't ever let a boy stroke you there," she said, "or you won't ever be able to stop." I really didn't want to go all the way until I was ready, so I never let a boy stroke me any of the places. It sounds amazingly square, and it was, so I didn't talk about it. By sophomore year, I knew I had a reputation as a prude, but to change it I'd have had to pay too big a price for my inner self to bear.

Every boy I made out with got such a fast heartbeat, went so out of control, that I felt sorry for them all. Just deeply, deeply sorry. Helpless, these poor guys.

Nanny laughed, her eyes absolutely glistening with delight.

She ignited a rumble of laughs in me, but the whole thing wasn't entirely funny. I earnestly wanted to explain to Nanny the—the *vulnerability* behind my chastity. I hadn't analyzed it before, and since she obviously wasn't bored, I talked. In telling her, I was learning something about myself: something I'd never been able to understand until this conversation. I got back to the boy, making out. Whether I could have loved *him* or not, I didn't trust him to love me. Love wasn't part of this rocketing heartbeat. Also, though I passionately adored making out, my heartbeat never doubled like that. I felt so superior in my cool.

I had another kind of uncool, though. I didn't have out-of-control desire for sex, but I had out-of-control desire for love forevermore. I might not have been able to survive giving the ultimate, and—when his helpless hunger was satisfied—being brushed off. Other girls must not have connected baring their bodies with baring their souls, but I did. And I knew it.

It was too bad, because I needed to know about sex for academic reasons. In English classes we analyzed the sexual allusions in John Donne and Dante's *Inferno* and T. S. Eliot and even the Bible. I had no idea what the professors were talking about. One poet, I forget which one, talked about peeling an orange. It was obvious to everyone in the class that this was a sexual reference. All I could contribute to the discussion was, "duh."

"Have you read Barbara Cartland?" Nanny asked. She offered to give me the book she'd brought, when she was finished. "I think you'd like her."

I've always wondered if I would. I might.

The main thing all of us virgins in Sheila's room wanted to know, I told Nanny, was what an orgasm felt like. Sheila said, "It's like drowning in milk."

Nanny just rolled with laughter. "Drowning in milk!" She took out her hanky and dabbed off the tears under her eyes. "I've read almost every book Barbara Cartland ever wrote, and I've never heard that. She's more like those poets you were talking about. You need to bring your own bit to it, if you know what I mean."

Nanny was as much fun as the girls in the Pi Phi house freshman year.

But by sophomore year, the fun was gone. We didn't talk about sex any more because everybody but me had experienced it. Countless times. Mots did it legally: She got married. But she was unusual. By junior year I was the only person I knew, except my friend Trish, who was still in the dark. She and I were slow to mature. Everyone said it must be hell for guys to go on double dates with us because we laughed all the time. We had our own friendship and weren't that much interested in our dates. A rumor even got started that Trish and I were lesbians, in love with each other. That rumor was over with by our senior year. Trish got a boyfriend. She told me in detail, of course, what it felt like. And she agreed not to let anyone know the freakish truth about me.

As I told Nanny, until I finally went to bed with Tedward, I avoided the subject of sex whenever my women friends wanted to talk about it. "Well, how do *you* feel?" someone would ask, and I'd just say, "Well, I don't know, how do *you* feel?" or something lame. All my cells prickled with anxiety. I lived in terror that someone would press me and that I'd have to lie.

Nanny listened solemnly. I knew she'd understand when I told her I wanted to be sure I was loved. I wanted to be sure it was someone who wouldn't hurt me. I had total confidence that when the conditions were right, I'd love sex.

Nanny nodded. "A lot of men are no good, though. You want someone who'll take care of you."

Yes. That's part of it. I'm not sure in what sense Nanny meant this. "Take care of" might mean material support. But there's another sense, too. I need loyalty and cherishing.

It took me a long time to find Ted in the first place, and then to feel sure that he would cherish me, loyally.

Then I told Nanny what I've never told anyone. Not Mots, not Trish, and certainly not Ted: When I did feel sure, and we did go to bed, it hurt!

He, though, loved the novelty of having a novice. Someone to teach. He said, "Your pussy is all mine."

Nanny gasped. Then she leaned in: "He wanted to be sure of you too."

Maybe so. But I didn't like the way he put it.

Tedward took to giving instruction, in all the possible positions. But he insisted on perfect cleanliness. I had to bathe before we had sex. I had to douche afterward. We had to keep a box of tissues by the bed, to clean off the goo.

This seemed only proper to Nanny.

To me, it made the whole thing feel dirty. I didn't tell her about how he taught me to gargle, or why.

HE WAS ALWAYS COACHING me. While in the act, he'd tell me to move forward, to move upward, to roll my hips in a certain way. I'd try, and he'd tell me I wasn't doing it right. When I got the movement right, I didn't have the emotion right. I wasn't letting go. I wasn't experiencing joy.

"Joy!" Nanny said. "With all that pressure?"

It felt good to talk to Nanny.

Tedward kept coming back to tales about the greatest lover he'd ever had, an older woman. She was forty-three, he was twenty-five, and she had no inhibitions at all, she just flew into ecstasy, et cetera et cetera, and why couldn't I be like that?

"Ah, but you can't compete with an older woman, can you," Nanny said. "The French know that. Even the English know that."

I didn't know the French knew that. I didn't know the English knew that. I'd never heard it. But I suppose I might have begun to suspect it on my own, or why this creeping fear of Mrs. Haig-Ereildoun's possible power over Simon?

NOT THAT SIMON AND I are an item. I'm practically a married woman.

But I have to admit it. I don't know whether it's his Abraham Lincoln looks or what—his Adam's apple?—but sometimes just his presence almost makes me dissolve.

He's never touched me since that time he measured my hand against his. Oh. And when we cross the street. The cars always come from the wrong direction, and everything about the way they drive is terrible. He's probably saved my life about five times. Mrs. Haig-Ereildoun and Trevor have grabbed me and saved my life even more times. It's a wonder Mrs. Haig-Ereildoun trusts me with Claire.

One good thing is, when I'm with Simon, there's no internal debate about remaining faithful to Ted. I'm shocked at how every thought of Tedward flies out the window.

I suppose my conversations with Nanny helped me understand why I don't like it when Simon starts talking about sex. It's only natural that I'm uncomfortable with the subject. But the other thing is, I wish he'd stop talking and touch me.

33

"NOW, YOU NAUGHTY LITTLE pride and joy, it's time to brush the Hampton's Heath." Nanny has used the banister and one cane to pull herself up to the bathroom, to supervise Trevor's bedtime routine.

"But Nanny!" Trevor pretends to whine. "Someone's given my toothbrush the butcher's!" Peals of giggles, from both.

"Now listen to you!" Nanny chides. "You've turned into a holy friar. Use your mincers!" No one laughs harder than Trevor, when he laughs—except maybe Nanny.

They see Claire and me standing in the hall. The look on my face. Claire, too, is trying to figure out what's going on. This gets them laughing harder.

"Melissa can't understand us, Nanny, because she's a ham shank!"

Now they're choking, Trevor's slapping the knees of his pajamas, Nanny's red-faced. I don't like this.

"Claire doesn't mind, though," Trevor says, "because she's Mutt and Jeff!"

They throw their arms around each other and I'm afraid he'll pull her down on the floor.

"Come now, me china plate," Trevor says. "Be kind to Melissa. After all, she's living in our Mickey Mouse."

Now Trevor does fall to the floor, with a thwop, and Nanny grips the sink for dear life.

"You're right, Trevor," she says. "See her boat race? But we'd best be careful. It's about to turn to laugh and titter."

Between gasps for breath, I see Trevor start to take pity on me. "It's a secret language, Melissa. Nanny taught us."

"Not so secret," she says to Trevor. "Just special." She's beginning to sober up. "The people I come from couldn't read nor write, so they learned what they needed to remember by rhyming."

"Her people have grown to be quite Trevor!" says Trevor.

And the two of them are on the skids again. I don't see what's so funny.

"Ah, that's a good one, me pride and joy! Quite Trevor indeed you are."

"Do you know what pride and joy is?" says Trevor.

No.

"That means boy. A holy friar is a liar. Your boat race is your face. They're so good at rhymes," Trevor says, "the rhymes take the place of the words they rhyme with." Trevor's voice gets squeaky and high when he's this excited. "Tell her what it means, me china plate."

"China plate is mate," Nanny says.

"And in a minute I promise I'll brush my Hampton's Heath."

Oh. I see. I'm beginning to get it. "But he says someone's given his toothbrush the butcher's."

"That's harder, isn't it Nanny. She'll have to use her loaf of bread."

"Hah!" I say. I get down on my knees and hold Claire's head. "That's . . ."

"Hhheh!" says Claire. She's getting in the spirit. What a response she gets from that one. She puffs up her chest and shouts, "Hhheh! Hhheh! Hhheh! Hhheh!" Even I have to laugh.

"But what's this about the butcher's?"

"That means someone's stolen it!" Trevor shouts. "Given it the butcher's hook. But that would be too easy, wouldn't it, Nanny."

"So they gave it the butcher's? Meaning gave it the hook?" My loaf of bread was reeling. "So what about mincers? Does that have to do with the butcher's too? Like minced meat?"

"No, no, no!" Nanny is actually shouting. "Mince pies!"

"Which means eyes."

Of course.

"Doesn't Melissa have a bright pair of mincers, Nanny?"

"They sparkle in her boat race."

"But we'd best be careful, or they will turn laugh and titter."

Laugh and titter.

"Rhymes with . . ." says Trevor.

Oh, I don't know. This game is making me . . .

"Bitter!"

So I laugh and titter, instead of *being* laugh and titter. "But the part about ham shank. You said I was a ham shank?"

"That's a yank!"

Oh. Very Trevor. "And Claire is—Mutt and Jeff?"

"Deaf."

Oh.

NANNY AND I WERE babysitting. On the news, there was an interview of an engineer who'd built five bridges over five firths in Scotland, and all five had immediately fallen down. He'd just built a sixth, and the BBC interviewer asked him this way and that way why he believed this sixth one would stand. The engineer's answers were touchingly sincere, and touchingly unconvincing. Nanny and I got so tired from laughing that Nanny suggested we rebuild our strength by having a bit of Brie cheese.

She has been laughing a lot, ever since she got here. The laughing must relax her, because as we cut off great hunks of Brie to smear on great hunks of bread, she got into what I think is, for her, the most forbidden subject of all. Food. "Tell me about those dishes you make at the Cordon d'Or," she said. She hurried me through all the soups and stews and *epaules d'agneau* and so forth, wanting to move to the puds. "That's my weakness," she confessed. With the pungence of Brie melting in her mouth, she listened to my descriptions of gateaux, tarts, and mousses. Her raptness, listening, reminded me of the best food description I'd ever heard. It was when I was little, watching Julia Child on TV. She cut into an apple charlotte. "You see how it wobbles?" Julia said. "It's almost—*heartrending*."

"Oh, I know what she means." Nanny laughed. "Heartrending!" I love the way Nanny says " 'eartrending."

We got into cheese custards and savories. "There is one thing I do like better than butter, though," Nanny said, leaning in. "Have you ever tasted the egg of a duck? It's a rare treat. The ducks hide them, you know. Mrs. West and I go out for our constitutional around the pond with our eyes to the ground. One finds a duck egg ever so infrequently, but the taste of one is worth a month of walking. Milady disapproves, says the duck's egg can be deadly. Perhaps that makes it even more thrilling. When we find a nest with an egg or two in it, Mrs. West and I keep the news of our treasure to ourselves. We arrange a trysting time for boiling our eggs and eating them—lots of butter on the toast. And when we do! Now the color of the yolk. It's so deep you'd have to call it orange. And the flavor. I've tasted truffles, at one of those posh parties in New York, when Harry was married. We also had Russian caviar there. Nothing so good as a duck's egg. The flavor of a duck's egg, rich and a bit wild, you know—I'm sure your Julia Child would agree, it truly is *heart-rending*."

"Do you think I might try one, next time I'm at Phillingsford?"

She beamed her sparkling eyes at me. "Now that, me china plate, is asking a bit much."

BESIDES MANY MORSELS OF juicy gossip (like, I told her about the time at Troonfachan when Mr. Haig-Ereildoun got elephant trunk—i.e., you know what), Nanny and I have gotten into some serious topics, like my brother, Sam, living in the Christian commune in North Carolina ("But it's better than drug addiction, isn't it now"), and she told me about her brother's flight from Phillingsford. It was after he got out of the Royal Air Force—with "a 'ole chestful of medals for bravery. 'I'd never go back to being a footman,' he said." Nanny thought it was a great pity, at the time, because he had a future, a good chance at becoming a butler. "He was quick!" And a butler in a great house, she told me, was like being the chairman of a firm. "He could have managed it." Instead, he went to Australia and started a business of his own, delivering food to restaurants. Nanny is "a bit laugh and titter," because she hasn't seen him since. "He's done very prosperous. He could afford to come back and pay a visit. But he won't." She had me fetch a large envelope from her case. She'd brought a photograph of her brother and herself. He was tall, healthy, and smiling in his footman's uniform. But *she* was gorgeous—not fat yet, just pleasingly plump. Like me, halfway between the way I usually am and the way I am now. She was fair-skinned and fair-haired as Carole Lombard—but no bleach. Nanny, in her youth and in her own way, was as pretty as Pru, the little Renoir girl.

NANNY GETS A LOOK in her eye when she tells me about the Chipchase family. "A very historic family indeed. They have a castle in Scotland." I'd heard about this castle. We haven't taken a side trip to see it on either of our trips between London and Troonfachan, because Mrs. Haig-Ereildoun doesn't like it. It was built along the border between Scotland and England, in the year A.D. 600 or something, when England and Scotland were forever at war. Pru says Chipchase Castle is more of a fort than a house.

And Sir Chester. "He was a hero!" He was the youngest commander in World War Two. "I was a girl then, but my brother worked for him. The whole country heard news of him on the wireless. And he was a member of Parliament for most of his life, very distinguished."

She also told me about "an affair" Mrs. Haig-Ereildoun had when she was at Oxford. "He wasn't a proper suitor." Not even a student. He was a tutor. In his forties. "And he was not a free man!" ("You mean he was *married?*"—"Yes!") She said Lady Chipchase found out and was fit to be tied. Sir Chester never knew, though.

So. I thought so. Philippa may not be that conservative after all.

34

WE'VE ALL BEEN SAD today. We got a letter from Granny Aitchee.

"Dear Philippa, Pru, Trevor, Claire, Nanny, and Melissa." How nice to be included in the family. Mr. Haig-Ereildoun wasn't included, because Granny Aitchee knew that by the time we got the letter, he'd be on the sleeper to Scotland.

"I have sad news to report. Mary is dead." Mary, the sweet Scottish deerhound. "Bruce is grieving so painfully I can't think what to do for him." Bruce is Granny Aitchee's other hound. She said Mary was so old she should have been kept inside the garden, but "I had the lack of wisdom to take her out for a long walk with Bruce on a day that was uncharacteristically warm. I think it was too much for her, because when she returned, she refused to eat her supper. She simply fell by her bowl and slept."

"Yes?" Trevor was glued to the words as I read the letter. The reason I was reading it was that Mrs. Haig-Ereildoun and Pru weren't home yet, and Nanny said she couldn't read Granny's handwriting. Nanny has confessed to me, though, that reading anything is difficult for her. Her grandparents couldn't read a word. Her parents couldn't read well. They were in the first generation of English children who learned to read at all. ("Average children, that is," she said. "The members of the peerage, and so forth—that was different.")

"During the night Bruce nudged me awake. I couldn't imagine

what was wrong, but he was insistent that I go downstairs. I eventually obeyed him and put on my dressing gown. He led me to Mary, who seemed to be asleep on the kitchen floor.

"Puzzled, at first, I took a closer look at Mary. It occurred to me to check her breathing. Sometimes she sleeps so quietly that it's difficult to see any movement at all in her chest. This time I had to crouch down, to feel for the breath. And no breath came.

"As it was dark all 'round, and I had no one to help me, I fetched a rug and spread it over Mary. As I fixed a small pot of tea and stroked Bruce, he stood up and removed the rug from Mary and pressed his body to her, lying down with his chin tucking in her head."

I looked up from the letter and saw that Trevor had moved to the foot of Nanny's chair and had put his head into her lap. He faced Claire and me and let tears fall silently.

"When at last I went back up to bed, I tried to bring Bruce up with me. But he wouldn't come beyond the first stair. He went to Mary again and pulled the rug aside and pressed his warm body next to her dead one."

Now Trevor was openly heaving, and Nanny took her hanky to his tears and her own. She said, "There, there, me china plate." Trevor looked up at her and grinned, making a choking sound, halfway between a laugh and a sob. He buried his head again in her lap.

"Bruce was still beside her in the morning. When Angus arrives, he and his brother will bury Mary by the gate, under one of the rowan trees. The ground beneath the other rowan tree will be reserved for Bruce, in his time."

35

I TOLD SIMON TALKING about sex makes me uncomfortable.

It was last Thursday night, after a busy day with children and libraries, typing and posting my letter to Harvey, and another harangue from Mrs. Haig-Ereildoun. Simon had come over to take a walk after supper. He came all the way on the tube and couldn't stay long because his rooms are in such a remote outskirt of London that the tube doesn't go there after ten p.m. I've been there once, with Rupert and Mots. Very bleak. Rooms, plural, is an exaggeration. He has a bed, a small table, two straight chairs, an electric kettle, and a hotplate. No refrigerator. To turn on the heat you have to go down to the cellar and put coins into a meter. All that would be all right, if it weren't for the tidiness. It would be fun and Bohemian if Simon were a more relaxed housekeeper. As it is, the meticulous order of his bare necessities show the total lack of pleasure he's taken in his home. He'd make a good monk.

Thursday. We were walking on that little street that goes alongside the Kensington Palace when he said, "What does an orgasm feel like, to you?"

I stopped walking and told him what it feels like when he talks to me about sex. It's beneath him to try to be provocative in such an unsubtle, boorish way. That's what I said. More or less.

He'd talked about sex before, and I hadn't said anything. He'd asked if I could analyze the particular male features that attracted me (actually, I don't think it's physical features that attract me, but that means there's no explanation for the way his shoulders, or his hands, stir something inside me—but I didn't mention any of this to him). He'd asked if I found pornographic films erotically stimulating (I've never seen one but I think I'd be repelled). He'd asked if when I looked at *Playboy*, the female bodies aroused me (they do, a little, for some reason). About the last question, he was intrigued. He told me it seemed to be normal, usual, for likenesses of their own bodies to trigger in women some sense of anticipation—anticipation of the pleasures they could receive and bestow—a whole flood of feelings in one visual instant. This subject interested me, and it didn't make me squirm too much. But when he progressed to really personal things, like which parts of my body were the most vulnerable to the touch, I ignored the questions.

Apparently cold silence wasn't a strong enough statement. What does an orgasm feel like? Simon, I don't like talking about this!

So he stopped talking about it. Instead, he went into his work mode, his PhD candidate in psychology mode: He began studying me as if I were one of his rats. You can't cross-examine a rat, but you can try experiments to see how they react.

Last night, Friday, we were in Mots and Rupert's garden. It's a real garden. One of those walled London gardens, a deep oblong, with an arched trellis dividing the part with the paving stones and the table and chairs from the more private part in back, with the little box of lawn and most of the flowers. Rupert had sent us back through the arch to have a look at his clematis, which he's proud of but which is just finishing its bloom. "It's perhaps your last chance to see it until next May."

Rupert and Mots stayed inside, going over travel brochures, to plan next year's holiday. Can you imagine planning next summer's vacation before you've even gone on this one's? That's how thought-ahead their life is.

Back behind the trellis, with the Souvenir de Malmaison rosebuds promising to bloom, Simon told me first that it's called Souvenir de Malmaison and, second, why it's called Souvenir de Malmaison. It was hybridized by the gardener of the Empress Josephine and first grown at her estate, Malmaison.

Isn't that a funny name for a house? *Malade* equals malady, to be *mal* is to be ill. Sick house.

Simon cupped his long-fingered hand around a rose from a neighboring bush, the one rose in Mots's garden that had already developed into a full flower. It had white petals, not tight scallops but blousy and loose—layers crowded upon layers, but somehow giving the air of luxurious space between them; and when you looked deep inside it, you saw but barely saw, at the base of so many ruffles, a tinge of pink. "Do you know what this rose is called?" Simon asked.

No. But this one blossom, held so gently in Simon's long palm, became almost a world, to explore with your nose and eyes. "Is it called . . . Delicious?"

Simon smiled. "It's my favorite rose," he said. "It has quite a lot of names. I think most people call it 'maiden's blush.' "

Mmm. I saw the blush. And the maidenliness. It could be a girl in a first communion dress.

"It's also called 'virginale.' All the names people call it are sexy. Like 'la seduissante.' And 'incarnata.' The name I like for it, though, is 'cuisse de nymphe émoué.' "

"Thigh of the nymph," I said. But I couldn't remember. "What's *émoué?*"

"Aroused."

I wonder if my thighs were blushing.

I wonder if thighs blush.

Anyway, if my face blushed, Simon saw.

I was wearing a spring dress I'd gotten when I still weighed only about eight stones. Mr. Haig-Ereildoun is fabulously circumspect about not ogling, but even his eyes popped when I came down the stairs in that one. Mrs. Haig-Ereildoun frowned. The neck's low, and I'm afraid my breasts have swelled more than I realized. On my walk to Mots's Friday night, a taxi driver pulled over and offered me a free ride.

Simon put his hands in his pockets and let his eyes rest on my *poitrine*. Not for a whole second. Just long enough that I, too, looked down. Then up to Simon's eyes. They laughed.

"Simon?" I was flooding with a combination of embarrassment and—actually—desire. "Simon!"

"Mmm?" His eyes wouldn't leave mine. "Mmm?" he asked. Hands still in pockets.

I started walking back into the kitchen. He ambled slowly behind me, and I felt angry. Exposed. Because I was sure he was now taking in the jiggle of my hips. Yes, the dress is tight.

Inside, Mots was rinsing a colanderful of strawberries. Ripe, round, red. As she poured the cascade of crimson into her cobalt blue bowl from Finland, I said I'd never seen anything so pretty. Simon, frowning at the strawberries, made that that tst!-tst! shame-on-you sound.

Why?

Mots immediately knew why and took offense. "Simon, just because you're so thrifty doesn't mean I have to be. I have a right to buy the first strawberries of the season if I want." (I've noticed the price, in the street market stands. Each strawberry did probably cost about ten or twenty pence.)

"For shame," he said.

Annoyed, Mots took the bowl to the table, sat down, and said, "It's a treat. You should learn to sin, Simon."

All of us now at the table, he was the first to choose a berry, the biggest one. He reached across the table to me and held it in front of my mouth. I took a bite. I pretended not to notice his eyes almost burning me and licked juice from my lip to take another bite. It was very sweet. Almost as red on the inside as on the outside. Two-thirds gone. As I nibbled the edges around the stem, careful not to bite his thumb, I felt my face turning something much less subtle than maiden's blush. It was a yearning I felt, and almost a sense of shame, because he—and everyone—could probably see that I was *émoué*.

TODAY, AFTER MY SATURDAY morning Picasso class, he called to say he'd borrowed a car from someone at the lab. Could he come by after I'd put Claire to bed and take me for a spin?

My heavens. Three nights in a row.

I checked with Mrs. Haig-Ereildoun. She was vexed. "I told you I might need you to sit the children."

"I remember. That's why I asked. Did you decide to go to Mrs. Threshfield's?"

"No."

"Well then?" I asked.

"I've had them all *morning* while I let you go to your class, and I thought you might give me some relief in the evening."

"Simon? Tomorrow would be better. Will you still have the car?"

36

TONIGHT HE CAME AND picked me up in his friend's Renault.

This just happened. This very night. I don't *think* it was a dream.

"Where are we going?" I asked.

"You'll see," he said.

He drives fast. Everyone in London does. It scares me to death. And they drive on the wrong side of the road. Every time we came to a light I reflexively lifted my foot and jammed on the imaginary brakes on my side.

"Thank you for helping me," he said. His eyes. When they make fun of me.

Pretty soon we were on the A-whatever, heading out of London. It stays light incredibly late here. I think we're at a high latitude. And it's getting close to the longest day of the year. The puffy clouds were only just getting a touch of pink when we exited and found ourselves in a wooded place, on a road that meandered. He slowed his driving. A pebbled driveway led to a big metal gate, in a very tall fence. Simon parked. He selected a key and unlocked the gate.

"Where are we?" There was a strange cheeping sound in the air.

"Come along" was all he answered, leading the way up a tree-covered path.

The cheeps got louder as we got closer to what turned out to be a destination. The cheeps became shouts. In one of the trees I noticed a monkey, just sitting on a branch. As my eyes got used to the sight, I noticed more and more monkeys, in various trees.

I looked at them and looked at Simon. He was smiling down at me. Absorbed. I looked over at the first monkey, slowly, slowly scratching her knee. With a whish, another monkey flew through the air and landed with a thwump! The branch rocked. This second monkey, bigger, grabbed the first monkey's head. He pulled it. The smaller monkey fought the big monkey, and the big monkey smacked it. There were violent screeches, scarier than Mrs. Haig-Ereildoun. Much more violent. The tension, as they fought, froze me. I didn't take my eyes off them to look at Simon. Because there was something more than fighting going on. The smaller one was resisting, but she was so magnetized to the big one I could feel the pull in my own body. The branch shook and swayed, and it felt like the ground underneath me shook and swayed.

I don't have any idea how long the struggle lasted. Time stopped. The male took the female from behind and the fighting got rougher. I was afraid the branch would crack off the tree. The sounds they made were hideous.

Then, in a breath, they were still.

The branch swayed to a slow stop.

The two monkeys sat with their legs and arms around each other. Adoring each other. Picking fleas out of each other's fur. Again, the clock didn't tick. I'm not sure if Simon or I continued to breathe.

HE DROVE ME HOME. The sky had gone from baby blue to powder pink to almost fuchsia to starry black. Not a word was spoken.

37

YESTERDAY, BEFORE WE WENT to see the monkeys, I chopped vegetables and stuffed fish fillets and made Arabella Tuckett's *gateau cerise.* I worked fast and sweated and planned out how to tell Tedward about Simon. Not that there was anything to tell. But I thought it was about time to air this. I sometimes wonder whether Tedward would be all that upset to lose me, after all. In letting me come here, he must have known he was taking a chance.

After the afternoon dinner, a few minutes before Simon was due, I made my collect call. Instead of the woebegone, whining voice he's had almost ever since I've been here, his voice sounded happy. One of the main things that attracted me to Tedward was this music in his basso voice. You know how some people have a twinkle in their eye? That's what he has in his voice. Usually. Then it was gone. For a long, long time it was gone. It left way before I came here. Yesterday it was back. He had news. He's been asked to do a one-man show at a gallery on Maiden Lane! It's the one where we saw Keanu Reeves buy a painting for sixty thousand dollars. Tedward's show is going to be all nudes, which means I'm going to be in it. Disguised, of course. He makes my face and hair so different no one would recognize me. One person did, though, once. My old boss at the advertising agency. When a bunch of us went for a drink after work

I showed him one on the wall at the Iron Horse, and he said he'd know that body anywhere. I'm glad I'll be out of the country for this.

"When are you coming over?" I asked Tedward. His voice, when he's happy, is also sexy. I started feeling a buzz. August isn't that far away. He said he didn't know, now, when he could make it. The show opens August 23, and he has to have a dozen canvases. That means four new paintings, plus revising six others.

You couldn't imagine how much this means to him if you hadn't been dragged from gallery to gallery every weekend of the year, getting informal little lectures on this guy's technique vs. that guy's, gimmicks that so-and-so likes and Tedward hates, artists that Ted would give his "left bun" to paint like, and so on. I think spending all my spare time in galleries, hearing analyses, is one reason I was a little depressed last year. It was like having no spare time. Is this all there is, I wondered, for the rest of my life? But even if I can't share it, I respect his passion for painting. He paints from the time he wakes up (ten) until it's time for dinner. He has a studio on one of the piers, and that is his real home. That must be why he can stand to live the way he does, in his apartment. The studio is nice. Raw wood and canvas stretchers and paint all over everything, including Tedward. He wears an apron! Instead of looking like a Fauvist, he looks like a cobbler. But all these years he's been painting behind closed doors. Some of his nudes have hung in restaurants, if you call those places restaurants. They're the dark kind. To suddenly show at the Maiden Lane gallery is the adventure of his life. He says some collector, drinking in the Iron Horse, bought one of his paintings for a thousand bucks. He wanted to see more, went over to the pier, and one thing led to another.

"Who will you use for a model on the new ones?"

He said he'd found someone through the Art Institute. He says she looks the way I would if I gained fifteen pounds. He laughed with that lecherous leer he has. I didn't tell him I've already gained fifteen pounds. More, actually.

"So when will you come?" I said. I think September sounds a lot better than August anyway. Pru says it's hot in August. But I need to know these things. "I have to give Mrs. Haig-Ereildoun as much notice as possible, so she can arrange for another au pair."

He said September sounded great.

"I've heard it's the nicest time to be in Paris," I said to him. "The tourists are gone and the weather is lovely."

"Love-lih," he echoed.

I never did tell him about Simon.

I'VE BEEN THINKING A lot about Mots and Rupert's thought-ahead life, planning their summer vacation more than a year in advance. I'm so the opposite. I don't even know what my last name will be in September. In September he could so easily have some other reason to postpone his visit. For instance, his fear of flying. He could get a psychogenic rash so bad they wouldn't let him on a plane. I don't know what I'll be doing once I get back to San Francisco, except get pregnant. And if I know Tedward, he'll put that off as long as possible. I'll have to get a job. Advertising?

Maybe I could work for the *Chronicle*. I think I'd like that.

But then, I thought I'd like this.

I live completely in the moment. I'm sure that's why I eat so much. If I thought, while sticking my hand into the biscuit tin, of how much tighter my jeans will be next week, I might take my hand out of the biscuit tin before touching a biscuit. But who cares if my jeans are too tight?

I don't like getting this fat, though. I can walk around here fine, because the streets are flat. I can run up and down the stairs, because there are only four flights in this house. But when I get back to San

Francisco, I won't be able to make it from the bus stop up the hill to home, because I'll be huffing and puffing like Nanny.

I suppose Nanny lives in the moment too. She has no goals. Of course, at her age, nobody does. But she probably never did have any. Her life was charted out for her, without a lot of choices. She's probably never had a reason to look sensational, for a job interview, say, or even a prom. But think of how white her cardigan. How prettily fixed her hair. She cares about looking nice. It must bother her to be fat. But that doesn't stop her from preferring the pleasure of the moment when she's alone in a room full of food.

And then, she lies about it. A closet eater.

At least I eat openly.

Except in the middle of the night, like right now, when I start remembering how delicious those digestive biscuits tasted at tea. The sweetness is so subtle—so frustratingly not-quite-enough—you're tantalized at the same moment that you're taking your satisfaction. I think I'll tie on my dressing gown and feel my way down the stairs. I know my way very well, by now, in the pitch-black night.

WELL! THAT WAS SOMETHING. I was feeling my way down the banister when I hit a hand feeling its way up. Two screams rang out: mine, and Mr. Haig-Ereildoun's.

The people here must sleep like bears.

"Melissa!" he gasped. I tiptoed down and lit the light in his office—enough for us to see each other but not enough to be seen upstairs. (I'm experienced at this.) He was wearing his tux, carrying his patent leather pumps.

"Just going for a glass of warm milk," I said.

I think of myself as a person who doesn't lie, but I'm completely aware that I make exceptions.

Mr. Haig-Ereildoun is different from me. He skips the explanation.

After enough time to know I was safe, I did get a plate of digestive biscuits and brought them up here. No milk. Milk is full of calories.

ABOUT LIVING IN THE moment. Just about everything I do, I do spur-of-the-moment. Like coming over here to do this nanny job.

And now that I'm in this nanny job, I seem to view it as if it were my career. I work longer hours than I did most days in my advertising job.

But I never planned to make that a lifelong career either. When my old boss said, about the high-paid receptionist, Lenore, "It's the end of the line for her, isn't it," I did realize that perhaps my low-paying job would lead to a job paying more than a receptionist's. But the amount of pay didn't mean much. I just liked the job, for the moment, better than I'd like the receptionist's job. I worked hard because I had work to do. And the work absorbed me. Moment to moment. I never thought of any future beyond the next deadline.

Except. One possible future I did imagine was getting fired. I wasn't clever enough. You really, really have to be clever. Otherwise off with your head.

I was hired on a month's probation. The last day of the first month my boss called me in and told me, in effect, that I'd stopped the guillotine blade mid-slip. He said that in four weeks I hadn't earned even my paltry paycheck, as far as he could see. The management had decided to let me go. "And then last night I took home those three commercials you did yesterday. Genius!" He said his wife, who was right on, as far as our target market was concerned, couldn't resist these commercials. She wanted a carload of the product. My boss didn't know how I'd thought up the concept: *He* couldn't have come up with it, and he doubted if anyone else in the world could have in a thousand years. It seemed to me he was a little over the top. The commercials were okay.

I also hadn't realized that they'd made up their minds to let me go. We'd all liked each other so much. It had felt like a family.

They put me on another month's probation, and when they finally decided to hire me officially, I lived with a secret: You had to be "genius" and I wasn't. I always rang in just in time with something, and I fooled everyone by getting all those awards. But I knew sooner or later they'd put two and two together.

When they did, though, believe it or not I wasn't prepared. I couldn't have imagined the chemicals that would rip through my body. The residue they would leave.

I wonder if Mr. Haig-Ereildoun is prepared for those chemicals, and their residue, if he fails in his last chance to keep publishing. The sound that comes from his typewriter is silence. I resisted peeking in until one day, when I realized he wouldn't notice. Over the typewriter, his hands clasped the top of his head, a cigarette clenched between two fingers looking like a little white chimney. He took one hand off his head to reach into his bag of Pascall mints and, nervously fumbling his fingers, unwrapped it. It was quite a project, with one hand. He didn't see me, the mint, or the cigarette.

AT HOME THE ONLY thing that saved me, when my failure became clear, was Tedward. He would never dismiss me. In return for the certainty he has offered, I owe him the same certainty. I'm not sure if Mr. Haig-Ereildoun has, in Mrs. H-E, the same solid base that I have in Ted. If he lost his ability to support this family in even the on-the-edge way that he does, she might decide she's had enough. The silence from his typewriter reactivates all the fears I felt for myself every time I was faced with a blank computer screen. But at least I didn't have to worry about losing Tedward, too.

Certainty of love is an absolute need, as a home base. And here I am, a person who lives moment to moment, promising to give Ted that certainty in return for what he's given me. To marry Ted and his furniture. Of course, I have some sense of hope about getting rid of the furniture. I suppose I'm thinking ahead there, a little. But this promise to be true for the rest of my life. How can a person like me make such a promise?

38

"MELISSA." THE HORRIBLE, HISSING command tone. "Melissa, you're going to have to buy yourself a new pair of jeans."

"Why?"

"Because our trip to Crete is coming up. You'll be taking the children to Phillingsford for a long weekend, and I'm afraid I can't have you wearing those jeans. Not at my mother's house."

I didn't have to ask what's wrong with them.

Mrs. Haig-Ereildoun's eyes went over all my inches. I felt violated. When I was Claire's age, the pediatrician had stuck a thermometer in my bottom. I didn't have the power to squirm away from his horrid, unthinkable invasion. After, fuming in my crib, I thought up the revenge I would present to Dr. Fitch if he tried that again. This humiliation, and the rage rising out of it, were what I felt toward Mrs. Haig-Ereildoun.

This was my new pair. I'd bought them at Troonfachan at the end of March, the day we drove the ten-mile journey to the nearest town, because the jeans from California—well, they had shrunk. Even leaving the top three buttons undone to accommodate the fat pushing up from below (under all my sweaters, of course) didn't give me enough room. I think the weight gain has plateaued since we've been in London, but my intake of sweets hasn't. It's lucky that Claire can't talk, or everyone would know that on the way to the park, or

Mots's, I steer the pushchair up to one of those little corner stores where they sell candy bars. I can hardly pass a newsstand without buying some kind of sweet. I always give Claire a tiny bite, but not too much. I don't want to ruin her teeth.

The only thing that keeps me from rolling up an eleventh stone is all this scrubbing, vacuuming, and walking.

"You can pay for the jeans with your newfound wealth," Mrs. Haig-Ereildoun smiled. Her ironic smile. She sees the window envelopes arrive.

I PAID FOR THE jeans not with my nouveau riches but with my old money. I still have packets of traveler's checks. On the morning of my Cordon d'Or day, I walked all the way to the King's Road, in Chelsea. I love it there. Old Rolling Stone songs alternate with new Doll and Gun Show songs, in a swish of velvet capes, ripped jeans, rhinestoned lips, and Penny Lane trumpets.

Everything's expensive. But that doesn't bother me. The sizes don't bother me either. I don't have to be shocked that I need a size fourteen, because all the numbers are different here. Untranslatable. For instance, I wear a size three shoe.

I left the shop in my crispy new jeans, carrying my old ones in a bag. I may lose weight someday. Then I took the tube all the way to Threadneedle Street. It's in this financial part of London I hadn't seen before. Such different worlds, in this one town. Here all the buildings are massive, like temples to money. Dark stones, honed to a shine. Imposing columns. Everything quiet. I went to Threadneedle Street to deposit four hundred dollars in the London branch of Wells Fargo Bank. I could use any old ATM to get money out, if I were taking money out; but the ATM won't take deposits of dollars in a bank six thousand miles away. It was nice in Wells Fargo. The guy there said, "Howdy."

I can't get an English bank account. Mots laughed when I told her I was going to open a savings account at Midlands Bank, or Barclay's. "They won't take your money."

I turned to Rupert, who was born here.

"You're living in the past," he said to Mots. "It could be different now. One doesn't know. One already has a bank account."

Mots didn't know for sure, either. (She got hers by marrying Rupert.) She just said that she was pretty sure you had to have fabulous credentials to get a bank account. "They might give you one, if you had outstanding references, and if you could prove large assets. But it's quite an involved process. It could take far longer than you're planning to stay."

MONEY IS FUNNY HERE. One night at Phillingsford, Sir Chester had got on the subject of banking. "I know my overdraught has grown rather large when my banker asks me to lunch. We go to a restaurant, and of course money is a topic that never comes up. I know my overdraught is *dangerously* high when my banker asks me to supper."

Another night at Phillingsford, Sir Chester addressed me from his end of the table. "In America, anyone who likes can buy land, can't he. As long as he has the money."

Such a strange question. "Yes," I said.

"A dreadful practice. And I'm afraid it's now spread across the Atlantic." The volume of his voice was going up. His enunciation got the way I imagine Winston Churchill's went when he talked about blood sweat and tears. Because Sir Chester pronounced, "It takes more than one generation to make a landlord." He slapped the length of his palm on the table: "And that is a fact." Another resounding thwack of the palm, his forearm giving even more leverage to the second blow: *"That . . . is . . . a fact!"*

Who could buy land, then? Before our dreadful practice spread across the ocean?

I didn't ask.

AND I FIGURED OUT the Haig-Ereildouns don't live on Mr. Haig-Ereildoun's salary plus novels. I was just *imagining* a crucial need for the publising income. They live on the income from each of their inheritances. I happened upon this conclusion from a conversation with Mrs. H-E, and confirmed it by talking it over with Mots.

My clue from Mrs. Haig-Ereildoun came one afternoon after she'd been out with Mrs. von Tepliz. Mrs. v.T. loves a good gossip and can make anyone feel relaxed. Mrs. H-E seemed philosophical and a little dreamy as she sipped a cup of tea and watched me clean the refrigerator. She was in the same state as when she told me she liked Mr. Haig-Ereildoun's body. "I think that when couples have problems," she said, "it's very often when the wife has more money than the husband." She seemed to feel a kind of smugness about the happiness of her marriage.

So.

"Mrs. Haig-Ereildoun must have money," I told Mots. "And Mr. Haig-Ereildoun must have more."

"I should hope so," said Mots.

"What do you mean?"

"You can't live, in this country, without money."

I just looked at her. "That's true in every country."

"In this country the word 'money'," she told me, her dull pupil, "means inherited money."

"Do you know anyone who doesn't have inherited money?" I asked. (I know she has some, and that Rupert does.)

She thought and thought and came up with someone. "Yes! Rupert has a friend named Robert Pumphrey. Robert has no money.

His wife has no money. This is someone who went to Cambridge with Rupert. He went on to be a doctor."

"Oh. But he *makes* money."

"No," Mots said, patiently, "doctors don't make money here. Not like at home."

"But he's still a friend of yours? In your group?"

"Yes. But I feel sorry for Robert and Meghan. They don't go on holiday, they don't go to the theater, or to restaurants. Their children have to go to state schools. They can afford to give, I'd say, one small dinner party a year."

That was when Rupert came down from his study and asked if we'd like a brandy. Mots, who was ironing as usual, took hers at the ironing board. Rupert opened a huge cardboard box that had been sitting in the corner and began reading directions for assembling a swing thing for the baby. He showed us the picture on the cover of the booklet. The swing thing hangs from the ceiling on a spring. The baby can make it boing-boing up and down. Supposedly babies love these.

"Does Simon have money?" I asked Mots.

"Of course," she said.

"Why of course?"

"His father. You don't get to be an ambassador without a lot of pull. Which means, money."

"Then why doesn't he have a car?" I asked. "Why doesn't he have a phone?"

"In case you hadn't noticed," Mots said, "Simon is a scrooge."

Rupert, without looking up from his instruction book, said, "One doesn't like to show." He always defends his friends. "We don't own our car," he said. He has this funny, educated mumble. You have to work to understand him, but he's easier than Claire. "It belongs to the firm."

"I've heard," I said, "that a lot of people don't have dishwashers?"

"Of course not!" Rupert said. He seemed irritated.

"That's amazing," I said. "The Haig-Ereildouns have their own car and a dishwasher and a video, and they're poor."

"Poor!" Rupert said, not mumbling a bit. "That's ridiculous." He tossed his instruction book on the table and left the room with his brandy, not even bothering to put the box away.

"He's mad at me," I said to Mots.

"Oh, it's not you," she said. "He hears this sort of attitude from me all the time, and you're confirming it. Things were pretty pinched when he was growing up. For most people."

A new question hit me. "How is it that Rupert has money? His parents are still alive."

"They get it for their twenty-first birthday," Mots said.

"Oh. Everybody?"

"Well, everybody except Robert Pumphrey."

Maybe this rich-country-poor-country heritage is part of why Mrs. Haig-Ereildoun doesn't like me.

Yesterday, she got home from visiting an American down the street, a woman named Jackie Kelly, who once was Miss South Carolina in the Miss America pageant. This woman had been invited to the same country-house party the Haig-Ereildouns are going to for a weekend. Mrs. Haig-Ereildoun said to me, "You know that book you were thinking of writing about the difference between American and English?" (Actually, *she* had been thinking I'd write this book.) "Well, you're absolutely right. They're not the same language. Mrs. Kelly just asked me, about the party, 'What do you think I should wire?' I thought and thought. Wire? Finally I asked her, 'Why would you wire anything?' She looked quite shocked. Then she laughed and laughed. Eventually we put it together. She'd meant 'wear.' But she pronounces it 'wire.' "

About the party, Mrs. Haig-Ereildoun said, "I suppose it will be quite lavish. These people have masses of money." Then she gave an embarrassed look and almost whispered, in kind of a scandal-revealing hush, "I think it's *American* money."

39

I MUST SAY, SIMON is an honorable man. He's restrained himself from calling me. It's a shame that this sexual thing has had to enter into our friendship, because I miss him. Mots and Rupert haven't seen him either, but they say that it's normal for them to go months without seeing Simon. I won't be here many months.

"MELISSA DEAR, COULD YOU be an angel . . ."

Uh-oh.

"I overheard you on the pavement just now, talking to Pru. You used a word I've noticed you using before, but have hesitated to bring up."

I'm so glad I don't say "fuck" anymore.

"She asked if you liked her new shoes and you said, 'Totally.' You may not realize it, but you use that word quite often. Furthermore, you pronounce it 'todally.' I worry lest Claire pick it up."

She has already picked it up. It's one of her best words. "Ho-ha-hee," she shouts.

"I'd rather you wouldn't use it in front of her, or the other children, for that matter. It's not that I have anything against the Americans. Certainly not. But I do try to keep the children away from Americanisms."

Thank God they're going to Greece. Three weeks without her, and I may even recover.

It may be normal, or on the far edge of normal, that when she flies out in anger, my body goes into crisis mode. I think the major enzymes released have to do with fear. But the little insults, to me and my kind. And as Lord Chesterton wrote to his son, "A gentleman is never unintentionally rude."

IT'S TOO BAD THAT Mr. Haig-Ereildoun is almost always gone now. His schedule is all discombobulated. He flies to Brussels twice a week. He's working on the Euro and all the details of advancing the European Union. He's been excited about this United States of Europe idea since long before anyone did anything about it—since before he went to university, even. "It's the only way we can survive economically," he says he has always said. "I don't like it," Mrs. Haig-Ereildoun says. "I've never liked it. What I dislike most is having the professional standards and licensing of each country accepted across the board. So, for instance, if I should become ill, I might have to go to an Italian doctor." I must say, that sounds dangerous. French people don't like the E.U. because countries like Britain insist on putting a high tax on spirits and wine (to discourage sinning); the French view wine as food and think it's immoral to tax it. Mots doesn't like it because she thinks dogs with rabies might be let in. Even this microchip solution they've come up with, ensuring that a dog has current vaccinations, doesn't appease Mots. A lot of English people are upset about having had duties removed, because now they have to compete to sell their own products in their own country. An old man I met in Kensington Gardens said, "It was vexing enough when goods from the Commonwealth, like New Zealand butter, were allowed to be sold at a price that made English dairy products far too dear."

The Scots, though, are the most stubborn. If the bathwater situation makes me see that the English got used to being poor after the World Wars, the Scots were always poor. They say the common market, with more or less common prices in every country, makes everything too expensive. Even the mutton and wool they produce locally is sold to them "at Paris prices!"

"I understand your concern, Madame," I heard Mr. Haig-Ereildoun say on the phone today. "But our democracy is based on elected *representatives,* rather than delegates." (Pause.)

"Yes, yes. I quite understand. And I sympathize indeed." (Long pause.)

"You understand, though, Madame, the distinction between a *delegate* of the county and a *representative.*" He's very polite. He listens and listens.

"Yes. I'm painfully aware of the hardship. Acutely aware. There may be one or two more difficult years as things are sorted out. However, my responsibility is to see the long view, in as educated and sensitive a manner as I . . ." He held the receiver out and looked at it, then at me. "She rang off."

I'm in awe of his cool. And his unflinching candor. My idea of a politician is of a person much more devious and sugar-coating than he is. Especially when such droves of voters send him angry letters and postcards. You can't see his desk!

I'm very lucky, to be so close to this part of history.

Ahem. I remind myself of Nanny.

DID I ENJOY THE queen's birthday party? Yes. The Friday before, Mr. and Mrs. Haig-Ereildoun left for that house party—the people with the American money. Pru was picked up—off to stay at Camilla's country house. So I had Trevor and Claire.

I worried. One thing I don't write much about here is how

naughty Trevor is, half the time. How gleefully naughty. Also, Claire. I didn't know how grand lords and ladies might react if she took it into her head to march around shouting, "Shut up!"

So I was totally amazed. The night before the party, a hush of excitement. Trevor got all his clothes laid out (he never does that!) while humming what sounded like "My Country 'Tis of Thee"; and I suddenly remembered that melody also goes, "God save our gracious Queen . . ." Trevor got out the tube maps and rehearsed our route to Parliament Square, working out the times and suggesting that we leave early in the morning, allowing an hour to spare, just in case. He double-checked me to see that Claire's clothes were laid out, down to the shoes being polished. He reminded me that there would be hors d'oeuvres, and that I must be careful not to be greedy. Me?

"I don't think we'll meet her," he said. "But lest we do, do you know how to address her?"

"Your Royal Highness!" I replied, proud as Claire saying "hhheh."

"No. One calls her Mom."

"Mom?"

He meant Ma'am. "Everyone knows this," he said.

As soon as we walked up the steps and into the room where the guests assembled, we were greeted with great enthusiasm by almost everyone we were introduced to. No one said how cute Claire was, but everyone obviously thought it. With her hearing aid wires trailing to her pocket, she is the cutest of the cute. And there were many side comments to me about what a fine boy Trevor is. How well-mannered. Trevor! Everyone there knew the Haig-Ereildouns and were fond of them—especially of—guess who? Mrs. Haig-Ereildoun's public personality is convincing.

The down side was, the queen didn't actually come into the room. She just rode by on a horse, with a great long procession of bands, those tall furry hats strapped to their heads with chin bands. Some wore kilts and played bagpipes. There were sedate parties going on in all the fine apartments overlooking Horse Guard's Parade that gray, humid day. She probably went inside to one of them, after the ceremony, but she didn't come into ours.

When the festivities started, some people stayed in the drawing room, but we went out to the balcony to get a better view. The music swelled, and my heart filled to bursting. The importance of this. How I love this country. I was taking out my Kleenex when the woman behind me said, "My God this is boring." Everyone laughed.

My tears dried right up.

Once we were home, I wished for the first time that we were back at Troonfachan. Because if we had been, I might have written a note about it to Simon. Since we're in London, there's no reason to write. He might have been at the lab, but I decided not to call him. Instead, I wrote an account of the day to Harvey. This time it wasn't a column to be published, I just like telling Harvey things.

MAYBE THE WARMTH OF the guests at Queenie's party (Rupert and Simon call her Queenie) got my hopes up for enjoying Mrs. Haig-Ereildoun's long-planned supper party. Beforehand I fretted more than she did about the house. I've finally become nearly competent at dusting (almost "a dab hand," as Nanny would say). For the party, I did a terrific job. Unfortunately, though, I made a faux pas. Two days before, after I'd made the beds and swept, I decided I'd looked at that greasy yellowed pegboard and those tortured insects long enough. I took down all the pots and pans and scrubbed them. While they dried on the drain board, I stood on the cooker and used all my muscles to scrub away that guck. It was another warm day, and my clothes were drenched with sweat by the time I was finished. But amazingly enough, the pegboard turned out to be white. I hung the pots and pans back up and admired the miracle I'd just performed.

I then laid the table, and when I heard her come in the front door, all cheerful with Claire, I started setting out the lunch.

At the doorway to the kitchen she stopped. "*What* have you *done!*"

Oh. "I finished the cleaning early, and the lunch today is easy, and I had some extra time, and . . ."

She was furious. "Have you washed down the walls in all the children's bedrooms?"

What?

"Have you?"

She told me that thenceforth I must scrub the walls of each child's bedroom, as well as the nursery, every day. "They could be ill. I'm amazed you haven't been doing it all along. Unsanitary conditions in the room where children sleep can cause any number of illnesses. They might even be fatal."

I was shaken. As she went on about my having endangered the children's lives, I thought: At least I have Mots. I couldn't wait to tell her about the latest proof that Mrs. H-E really was "mental." But at Mots's, before I'd finished the first sentence of the story, she left the kitchen. When she came back with the iron, I finished the sentence. Mots didn't respond, she just left the room again. She got back with a basket of baby clothes, and I told her how hurt I'd been. She plugged in the iron and didn't look in my direction. "Well, wouldn't you be hurt?" "Mmm." When I tell Mots anything about Mrs. Haig-Ereildoun now, the only word she says is "Mmm." Thank God for my blue notepads.

And before I'd finished composing the first sentence about this incident for my diary, I figured out why Mrs. H-E had blown up on seeing her clean kitchen. I felt a rush of shame for myself, and of sadness for her. I suddenly remembered how I used to feel when my mother gave up nagging me to clean my room and stepped in and cleaned it herself. It was the ultimate humiliation. I felt sorry I had hurt Mrs. Haig-Ereildoun. I'm still sorry.

The day of the party she was gone before breakfast—to her mother's house way up in York. Late in the day she arrived with the station wagon full of flowers. I helped her get them in, bucket after bucket, then served the tea and went outside with Trevor and Claire while she arranged huge bouquets. When I got back inside, it was a new house. I swear, with roses and peonies filling each room, I couldn't see the grease spots on the chairs or the spewing upholstery stuffing. The caterer arrived with trays and trays of food, and all Mrs. H-E's smokie mousses had thawed, and the caterer set out the glasses; she did everything. In other words, I was a guest at this party. So was Mrs. Haig-Ereildoun.

The first other guest to arrive was Lady So-and-So, who amazed me by knowing all about me. "I understand that you're engaged to be married. Will the wedding be held in England?"

"Well, I'm not sure," I answered. I told her how we'd originally planned to be married at home, in February, but then a problem had come up, and we'd decided to postpone the wedding, and that we thought we'd do it in France, but that I actually hadn't been able to pin my fiance down to an actual date, because he was very busy with this art show . . . The more I talked, the more uncomfortable she seemed to be, so I kept explaining more details, to cheer her up, until she shook her head sympathetically and said, "Sounds rather dreadful" and walked off.

The next person to arrive was Mr. Heepton, father of Pru's friend Camilla. Divorced. Red-faced and triple-chinned. Mrs. Haig-Ereildoun had hesitated to invite him; I gathered he wasn't quite up to the guest list. In the end she'd decided to include him, because it would mean so much to him. Mr. Heepton's smile was so continuous that his manner seemed a bit un-English. He was absolutely thrilled to meet me. "And what brings *you* to this gathering?" When I told him I was the au pair, he beamed: "Wonderful! How do you like Engl—Hmm!" (He looked around.) "I wonder who else is coming."

Monsieur and Madame du Dordoigne arrived, France's minister and mistress of culture, a tiny tiara around her topknot and a brown silk cloak sheathing her elegant form. The wife of the UN delegate was also regal. She didn't talk to me. The only ones who were nice to me were the queen's cousin (called Adam), his wife (called Penelope), and their guest, whose name I can't pronounce or spell but who I spent most of the evening with. First, Adam. What a good-looking man. He told me San Francisco was one of his two favorite cities in America. "What's the other?" Detroit. That got laughs from everyone, especially me, and the question, "What do you like about Detroit?" For his answer, he had good stories—and summed it up with, "I suppose in the end the thing that makes one like a place is one's affection for the people one knows there." His wife, Penelope, is the only English woman in this set who I've seen wearing makeup. Makeup is, as Mr. Haig-Ereildoun might say, not on. But Penelope had the tiniest touch of gray eyeliner. These members of the royal family are, Mrs. Haig-Ereildoun once told me, the only couple they know who send their children to state schools. I'll have to remember to tell Mots that. Their guest, with the unpronounceable name, was being trained to rule a small kingdom in the Himalayas. Instead of a tux he wore floor-length red robes, with lots of embroidery and set-in jewels, and a red bejewelled cap. He was studying at some special institute in London. He spent the evening telling me about his country's absolute monarchy, and how the king didn't want a monarchy but the people did. This man in red had been delegated by the king to rule during the transition, where the hope was that the people would learn to like democracy. Persuading them would be his challenge.

Mrs. Haig-Ereildoun had told me that after supper, the women go upstairs to powder their noses and talk in the drawing room, and the men remain in the dining room to smoke cigars. ("Rather the way it was done in New York, when I lived there, except that there were no cigars. The men just went off to one corner and talked about business, or something, and the women congregated somewhere else, to talk about what interested them.") The husband was supposed to invite the ladies back down, eventually, to rejoin the gentlemen. She said Mr. Haig-Ereildoun tended to get so involved in the smoking room that he forgot the women until it was time to go home. So Mrs. Haig-Ereildoun had worked out a system where, at a certain moment, she could ring Mr. Haig-Ereildoun from upstairs and tell him the women were coming down.

Experiencing this phenomenon, of the men segregating themselves to smoke, was the thing I'd looked forward to most about a supper party. But I missed it. I was so engrossed in how this man in red and jewels hoped to convince his king's subjects that they'd like democracy that I didn't notice the women leaving the room, and neither did he. I didn't notice them coming back, and neither did he. We didn't even hear the phone ring. This man was not only the most beautiful, but the most interesting and intelligent of all the guests. The reason he and I spent the evening locked in conversation was that none of the English people wanted to talk to either of us.

I'D CALL SIMON, IF he had a phone. Well, he practically lives at the lab anyway, and I could reach him there. I just think he should call me.

WEEKEND BEFORE LAST WE had a picnic on the grounds of Windsor Castle in the sun. Last weekend our picnic was at Henry the Eighth's house in the rain. So funny, it was, to see all these English families with meals spread out underneath black umbrellas. Henry the Eighth's house has a maze of very tall yew hedges, and I lost Claire. Trevor, Pru, and I spent an hour finding her and losing each other. I would never go into that maze again. King Henry's house had a kitchen: a full basement floor, with room-sized fire pits, kettles suspended on chains, shaped like woks without handles, each big enough to hold a couple of cows. Maybe I should do some reading on historical recipes and send Harvey a letter about that.

I've now had four more window envelopes. Pretty soon I'll have the capital to open an English bank account.

CLAIRE CAN NOW PUT a few words together to make something like a sentence: "Heh-hah, hhhgho ah-*hay!*" (Trevor, go away.)

For the pronunciation, and other things, I've started taking her every other Tuesday (she skips school) to University College Hospital ("UCH" it's called), to see Miss Gilbert. We go on the Underground. Miss Gilbert has a strong stocky body and always wears gray. Her hair is gray. She makes me feel almost loved.

Sounds funny, but she does. She'd met Claire before, with her mother, and she can't believe the improvement. "You've been good to her," Miss Gilbert said, with great, energetic warmth. "I'm frankly amazed at her progress."

She tells me to hold a piece of paper in front of Claire's mouth, to teach her consonants. A "p" will make the paper fly straight out. A "b" also moves the paper in almost the same spot, but less emphatically. A "d" will blow the paper in another place, a "t" in the same place but more forcefully. It's sort of like what I've been doing by holding Claire's hand in front of her mouth, but the paper gives her a visual sense as well as a touch sense. She does like to see how her breath and her mouth movements cause the paper to move, but it doesn't take much of this to be enough. Which is fine. It bores me, too. I think it's a little like teaching someone grammar rules and verb conjugations before they have anything they want to say.

Miss Gilbert explained to me—actually by way of asking questions—a little more of what's wrong with Claire. Mentally. I didn't like to hear this. One of her questions was, "Does she often lash out and hit?" Once in a while, but not often. "Scratch?" Not since my first week in Scotland. "Kick?" Rarely. Only Trevor. "Bite?" No, thank heavens. Apparently being unable to communicate leaves a person frustrated, lonely, and aggressive.

I can attest to that.

"Does she seem to have vast amounts of energy, that must be expended if she is to be at all civilized?" Yes. "Not having words to work with gives one few thoughts to work with," said Miss Gilbert. "A normal person spends a great deal of energy thinking. Children even more than adults. Since Claire's ability to think is limited, she has an excess of physical energy. If this isn't spent, a kind of anxiety grows, and the length of a day becomes intolerable. One can almost grow mad." I certainly have noticed that about Claire. I just thought she'd inherited it from her mother.

"Does she often seem fixed on something you can't see, absorbed in something not apparent in her immediate surroundings?" Yes. "Children who don't have words tend to create a world of their own, in their heads." Miss Gilbert pointed her index finger at her own head and buzzed circles—international sign language for "nuts."

It's apparently *very* important that we teach Claire language, as quickly as possible.

It would be interesting to talk to Simon about this.

I'VE BOUGHT MYSELF THREE wedding presents. My grandmother sent me a hundred dollars for that purpose. The unspoken stipulation in our family is that if someone gives us money, we buy specific things and tell what they are in the thank-you.

The first thing I bought was at the cookery shop next door to the Cordon d'Or: a huge copper bowl for beating egg whites. It cost a quarter of what it would have cost at home. When I showed Mrs. Haig-Ereildoun, she looked at me pityingly. "You shouldn't waste your wedding present money on new things," she said. "They have no history. They won't hold their value." We were in the drawing room, and she went to the fireplace. "This was a wedding present," she said, picking up the little brass clock and fondling it in the palm of her hand. "My father's constituents went in together and bought it. It must have cost six or seven hundred pounds at the time. Now, I imagine it would fetch five or six thousand at least."

Huh. That plain little clock.

So last Saturday I skipped my Picasso class and went to the Portobello Road Market. At one of the street stalls I bought a copper colander that the owner of the stall said was Elizabethan. I loved to think of someone like Anne Hathaway using it, but what really attracted me was the colander itself. It was pretty, a little dented and with irregular-sized holes, and slightly misshapen domed screws holding on the hook, a heavy brass ring. At another stall I bought a copper kettle that the dealer said was "Georgian." One of my fellow customers, milling with the millions along the pavement, looked over to examine it and said, "Quite so. One can tell by the screws. Georgian." I suppose he meant the George who lost the American Revolution.

Tedward actually sold another painting for a thousand bucks. ("So I can pay my phone bill," he said.) Each time I talk to him he's more frantic about his show, which gets closer and closer. He complains, but instead of a whine, there's energy in his voice. I haven't told him about Simon because there's nothing to say.

. . .

I'VE HAD A LONG weekend off. Four days, because Mrs. Haig-Ereildoun couldn't spare me until I'd had six consecutive weeks on. I took the train to Stratford-upon-Avon and saw Anne Hathaway's house.

It's interesting that those words popped out on this paper: "Anne Hathaway's house." I saw two plays done in the way they were done in Shakespeare's day (no costumes, no sets, only minimal props); but what was really important was Anne Hathaway's house. Half-beamed, Tudor. Very low ceilings, because people were small. A huge copper kettle was suspended in the fireplace. Houses mean more to me than Shakespeare.

That's partly why I'm so upset by Tedward's furniture. That's also partly why I'm tired of being here. I want my own apartment to fix up.

40

SOMETHING ODD. Although he hasn't called, or been to see me, he's been here.

The one bed in the house I don't make is Mr. and Mrs. Haig-Ereildoun's. I never go into that room. But tonight, after my cooking class, I had to babysit (again). Pru was looking all over for her book of Greek mythology. I saw Mrs. Haig-Ereildoun with it this morning. She's started reading a little, probably skimming, doing homework for her trip. "Why don't you look in your parents' room?" I asked Pru. Oh, no, she said, it wouldn't be there. She thought she'd left it at Camilla's house. She absolutely positively had to have it. I said just let me see, and I went to the top floor, and on opening the door, what was the first thing I saw? The aged Greek book with the leather cover, the one with the ring from a glass circling the gold title, the one Mrs. Haig-Ereildoun had lent Simon. This was a long time ago. Before the monkeys. The night of the monkeys, he definitely didn't have that book with him. I met him at the door that night, and she appeared long enough for the two of them to exchange hellos, but no book. Now here it was, with its wineglass stain on the leather, lying open in Mrs. Haig-Ereildoun's bed.

Apparently she doesn't make her own bed. Why would she? She just gets back into it at the end of the day, hours before he gets home. The door to that room is always shut, so who's to know?

Much more important, though: How did that book get here, between the pillows and the sheets?

"Trevor? Trevor!" He was in the nursery, looking through a toy soldier catalog. "Trevor, has Simon been here lately?"

"Yes." He turned to a new page.

"When?"

"Today."

"Why did he come on a Wednesday? He knows I have my cooking class on Wednesdays."

"Can't say," said Trevor.

"Did you talk to him?"

"Not really. He and Mum were having tea in the garden when I got home. They were talking about a book. Mum asked me to do tea for Claire in the kitchen and exercise her, as she didn't have time. I taught Claire soccer in the street. She's really fast, Melissa. I got incredibly tired."

"Did Simon come out the front door while you were still playing?"

"Of course."

"Did he say goodbye or anything?"

"Of course."

"WAS MY BOOK IN Mum's room?" Pru asked.

Book?

"My mythology. Honestly, Melissa, sometimes I think Mum's right about you."

Honestly, Pru, sometimes I don't like you either.

I ran back up four flights and, of course, found Pru's mythology book on Mrs. Haig-Ereildoun's secretary. There was a bookmark in it. I opened to the marked page: the middle of a chapter on Aphrodite. Heavens, she is something.

Practically all evening I've been sitting with my hand on the receiver. I really should ring the lab.

What good would it do?

Just to hear his voice, to get some reassurance.

I pick up the receiver, listen to the honking English dial tone, and put the receiver down. I do this again. I do it again.

Yikes! My letter to Harvey. Simon sneaking over to see her behind my back (???) has me so rattled I almost forgot to be responsible.

My notes are in the kitchen. Which is handy. Because I'll need a biscuit or two to get going.

DEAR HARVEY, "Cookeeng ees about more than receeps and technique." These are the opening words of Michele Giverne, guest celebrity chef at the Cordon d'Or. "Cookeeng ees emotion."

When he announces, "Today I prepare a receep of foie gras," voila! Sounds of emotion—two kinds in the room. Sighs of pleasure from the professional cookery students in starched white chef's coats and black-and-white checkered pants. And from a couple of others—well-dressed London ladies in hats—huffs. Their chairs scrape, then their heels clack toward the door. To a lot of people foie gras represents cruelty to animals—and the English love animals.

The two women pick up their pocketbooks, and Chef Michele smiles. The smile seems to say, "I respect your right to your opinion." But it adds, "I feel sorry for you."

Real cooks have hard hearts.

One of the women notices, takes off her coat and goes back to her chair.

"We do not force-feed," he explains to those of us who remain. "This is a misuse of words. The goose see the food we offer them and run after us. They say 'give me more!' "

I've read that the keepers insert wire cagelike gadgets into the goose's throat, to enable him to consume an unnatural quantity of figs and prunes and milk-soaked bread, but Giverne doesn't mention it. "The goose is happy," he assures us.

"In France," the chef continues, "they like the foie gras from the goose whose papa is the Barbary (Bair-bair-eee) and whose *maman* is the Peking. Other countries like different races of geese. They remove the liver in different ways but it is always, as we are to find out, so fat it is like pure butter."

"Watch!" Chef Michele commands. He shows us how pliable a goose liver is by fitting a whole liver into a terrine as neatly as you would fit bread dough into a loaf pan. He puts that one in the oven for slow cooking. "No seasonings," he warns. "It taste good just as it come from the goose. No butter," he goes on. "Bake it, fry it, you do not want to use butter. The foie gras is fat enough."

"Cholesterol," comes a whisper from the audience. He overhears it and chuckles. "In all food, it is the fat that bring out the flavor," he scolds. "If you are cooking low fat, you are cooking in an 'ospital!"

Before moving on to show us his favorite recipe, he tells us, "The old chefs drown the foie gras in bechamel and bearnaise. Do not do it! And whatever you do, no cream! Simplicity is the best. A great natural ingredient should be enjoyed for itself."

He holds up the foie gras he's chosen for his favorite recipe. "Little is grade C," he says. "Then B. Biggest is grade A." This foie gras must have been grade A, because it is huge. It's almost impossible to believe that a creature only the size of a goose could produce such a gigantic liver. I think of a chicken liver, it doesn't fill a serving spoon. This goose's liver is hefty enough to fill a medium-size cast-iron skillet, a pink mound of plumpness.

Chef Michele smiles affectionately at the pan. "I like a cast-iron skillet." The way he says just those words conjures up a love in me for all cast-iron skillets.

His recipe includes a handful of special white grapes from the foot of the Pyrenees, some peeled and some not, "as the skeen of the grape add flavor to zee wine, so eet ees with zee sauce"; some baby capers ("nonpareil"), two handfuls of chopped fresh porcini mushrooms, a shallot or two minced fine, and a big splash of sweet Sauterne wine.

"First, I *cotay reesay*."

"Cotay reesay?" I got A's in French, and I'm proud of how much I remember. "Coté?" "Side." "Risay?" Something to do with rice? Risotto? My brain goes through a snarl of effort but luckily the Cordon d'Or's proprietor, Arabella Tuckett, is at the back of the class and saves the day. She can be a little snippy to her assistants and to her students, but she doesn't make it obvious now that she can't understand "cotay reesay." She just asks him a few questions. When she figures out what he means, she has the tact not to translate and embarrass Chef Michele about his English. Instead, she says to the class, "Did everybody learn that? When you go to apply for a job, you say you learned to cauterize the meat."

Sizzle! Steam! What a reaction when he eases the foie gras into the hot skillet. "You touch eet the meeeneeemum of time," he warns. "You turn only one time." The assistant rushes to hand him some tongs. He looks at the forceps with horror. "The enemy of French cooking!"

"Why do you say that?" Arabella asks from the back of the room.

"You know why? Because cooking is feeling. Your hands are your best tools. When you need others, choose them to be an extension of your own hands. When you poke with a fork, you feel, through the instrument, how the skin resists. And then, you know how much soft, how much firm, inside. It come through to your fingers." He explains that since the point of cauterizing is to seal the juices into the meat, he can't prick the foie gras with a fork. The next best thing for feeling is a spatula. He slides it under for one quick turn. "The meeneemum of handling," he reminds us.

By then the liver has shrunk a bit, making room in the skillet for the other ingredients. Tossing in the shallots, grapes, capers, and mushrooms, he lets them brown a moment. When he splashes Sauternes into the skillet to release a hissing cloud, he uses a spatula to get at the "jzoot."

"The what?" asks Arabella from the back.

"The jzoot. You know. The brown bits at the bottom of the pan. What is the English word for that?"

She thinks. "We call that 'the brown bits at the bottom of the pan.' "

Slipping the cast-iron skillet into the oven, he says, "There is no need to baste. Normally, basting is essential, it make the meat taste good, but foie gras have so much fat, it baste itself."

As the foie gras slowly cooks in the oven, Chef Michele takes questions. How often does he usually baste meats or chickens? Every five minutes. What nationality are the best chefs? "Not the French! They know everything. Very difficult. Me, I find Latin Americans make the best cooks. I think it is because they grow up with someone at home in the house and always the smell of things cooking. They have deep love for food."

The professional cookery students have urgent and more down-to-earth questions. "What do you ask a job applicant on an interview?"

"Usually it is 'What did you have for dinner last night?' "

That amazes everyone, even Arabella. "Why that?"

"Because what is most important to find out is a cook's feelings for food. The most vital quality is passion. Because in cuisine there are many 'tanshuns.' You know. Eet ees hot in the kitchen. If you do not have passion, you burn out."

The assistant has a stack of plates and a small knife. She dispenses slices the size of fifty pence coins, plus a spoonful of sauce, and with each serving a grape or two, a chunk of porcini and some capers. Oh, those brown bits! Specks of buttery crust from the foie gras membrane blended with the sweetness of the Sauternes, with the tang of those grapes cooked in it. The juicy fresh porcini is even wilder next to the zip of baby capers. The foie gras itself is so creamy it gives the teeth barely any resistance. That richness with a texture must be where the word "toothsome" comes from.

Each of us gets only two little pieces. Each of us could eat the whole skilletful. More! we yearn. The woman who'd almost walked out smacks her lips and he gives a wicked smile. We are all like those geese who would die for the pleasure of eating.

I LIKE WRITING. IT takes my mind off everything else. I didn't think of Simon again and I didn't hear the Haig-Ereildouns come in until they knocked at my door on their way upstairs. I gasped. My gasps are like Mrs. Haig-Ereildoun's shrieks.

"Mustn't concentrate so hard, Melissa," Mr. Haig-Ereildoun grinned, devastating in his tux.

"When you're so far off in another world," she scowled, "I fear for the children, lest a fire consume the entire house without you noticing."

I could see his nostrils twitch, smelling unpleasantness, and he disappeared up the stairs. She was wearing one of her silly long dresses. "I daresay you've smoked quite enough cigarettes this evening." I followed her eye to my ashtray, not exactly overbrimming. I'd smoked two cigarettes.

41

IN THE MORNINGS, WHEN I have the house to myself, I sometimes turn up the wireless and sing along, loud. Sometimes I splash the water in my bucket and vent my anger at all this maid's work. Washing down the walls of the children's rooms every day is a punishment I don't deserve, and today I worked myself up into quite a fury. I stomped down the stairs and *threw* my stuff in the broom closet. I slammed the door so hard I'm amazed the house didn't collapse.

"Melissa!" Mr. Haig-Ereildoun gasped. He was peeking his head out from his office door.

I screamed! I thought he was in Brussels.

He clicked his tongue at me, his eyes registering both shock and merriness.

SO. NOW HE KNOWS. I felt a thrill. It lasted all day. I still feel it.

42

THEY FINALLY WENT TO Greece. At first nothing bad happened except Pru broke her leg the first day; the next day Trevor came within a millimeter of being killed (I still hear the brakes, the screams, my screech, going on and on and on); later in the week Trevor and Claire got stomach flu and for three nights I had no sleep, running up and down stairs from bed to laundry room, a perpetual-motion machine, changing sheets. Then, just as relief set in, the nightmare. We lost Claire.

One day early on, just after Pru's being taken to the hospital and Trevor's nearly being run over, Simon said to me, "What are you afraid of?" When I didn't answer, Simon said, "Afraid they'll come home to a dead kid?"

I've lost my sense of humor. What he said was the clean truth. I was almost sick. I've been that way since the Haig-Ereildouns left. I close my eyes and see a street smeared with blood, body parts strewn. I squeeze my eyes shut hard and shake my head. Everyone on the block was rattled except Trevor. Every horn in Kensington High Street honked, the most blaring noise. People parked right in the middle of the road and got out of their cars to shout and shake their fingers. I honestly do think Trevor has no fear of death. He's lost in a daydream. A thought hits him that he should dart across the street, and he doesn't look to the right or the left, just shoots. He'll do it again.

Compared to that, Pru breaking her leg was ho-hum. I've always thought she shouldn't be allowed to ride her bike in London traffic. Luckily, I wasn't there for that one. She was over at Camilla's, and Camilla's mother got her to the hospital. It was actually a relief to get her tucked away there for a couple of days. Thank heaven for the National Health. And Robert Pumphrey, Rupert's doctor friend with no money. That poor man averages a ring a day from me. We've never met in person, but he treats me like his cousin.

Pru had just got home from the hospital, I'd just changed the nursery (ground floor) into a bedroom for her in her cast when Trevor said, "Melissa, I don't feel very well" and almost before the words were out, projectile vomit shot across the kitchen table. I put him to bed with a saucepan, to throw up into, and went down to the kitchen to have a look at Claire. Did she look a little white? I couldn't tell. "Melissa?" I ran back upstairs to Trevor, who said, "I'm afraid I'm throwing up at both ends."

And thus began the changing of the sheets. There's no dryer in this house. In fact, we don't wash sheets at home. A linen service picks them up every Wednesday and brings another load back. The turnaround's a little slow, in a crunch. The supply of clean ones is always low, and within the first two hours we'd run through the whole stack of single sheets and started in on doubles. About three a.m. Claire started throwing up at both ends too. By morning I had taken the sheets off my bed and the Haig-Ereildouns' and had put them on Trevor's and Claire's beds. I had wet sheets and diapers and pajamas and nightdresses spread all over the house, hoping some would dry by the time one of the children needed a new set but knowing they wouldn't. I called Mots. She has a dryer. And a car. (Even though Rupert's car belongs to the firm, he takes the tube and she drives.) She drove over with an armload of her own sheets, stepped in the front door, and said, "Pew!" She held her nose as we picked wet sheets off tables and chairs and sofas. She drove them over to her house to dry and brought them back, picking up a new load, etcetera etcetera, for three days. Mots has really worked hard for my pocket money this week.

Trevor got well, but Claire didn't. She stopped throwing up, but she didn't get well.

I don't know why God decided to spare Pru this sickness, but I take off my hat to Him. Also, it sure is lucky I didn't get sick. I worked on that part, though. Prayers every minute.

THERE'S A LAW IN this country that you can't leave children under twelve alone in the house without supervision. A law! And yet Pru and I needed food. Even if I'd had a car, I'd have had to leave them. But with no car, I had to run (!) up the winding streets and lanes to the tiny grocery in Binsbury Place, the shop that also has a post office in the back. There's only one person there to help you, and she's often behind the post office window taking care of people who need stamps. And she encourages stamp collection. She'll spend half an hour with a customer, pointing out which stamps are apt to be valuable a few years hence, and on and on, as more and more people cue up. It's not the kind of place where you walk the aisles, picking out what you need. It's the kind of place where you go to a counter and tell the woman what you need and she goes to get it. Then when she finally gets there to help me we have confusion. "I'd like a small jar of mayonnaise," I say, pointing to the small jar of mayonnaise. "We don't have small," she says, with hostility, because (I can only assume) of my American accent. "Yes you do," I say politely, still pointing. "That one is small . . ." She huffs: "That is the large size, Miss." Heavens. A tiny jar of mayonnaise. They buy everything in minute quantities here. But the clock is ticking. She asks for my basket. Basket? Oh, rats. They all carry shopping baskets here. The grocery store doesn't have a bag. So I run (!) home with my hands and purse and arms full of tiny jars and cans, chanting, as I run forward, "At my back I always hear . . ." and, as I dip backward to pick up a dropped jar, "Please, God . . ."

I don't know what would've happened if they arrested me.

But that leads to the worst thing. I've discovered something despicable about my character. Instead of being afraid that the children may suffer, may die, I live in fear of what may happen to me. My real concern all day, and each of the times I tiptoe into their rooms at night to see if they're still breathing, is myself. What I hear, in my mind's ear, are Mrs. Haig-Ereildoun's shrieks. "Can they sue me?" is a question I keep asking myself. Such a stupid question. What could they get? My six hundred dollars in Wells Fargo bank? My traveler's checks? I suppose the point is punishment. How bad will the punishment be?

SO. THE REAL TERROR. Claire.

By the way, Simon never did call me. When things got really scary, just the broken leg, the accident, the flu, the law I broke, I called him. He was a champion. He came over and helped me. Not with sheets. I didn't call him till that part was over. He just helped with moral support. And even though I had to miss my Cordon d'Or class, thanks to Simon I did get a letter off to Harvey. I wrote about buying cookery things in London, using Mr. Haig-Ereildoun's books about the history of furnishings to enrich the part about Elizabethan and Georgian kettles and colanders. Simon knows a lot about street markets that are better than the Portobello Road. I just took his word for it and wrote the things he told me as if they were first-person experiences. I think this was one of my best columns, because Simon is pretty funny. Without him, I could never have written anything that wasn't tense and morose.

He invited us all to the zoo on Sunday. Recovery had begun to set in for the children, and the weather was good. Simon borrowed his friend's Renault again and picked us up: Pru on her crutches, Trevor in the pink, and Claire with doctor's permission. Robert Pumphrey knew she had a fever of a hundred and one, but he said the fresh air would be good for her. The English are amazing about illness. The cure for anything seems to be a bike ride in the rain—any kind of exercise in the fresh air.

And fresh the air was. A beautiful day. At first it was great to be at the zoo. I could tell most of the people thought these must be *our* children, Simon's and mine. I suppose they couldn't have thought Pru was mine, or Trevor. But to someone who can't guess ages precisely—Simon could pass for thirty-five, maybe, although he's twenty-eight—Trevor and Pru could conceivably be his, with me as the young stepmother. Not the evil stepmother, either. I could tell people were thinking I was nice. Which I am.

Claire, though dull and out of it ever since her parents left, got a little hit of excitement, at first, showing off her vast vocabulary: "*Eh*-ah-fuh!" (elephant); "*High*-huh!" (tiger). "*Uh*-hee" (monkey). This was the first time she'd seen her friends from books in real life. I held her hand, Pru hobbled along happily, and Simon and Trevor walked circles around us, Simon pointing this and that out about the animals. Lots of facts we learned. Trevor, like Simon, is fascinated by facts.

We were standing by the monkey mountain, a big island of rocks in a lakelike thing, with waterfalls, I think. I had Claire's hand gripped, but I noticed something about one of the monkeys. "Look, Trevor," I said, letting go of Claire to point and say whatever I had to say about the monkey. When I reached down to take Claire's hand back, it wasn't there. I'm always on automatic pilot with Claire's hand, my hand and hers always re-clenching after a few seconds of letting go. When the hand wasn't there I looked for it.

"Claire!" I shouted.

Then everyone started saying, "Where's Claire?" Our feet stayed nailed to the spot as we turned our heads and bodies. There were lots of people, but no Claire.

"Let's break," said Simon, "and meet back here in fifteen minutes whether one of us has found her or not. Trevor, you go that way, Melissa that way, Pru over there, and I'll run round to the other side of the lake." We dispersed, all shouting, "Claire!" all knowing it did no good to shout "Claire." I can only speak for myself, because I was searching alone, but it took me only two shouts of "Claire!" to feel more frightened. I ran from person to person shouting, "Have you seen a little blond girl in a blue dress, with a hearing aid?" I assaulted group after group, interrupted dozens of conversations, feeling crazed. Nobody had anything for me but a blank look.

In fifteen minutes we met back at our starting place, everyone except Claire. We decided to make wider circles this time and meet back in half an hour. Simon went to find a zoo official.

"Have you seen a three-year-old girl, blond, in a blue dress with a hearing aid?" takes a long time to say. I said it so many times, so many times. The crowd seemed thicker, thicker, thicker. When we met back in half an hour, a zoo official was beside Simon, explaining why they couldn't make an announcement that would ring through the crowd, something about the PA system. Everything's always broken in England. Have you seen a blond three-year-old girl in a blue dress, have you seen a three-year-old girl in a blue dress, have you seen a little girl in blue, a little girl in blue, little girl in blue, girl in blue, girl, blue, girl blue? A beautiful, warm day, running, running. Sweat-drenched. Little girl in blue?

People take forever with their answers, raising hopes. But no. And yes! Running that way for the little girl in blue.

There are lots of little girls in blue.

Little girl in blue with a hearing aid? There are lots of little girls in blue, and people don't always notice whether they have a hearing aid.

IT WAS COOL IN the pachyderm den. Dark. Hushed. No throngs of people, just a handful. This was a man-made cave, doming a huge pit of water, a lake surrounded by steep walls of concrete, a slippery near-vertical pitch into slime with two-ton animals wallowing. Sharp horns. Wrought-iron fence around the hole. On the other side of the lake, no people, except little girl in blue with hearing aid climbing over wrought-iron railing.

I run! When I get a quarter of the way around the lake, she's in crawl position atop the rail. She looks confused as she tries to find a place to set her foot. There's no place, because the cement wall pitches down, down, into the pit. She's inside the fence, one foot on the solid rim above the pool, the other foot wagging.

I get to her just as she loses her balance and hangs in the air, one hand sliding down the rung. Through the rungs I grab her forearm. Grip it tight. Leaning over the rail, I get the other arm. Scrambling her arms and body around, I can't lift her. I hold on. Pull. She flails. Confused. I finally hoist her over the railing and hug her. When I look at her face and say, "Claire!" she doesn't respond. I bring her in close for another hug. "Claire! Oh, darling Claire!"

Eyes vapid. Skin pallid. No response.

I shake her gently.

Eyes vacant.

So I just hug and hug.

Outside, the light dazzles. Hugging Claire, I run and run. Were we supposed to meet back at the monkey island?

Nobody there. Well. Strangers.

. . .

I FELL ASLEEP HERE. It must have been about ten P.M. I started writing after I got Claire to bed, and I let Trevor and Pru put themselves to bed. I did go check, and they were angels. Breathing. Now it's about two in the morning. I wake up often in the night, scared. Scared of I don't know what. There are so many things to be scared of.

I remember one time when Mr. Haig-Ereildoun gave me a ride to Mots's, on one of those nights when he'd come home before voting and was headed back to the House of Commons. I prickle with anxiety when I'm with him, only able to talk small talk. This night (I say night, but you know how blue the sky is at eight-thirty), I chatted away about nothing as usual. The nothing I said was true: I never realized what a hard job it is to bring up children. "Oh," he said, shaking his head as he tore his car down Selwood Place at about a hundred miles an hour, "it is a job. I daresay, it is a job." How would he know, I wondered then. Now, now that the whole responsibility is mine for a few weeks, I really wonder: How in the world would he know?

"ARE YOU SURE THAT being deaf is all that's wrong with her?" Simon asked me. This was in the aviary, before we lost Claire. Trevor and Pru had taken her a few paces off, encouraging her to make peacock sounds back at the peacocks.

My reaction was hurt feelings. I wanted to say of course that's all that's wrong with her. I wanted to convey how bright she usually is. What a strong resilient spirit she has. At the moment, she has a fever! But she's been, honestly, so dull lately. She had that dazed look long before she got the flu. She didn't have it before her mother left. I tell myself that. But, you know how I tend to live in the moment. It's a handicap now. Because I see Claire, day after day, so mentally off. It's hard to remember the way she usually is and keep the big picture in mind. She is in a fog, she actually stumbles when she walks. She responds to nothing. It is terribly hard to like her.

I wanted to confess these feelings. I wanted to tell Simon all the things Miss Gilbert has told me. All the things I worry about. And then Trevor and Pru stepped back to where we were and we couldn't talk anymore. And then losing Claire must have rattled him, too, because when we got back to Lettering Lane he just dropped us off. Goodbye, goodbye. Goodbye.

My real fear (another of my real fears) is that Simon is beginning to feel about me the way I've been feeling about Claire. It may be hard to like me. The way I am now.

About Claire, I thought I loved her. The trouble is, I somehow seem to require something of her. I require that she give a response to me. When I love her, it's not only because she looks cute but because there's something going on between the two of us. When she's locked in this blankness, I can't find much to like. In fact, the way she is now, she doesn't even look cute.

I think Simon feels that way about me. Now. My nervous system has gone off, like Claire's. All the worrying I do makes me remote. I'm remote even to myself.

IT'S EASY TO BELITTLE the mother-daughter relationship here. I'm the one who's spent I forget how many hours a day talking, casually and deliberately, to her. I'm the one who's taught her most of her vocabulary. But that half hour of cuddling is a lifelong constant. Starting even before she was born. Who knows what indelible mysteries go on when the babe is in the womb. I'm a newcomer to her. I even think it's in Claire's consciousness that I'm here today, gone tomorrow. I think it registers that Trevor and Pru are constants, too, but she doesn't have that daily cuddle with them. Claire is addled without her horrible witch of a mum. The witch who turns soft when she cuddles Claire.

IT WAS AFTER SIX when Simon dropped us, slightly past time for my once-a-week call to Tedward, but still, I brewed a pot of tea for myself and spaced out for half an hour. Claire and I had a cuddle at the kitchen table, where her mum cuddles her, Mrs. Haig-Ereildoun probably lost in her own thoughts the way I was lost in mine. It wasn't till Trevor came into the room and asked if he could cook the supper that I came to. He wanted to do scrambled eggs. "Sure," I said. That got a laugh. They all think the word "sure," instead of "yes" or "certainly," is one of the funniest things Americans say.

Ready to rejoin the world, I set Claire down at her brother's feet and ventured into Mr. Haig-Ereildoun's office to pick up the phone. I told Tedward about Simon. I told him how much I like Simon. What a friend he's been.

Tedward sprang like a cobra. "Who is this guy?" (His tone said, who is this jerk.)

I tried to smooth his riffles, but the conversation progressed to the point where Tedward actually said, "I don't want him sniffing after my pussy."

I usually let words like that pass, cringing only internally. This time I told him I don't like that word and I don't like his perpetuating this misconception that he owns me or any part of my body. This time, we didn't end the conversation with "Love you."

TREVOR SHOWED ME HIS special way of scrambling eggs. I thought it wouldn't work, I wanted to tell him what he was doing wrong, but he worked so merrily that I just watched, amused. First, he takes a deep saucepan, the kind you'd use to heat up a few cans of Campbell's soup. In that he breaks two eggs per person (eight, for the four of us). With the yolks still bobbing around whole, he cuts about a quarter-pound hunk of butter from the pound slab and plunks it in to swim with the yolks. Then he pours in practically a pint of milk! He turns on the cooker, low, and stirs the whole thing with a wooden spoon. When the butter's a little melted and mixed in, he puts a lid on the saucepan. "I'll lay the table, too, Melissa. And warm the plates and make the toast. You can get Pru and Claire in ten minutes."

Ugh, I think, this should be an awful meal. But I love his enterprise.

And how wrong I was. These eggs were like a savory warm custard.

We were all congratulating Trevor when the telephone rang. I jumped like a cat. That's my reaction, now, to any unexpected sound.

It was Tedward. And it was, as the ring had made me fear, more bad news. He's coming over. He's made plane reservations for next week.

"Your show!" I said.

"Fuck my show."

"Don't talk that way." I never liked that way of putting things before, but now, being free of it for so long, it sounds unspeakably ugly.

"You'd better cancel your reservations," I said, "because I won't be here."

This is true. We're going to Phillingsford next week. I can't tell you how much I'm looking forward to it. For one thing, I'll have the support of Granny, Grampy, and Nanny. But it's even more than that. I feel so honored, because Sir Chester and Lady Chipchase have actually invited a young American couple they know, both professors at Wellesley, to be there at the same time. In fact, this couple is picking us up and driving us. "I think you'll enjoy them," Lady Chipchase said on the phone. "I'm quite certain they'll enjoy you." I was flattered pink.

Tedward, with his terrible language and his hicklike manners, would ruin the whole thing.

I didn't get specific, just told him we were going to be in the country.

"With that prick?"

I felt drained of blood when I went back in to my cold scrambled eggs.

I'VE BEEN HELPING TREVOR write stories, for school. I don't think it's right to write his stories for him. The way I help is not even to say, "You could write about an Iroquois boy" or "You could write about Claire getting lost at the zoo" but to ask questions. "Has anything scary happened to you lately?" "Have any of your books taught you about something that you'd like to delve into, with your imagination?" The Iroquois boy is what Trevor came up with when I asked that question. Losing Claire is what he came up with Sunday night, after Tedward rang.

He usually thinks up a range of subjects before he settles on one. When he's chosen, I sit with him as he speaks each sentence, before committing it to his lined composition paper. After the last word (always "Finis"—he likes to end each story with Latin), I sit with him as he grinds his teeth and tells me how much he dislikes the story. "It's not good enough!" he says. "I want a moral story. I want people to learn something about life from my story." The more I tell him how good I think his story is—that I've learned something about life from it—the more stupid he thinks I am. He stomps around the room. "It's *not* good. It's not *important!* I want to write something with *meaning.*" He seems about to cry. He says, "Melissa. I want you to write my story for me."

"Then it wouldn't be your story."

"But it would be better."

"No, Trevor. Your story is better than anything I could write because, in the first place, it is good. And in the second place, very special. Because it comes from you."

Sunday night he whined, "I wish my mother were back!" He banged the hard soles of his shoes on the linoleum as he marched off to brush his teeth. "Mummy would write my story for me." He didn't speak to me again until he was under his covers.

"Melissa?" he called out. I went upstairs to kneel by his bed and he threw his arms around me. We locked, and rocked, and chuckled.

SINCE THE HAIG-EREILDOUNS LEFT, I've only once or twice fallen fully asleep for a few hours. It must be an instinct, to keep one ear open. I leave my door wide open, and the hall lights on, as well as the light in Mr. Haig-Ereildoun's office, to scare away the bad guys. That way, I can half-sleep. At about three A.M. Sunday night, a blast rang through the house. Ring-*ring*! Ring-*ring*! These English phones are like nightmare alarm clocks.

Tedward, of course.

Sometimes I wonder if God really listens. Because Tedward had calmed down. He apologized. He said it probably wasn't a good idea to come now, so soon before his show. (He didn't mention his fear of flying.) Still, he wanted reassurance about Simon.

That was easy. "He's never touched me."

"Not once?"

"No." I sort of lied. I couldn't see any reason to get technical.

"But will he?"

That one was harder. It doesn't look like he will, but I couldn't put it that way.

The silence while I tried to phrase my answer got Tedward jumpy all over again. "Okay, I'll be on the plane after all."

"No, Tedward, it's not that way."

"What's the matter with him? Is he gay?"

Aha! An opportunity. "I really don't know," I said. "He could be. I don't know that much about him." This was certainly the truth.

"Are his wrists limp?"

"No!"

Tedward laughed. I laughed. "He lisps, though," I said.

"With an English accent?"

"Mmm," I said. "Quite thoh."

We ended up laughing, and the whole memory of how much I used to like Tedward, of how he makes me laugh, melted through me like butter on toast. After we'd rung off, I fell almost sound asleep, for the first time in weeks.

43

PHILLINGSFORD. BLUE SKIES, SUN on the bricks. Roses climbing the walls. Roses reflected in that mirror bowl in the circle of lawn the drive wraps around. Posy-lined paths winding all through the grounds, the paths as pretty as what they're leading to. Phillingsford in summer is like the world's biggest flower arrangement.

At the moment, everyone's playing croquet and badminton (there are lots of people here), and I've come up to my room to write a letter to Tedward.

For Tedward, I made a sketch of my room: They've put me in the Blue Room this time. The blackened brass plate on the hearth says "1599." So it must have been one of the earliest fireplaces in the house: an important room. It's big, with windows looking slightly to the back (the aviary) and to the side (the arbor just before you get to the badminton court). The arbor has a long straight path, the whole length arched over by a trellis dangling bell-shaped flowers to make a ceiling. I look down on the top of that, and the foliage leafing out beyond it. My Blue Room has lots of Chinese carpet between each piece of furniture. I love the furniture. This desk is very old, very waxed, walnut. (I think. I think I'm getting to know walnut from oak.) The legs bow out, really graceful. On top of the desk, as if built-in but not, is a box of the same waxed wood, with a lid curved like a bass clef, opening to compartments for pens and paper and whatnot. I see desk boxes like this in the antique shops and the market stalls, with huge pricetags. No pricetag here. This is free. It's in the setting the antique dealers got these boxes from. The customers probably hope to evoke, in a vignette, a setting that harkens to this. There are blue-and-white pots of rosy-red cyclamen on either side of my bed, and one on the coffee table in front of the settee facing the fireplace. The blue and white pots are not antiques, I know, because I've seen the exact ones in the Conran shop in South Ken: they're from Portugal. Cheap, too. And so pretty. It's hard to imagine Lady Chipchase shopping in London. Maybe one of her daughters-in-law gave her these blue and white pots from Portugal. On this desk there's a small crystal pitcher (old, I'm sure) of just-picked anemones, each flower like a face.

The first moment I had free here, I sat at my desk, took a pen from the waxed walnut box, and wrote Tedward that as soon as I get home, we're going to have to start looking for a house again. I want one just like this.

Of course there are no houses like this in California. Even if there were, Tedward would have to cash in his whole trust fund. I don't think he's allowed to do that. But I'd be happy with a house with just one room like this one, and a garden like just *one* of the gardens here. (The gardens at Phillingsford are like rooms. Walls of hedges.) Actuallly one garden like one of these wouldn't be impossible. I'm remembering some of the houses we didn't buy, in Sausalito. Beautiful houses. Not like this, but beautiful. Bay beyond. As Mr. Haig-Ereildoun said, San Francisco may be the most geographically blessed city in the world.

Ah, but Phillingsford.

Yet. I long for home. My own home. Maybe, with some of Harvey's money, I could get a box like the one on this desk, to take home and create a vignette. I wonder how my English vignette would fit with the pillows I made out of coffee sacks. It will take some thinking.

And of course, it will take real genius to find a way to get rid of Tedward's furniture.

If we don't get a good enough house at the moment, we will have to get a bigger apartment, anyway. (Don't worry. I didn't broach this in my letter to Tedward.) But my mind is work-work-working away. If I could work for Harvey, I wouldn't mind working. And we could safely rent a place with two bedrooms.

We'll need two bedrooms, because Nanny is coming.

It turns out she's barely spent a half penny since she started working for the Chipchases at the age of fifteen. I wonder how many pounds she got a week, by the end of her working days. More than me. After all, she was a proper nanny. They earn more. Invested, this could add up. Oh. But Mots told me Engish people didn't buy stocks until recently. Not ordinary people. Maybe it took even more credentials to buy stocks than to open a bank account. Or else they just didn't think of buying stocks. The mentality used to be very excluding here. Oh well. Nanny says she has enough savings to get to San Francisco. She has enough to get to Australia! That's where she wants to go. Her brother is there. He's offered to pay her way, but she says Piffle! She'll pay half. She'll stop off in San Francisco, and since we've invited her, she can stay as long as she wants without the expense of a hotel. "An hotel." Everyone here says "an hotel," not "a hotel." They really are closer to the French, in many ways.

Tedward and I will have some logistics to work out, like the guest room. (Nanny can't sleep in the living room!) But there'll be time. She thinks next spring.

THE WELLESLEY PROFESSORS, CAROL and Phil, make dinner so much fun. He's history, she's French lit. They stimulate Sir Chester and Lady Chipchase. Sir Chester tells his old chestnuts ("How does a porcupine make love?—Ved-hih, ved-hih cah-ful-lih") and Lady

Chipchase chuckles and turns pink, as if she's never heard the joke. Mrs. Haig-Ereildoun's young brother, the unmarried one whose room I slept in before (the plaid one), is here now. Sleeping in the plaid room. I'm not sure I like him. Also, the oldest brother, Harry, who'll inherit Phillingsford by primogeniture, is spending his days here, with his wife and their four children. The middle brother is here too, with his wife and their four children. They normally live in Surrey. So the nursery is filling up: seven children to sleep, plus Nanny plus two young nannies. The middle brother must have done well, to afford two nannies. (Harry's four children, of course, sleep at their own house, across the fields.)

Must go out and play croquet. Or badminton. Or tennis! Did I mention the tennis courts? They're not all cracked and mossy like the one at Troonfachan. I've brought my racket.

ON THE WAY UP, Carol and Phil wanted to hear about my advertising career. They're quite a bit older than me, but younger than the Haig-Ereildouns. They're eastern (Connecticut and New Hampshire), but they're Americans. It's a relief.

I told them I felt guilty, working in advertising, but it was the only writing job I could get.

Guilty? Why?

Well. I told them about my favorite teacher in college. Mr. Hanzo. He's the one who changed my life, by stunning me with the fact that I could write. He somehow gave me license, by his appreciation, to take extra time and do my best on every assignment, not only in his class but in every class that included writing. So even in zoology, even math, I got A's every time we had to write a paper. My professors ended up reading my papers to the entire lecture hall. Thanks to Hanzo, I changed from a C student into an A and D student. One day he read one of my papers to the class and shook his fist. (I only heard about this, because I'd cut class that day.) People told me he said, "*This* is the kind of student I've wished for! Someone who understands James with depth and spirit!" This same professor arrived late to class another day. (This day I showed up.) He was in another one of his passionate rages. He'd just come from a lunch with some alumni, a group of men who'd done quite well—in advertising. The four of them were donating some money to the university, so Hanzo had to be nice to them. "Do you realize!" he ranted to the class, when he got there. "There are people in this country who earn a *living* by trying to convince other people that one *toothpaste* is better than another?"

Carol said, "Why is that worse than earning a living trying to convince people that one novel is better than another?"

TODAY SIR CHESTER TOOK me to a house he owns, on the edge of his acres, a house he lets. He's between tenants at the moment, so he's fixing it up. He's so old, and so aristrocratic, it's funny to see how he loves to work with his hands. At Phillingsford he spends hours a day in his own special room with a table as long as the dining room table, building ships in bottles. And now, this little house. He was going there, in his tweeds, to rewire it. Himself. Most of the refurbishing was finished (a lot of it by him personally), but he brought some lighting fixtures and copper wire, and new plugs.

I had to scrunch to get into his sports car, a shiny red Jaguar. He keeps it in what used to be the stables, below the apartment they've converted for Nanny. The old stables are brick, with arched openings for doors like big gates. The car speeds! His long body fits into it lithely. He puts his cane behind the seat so he can man the gears with flourish. We purred across the wolds. The road was normal (asphalt) until we got to the drive winding through trees to his rental.

There we hit cobblestones, and through an opening in the thicket we saw . . . wow.

It was almost exactly the house I saw in the You're Out Walking game. Describe the house. It's an old house, English. Thatched roof. Half-timbered. Pretty garden. This was that house.

It's Elizabethan. I learned today from Sir Chester that the little dormers that peek out of the roof are called eyebrow windows. They are shaped like eyebrows, little curve-topped slits cut into the thatch that slouches over the housetop like a hood.

Inside, my head almost bopped the beams. Sir Chester had to stoop like a hunchback. Funny, to think that people in Shakespeare's day were so little. Think how small the aristocrats who lived in Phillingsford (also Elizabethan, therefore short) must have felt, with rooms so big, ceilings so high. I wonder if the aristocrats built houses like Phillingsford to make themselves feel bigger, or to cut themselves down to size.

Sir Chester worked with his wires, and I dreamed. This is my house. Much, much more exciting than Anne Hathaway's house. Hers is a museum. This one is real.

I didn't ask how much is the rent.

I'll have to write Tedward. In fact, maybe I should call. Collect. I'm sure the trust fund could easily mail his check here, every month. He can paint. I can write. In between, we can garden together.

But about babies. I'd like to wait a while. I'd like to recover from this. I now know that having children is much more work than working.

I JUST CALLED TEDWARD. Collect. Even though it's the middle of the week. "You've got to come right over!" He thought I was crazy. His show. His finances, because of the phone bills. He said the trust fund couldn't afford a trip to England.

. . .

THE YOUNGER BROTHER. HUMBERT. Plaid bedroom. I think people are thinking Humbert and I might be attracted to each other. They don't know me. Disloyal is one thing I am not. Besides. Humbert.

We found ourselves alone in the morning room today. Afternoon, not morning. The sun, by the P.M., had gone somewhere else. Still, the light was pretty. Long shadows outside. Humbert sat in a chair with huge arms, resting his hands. He pointed out which things were Chippendale, which were Sheraton. His voice showed awe, but I think also something like greed. I've glossed through some of Mr. Haig-Ereildoun's history-of-English-furniture books, but they don't touch the subject of prices, except to make it clear that Chippendale and Sheraton are in demand. Which fits in with Humbert's air of gloating. Trouble is, he's the youngest. I don't think he'll get any of it.

After going over most of the pieces of furniture, as if reading from a catalog, Humbert had exhausted that subject. Especially since all I could add to the conversation were words like "Mmm!" and "Oh!"

He said, "You haven't any great writers in America, have you."

"Huh?" I said. Or something like that.

"I mean, your culture has never produced one."

Huh?

"I wonder what the reason is," he said, fingering one arm of his chair.

His statement, about no American writers, didn't make me feel defensive. I just wondered. "What do you study, in England? Do you read any Hawthorne or Twain or Hemingway?"

"Rather not," he said.

"Emily Dickinson? Edgar Allan Poe? William Carlos Williams?"

"Who?" he said. His nose seems permanently tensed, as if everything smells bad. "Not on, I'm afraid."

"They're pretty good," I said.

"Mmmm."

"You might want to try one." I wasn't feeling combative. I was actually wondering to myself if these writers would hold up to his standards. As for his standards, I must have read them. Milton, Pope, Shakespeare, Defoe, Austin, the Brontes, Woolf. Of course they have more of them than we do. But we have some. "You haven't read Hemingway?" I wondered if he might concede a little.

"Mmm. Can't say I've had cause to read the Americans."

"Mmm," I said.

"Can you speculate," he asked, "why your country has contributed so little to the arts?"

Mmmm. "Maybe we're a new country. So much energy has gone into setting it up. Most of the people who first got to our country came from your country. I once read that Jefferson, I think—have you heard of Jefferson?" (He nodded.) "Jefferson or someone said, 'We are farmers, so that our sons may be doctors, and their sons may be artists.' Maybe it takes a long time."

"Mmm," he said. Then he said, "How far back can you trace your family history?"

Gosh, I was glad he asked. Not one person has ever asked me. In America (or, I should say, in Oregon or California—I now know I know nothing about America), no one has ever asked me one thing about my fabulous pedigree. If they did, they'd probably respond the way I responded to Humbert's Chippendale and Sheraton.

I eased into my answer, so as to seem humble. "Well, on my mother's side, we're Norwegian. People don't keep much track of these things. I do know we're descended from King Cnut, and from studying history with Trevor, I understand he was a good guy. He ruled in England, too. Long time before William the Conqueror got here. But the Norwegians don't seem to care a lot about nobility.

Royalty and regular people marry each other all the time. Probably everyone in Norway is part royal."

His eyebrows twitched up, but not much. He sat smug, making circles on the arm of his chair by, no doubt, Chippendale. If Chippendale made chairs.

"But on my father's side," I said, "we're English. And all the branches have published thick books of genealogy, weighing about four pounds apiece. So I know that, on his side, all four great-grandparents go back to William the Conqueror."

Humbert's eyes, half-lidded, widened a notch.

"How far back do you trace your family?" I asked, completely sure that the Domesday Book doesn't go further back than my pedigree.

"To William the Conqueror," he said.

I've been wondering how sweet, pink Lady Chipchase could ever have given birth to people as competitive and therefore wimpish as Humbert and Philippa. Those two begin to strike me as bad losers.

As for Lady Chipchase, the trip to Sir Chester's Elizabethan cottage and the time in the morning room with Humbert and the tennis games and Nanny's marmalade lesson in the kitchen (I haven't mentioned that yet) are all her doing. She's the fairy godmother. I'm not sure if she knows how badly I've needed a vacation. Lady Chipchase has had children, but she's had a nanny and undernannies, so I'm not sure if she knows how hard it is. I can't imagine that anyone could have the imagination to sympathize completely.

I remember how she used to watch me. Worried I'd be a zigzag eater. Possibly worried, I now have to admit, that I'd seduce Mr. Haig-Ereildoun.

She still watches me. I catch her at it all the time—but now she gazes with a different expression on her soft face. I catch Sir Chester watching me too. Today I was in the entry hall, or whatever you call that huge room at the bottom of the staircase, holding Claire in my arms. Claire has pepped up, being here. The fever was still over a hundred in London, when we all got in Phil and Carol's car, but the morning after we arrived at Phillingsford the thermometer came out a touch below normal. Today, as she wrapped her arms around my neck, my arms supporting her back and behind, we were talking, I with deliberate lip-speaking and she with exuberant gutteral gibberish. Lady Chipchase and Sir Chester were watching and listening. I saw him touch her shoulder.

44

MOST THINGS ARE GOOD here, but two things are bad. One of them is my fault, but I tell myself I have no control. The other is not my fault, but I feel guilty.

First, the one that's not my fault. It's the nannies. After I've bathed and dressed for dinner, I go into the nursery, looking nice, and help Nanny and the young nannies (proper nannies—they wear uniforms) get the children ready for bed. I take orders from Nanny. "Do all you Americans use half a tube on your toothbrush? You're in England now. Don't you let him do that!" To Trevor she says, "Waste, my pride and joy, is very un-English." The young proper nannies are more subtly bossy. ("Melissa, Claire is washing with Pru's flannel.") I usually have time to let Claire read me a story (that's how we do it—an opportunity for her to show off her words) and get her tucked in with a dozen other books. By then all the toddlers and babies are down and the older children are settled at their various before-bed doings, and one of the young nannies fixes a pot of tea for us all. We're all getting into a chat, usually about our boyfriends ("we say beaux!" Nanny corrects)—and even Nanny had a beau once. The gossip is just getting good when the knock comes at the door. Mrs. West. "You're wanted downstairs, Miss." To me.

Silence fills the room.

I feel sunken with shame as I follow Mrs. West down the back stairs, through the kitchen and dining room into the drawing room. All along the way I tell myself it's not my fault I'm lucky. And it isn't. I tell myself at least this isn't *my* system. I'm American. And then I step into the drawing room, thank Sir Chester for my cocktail, and I don't give another thought to the nannies exiled in the nursery until the next night, when it happens all over again.

Simon once told me Americans are the only people in the world who feel guilty about not feeling guilty.

NEXT. THE SHAME I supposedly could do something about but can't seem to. The cookie-thief thing. Every night, when everyone's in bed and I'm alone in the Blue Room, writing on my blue paper, I start thinking about all the pudding that was left over after supper. Always we have something incredible—like Mrs. West's gooseberry pie, or the apple charlotte she made tonight, with that English double cream, so thick you have to scoop it out of the pitcher with a spoon. I even like the treacle pie we had at tea. In fact, I like treacle. Right out of the crock.

It's a long walk to the kitchen, and the old floorboards upstairs groan through the silence like bagpipes. I tiptoe, in socks, wearing my coat over my nightdress, my heart thrum-thrumming. I grip the banister and, wincing at all the noise I'm making, put my foot forward to feel for the steps. twenty four, twenty-five, twenty-six. Once I hit the ground floor, it's safer. The floorboards hardly creak. I'm getting expert now at feeling my way to the dining room, the kitchen, the two pantries. Mr. and Mrs. West sleep in a cottage past the aviary, so no one on the whole estate can see if I turn on the light in the second pantry. Usually I don't do it anyway. I can see pretty well just by keeping the refrigerator door open.

Can you imagine what would happen to me if I got caught?

. . .

I THOUGHT THAT WRITING this might have some effect on my conscience. Instead, it whetted my appetite. I couldn't find the apple charlotte, but I must say. Treacle is a treat.

And I did resist one temptation. There was a small bowl of beautiful eggs—four of them—stone-colored, with speckles. They looked like big, smooth, egg-shaped pebbles. I'm almost sure these were the duck eggs Nanny told me about. There just happened to be a little saucepan near the sink, and a loaf of Mrs. West's own bread in the breadbox. Even the bread knife was handy. I was dying to try one of these little eggs, on a piece of toast with some butter. Are the yolks really orange? No one would find me out. I actually put the water on and stood licking the treacle spoon till the water bubbled. Those eggs had to be for Mrs. West's secret feast with Nanny, but if I ate one, there'd still be one and a half for each of them. This might be the only chance I'll ever get to taste a duck's egg, I reasoned. Then my conscience came to my rescue. I emptied and dried the saucepan and put it exactly where I'd found it. I crept upstairs actually feeling a little virtuous.

45

THE DEW IS STILL drying on the croquet court. The peonies are opening, doing their morning stretch to the sun. Keats's globèd peonies. I must say, I'm not glutting my sorrow on the morning rose today. Today the morning rose makes me nothing but happy.

Nanny is having a lie-in, but the two younger nannies have the children's mallets hitting the ball instead of each other. Pru is entertaining everyone by using her crutch to knock the ball. It's all peaceful. I can sit out here and write. I'm warming up for my letter to Harvey.

Since I had to miss the Cordon d'Or, I'm going to write Harvey about Nanny's marmalade lesson, yesterday in Mrs. West's kitchen. I doubt that anyone in San Francisco has ever seen as huge a kitchen as this. Miles of tiles, light green and white, some of them chipped—this kitchen is old-fashioned and not pretty. The window looks out on the kitchen garden, which is also large and functional and not pretty. I hope I can paint the picture, the rows of vegetables outside and the lines of jars filling up with the bitter richness of Nanny's marmalade. It starts out orange, and sweet, and liquid, but it ends up bitter, thick, and brown. The more you cook it down, the less sweet it gets—and the less orange. Nanny says she tells everyone the secret is Seville oranges, but she confides to me that the real secret has to do with bravery—daring to let the concoction in the kettle get as close to burnt paste as you can without actually blackening it or turning it to glue.

So. I switch to my other notebook, and, tah-tumm! Here goes, Harvey: Nanny's Risky Brown Marmalade.

I STARTED TO WORRY when Lady Chipchase didn't come to dinner.

"Nonsense!" blustered Sir Chester. "Your grandmother is in the pink of health. She's simply in her Florence Nightingale mode. As you know, she's famous for it. Always insists on sitting with anyone who catches a bug. Manning the teapot. Preparing her dreaded milk toast."

"Who's ill?" asked Pru.

"Nanny, I'm afraid," said Sir Chester. "I'm told she looks a bit green at the gills."

Without taking his eyes from his plate, Trevor said, "What's the matter with Nanny?"

"I should say it's a tummy thing," said Sir Chester.

Eeeyikes. The flu Trevor and Claire had. At Nanny's age this could mean even more nights of changing sheets than we had with Trevor and Claire. "I think after lunch I'll go over to Nanny's and relieve Lady Chipchase," I said.

"I'm going with you," said Trevor.

"Here here!" Sir Chester scowled, the commander in him coming out. "Melissa may go, but not you, young man. The last thing we need is another patient."

"But Grampy, I'm immune!"

"Melissa may go, but children may not. And that. Is. A fact."

CROSSING NANNY'S THRESHOLD, I felt relief: a sense of all's right with the world. Her glorious windowsill garden, with pots of primulas and big fat begonias, was getting a sunbath. Birdsong was the only sound in her big double parlor. A breeze puffed the curtains. Shadows from the trees outside shuffled and danced on the patterned rugs.

Then, through the quiet, a grotesque roaring retch from behind the bedroom door. Shouted retching. A scream of a groan, cried out through torn vocal cords. Chokes. Another retch, louder. Coughs with tears in them.

I stood paralyzed. I finally called out, through the sound of pain, "Nanny?"

Lady Chipchase, face the texture of torn white bread, opened the bedroom door. "Darling Melissa," she said. "The doctor hasn't arrived yet. I assumed it was a flu and didn't press him, in the morning. But it's grown quite violent. I called again at half past twelve. The nurse said he'd gone off on his rounds and had, in fact, planned to stop by. If so, I can't imagine what's keeping him. I fear we can't wait any longer. We're going to have to get Nanny to hospital. I have her dressed. Could you run fetch Mr. West?"

Another wail of gagging and tears, another putrified wave of odor exuded from the bedroom and Lady Chipchase rushed back in. I ran to find Mr. West, enlisting Trevor, Pru, and Phil to find him. Carol said she'd stay in with Claire. Humbert turned a page of *Country Life* and said, "Such drama."

We found Mr. West in the aviary. He dropped his pliers and ran to the stables and up the stairs, Phil following. Sir Chester moved his cane fast toward the Jaguar.

Nanny struggled, with tears down her face, against Phil and Mr. West as they shared her great weight between them. "I want to stay!" she cried, convulsing. "Oh, my frock!" she sobbed, as vomit spilled from her mouth.

Three men could never get Nanny into that little Jaguar. Phil ran for his station wagon as Nanny pleaded, "I'm remaining here! Please, please. Let me stay. This is my home."

Trevor stood tense. "Oh please, Grampy. Don't make her go."

"Chester," said Lady Chipchase. "Perhaps we should listen to Nanny."

Just then a small black car rounded the drive. The doctor. Reaching to the backseat for his black bag. Trotting over. Taking the stethoscope from his pocket. Taking Sir Chester by the arm. Lady Chipchase following. All of us stood with our feet planted as the three conferred. We couldn't hear them.

Trevor was the first to move a muscle. His hand went up to brush a tear from his cheek. I moved toward him to brush against his shoulder, so he'd know I was there.

When the three of them broke, Nanny, still held between Phil and Mr. West's shoulders, was pitifully covered with sick but momentarily collected: "Please, I don't want to go."

Sighs all round. The doctor, looking at the ground, shook his head. "I'm not sure she isn't better off here," he said. "At least I can better examine her upstairs."

Nanny, with Mr. West holding her under one armpit and Phil gripping from under the other arm, allowed herself to be lugged up the stairs to her beautiful new flat. The doctor followed. She mumbled something, repeating it like a chant. I strained to make it out. "This is my home. This is my home."

SUPPER WAS NOT A cheerful meal.

In the nursery, even the small children were quiet and somber. Claire tried to raise our spirits by leaning across the table to Trevor and saying, hopefully, "Shut up." This didn't get a smile, so she tried, "Totally." This got her a small smile from Pru and an absentminded pat on the hair from Trevor. He moved his banger and mash around the plate, mixing but not moving his fork to his lips. When one of the young nannies told him to eat, he said he wasn't hungry. "Nanny would want you to eat," I said. "To keep up your strength in a difficult time." He ate one forkful.

Supper in the dining room wasn't any better. Lady Chipchase was missing, of course. Sir Chester made only a feeble attempt at leading conversation and stopped midsentence a couple of times.

After the meal he said a prayer: "Thank you, dear God, for each other."

46

SIR CHESTER WAITED TO speak until everyone had gone to the sideboard to fill their bowls with cornflakes, and the nannies had served the babies in highchairs, as well as themselves. It was unusual to have babies and nannies at breakfast in the dining room. This was the first time I'd seen the table set to capacity, with the aunts and uncles, cousins and nannies, Phil, Carol, and me. There was nothing but cereal, sugar, and milk this morning. Resting both hands on the edge of the table, Sir Chester said, "I have something of the utmost sadness to tell you children." As he drew a deep breath, my eyes shot to Trevor. Sir Chester said, "Your Nanny died in her bed last night."

Trevor stared at Grampy, his expression frozen. Ever so slightly, his eyes narrowed. "No," he said, his voice very quiet. Sir Chester started to say, "I'm afraid it's . . ." but Trevor interrupted, louder, "No."

Lady Chipchase walked from her end of the table to stand behind Trevor's chair, touching his shoulders. He twisted out of his chair, and I thought he would run from the room, but instead he twirled himself into his grandmother's arms and held tight, muffling his outcry in her soft chest: "No! No! No."

Around the table, all the children, even the babies in high chairs, looked stunned. Claire, with fear in her eyes, got out of her chair to tug her grandfather's jacket, to be picked up. Pru had begun eating her cereal and had her spoon locked into her mouth. Her lips, in a tight line, were moving down, down, down at the corners. She made no sound, just watched Claire and Grampy, Trevor and Granny, big tears rolling from her eyes down her cheeks. I watched Lady Chipchase's face as she hugged Trevor and moved her eyes from grandchild to grandchild. She held herself collected, but her face was swollen. The skin around Sir Chester's eyes, too, I noticed, was puffed out, the crinkles reddened.

"I was with her when she died," Lady Chipchase said, such a hush in her voice that we strained to hear. I looked over at Humbert, sitting stiff, looking into his cereal bowl. "At the end she slept. I kept my hand on the counterpain, and held hers, when it was comfortable for her. At one moment she stirred—and gave my hand a squeeze so slight—I might have imagined it. Then, with her eyes closed, she spoke. I leaned in. She said . . ." At this point Lady Chipchase had to stop talking. She bit her lips and made several attempts at sound before she was able to continue. "Nanny said, 'This is my home.' "

"SORRY," HUMBERT SAID, PUSHING his chair back and leaving the room. Lady Chipchase stroked Trevor's back and said, "Darling, stay here and be a friend to the others." She left the room.

Sir Chester cleared his throat.

"Nanny would want us all to eat our breakfast," said Trevor, putting his spoon into his cornflakes. Claire allowed Grampy to set her back into her chair. By the end of breakfast, everyone was edgy to leave the room. Everyone had to cry, and talk.

"First the prayer," Sir Chester said. All of us closed our eyes, but I peeped from under my eyelids, to pray sincerely but at the same time see the other people—to register their feeling as Sir Chester spoke, asking us to accept "God's most baffling mystery." He prayed, "We may not hope to understand, but give us the strength to accept

Thy way. Give us the strength to remember our thanks, as we face our sorrow: our thanks for Nanny's life, and for the joy she has brought to our family since the day she came to join us, years before most of the assembled were born." Pru's eyes were squinted shut, squeezing tears from the corners. Her hands gripped each other tight, whitening the skin underneath the fingernails. Claire bowed her head, her hands interlocked fists. Trevor scowled to concentrate on Grampy's words: "We have been blessed with Thy love, through Nanny. And through her may Thy love last in our hearts forever and ever. Amen."

A gust of children's sobs and adult coughs. The scraping of chairs, the pat of feet. Clearing the silver and cereal bowls to the kitchen, the question: "How did it happen?" "Poison?" "Why Nanny?" Lady Chipchase came into the kitchen on Humbert's arm, his face grave, the two of them exchanging words we couldn't hear. "We'll have to pitch in with the washing-up this morning," Lady Chipchase said to all, "and with the dinner, as well. I'm afraid Mrs. West deserves a rest today."

"How is Mrs. West?" Humbert gasped. Apparently he, like me, hadn't noticed she wasn't there until her name was mentioned.

"Not at her best," was Lady Chipchase's reply.

Fright struck.

"No, she's not ill," Lady Chipchase assured us. "She is simply overtaken with grief."

"Mother," said Humbert, rolling up a sleeve, "where does Mrs. West keep the soap?"

Lady Chipchase fetched the Fairy soap from under the sink and handed it to Humbert, plus tea towels for Pru and me. When Phil and Carol came in Lady Chipchase assured them we had an ample crew, and they went outside. Claire reached up to pull Granny's tea towel, and she gave it to her, getting another one from the drawer for herself.

"How did it happen, Granny?" Pru asked. "I heard someone say poison."

"That's what Dr. Garrett said," Lady Chipchase told us. She stopped transferring clean bowls to the pantry and stood still, talking. "He said it was clearly poison, and by the time he got here it had already worked its way through her body. It had damaged her organs sufficiently to make recovery a virtual impossibility. It was he who made the decision to let Nanny spend her last night in her own bed, at Phillingsford."

"I'm glad," said Trevor. And he tucked his head down tight. His body began to convulse.

"Trevor?" I asked. "Would you like to go to bed for a little while? Maybe take a book?"

"Yes, please," Trevor said. Claire was too happy helping in the kitchen to leave Granny, but Pru came with us. We took the outside route to the nursery and passed two groups of cousins and nannies, sitting and talking on different parts of the lawn. Upstairs, in the big linoleum hall, so sparsely furnished with miniature chairs and tables, Trevor and Pru went through the little bookshelves in the children's library. "Nanny gave me this prayer book," Trevor told Pru, opening it to a picture of an angel. "I remember. Can you find the bible she gave me?" He helped her look. Each with a book, they disappeared into their separate sleeping compartments. When I left them in their bunks, their heads and bodies were under covers, big lumps, heaving. Wailing. Even with a wall between them, it was good they had each other.

THE WASHING-UP WAS DONE by the time I got back to the kitchen, and Lady Chipchase had her head in the fridge, handing things to Humbert. "The mutton's in the pantry cooler, darling . . . Oh. Look here. A couple of ducks' eggs!"

A couple. There had been four. Of course, that was night before last. Long time ago.

"When I was a child a man in our village died from eating a duck's egg." Lady Chipchase tossed the eggs in the trash can under the sink.

Humbert smiled. "I've eaten dozens."

"I'VE NEVER SEEN MRS. West this way," Lady Chipchase told me, as I helped her lay out cornflakes and milk again this morning. "She has taken to her bed, but she says she's not ill, she is simply too upset to carry on." She set down a stack of cereal bowls and mused. "Best chums for thirty years, those two. Ever since the Wests came to us, just married. 'Kids,' as Sir Chester would say. Nanny became like an elder sister." She loaded more stacks of bowls on her tray. "Mrs. West may take some time to recover."

Especially if she had something to do with it, I thought. I'm afraid she probably did.

"Do you think she would mind seeing me? Maybe I should take a lunch tray over to her today."

"Oh, never mind, Melissa. That's my job."

"Well, I was thinking. She might like someone new to talk to, to take her mind off Nanny. Maybe I could bring Claire and eat with Mr. and Mrs. West in their cottage."

"She might enjoy that! As it happens, Mr. West has gone into town. She might welcome some conversation. We can pack a basket with cold mutton. I'm planning my special potato salad." I started in on a cold green bean salad, part of a recipe I'd learned at the Cordon d'Or. Lady Chipchase made the mayonnaise—exactly the way Arabella Tuckett taught us. Which is exactly the way Julia Child used to do it on television. At least one thing stays.

. . .

I'D NEVER HAD A conversation with Mrs. West. All the way over I kept wondering what I'd say. When you have just one thing on your mind, you want to get to the point.

Claire hadn't wanted to come. More and more, she wants to cling to the permanent people in her life. Granny persuaded her that she was needed, to "help" me carry the basket. This made the trip to Mrs. West's a long, slow journey. It gave me time to get stage fright.

The Wests' cottage is very private, past the kitchen garden and the chicken coops, on the far side of the aviary. It's so ensconced in a little glade of its own that on my first two visits to Phillingsford I didn't notice it at all. It's brick like the big house, but built some centuries after—in the 1700s I think. (Georgian!) It's small. I'd never seen the front, which faces away from the aviary. The brick wall around the garden is taller than I am. Unlatching the iron gate, I absolutely gasped. Enchanted. Claire's eyes sparkled with interest. Part of the drama comes from packing so much color, and so many textures of leaves and flowers, into such a small space. Mr. West must have been working on this garden the whole thirty years they've lived here, to get such an effect of cheerful disarray. Roses cover the front wall, with hummingbirds buzzing. Stepping stones lead through beds that fluff out with yarrow and rue and hollyhocks and storybook flowers. One tree is heavy with plums like giant garnets. I knocked at the front door.

"Claire!" Mrs. West was dressed not in her dressing gown but in her tweed skirt, a flowered blouse, and a cardigan. She picked Claire up and carried her inside, inviting me to follow, delighted with Claire's "Heh-oh!" Claire responds to Mrs. West more than she does to me now. She lights up with her the way she did with Nanny.

"Lady Chipchase made us a picnic," I said. "She said you have plates. And tea."

"Ah, she's good to me. I'm feeling far better. I'll be cooking the supper tonight."

"Oh, I don't think so," I said. "We have it pretty much done. Lady Chipchase is feeling creative." We laid the table, Mrs. West found a fat cushion for Claire, and we all sat down for our feast. Mrs. West leaned across the table to cut Claire's meat. "*Haggkh*-hoo," Claire said, beaming up into Mrs. West's face. "Meeh!" she said, conversationally, lifting some meat onto her fork. "Po-hay-ho!"

"Oh yes! Potato!" said Mrs. West.

"Bee!" said Claire.

"Yes, yes! A bean! Well done, Claire."

I must say, she's getting her p's and b's. But the main thing I said to myself was thank heavens for Claire. She took the burden of conversation off me. Mrs. West was just tickled with her. "We heard all about Claire's talking from Nanny, after her last visit to London. But seeing is believing. Or, rather, hearing is." And this led *naturally* into the subject of Nanny. Mrs. West must be like me: When you have just one thing on your mind, you want to get to the point. She bowed her head and spoke so softly I wasn't sure I heard: "I'm afraid I may have killed Nanny."

"What?"

She repeated it.

Thank heavens Claire is deaf. Or Mrs. West couldn't have said it.

"You see, Nanny . . ." Mrs. West's voice broke. She sat silent, struggling to speak normally, her nostrils expanding and contracting, her lips pressed together as the corners of her mouth twitched and emotion appeared in red patches on her throat, like a rash. One look over at Claire seemed to be what she needed to pull herself together completely. She took a gulp of fresh air and spoke in a firm, confident tone: "A cold dinner is just what the doctor ordered, on a warm day such as today. Is this due to your American influence?" The only sign of emotion that stayed was the reddened skin on her throat. Evenly she said, "We so rarely have cold dinners, here."

Now I wished Claire hadn't come. Mrs. West would never risk breaking down in front of Claire.

"Do you have any toys in the house?" I asked.

"No. Sorry, no toys."

"Picture books?"

"No, sorry."

"Paper? Pens or pencils?"

These she did have. "Perhaps we can put Claire to work after dinner, drawing," I said. Deliberately, so Claire could read my lips, I turned my face to her: "You're very good at drawing, aren't you Claire."

"Ehh!" Claire said, nodding yes.

"It's odd," said Mrs. West, now getting actually involved in conversation, instead of pretend-involved. "You seem to lose your American accent when you speak to Claire." And so we continued on the subject of Claire until Claire and I had finished our frozen mousses (Mrs. West didn't want hers) and could set her up at the garden table with lots of pillows on her chair and a thick notepad for drawing. Making a page of crude sketches, I assigned a long list of flowers, windows, clouds, trees, and birds for her to draw. At first she wanted to stay inside with us, but Mrs. West went out and coaxed her to make some pictures. She was so pleased that Claire could read her lips that Claire seemed enthused about earning more praise. We two women left her busy and went in for a cup of tea at Mrs. West's table. Passing the milk and sugar cubes, she burst right in. "I meant no harm! You can believe me. But you see. One thing Nanny and I have always shared is a love of the duck's egg. They're quite a delicacy for them that like them, though not all do. Some folks say they're dangerous. They can get a taint, sitting by the pond. But they've never hurt Nanny or me before!

"They're a rarity as well, as they're quite difficult to find. The ducks hide their nests, you see. So it's not as much as once a year as I come across one." She smiled to herself. "If there's only one, I have a struggle with myself as to whether to give it to Nanny or have it myself. But this was one time I had no struggle." She curled her lips into her mouth, clamping them inside her front teeth. The blotches of red were back, coloring even her forehead, so that she looked about to explode with sadness. It took her forever to get her voice back. "I took my walk by the pond, over near Harry's home, and it was my lucky day. Or so I thought!" Now tears poured out freely, but the words took forever. "That day I found four!" I let her cry, refilling our teacups and fetching the box of tissues from behind the sink. I felt an ache for Mrs. West, and for Nanny—for everybody; but I haven't cried since this happened. Mrs. West said, "I was going to surprise her, at tea. But that day she had your marmalade lesson! After that she had you to tea in her flat. I couldn't offer *you* a duck's egg! You wouldn't have appreciated it. It's something just Nanny and I have between us." She was blowing her nose between every sentence, but here she stopped talking entirely, to sob. "I should say," she said, "something Nanny and I *had* between us."

Since she really couldn't speak for a long while, now, I went into the kitchen and got the mousse she hadn't eaten. "You're sure you don't want it?" I asked. She didn't hear the question. "It's melting." Her look indicated that this was the last thing she was interested in, so I picked up a spoon. "In London," I told her, between bites of mousse, "Nanny and I had great long talks. She told me about how she used to hunt for them with you, back when she 'had her legs.' And then, the night Nanny must have got sick, I went down to the kitchen after everyone was asleep and found four duck's eggs. I was tempted to eat one!"

"Nanny's egg?" Mrs. West was horrified.

"I wasn't sure it was Nanny's egg. And there were four of them. I was only going to eat one . . ."

"You wouldn't have done that, would you?"

This was a painful confession, and Mrs. West wasn't making it easy on me. "No," I lied. (I'd boiled the water and everything.)

"You would have been punished!" She went into more tears.

I poured the last of the tea into our two cups. I was sorry to be getting down to the bottom of the mousse cup. When I'm really emotional, I crave food. That's my way of being what Mrs. Haig-Ereildoun calls "mental."

In almost a whisper, Mrs. West said, "Nanny was greedy, you know."

I knew.

"She couldn't control her appetite."

"I have the same problem."

She wasn't interested in my confession. "I was saving those ducks' eggs for her tea the next day. I didn't breathe a word to her. She must have come down to the kitchen in the night, after you did! Only Nanny must not have been able to resist the temptation. Even though she must have known that I'd have taken pleasure in treating her."

"But there were four. Apparently that's unusual."

"Yes, but she ate her full share on her own, without me."

"She was probably going to beg your forgiveness in the morning," I said. It was hard to get those words out, because that part hit me. Only I knew how Nanny's own pleasure in eating the treasured eggs must have been ruined by shame—probably an elaborate concoction about what had happened to the duck eggs. She might lie awake wondering if she could get away with an assumption that somebody else in the household must have eaten them. If she allowed Mrs. West to assume that, she'd have to sit there feeling Mrs. West's disappointment that each of them would only get one egg. She might have lain awake wondering whether to confess or not. It's a shame I can't tell Trevor this story. It would give him a moral tale for his next composition.

"And I didn't know they were poison!" Mrs. West vowed. "I never meant to kill her!"

I handed her more tissues. I didn't know her well enough to put my arms around her. I didn't want to keep staring at her with compassion all over my face. I certainly didn't want to mention that I was glad *she* hadn't eaten any of the eggs. (It didn't even hit me till now to be glad that I hadn't eaten one.) All I could do while Mrs. West cried was clean out the inside of my frozen mousse carton.

"You won't tell the others, will you?"

"Of course not!"

"I don't know," she said. "Perhaps *I* should. I don't know how I can live with myself."

I felt such relief for her when she said that. Of course she should tell. "No one would think less of you," I said. "It would make everyone feel better." I said this with my back to her, because I was taking my spoon and the mousse cup back into the kitchen, using my finger to swab the last drop of mousse from the carton and lick it clean.

LATER, WHEN I'D HELPED serve tea in the nursery, I left the children and the young nannies and went down to help Lady Chipchase with supper. At the kitchen door I saw Mrs. West with her, not cooking. They sat at the table Nanny and I had used when we jarred the marmalade. Their voices were low, their faces serious. I left before they could see me.

47

SIR CHESTER, THE CHILDREN, and I paced the cemetery today. There's hardly an inch to spare between the tombstones. They will have to move out a body. Sir Chester had a hard time deciding which one. Mr. West will do it, and rearrange the tombstones, crowding them even more. Trevor said, "Oh, I see. This has been done before. I always wondered how they could make so many coffins so skinny. I mean, people in history were smaller, but not that small." Sir Chester didn't say anything. Trevor said, "Don't mind, Grampy. They're not in their bodies anymore."

The services won't be till next weekend. We can't have them without Philippa. I can't believe she'd go off for three weeks to a place where she can't be reached. What if it had been one of her children?

Lady Chipchase says there won't be many people in the church. Nanny's circle was small. On the telephone from Australia, her brother said he'd be unable to get here on such short notice. When Lady Chipchase said we could have a small graveside burial now and postpone the services to a time that suited him, he admitted that the real factor was cost. When Lady Chipchase offered to buy him a ticket, he wouldn't think of it.

I think he just doesn't want to come. Nanny said he'd "done very prosperous" in Australia. If he offered to pay Nanny's fare to get to him, he could pay for himself to come to her. I think I understand, though. He probably doesn't like rubbing so close to the old class system again, with his sister honored as the beloved servant. He might even be bitter. Or afraid. Afraid he might lose all the self-confidence he's built up over this whole quarter century. He might think if he got back in this environment, he'd see himself as a footman again, instead of as the proud manager of his own business. Whatever the reason, he won't be coming.

And we won't be staying. We'll come back next weekend for the service, but we're going back to London tomorrow as planned. The Haig-Ereildouns get back Tuesday.

Packing to go home must be the worst part of any trip. Especially if you have to launder the clothes of four persons and fold every last pair of underpants and organize everything into cases, gathering all the books and toys and hearing-aid batteries and not forgetting anything. The only thing good about the chore of packing is that it gives you something small to be irked about, instead of the big thing: I'm sad to leave.

MRS. WEST COOKED THE dinner today. She seemed glad to be back on the job. Since it's our last day, and Sunday, the whole family ate in the dining room. Trevor said, "It feels funny without Nanny." Sir Chester said this was the first Sunday dinner they'd had in this room without her in forty-four years. Everyone felt the vacancy. After placing a basket of rolls on the table near Humbert, Mrs. West touched his shoulder, for just half a second, with her hand. He blushed. She sped from the room.

TONIGHT AFTER THE GROWN-UPS' supper, I went up to the nursery to see how the young nannies were doing. Trevor and Pru weren't in their night clothes yet, and Trevor wanted to take a walk in the orchard. Pru too.

It stays light late here. Later than London. Like Alaska, almost. The sunset was just disappearing, and Trevor said, "Look! The wishing star."

"Make a wish, Trevor," said Pru, closing her own eyes and wishing.

Trevor squeezed his eyes tight and seemed to be wishing with all his might.

"You can't make a wish that can't come true, Trevor," Pru said. The authority.

"You don't know what I wished."

"Yes I do. You wished Nanny were still alive."

"No I didn't," said Trevor. "I wished Mummy would come home."

"So did I," said Pru.

48

MRS. HAIG-EREILDOUN GOT home today, and I quit.

Yesterday, everyone in the back of Phil and Carol's station wagon waved goodbye, goodbye, goodbye to Granny and Grampy and didn't stop waving until we got to the pillar box at the main road. Then Claire started to cry. Loud. By the time we got to the highway, she'd stopped crying, but she'd gone into that glazed look. We got home to a dozen bottles of sour milk on the doorstep. I'd forgotten to cancel the milkman. The front hall was so heaped with newspapers and post you could see linoleum only around the edges. I still haven't had time to sort it, though I could see lots of envelopes addressed to me. London soot had piled up on the windowsills, and even the floors were gritty. I groaned to see how much cleaning would have to be done before Mrs. Haig-Ereildoun got home. At supper Claire took pleasure in taking her egg from her eggcup and throwing it with all her might across the table, making a mess on Trevor's shirt, which I'd just washed and ironed. She ran for Pru with butter and marmite on her hands and ruined the clean blouse just ironed by me. She splashed all the bathwater out of the tub and drew blood from my face with her fingernails—the first time since Troonfachan. She wouldn't put on her nightdress, and when I finally won the fight she wouldn't stay in bed. Leaving the supper dishes on the table, I spent an hour holding her, rocking her, reading to her, and she still wouldn't stay in bed. So I let her watch television, babbling and running across the room to attack Trevor or Pru or me with her nails. Pru was the first to leave the room. She's fit enough to be back in her own room, on the top floor, and she makes her crutches almost skip. Soon Trevor went to his bed, too. But it wasn't till after the last channel had flickered out that Claire finally fell asleep in her chair, so that I could carry her to bed and go downstairs and do the washing-up and lay the breakfast table. Before sunrise, at about five, she was up and tearing the house apart. It was better when she had the flu. No one had school, so I had to take them all shopping with me to restock the food supply. Trevor ran in front of a bus and nearly got killed again. His basket flew across the road and a dozen eggs splattered. Peaches and apples rolled everywhere. He darted back into the traffic to pick up the fruit! A woman got out of her car to yell, causing a traffic jam. When we got home a neighbor I'd never seen before marched up to the door and scolded me for going away and letting milk pile up and spoil on the doorstep. "You Americans are famous for waste," she said. Lunch was the only break in the day's unpleasantness. I took the mince and made hamburgers, using bakery rolls as buns. Pru couldn't get over the thrill of having her first American hamburger. With lettuce, pickles, tomatoes, and onions! Between unpacking and cleaning and mopping I got Claire to the park for three hours, where she ran absolutely wild but didn't get tired in the least. I was about to drop when the front door opened and Mrs. Haig-Ereildoun walked in with her arms open ("Hello, my darlings!"), followed by Mr. Haig-Ereildoun ("Cheerio!") carrying the bags. "Darling darling darlings!" she chanted, as Trevor and Claire moved into her arms—a rare show of affection from Trevor. "Oh, Melissa," she said to me joyfully, over her armload of children, "one thing you'll find when you're married and have your own family is that you don't *dislike* coming home from holiday. You can't wait to see your children! Oh, how I've missed you," she said to Trevor and

Claire. "Now tell me all about what you've done. Was Phillingsford beauti—*Pru!*" Pru has become quite agile on her crutches by now. Of course, what Mrs. Haig-Ereildoun saw wasn't improvement but the opposite. She glared at me. *"What,"* she gasped, "is *this?*"

"It happened at Camilla's," Pru said. The most welcome words I'd heard all day. I do think Pru inherited some of her father's sensitivity to the underdog.

Trevor's news (a bald "Nanny's dead") came next. Mrs. Haig-Ereildoun went to a chair in the kitchen and pulled Claire into her lap. As Trevor and Pru gave the details, she shook her head gravely, probably too stunned to cry. By now Mrs. West had told everyone about the ducks' eggs, so at least the poison mystery was solved. As everything was explained to her, down to the scheduled burial and the brother in Australia, Mrs. Haig-Ereildoun kept her head down, rolling her chin against the top of Claire's head. Eventually other subjects were added to the conversation, such as Phil and Carol, Harry's cute baby, and Pru's great excitement for the day, her "American hamburger." Mrs. Haig-Ereildoun shot me a look of absolute hate and said to Pru, "I can't say I approve. Never mind. I hope you enjoyed it, Pru darling, because you shan't have another in this house." The phone rang and I ran for it, as usual. I've gotten into the habit, since she's been gone. She slid Claire off her lap and grabbed the receiver out of my hand with a look that said, "Whose house do you think this is?" Then, in her chirrupy voice, "Hel-lo?" Then, extra chirrupy, "Oh, hello! [Pause.] Oh, it was heavenly. I enjoyed your Richards book so. Also your Xanthos. I just sat on the beach and read for hours and hours every day, getting quite brown. [Pause. An intimate laugh.] Exactly! So tell me. When are you coming round? [Pause.] Excellent. I'll see you tomorrow then. [Calling out pleasantly and holding the receiver out to me.] Melissa? It's for you."

Simon. He said he was coming over tomorrow. I said, "I won't be here." (It's my Cordon d'Or day, and I have to write my letter to Harvey.) Simon laughed. "Playing hard to get, are you?" I told him I really wouldn't be here, but he could come see her.

There was no other conversation between us.

THE HORRIBLE THING HAPPENED after I'd served the supper and had put Claire to bed, but she wouldn't stay there, even after the others had been sound asleep for an hour. She escaped and ran to her mother's chair in the drawing room, shouting her version of "Mummeee!"—scattering the stacks of post Mrs. Haig-Ereildoun had been organizing on the floor in front of her. Mrs. Haig-Ereildoun looked at me and snapped, "What *have* you been doing with her!"

At that moment, all the tension of the last three weeks burst to the surface. I almost bared my teeth. I said to Mrs. Haig-Ereildoun, slowly but fiercely, *"She is just . . . happy . . . to see you."* I stood tall, even though I was shaking, and said, "No one has ever spoken to me the way you do. I do not like it. And I am not putting up with it anymore."

Then, all the tears I hadn't shed for Nanny or anyone broke out. All the tears I hadn't shed for myself. Those were a lot of tears.

Mrs. Haig-Ereildoun said she was sorry, but actually the sigh she heaved was of exasperation.

I said, "I don't like this job, I don't like housework—I'm not *good* at it! And I don't like living in fear of you. I'm not going to do it anymore."

"I am sorry," she said again. This time she said it angrily. As she continued she grew more angry. "I think the main thing is that I *walked* into the nursery and saw all the backload of *ironing* piled up and . . ."

"Ironing!" I said, furious. "*You* can't run this household yourself. If you had to do all the work without me, not *one item* would *ever*

be ironed. How do you expect *me* to do what you have never done and could never *possibly* do?"

The only thing I wish is that I hadn't been crying.

BEG IS WHAT SHE did next. She did beg. But it wasn't a humble kind of begging. It was a tired, look-what-I-have-to-put-up-with kind of begging, like the way people will beg a cat to climb down from a treetop sixty feet above the lawn. Desperate, self-pitying, and fed up. In the end I said I would stay, "for a little while. We'll see."

Mots is going to kill me.

As for Simon. It maddens me that he doesn't have a phone. I want to call him and tell him about this.

If he comes tomorrow night it will prove he's not really coming to see me. He's coming to see her. To see her tan.

I hate how great she looks with a suntan.

AFTER MY COOKERY CLASS I went to a place called the Swiss House for a salad, with my notepad. It's a good place for writing my letter to Harvey: clean, light, no hurry. But tonight I couldn't get into the spirit. I was nervous about Simon. Would he or wouldn't he come over to see her? When I made the decision to pick up my notepad and go home, I was in such a hurry to get there that I actually let a taxi give me a free ride. I remember how it used to surprise me, when cab drivers offered. Now I'm surprised if I go somewhere and at least one big black taxi doesn't pull over and open its back door. I've never taken one up on it before. This one didn't want anything in return except some conversation. I must confess he did make me aware of a certain lusciousness about me. Round and voluptuous, as Tedward would say.

When I walked up the stairs to the drawing room, around eight,

Simon wasn't there, but Mr. Haig-Ereildoun was. For some reason. Maybe he's got out of the habit of hanging around Whitehall all night. They were having a drink. She was wearing sandals and the black linen shorts. She'd painted her toenails the subtlest of pinks. I said hello.

Trevor was just coming down. "Oh Trevor," Mrs. Haig-Ereildoun said, actually gushing. "Trevor, come and talk to us for a moment." When he got closer she reached for his hand. "Trevor. Do you realize what a lucky boy you are, to have someone as wonderful as Melissa here, taking care of you?"

"Yes," he said, looking baffled. "Of course."

"Good," she said. "Because you are a very, very lucky boy indeed."

"May I go now?"

"Of course, darling. Melissa?" Her pronunciation of my name was sweet. "Won't you join us for a gin and tonic?"

"No thanks," I said, grinning to myself and continuing up the stairs.

Join them for a gin and tonic! I could already hear Mots's laugh: the laugh she has when she's really laughing. It sounds like big round bells. "You should quit more often," Mots would say.

In my room, I was just getting into the mistake Arabella Tuckett's sous chef made on the moussaka when the doorbell rang. I froze. I heard Mrs. Haig-Ereildoun's sandals going down the stairs, and pretty soon Simon's voice in the hall. And hers. And two sets of feet coming up the stairs. "Melissa," she called up to me. "Now you really *must* join us for a drink. Simon is here!" She sounded as thrilled as Pru when Pru had her American hamburger.

I finished my sentence. I finished my paragraph. I started a new one.

I brushed my hair and put on lipstick and fished my shoes from under the bed. I took one last look in the mirror, at my huge breasts bulging out of the scoop neck of my little summer dress. It sure is little, compared to me. I don't know if I look luscious or fat. And after all these months in England, I now have no tan whatsoever. Even the freckles are faint. But at least I have no more pimples, either. I opened my door and a burst of laughter came from the drawing room. Mr. Haig-Ereildoun was saying some words in Greek. More laughing.

COMING DOWN THE STAIRS, I saw Simon before he saw me. His wide, bony shoulders.

His head was down, looking into his glass, which he held pressed between eight long fingertips, his elbows resting on his spread-out knees. My heart did a flip. Why should his *posture* affect me this way? He is just—cool. When he looked up it was not toward me but over toward the sofa. I walked in and saw the long tan legs of Mrs. Haig-Ereildoun. She was standing barefoot on the sofa, adjusting that little painting of the dog howling at the moon. It's been crooked ever since she painted the room and tried to center it there. Simon's presence made her notice.

She has that kind of tan that very fair people can get with only studied restraint. She must have used an egg timer. There wasn't a hint of burn or ruddiness, just a powder-soft brown, like a slightly toasted magnolia petal. So underdone it's tantalizing.

"Lime?" Mr. Haig-Ereildoun asked, handing me a tall fizzy drink with no ice. My eyes on her legs, I only *heard* that the drink fizzed, that no ice clinked, that he plunked in a wedge of lime. I looked up to say thank you and saw that his eyes, too, were upon Philippa's legs. Simon, though, was now standing up, smiling down at me from his height. His hands on my shoulders. A kiss on both cheeks.

I've never gotten used to this two-cheek kissing and am not good at it. On tiptoes and so close to Simon's blue eyes, looking at me as if he were drinking me, I missed his cheeks completely. He laughed and held my face. "Let me give you a lesson," he said. "You aim for the cheeks, not the nose." Again he kissed both of my cheeks. Still holding my head he said, "Now, don't expect me to present my cheeks to you. You have to stretch your neck."

There might as well have been no one else in the room. I got high from the touch of sandpaper brushing my lips.

Tedward has sandpaper too. So did Dad. How I loved it, and love it.

They didn't speak Greek. Mr. Haig-Ereildoun had some good stories, and Mrs. Haig-Ereildoun laughed with abandon. Maybe they had a good holiday. Lots of spanking books.

Or maybe she's in top form when she has two admirers. Of course I had two, too. With Simon there, Mr. Haig-Ereildoun could be free to pay attention to me without making her mad. I could pay attention back. *She* brought up the subject of my "column." Simon asked if I'd had any fan mail for the one he helped me write. I said I hadn't had a chance yet to look at my post. He teased me: "One month ago you'd have called it your 'mail.' You'd better watch out. You're turning English." "I don't have an English accent though, do I?" I asked in fear. All of them laughed. "Far from it." "You'll never have to worry about that." (In an exaggerated American accent, like Johnny Cash.)

I DESERVE A MEDAL for getting my letter to Harvey done. One thing, though. I wasn't tempted to sleep. And I'm still not. It must be four o'clock. If Mrs. Haig-Ereildoun isn't sleeping, she deserves a medal too, for not banging on my door and reminding me that I have a busy day tomorrow. I do have a busy day tomorrow! But not working for her. She announced at supper (we ended up having supper in the drawing room) that I get a day off. And Mr. Haig-Ereildoun has arranged to get me two tickets to Parliament. Simon is taking the day off too, so we can go together. She'd actually called him at the lab and set it up while I was in class. It was their surprise. I suppose I shouldn't be surprised that she's so nice all of a sudden.

The other stroke of luck was that the dinner was moussaka. The Haig-Ereildouns, Arabella Tuckett, and Simon all pronounce it MOOSE-a-ka. I thought it was pronounced moo-SAH-ka. They laughed. Anyway, Mrs. Haig-Ereildoun makes it completely differently than Arabella Tuckett does. Mrs. H-E uses lamb mince—raw lamb ground like hamburger. Arabella uses leftover leg of lamb, diced. The two of them do the eggplant differently, everything, but especially the potatoes. Arabella puts the mashed potatoes into a pastry bag and makes fancy fluting all around the edges, like a birthday cake. The flutings get brown and look like a photo in a magazine. Mrs. H-E just heaps mashed potatoes all over the top, making something that browns like a peasant dish. Arabella's looks better, Mrs. H-E's tastes better. Contrasting the home version with the Cordon d'Or version made my letter to Harvey easy.

The only hard part was the stiff upper lip of Mr. Haig-Ereildoun when he urged me to use his typewriter in the morning: "I have no use for it."

I suppose he doesn't need to publish to keep food on the table, and I don't feel so scared that she'll leave him (I do tend to live in the moment); but behind the smile I thought I saw a combination of fear and resignation in his eyes.

49

I'M TURNING OUT TO be a person I can't trust. In heart and mind I betrayed Tedward as if he didn't exist. I forgot that he did. I keep doing that.

Simon and I met outside the Westminster tube station, under Big Ben. Noon. The sun beat down, and the air steamed with petrol fumes. A line of loudly dressed people in Bermuda shorts and gaudy shirts circled the block around the houses of Parliament. They were talking loud too, in those John Wayne accents the Haig-Ereildouns like to imitate. I felt embarrassed to be from their country.

Something historic was supposed to be debated today, having to do with the European Union, and everyone wanted to say they'd been there. They were willing to suffer for it. Simon and I walked right past them and pushed open the immense doors of Whitehall.

A hush of cool. White marble forever. No one in there but us. No sound but our breathing. In that moment our two spirits, and our bodies too, it seemed, commingled and we were one. It was the most heart-stopping moment of my life. More sexual than the monkeys. Isn't it mysterious how an event like that is so short, but you know it's for a lifetime.

After the silence, the ring of our footsteps on marble. Repeated in echo against the marble encasing us. Our feet sang out in all that air, the works of a musical instrument five hundred years old.

Inside the hall, where straight rows of seats face each other, people began to collect. Speakers began to speak. This was the comedy part of our drama. No one got around to talking about the European Union, because the first subject on the agenda was dogs. How the law must prevent people from abandoning dogs by the side of the road. This subject was far more emotional than anything that could change the history of the world. Of course, I agree that dogs are more interesting than the E.U. Aristocratic little old ladies, hot-blooded Cockneys, and caricatures of Eton twits (like Humbert) stood up and satirized, wept, shouted, and intoned. The debates got hot, comical, insulting, fraught, and endless. No other subject came up.

We exited with the crowd and joined another crowd underground, waiting for the Circle line. Simon wanted to take me to bookstore row—this part of London that is blocks and blocks of antique bookstores, all many stories tall with ornate facades, all loaded like stacks in the library. He was looking for, of all things, a certain aged edition of *Fowler's English Grammar.* We found many versions that didn't satisfy him, but finally he found the one he liked, absolutely cube-shaped, almost too heavy to hold in one hand.

The old bookseller approved of Simon's choice. They were fellow aficionados. The man, in tweed as old as he was, looked at me through his thick glasses. "You'll be happy he bought this, one day." He included Simon in a beneficent wink: "Your children will enjoy the use of it. Then, your grandchildren."

I stopped breathing.

I didn't want Simon to see my emotion, so I didn't look up at his face to be sure he was feeling what I felt. All I know is, the air was thick with it.

I've decided not to go to Phillingsford this weekend for Nanny's services. I have to think.

I'm not worried about whether Nanny would mind. Wherever Nanny is now, she knows I'm with her.

Trevor and I talked about it. This belief. About the dead. We seem to feel the same thing, and to believe it so naturally that it doesn't seem a question. What we believe is that this life is only a part of our lives. That before we were born was another part of the big life and that after we die is another part, and we don't know how many parts there are or what the other parts are like. All we can know is that we don't know. And that it's not our business to know, yet. I told him what Thoreau said (first I had to explain who Thoreau was) when someone asked him on his deathbed if he believed in the afterlife. Thoreau said, "One world at a time."

Seeing Trevor's reaction (a calming, a relief, a recognition) made me remember how much sense that had made to me, the first time I'd heard it.

Trevor and I admit we don't know, but we sense that in dying, Nanny has become more fully joined with us now than she was when she was alive. She's integrated into Trevor now, into me now, more than any living person could be. She's in us, and we're in her. She's not just the unit called Nanny anymore but part of nature's swim. She is part of God now. I told Trevor about an old man I knew who once in a while talked of "what, for want of a better term, we call God." This struck a chord with Trevor too.

Since Nanny is now part of what for want of a better term we call God, she knows how we feel, how we think, when we're wrong and when we're right, more than we can. If there is such thing as right and wrong. After all, there are always reasons for all wrong. Understanding the reasons includes forgiving. I'm not going to Nanny's services, and Nanny knows I love her. She also knows I have reason.

Maybe Nanny will help me think.

50

I FOUND JUST THE right hotel. I can't stay in Lettering Lane, even though the Haig-Ereildouns will be at Phillingsford until Tuesday night. I need to be away. To be not in their house. I need something "my own," in the sense that I'll be paying the rent.

I couldn't stay in one of those cheap hotels that line the roads near Victoria Station. I needed something uplifting. But definitely not the Ritz. One of the grand old hotels looking out at Kensington Gardens or Hyde Park would be too expensive too, and also, I imagine, dingy. They look so uppity and dull, standing there with their faded awnings and deadpan doormen. There's a small hotel I sometimes pass on my walks that's old and brick and, oddly enough, called the Phillingsford. Simon first spotted it, on the way home from something, a long time ago. I've always wondered what it was like inside. Yesterday I took a detour on the way to the park and wheeled Claire into the lobby. The price was surprisingly okay. The hotel has a pretty parlor, like a smaller cheaper version of the morning room at Granny and Grampy's. I'm sitting in the parlor right now, at an escritoire that must be somebody's heirloom. It would be really something if it were refinished. The window in front of me has leaded panes, and through the wobbly glass I see the construction site across the street. All of London seems to be a giant wrecking yard. And it's

August. Horribly hot and sticky outside. It's hot in my room on the fifth floor too (no elevator—maybe that's one reason for the low price), but it's cool down here. I must say, I've found a comfortable place for my think.

I HAD A REVELATION yesterday, walking Claire down the Gloucester Road. It hit with the force of a mystical experience.

There's a scale in front of the Boots we always pass (me sometimes stopping for candy bars), and the face of the scale is a mirror, shoulder-high. I'm very used to seeing my reflection as I pass, but yesterday what I saw was different from what I'd noticed before. Or maybe I should say that yesterday I recognized what I've been seeing all along: a fat girl.

My whole body flooded with shame. In one second I relived the party the Haig-Ereildouns had, where almost everyone found talking to me a chore of politeness. Where the man asked me a question and rushed on to say, "I wonder who else is coming." Looking at my hefty, husky reflection in the mirror on the scale, the words that came into my head were, "No wonder you have no credibility."

Funny word. Credibility. Why credibility? I guess what it meant was that no one takes me seriously. No one who doesn't already know me, anyway. No one who doesn't have some special reason to like me, like Miss Gilbert or Nanny or Lady Chipchase.

And words—the ones that pop first into your head—are so often not exactly what you mean. Like "seriously." Being taken "seriously" isn't what I care about.

I know a lot of people, like Freud, say that the first word that comes out, unchecked, is what you really mean. Ah-hah! I think they're wrong! (Another revelation.) Maybe when you state a problem, to yourself, you hedge a little by using the wrong words at first, so that if you're going to face it, you face it slowly—giving yourself a choice about whether to look it in the eye. I want to look this problem in the eye, by slowly working out the right words.

What I feel is not so much that I have no credibility, or that no one takes me seriously, but that no one sees me as the person I see myself as being. (Oh, heavens. There I go again, exaggerating to avoid the literal truth. Granny Aitchee sees me as the person I see myself as being, I think Mr. Haig-Ereildoun does—there's a long list. But a lot of people don't.) One great reason is that I am fat. Not like the fat lady in the circus, but I could be described as "overweight." In fact, that's probably the first word a person would choose to describe me. "Overweight" or "big" or "heavyset" Or, to be polite, "robust" or "Brunhild-like." I didn't have to put one pence in the scale to find out if I really was overweight. Anyway, we'd passed the scale by the time these thoughts chugged through my brain.

Chug *is* the right word. That's exactly how the thoughts moved: regular, matter-of-fact, undramatic, and going somewhere. Where they went was here: I'm not going to be fat anymore.

Chug-chug is how I will arrive at the reality of being not fat, and how I will remain not fat. The extra stone and a half didn't melt away the instant I saw that reflection. But in that instant I knew I would not be buying any more candy bars.

I knew I'd be a little radical about starving for a few days and that after that I would eat good food, inconspicuously limiting myself to quantities smaller than it takes to maintain my current heft. I knew I would become, visually, the person I see myself as being. Not thin, like Mrs. Haig-Ereildoun. I'd hate to be thin. It wouldn't be me. I'm just going to look like me again.

Last night at the Haig-Ereildouns' I had a poached egg and an orange. For breakfast today I had one of Mrs. Haig-Ereildoun's horrid one-minute eggs and a glass of orange juice. After I checked into the Phillingsford, I had an apple for lunch. Tonight I'll have a plain yogurt in my hotel room, and maybe a peach. When I return to normal life, with people, I'll eat what they eat but leave a little on my plate. I'm not going to discuss this with anyone.

It's so funny, how fret-free this feels. It'll be life as usual, but with this aspect of it chug-chugging. Not to pun, but a weight has been lifted.

MRS. HAIG-EREILDOUN WAS UNDERSTANDING about my intention to stay in London instead of going with them to the country. One thing they will have, this weekend, is plenty of nannies in the nursery. Yesterday was packing the children's cases, getting library books, and cleaning the refrigerator, as well as the usual, like exercising Claire. The one different thing was Claire. Claire holds fast to her mother as never before. With her mother she's bright and alert. With me, she's not hostile, the way she was when we first got back from Phillingsford, but she's dull. She doesn't want to "talk" anymore. She doesn't want anything to do with me. She must associate me with her mother's disappearance. With Nanny's disappearance. She doesn't respond to me. I wonder how long it might take for her to forgive. Or forget.

Mrs. Haig-Ereildoun said she'd be off running errands until mid-afternoon, and since we were so busy I decided to make just sandwiches for the children's dinner. For myself, too. (This was before the incident with the scale.) I made extra-good tuna sandwiches, toasting the bread and loading on lots of lettuce and thick tomato slices. I served the sandwiches on plates (this is not a slum house) and was amazed at Pru's delight. "Is this really what sandwiches are like in America? No wonder that's how they look in the cartoons!" It was upon those words that Mrs. Haig-Ereildoun walked into the kitchen. Furious. "I thought you understood," she said to me. "No American hamburgers and no American sandwiches." Until this moment, I'd completely forgotten what English sandwiches are usually like: little shavings of meat or cucumbers between two thin slices of bread, and thick layers of butter or mayonnaise. She whipped the plates right off the table. Threw open the cupboard doors. The refrigerator door. Searching. Rattling jars, banging bottles. "*Why* haven't you stocked the kitchen with proper food?"

It was my job to stock the kitchen while she was in Greece, but not now. She hasn't even given me any money to shop with. I told her this, that uncontrollable tremble in my voice. "*Why* didn't you inform me, then, in the morning, that it was either starvation or American sandwiches. I'd have *given* you some money!" You'd think, after all the times we've been through this, that I'd have developed nerves of steel. But my nerves don't seem to build up like muscles. In fact, they seem to wear down. I was at least as shaken this time as I had been that first night at Troonfachan, when she screamed at me for not having made up the cot. As she hurled our plates back at us, and Pru went through the business of ascertaining whose partially eaten sandwich was whose, Trevor looked at me with wry sympathy. "Poor Melissa." He said it with his mother right there. "When you were little, you couldn't wait to get big, so your mother couldn't boss you anymore. Now you're grown up, and *my* mother bosses you."

We all laughed, except Mrs. Haig-Ereildoun. I don't know which helped me more, Trevor's understanding or the relief of a little chuckling. After everyone had left the kitchen, Pru stayed to watch me do the washing-up. She said, "You know, Melissa. You're the *free-est* person I've ever met." Me? "You are. You don't need this job. You are free to go wherever in the world you like. Trevor and I are just happy that we've had a piece of your life."

WHILE I WAS OUT with Claire, another courier letter came. Again, urgent.

This time Mrs. Haig-Ereildoun knew better than to call Mots and ask if she thought it would be best to open it. She just opened it. "I hope you don't mind," she said, handing me the torn-edged packet.

Harvey again. "Hey, kiddo. Get back to work. I got you a job with big bucks. Twenty-five grand a year. Call collect. Make it snappy."

Yikes! That's over two thousand dollars a month.

I didn't call him, though. I have to think.

THIS AFTERNOON I WALKED. I walked by Cadogan Gardens and the old stone church, square like the Phillingsford church, at the end of Selwood Place. Nanny's services will be held in a stone box just like that, the same number of centuries old, except two hundred miles away and in the country. Maybe tomorrow, while Nanny's services are being held in the Phillingsford church, I should go to a service at this South Kensington church and think about Nanny. I walked by the Anglesea Pub and saw a million happy people with frothy mugs of beer and shandies out in the garden. I walked by Mots's house but didn't stop. I don't want advice. I walked to the river and looked over Battersea Bridge at all the smokestacks and thought about all the people who worked there and got lung diseases. I continued downriver to the fancy, fanciful Chelsea Bridge and crossed, but only to the middle. How blue the Thames looked late this afternoon. You didn't even notice the grime. I walked back up into Chelsea, the smart little lanes and mews, and wondered what it looked like just a hundred years ago, when Chelsea was all cherry orchards, and Mots's smart little house was housing for cherry pickers. I imagined when the mews houses were stables and horses pulled carriages. A lot of those houses still have brass boot-scrapers at their front doors. I wondered how I could bear to leave all this history.

In the arcade of the South Ken Station, I looked in the rug merchant's window. They have ongoing going-out-of-business sales here, too. I passed the booth where I usually buy candy bars and looked at the sign with the tube map. Bakerloo! I took the ramp down and caught the Circle line and figured out how I'd get to the Bakerloo and bookstore row.

It was late when I found the store Simon had taken me to. They have shelves and shelves of used paperbacks, too, and I found just what the doctor ordered: an old book my mom said she liked. It became a movie, and she told me it was the only time she'd ever seen my dad shed a tear in a movie. *Love Story.* At the cash register, the same old man, with the same old tweed and the same thick glasses, recognized me. He took in the title of the book and gave me a smile that embarrassed me.

IT WASN'T NEARLY DARK when I got back to South Ken, but the restaurants had started filling up. I've always wanted to eat in one of these trattorias, to see if English spaghetti tastes horrible or wonderful. But I've never felt free to spend the money. Now, of course, I don't eat spaghetti. I walked by the Bistro, with the smart green awning and all the brass coffee-making gadgets gleaming, where I've always longed to have lunch or dinner, and had planned to, when I could afford it. I don't know what being able to afford it is, since I have enough money in the bank for a month of lunches there. But of course now I won't be having lunch or dinner or even a breakfast pastry at the Bistro. I'm slimming. Speaking of words. Isn't that a good word, for saying exactly what it is. An adjective made into a verb and in a tense that says "in progress."

Instead of having a yogurt and a peach in my hotel room, I bought a yogurt and a mineral water at one of those corner places and took it to the Chelsea churchyard, or whatever that little church with the big yard in Chelsea is called. There are marble benches set among the gravestones. I sat on one with my yogurt. The wishing star came out. I concentrated on it with all my might and wished the first thing that came into my head. The words that popped into my head as the star popped into the sky were, "I wish I knew what to wish for."

I guess that's a wish. My wish. I wonder if I'll get it.

I worked up my mind to think about Tedward. I worked my way back to the real seed of my love for him: He needs me. No one else has ever needed me the way he does. Simon certainly doesn't need me. I thought of Tedward's father dying a long time ago, then his mother, his sister, his brother. I felt the empty places in his heart taking over the full ones, till almost all was empty. And then I came in. I thought of how I'd filled his heart, enough to collapse his whole body if I should leave. I laid my whole body on the cold marble bench, and I sobbed. For all the dead to hear.

When I got back to the Phillingsford, I'd cried enough to fall asleep without opening *Love Story*.

SUNDAY. I DIDN'T GO to the little stone church at the end of Selwood Place today. I spent the whole day walking. Almost everything was closed. I love that about Sundays in London. It's a family day. Even if you don't go to church, it's a holy day.

In the afternoon I didn't write in the parlor, because when I sat down at "my" escritoire, a group of Englishmen came into the room. They were saying that since you can't buy a drink in England on a Sunday, it was lucky they had their flasks and this hotel. One asked if I'd like to join them. Any other time I might have. They seemed nice. But now, I don't drink. And besides, I'm thinking.

I thought all day about Tedward.

Tonight, in my room, I count chimneys. Outside my window I see that every building has a minimum of six small chimneys lined up along the roof, rectangular chimneys, most made of stone. One building has sixteen chimneys.

It's Sunday, but I didn't call Tedward collect today. It's early there—it's still light here. But I'm not going to call him, because I don't know what to say.

51

I STAYED UP ALL night. *Love Story* isn't that long, but I had to read intermittently. My eyes kept flooding, starting the moment I read the words, "This is the story of a girl who loved Bach, Beethoven, the Beatles, and me."

Past tense. So you know right away she's gone. And how the guy must have been elevated by being loved by a person like her. I read this as a book that could have been written by Tedward.

The woman in *Love Story* died. I'd just be leaving. But in a way it'd be the same, as far as Tedward was concerned. "Passing on" is the phrase Mrs. West used about Nanny.

My eyes were still swollen this afternoon when I woke up from the snooze I took after my all-night cry. I needed an ice pack, but this isn't the kind of hotel that keeps ice. I was embarrassed to go out on the street, but then I thought, who'll see me? It's sunglass weather anyway, and there's a chemist right on the corner. I got some sunglasses and walked to the Bureau de Change in the Fulham Road. I cashed sixty dollars worth of traveler's cheks into ten-pence coins. The man at the exchange searched around and found me a big shopping bag. I didn't even know if that sack of money would be enough. For once I wasn't calling collect.

I walked to the phone booth outside the Anglesea, lugging my coins. Her Majesty's shiny red call box is out in the garden. The outdoor benches and tables were empty in the morning, and hummingbirds flittered with butterflies around the hanging flowerpots. This was a pretty place for my mission. Tedward would just be getting up to go to his studio on the pier. He says he gets out early now, since he has so much left to do for his show. I tried to picture him, brushing his teeth. Carefully combing his hair to cover the bald part.

That American phone ring sound. The lifting of the receiver. "Hello?" The loading of coins into the slot, before I could speak. "Tedward?"

It was Tedward. Finding that out was all the stalling I did. "Tedward, I'm not going to marry you."

"I know, Baby," he said.

I didn't say anything about not liking to be called baby. "How did you know?"

"I just knew. I knew before we sent the invitations. You weren't happy."

"No," I said. "You weren't either, were you?"

He didn't say anything.

"I'm coming home," I said.

"When?"

"Soon as I can. I'm calling the airline, as soon as we finish talking. My reservation has to be two weeks in advance."

"Let me know," he said, "so I can meet your plane."

"Okay," I said.

"Love you," he said.

"I love you," I said.

And I meant it.

It's a funny thing, how reading that book must have given me what I needed. Reading it, I'd lived through the entire thing I'd been trying to keep from happening.

Next I called British Airways. When I walked back to the Phillingsford, the bag of money was almost as heavy as it had been when I'd left the Bureau de Change.

IS SIMON THERE? "Hang on," said his lab mate.

I was sitting on my bed at the Phillingsford. I'd come back because I wanted to be in a comfortable place for this call.

"Hello."

"Simon it's me. I'm going home."

"Where are you? I thought you were at Phillingsford."

"I'm not. Well, actually, I am, in a way." I didn't want to get into this. "Simon, I'm not going to marry Tedward."

There was a long silence. I didn't fill it up.

I waited. Waited. At last he said, "I can't marry you."

Heavens, how those words filled me with joy!

I laughed. "I didn't think I'd asked you."

He stayed serious. "I don't know how to explain it. It might be—well, say I was the kind of man who liked to whip women. I wouldn't be able to change it. Or to explain it."

"You don't have to," I said.

SO THAT WAS THAT. *Why do I feel so happy?* I asked myself as I skipped down the street to the corner odds-and-ends store to buy a yogurt.

I was enjoying the gnaw in my stomach, but I knew starvation was impractical. In the odds-and-ends store I bought a *Time Out*. Kenneth Branaugh is in a play at the Garrick. I have just enough time to bathe and get there. Oh, such a fancy hotel, with a phone and a bathtub.

Kenneth Branaugh was terrific. Kenneth Branaugh is always terrific. And I saw him in person.

After, I found another call box near the theater. I'd brought my bag of money with me to call Harvey. It was great to hear him say, "Hey, kiddo." This call didn't eat up all that many coins either. Probably no conversation with Harvey would. I'm starting Monday, exactly four weeks from today. (That'll give me a chance to fly to Portland and spend a week with Mom.) Harvey says I'll be on probation the first three months and in a sense for the rest of my life. C'est la vie, I said. "Yeah," Harvey said. "I'm amazed I haven't been canned yet." Also! He thinks if my flight isn't for two weeks, I should pop over to Paris for a little food research.

I didn't tell him I'm slimming.

In fact, I bet I could taste a few things and keep on slimming. Maybe I will pop over to Paris.

Funny. Harvey was just getting back from lunch. I'd already lived through the whole of one of the most momentous days and evenings of my life.

Still in the call box, I rang Mom.

As it turned out, this was where I really needed all that money. I probably spent more time putting coins in the slot than I did talking and listening to Mom.

She was just on her way to Jack's to get her hair cut. (How great it was, to hear that name. Jack. He used to cut my hair, too, until I went to Eugene, to college.) Mom let herself be late to Jack's. We had a lot to say.

"You don't sound like yourself!" was the first thing she said, distressed. "What's happened?"

"I am myself." We spent pounds of pence arguing over whether I have an English accent. I defended myself. "Everyone says I *don't*!" "You do, though." She didn't like it.

Finally I told her I'm not marrying Ted, so I can come home. Of course she was glad I was coming home, but I was surprised how glad she was that I wasn't marrying Tedward.

"When did you tell Mrs. Haig-Ereildoun?"

"I haven't yet." I explained about the funeral at Phillingsford. I told her a lot of the hurtful details about working for Mrs. Haig-Ereildoun.

Each time I recounted an incident, she said, "Oh, *no!*" It was great to hear the familiar sound of Mom saying, "oh, *no!*" It's what she says when something disturbs her so much she's speechless except for those two words.

"Why didn't you tell me? You should have left a long time ago."

"But I'd *promised* I'd stay through the summer."

"Oh, *no!*"

It amazed me that she felt that way. She was the one who'd taught me the importance of sticking with a thing. And even more, of keeping my promises. "And besides, Mom, I hadn't made up my mind about Ted."

"You should have stayed in a hotel. Traveled in Europe. Anything."

"But Mom, I didn't have enough money."

"You should have asked me! I'd have sent you some money. This wasn't good for you! You shouldn't have put up with it. I can hear in your voice that you're still emotional." She was very emotional.

We ended that I'd call her tomorrow. "After you've told Mrs. Haig-Ereildoun. And next time, call collect. We've wasted so much time with you putting money in that machine that I may upset Jack's day." Funny what a thrill it gave me, again, to hear Jack's name. I miss home.

IN THE STRAND, THE crowds had cleared from the street, but the restaurants were full. Supper after theater is the thing here. For them, but not for me. I found a nice little restaurant that wasn't too full, and I asked if I could come in just for a cup of tea and dessert. (I could see a couple eating raspberries. I was sure I could get some without the cream.) I think the headwaiter, like all those cab drivers, liked my body. (When I say it's fat, I don't mean ugly.) In any case, he did the un-English thing and broke the rules for me.

So here I am, with my ever-ready heavenly blue, a votive candle flickering illumination on the white linen tablecloth. I eat my raspberries one at a time, between paragraphs. My little pot of tea is real tea. I asked for herbal, because I want to sleep tonight. The waiter said they didn't have herbal tea. "It shouldn't be called 'tea,' " I heard him say to a fellow waiter. "It should be called an herbal beverage." They pronounce the "h" in herbal but still put an "an" in front of it. As in "an hotel."

Before the raspberries came, the gnaw of hunger in my stomach was joined by another gnaw: How am I going to tell Mrs. Haig-Ereildoun? I'll think about it tomorrow, I decided, and the gnaw went away. Both gnaws left, really, even before the raspberries arrived. My near fast may have contributed to my high. Enjoying each raspberry to the hilt, I sang to myself, "Simon's been thinking of marrying me. Simon's been thinking of marrying me."

I thought about what he said about whips. I'm sure he doesn't like whipping women. Well, pretty sure. I think I knew in a flash what he was saying, when he said what he did about whipping. Simon's perversion is, he doesn't like luscious. Or rather, he likes it, but he doesn't want to let himself like it. I don't mean the body thing. I mean the bawdy thing. Sensual pleasures. It means so much to Simon to be an ascetic. It's his aesthetic. But I might be able to teach him to let himself like luscious. It might be lovely.

Or, he may be right. Maybe we couldn't live happily ever after. I may be, to him, what some people say about New York: nice place to visit. I could drive him crazy. Because I would pay a fortune for the first strawberries of the season and let their juice dribble onto my chin.

52

WHEN I STEPPED INTO the Phillingsford, after midnight, guess who was in the parlor with a book in his lap.

"How did you know I was here?"

"It didn't take Sherlock," he said. "You told me, in your usual scatty way, 'I'm not at Phillingsford, well, in a way I am' . . ." He stood up and laughed down at me. I remember the time we walked down this street and he motioned to point out this sweet hotel. He didn't notice because it was sweet but because it had the name of our manor house.

"Would you like," I asked, almost losing my voice, "to see my room?"

AFTER, SIMON AND I were like the monkeys. Instead of sitting on a branch with our arms and legs around each other, we lay in a bed with our arms and legs around each other. We cleaned each other's imaginary fur and picked each other's imaginary fleas.

"You're out walking," I said. "You come to a house. Describe the house."

"Mmm. It's a lighthouse. High on a cliff, overlooking the sea on one side and the countryside on the other."

"You go into the house, and . . ."

"Slow down. It's a long climb up the rocks. There isn't a proper path, and it's a struggle to find the right rocks to get a footing. One takes a step and the rock tumbles, and one has to catch one's balance and try for a more secure rock."

"Hmm!" I was really taking this in. "Once you're inside, are you tired?"

"No! I'm quite fit, you know. I'm exhilarated."

"Great!" (Simon is really interesting.) "So. After a climb, with obstacles, you're in. Exhilarated. You look around. There's a table with three things on it. What are those things?"

"Ah. A spyglass. Rather a good one." He has his eyes closed, his hand tracing my vertebrae, the twitch of a smile on his lips.

I wait, and wait. "What else do you see?"

"Hang on. I'm still playing with this spyglass. It's rather complex. It seems to incorporate a periscope. But I'm not sure about this other apparatus here . . . Looks like I can turn some screws and make it into a kaleidoscope."

"So. Three things in one. Maybe those are the three objects."

"No-ho!" He sits up in bed, frowning. "You said three objects, and I see three objects. This spyglass is only one. Next to it there's a logbook, about a third filled with handwriting very difficult to read."

"What about the rest of the pages?"

"Pristine."

"Very interesting."

"Not very surprising. The log is in progress. Naturally. And the other item is a pen."

"A ballpoint?"

"Melissa. Are you daft? What would a ballpoint pen be doing in a setting like this? Of course it's a fountain pen. Again, rather special. An antique Mont Blanc, filled to capacity with indigo ink with a mysterious hint of green. Like the sea, on this dark day. I write the date on the first blank page, and find it writes more smoothly than any pen I've ever tried."

"Very good," I say. "Now. You look out the window to the backyard. And amazingly enough, there's a bear out there. What do you do about the bear?"

"In the first place, this lighthouse has no backyard. It's perched solitarily on a tower of sliding rocks, so that a bear is very unlikely to be anywhere near the lighthouse."

"Well, somehow a bear has managed," I say. "It's at the back, which must be the side not facing the sea. It came up from the countryside. And it's here, and I think it wants to come in."

"Very unlikely," Simon says with confidence. "All right. I'll indulge you. A highly improbable event has occurred. A bear has battled the rough waters of the Strait of Whatsit to my Hebridean island and climbed the rocks to my back door. Is it a polar bear?"

"You tell me. But also, I didn't know this lighthouse was on an island."

"I should have mentioned it. Yes. It's very, very far out at sea."

"How does one get there?"

"By launching a skiff and taking one's life in one's hands. Very treacherous, these waters. One can see the skeletons of others who have tried to get here littering the rocks at water's edge."

"Heavens!" I say. The implications. "But the bear. What do you do about it?"

"I see this as an opportunity. I study the bear. Of course."

"Like your rats?"

"Yes. Ideally, I'll try to import a number of bears, so that I can find out not just about this bear, but about bearness."

"Very interesting, Simon! Will you write about it in your log book?"

"Perhaps."

"The next thing you see is a cup. Describe the cup."

"Ah. It's quite a comely cup—a bit out of place in the setting. Everything else here is quite masculine."

(Not to mention the phallic image of the lighthouse itself, I'm thinking.)

"This cup is quite sweet. The kind of cup one might find in a Cotswald cottage. Not the standard blue and white, though, but hand-painted with pretty cornflowers and hollyhocks and buttercups, all faded into soft colors. The cup fits in a saucer. Did I mention the saucer?"

I was enchanted. "What do you do with the cup?"

"Good question. I don't know what the water source is on this island. I am thirsty, though. If I plan to survive here, I'll have to find something to drink."

"So what do you do?"

"Well, first off, I check the cupboards. A good supply of tea leaves, here . . . There's a jug . . . but it's empty. And certainly no milkman makes deliveries here. But! I climb to the top of the tower, and—ah, what a view! And in the center of the floor, I spy a bottle of rum!"

"So . . . ?"

"Hang on. On closer inspection, it's not rum at all. It's brandy, and a very fine brandy indeed. VSOP."

"What's VSOP?"

"Very Special Old Pale. Worth a fortune. And the bottle's almost full."

"So what do you do with it?"

"You asked me what do I do with the cup. Not with the brandy."

"Right. The cup. What do you do with it?"

"I pour in an ounce of brandy and sip very slowly, exploring the nooks and crannies of the lighthouse. I go back for a little more brandy. I like the place. But eventually I face the fact that if I'm going to stay, I can't live on brandy. I set the cup down on the table, with the three other objects—is it fair to have four objects there now?"

"Yes." I feel like a fortune-teller seeing the most promising palm she's ever beheld.

"So. Leaving four items on the table, I set out on an expedition to find a spring on the island. I take the jug with me. I'm sure I'll find it, for the meadows are green. A lovely island it will be to explore, too. I may even find some potatoes growing. Perhaps a gooseberry bush and a whole apple orchard."

"Will you come back to drink from your cup?"

"Of course."

When I interpreted, Simon laughed. Especially when I told him the cup was his love. "I suppose you think I've described you rather well," he said.

53

Dear Nanny,

At Troonfachan I started a rule I always follow now, about opening letters. I never open one until I have time to answer it. That way, the person's news and personality is fresh to me and I'm excited to keep "talking" to them. It's like a conversation. So I didn't open the letters that had piled up at Lettering Lane until today, when I am at a small hotel.

Of course, you know this. You are now a part of the great swim. But I'm writing as if you were still part of the world I'm in, because I'm in it still. I'm writing for myself, and addressing you is, I hope, a way to get into a kind of meditation. With you.

I loved your letter, Nanny. I saw the postmark, York, and couldn't imagine who it was from. Lady Chipchase? Mrs. West? I had a lot of letters from home, and before opening them I went and got a bunch of postcards—mostly pictures of the queen, because some of those can be so funny—and I just wrote, "Coming home!" The only person I sent a real letter to was my brother, Sam, whose letter was postmarked Iowa City. He's hitchhiking home to Portland, so I addressed him a letter c/o Mom. The Christians kicked him out of the commune! He says he told them he thinks Christ is only one of the voices of God, that Buddha and Krishna Murti and some others are, too. The head of the group said, "Sam, you'd better leave. And don't come back till you have your head on straight." In his letter, Sam sounded relieved.

I JUST OPENED THE letter I'd saved till last, the one postmarked York.

Such a shock to the system to see that the letter was signed, "Nanny."

Do you know, I still don't know your real name. I now accept that your real name is Nanny.

I'M GOING TO COPY your letter on my heavenly blue writing paper. I have a friend at home who *types* the stories of his favorite writers. He says that by tapping the words across his keyboard, he gets deeper into the heart of the writer. He feels the rhythm of the sentences—a short one followed by a long one, and so forth. He copies a page of Hemingway or Cheever and gets exhilarated. "Look! I'm writing this!" By threading the words that went from your heart to your head to your hand to your paper, through my head and heart down onto my paper, you'll be in my heartbeat.

One thing, though. You say you're "not a dab hand at spelling." No wonder! You told me your grandmother and grandfather couldn't read or write at all. So, I'm sorry to take out the "colour and flavour," but when I write out your letter I'll change your spelling to my spelling

Hello, dearie.

We've just had our marmalade lesson, and I'm still bubbling along with the jam. I sit in my beautiful flat, looking past my lovely windowsill garden to the circle of lawn with the mirror ball, and all the lovely green country beyond. I think what a lucky girl I am. Odd to say, but even with my white hair and my legs, I think of myself as a girl still.

My mind dances. Think of the adventure we're about to have in San Francisco! Of course I'll be going to Australia, too. This may be even more exotic and mysterious than Frisco, but to me the stop in San Francisco is almost more adventurous, being so unexpected. My imagination is quite prepared for Australia. I've dreamed of it ever since my brother left Phillingsford and set up a new life in a new world. I know the "Down Under" is a part of the Commonwealth, but in my eyes it is as foreign as Tibet or Camelot. He writes scant, and so what I know of his home and his town is drawn for the most part from picturing.

It will be jolly good to see those wallabies, but I never thought I'd see San Francisco. It's an extra thrill since you're writing up my marmalade for your American paper. When I get there I'll be famous!

I so appreciate your generosity and hospitality. But, my dear Melissa, I want to say something in the letter that I can't bring myself to say face to face. We'll have a great chin-wag soon, when you're back at Phillingsford, but I don't want to wait till then to tell you what I've been thinking.

What I mean to tell you is please, do not marry on my account. I know you want to offer me a bedroom, and that you even plan to let a larger flat, to put me up. To do that, you will have to have the support of a husband.

Believe me, dear, I don't mind a sofa.

And here is the crux of my message. I think you'll not do the chap a favor by going through with the marriage.

I know I shouldn't be so blunt. I hope you'll forgive me. I make things easier for myself by writing on a piece of paper instead of speaking out face to face. But here it is. I do think you would make a muck of your life, and *his* life. Respect for the mate comes first. Just look at Milady and Sir Chester. The poor bloke deserves to find a woman like the dishy "older woman" he told you about, the one who adored him.

You may find a chap that suits you. If not, don't marry. Have affairs!

The worst that could happen is that you'll end up like me. And, as for myself, I could not have asked for a more joyful life. Devoted children, without the pain of childbirth. And now my "kids" have given me "grandkids."

Which brings me to Claire. She'll always be Mutt and Jeff. But who knows? She may speak like a lady one day. Look how far she's come in a few months. She's a lucky girl to have someone come along and talk English to her night and day.

I just looked out the window, dearie. The sun is at its trickiest slant. The shadows on the lawn are twice as long as the trees are tall. It's my favorite time of a day. Suppertime is no longer nigh, it's past nigh. The tray Mrs. West brought up has sat here long enough to catch bugs. I may just have to skip supper tonight. After I address your envelope for Mr. West to post, I'll do up a nice piece of toast and open up a jar of that marmalade we made today. If serious hunger pecks me, I can nip into the kitchen when it gets pitchy, and do a bit of nicking. You know how it is.

Always,
Nanny

P.S.: Milady and I sit by the hour, talking about you—about how very English you seem.

Nanny, your P.S. was the ultimate compliment. Hoi-hoi-HOI! Still, I confess I'm proud that the country I'm going home to doesn't have castles and lords and ladies.

When I'm Mrs. Haig-Ereildoun's age—or yours—I'll probably cherish this time of my life as much as you, looking back, savor your year in Paris. But as soon as I finish this letter, I'm going back to the Haig-Ereildouns' to drop off my key and pack up my things and bring them to this hotel. For once I'm going to pay for a taxi.

I've decided to leave a note, instead of telling Mrs. Haig-Ereildoun in person. I can't say no in person and stick with it. It sounds chicken, but it's really the opposite. I've faced my weakness, and this is one I can't conquer. Well, maybe someday. But not by tomorrow.

I think Claire has had enough of me, for the moment. Good timing. Trevor and Pru already understand. They've practically told me in words. I've explained the whole thing to Mr. Haig-Ereildoun nonverbally. (To make a long story short, I slammed a door once.) He and I speak to each other almost always without words. I've worried about him, that his nonsuccess at writing could lose him his self-respect and even his wife. She doesn't seem to look up to failure. For a long time he just sat in his office smoking and sucking mints at the same time. I've feared for him the way I fear for myself in this scary world. Then a couple of days ago, he told me by the roar of his typewriter ripping through the house like a train that he's just going to continue living dangerously.

I am going to Paris! With a man! But of course you know all that. Are you pleased that I'm following your advice? Not getting married, just having affairs? At least that seems to be what I'm doing. You never know. It all reminds me of your risky marmalade.

If I were Trevor, I'd close this with "Finis." But since I'm me, I'll close with

Love,
Melissa